LAURA KAY

Making It

Laura Kay is a writer living in East London. Her journalism and personal essays have been published in *The Guardian*, *Diva*, *Stylist*, *Metro*, and *The Bookseller*, among others. In 2018, she was selected for the Penguin Random House WriteNow program, where she developed her first novel, *The Split*, which was longlisted for the Polari First Book Prize. *Making It* is her fourth novel.

ALSO BY LAURA KAY

Making It

Making It

Laura Kay

VINTAGE BOOKS

A DIVISION OF PENGUIN RANDOM HOUSE LLC

NEW YORK

A VINTAGE BOOKS ORIGINAL 2024

Copyright © 2024 by Laura Kay

All rights reserved. Published in the United States by Vintage Books, a division of Penguin Random House LLC, New York, and distributed in Canada by Penguin Random House Canada Limited, Toronto.

Vintage and colophon are registered trademarks of Penguin Random House LLC.

Library of Congress Cataloging-in-Publication Data
Names: Kay, Laura, [date] author.
Title: Making it / by Laura Kay.
Description: New York : Vintage Books, a division of
    Penguin Random House LLC, 2024.
Identifiers: LCCN 2023053330 (print) | LCCN 2023053331 (ebook) |
    ISBN 9780593470077 (trade paperback) | ISBN 9780593470084 (ebook)
Subjects: LCSH: Artists—Fiction. | Depressed persons—Fiction. | Gender-
    nonconforming people—Fiction. | LCGFT: Romance fiction. | Queer
    fiction. | Novels.
Classification: LCC PR6111.A936 M35 2024 (print) |
    LCC PR6111.A936 (ebook) | DDC 823/.92—dc23/eng/20231117
LC record available at https://lccn.loc.gov/2023053330
LC ebook record available at https://lccn.loc.gov/2023053331

Vintage Books Trade Paperback ISBN: 978-0-593-47007-7
eBook ISBN: 978-0-593-47008-4

vintagebooks.com

Printed in the United States of America
10 9 8 7 6 5 4 3 2 1

For Rosemary Kay, who keeps us all going

A Note from the Author

Dear Reader,

This is a story about taking a chance on yourself and how love, of all kinds, is transformative and can be found in the most unexpected places.

I pitched this book to my agent as a "fun and sexy rom-com about depression and anxiety!!!" which is exactly the kind of thing a person with depression and anxiety would say, isn't it?

People experience mental health conditions differently, and they manifest themselves in so many ways that one person's experience can be entirely unrecognizable from someone else's. I cannot represent all of depression or all of anxiety in one character or one story. I cannot say whether the experience of Issy will mirror your own or even whether it mirrors mine (apart from all the fun and sexy bits, those bits are all completely real).

In this book I reference medication, but it is nonspecific

and unnamed. This is deliberate. I also reference therapy, but it is nonspecific and vague. This is deliberate too.

This book is not about how someone overcomes mental health problems but rather how she lives with them. She is not a problem to be solved. I am not going to try to fix her. Although, I can assure you, I do take very good care of her.

If you live with anxiety and depression, there are parts of this book that you might find tricky to read. But there are also parts of this book that might make you feel some hope or even, against all odds, make you laugh out loud.

Hang in there.

Laura

Making It

Welcome!

Please take your time, look around, move slowly through my life, and soak it in.

It is not possible for me to tell you that this story has a happy ending because it has not ended; it keeps going and going. But I am happy right now in this moment, and I hope that my happiness shines through everything you see today.

Isobel Bailey, the Artist

CHAPTER ONE

"We can't all be the main character," I said, my voice raised, battling to be heard over the sound of the radio and the motorway traffic.

"What?"

My uncle Pete has selective hearing, and he had been selecting not to hear me for most of the journey.

"I said, we can't all be the main character, otherwise who would be the sidekick? Or the audience? Or the reader?"

"What the bloody hell are you on about?"

I sighed. I don't know why I even bothered trying to make conversation. We were listening to talk radio, and there was a woman on as a guest—who two men were shouting over—talking about "main-character energy" and how you can "manifest" whatever you want if you try hard enough. And if you buy her book, I guess.

Uncle Pete was the one who had turned up the volume in the

first place, trying his best to look meaningfully at me while I stared resolutely ahead.

I couldn't see him properly because I had a huge cage on my knee, the white metal bars all the way up to the roof of the van. I was extremely aware of him though because he kept offering me his bag of mini Kit Kats through the bars like he was my keeper at the zoo.

"I just mean maybe it's OK that I'm one of life's observers rather than being an active participant," I said. "What if I was just fine staying at home, living with Mum, working at Glazed for the rest of my life?"

I was meant to be making a hypothetical point about the dubious premise of this woman's book, but my heart lurched involuntarily when I said it. The longing for home I had been barely allowing myself to feel ripped through me.

"Well, it's a bit late for that, isn't it?" Uncle Pete said, his mouth full. I just knew he was spraying wet crumbs all over the dashboard. I was starting to feel nauseous.

"You know what your problem is, Issy?"

That I think too much.

"It's that you think too much," he said.

I clenched my teeth.

"Maybe you don't think *enough*, Uncle Pete. Did you ever think of that?"

He snorted with laughter. More crumbs. More nausea.

"Maybe that's why I'm so happy and you're always in such a bloody grump, Wizzy."

"Issy," I said.

"Hmm?"

"Don't call me Wizzy. I'm twenty-eight years old."

"Our little Wizzy," Uncle Pete said, ignoring me. "Always bloody grumping about something."

Always bloody grumping is not quite the term I'd use to describe, quite literally, clinical depression.

Uncle Pete turned up the volume on the radio again before I could protest any further, the men now shouting at each other about a political landscape none of them seemed to understand. I wrestled my phone out of the top pocket of my jacket and groaned when I saw that we had forty-five minutes of the journey left. The cage was heavier than I'd realized; I had stopped being able to feel my legs before we reached the motorway.

I rested my head against the window of Pete's van and let it vibrate against the glass. As hard as I tried, I couldn't stop thinking about my mum standing in the doorway of our block of flats in Margate, waving us off that morning with her cardigan wrapped around her tiny frame. She had clearly not slept all night. Uncle Pete, her younger brother, gripped her shoulder just before we left and said something to her, but I don't know what it was. It might have been "I'll take care of her," but it could just as easily have been "Get a bloody grip, love."

Just when the satnav was telling us we were ten minutes away from our destination, we drove into the car park of a twenty-four-hour superstore.

"Careful!" I yelled, as Uncle Pete pulled into a tight parking space and slammed on the brakes. I clung on to the cage as I was thrown back in my seat.

"It's fine, babe," Uncle Pete said.

I still couldn't see him clearly, but I heard the effort of him slithering out of the driver's side door, grunting and wheezing, trying not to scratch the car next to us. Uncle Pete is not a small man.

I placed the cage gently onto the driver's seat and began the process of slithering out of the van myself. Maddeningly, I could hear Uncle Pete wincing, watching as the passenger door knocked against the car next to us, as if he was not entirely responsible for where we parked.

"Back in a second," I said through the window I'd left cracked open. The news kept saying it was "unseasonably warm" for September—or, put better, perhaps, by Uncle Pete it was "absolutely bloody roasting."

"It'll be fine," Uncle Pete said, slapping me on the back when I emerged from the gap between the cars.

"Not *it*," I said, "*she*."

When we got into the shop, Uncle Pete pulled out his phone and a pair of reading glasses with floral frames. He doesn't think he needs glasses but pinches my auntie Jan's every time he leaves the house. He held the phone as far away from his face as he could, and I saw that he was studying an essay-length text. He kept scrolling, and it kept going and going.

"What's that?" I asked, straining to get a better look at his phone as he picked up a basket and passed it to me before taking another one for himself.

"Shopping list," he said, without looking up but moving the phone farther away from me.

"For you?" I said.

"For *you*, you daft cow. What am I coming all this way to do my big shop for?"

Uncle Pete's voice was loud, and it carried. I smiled apologetically at a woman who glanced at us in alarm, disturbed from her task of pretending she wasn't squeezing all the avocados next to the sign asking customers not to squeeze the avocados.

"I don't know! But I don't want a big shop! What if no one

else did a big shop before they got there? I don't want to turn up with . . ."

I glanced over his shoulder at the text again.

"Twelve tins of tuna!"

"'Course you do," Uncle Pete said, putting a container of strawberries in my basket, which I immediately removed because I am severely allergic to them, something he has known my entire life.

I can't even tell you how many times he has nearly killed me.

"I don't like tuna! I'm trying to be vegan now, remember?"

"Vegans eat tuna," Uncle Pete said confidently. "I was listening to a program about it."

"Did Mum send you the list?" I asked.

He paused before answering.

"Yeah," he said, frowning as I picked up a box of posh granola. Not on the list.

"Is she very worried about me?" I said, a knot forming in my stomach. *More than usual*, were the unsaid words we both heard.

"No," he said firmly. He stopped, slap-bang in the middle of the world food aisle. "She's not very worried; she's a normal amount of worried. You're not to worry about her being worried, do you understand me?"

I nodded. My brain understood. My writhing stomach, my jelly legs, the tingling in my fingertips did not catch on.

My body is always one step behind.

"Do you think I should just . . . ," I started.

"If you say 'go home' right now to me, Isobel, I'm putting these Twixes right back. No Twixes for you."

"I can't eat Twixes anyway," I said, "I'm ve—"

"You know what I mean," Uncle Pete said, holding the packet dangerously close to the shelf.

I nodded. "I know, yes. I know."

We somehow managed to fit everything into the van. It was quite satisfying actually, slotting individual boxes and cartons into the perfect-size spaces between everything I owned. I wriggled back into my seat, pulled the cage onto my lap, and despite having spent the entire journey desperately waiting for it to be over, I treasured the final ten minutes in the car with Uncle Pete, listening to him swearing at the satnav. It flew by painfully quickly.

We pulled up slowly in front of a large terraced house on a tree-lined street in Hackney. There were two front doors very close to each other: 47 (blue) and 47A (yellow). The upstairs flat was 47A. A maisonette, it was called in the advert—47A was home. The windows were single-glazed and the wooden painted frames were peeling, but the front door looked new at least—like, yes, I could probably kick it in with little to no effort, but it had had a lick of canary-yellow paint, which was cheering. There was a bicycle chained to the lamppost outside with both wheels missing.

"This is it," Uncle Pete said, and for the first time since this whole ridiculous idea was mooted all those months ago, I watched as his cheerful veneer slipped. A flash of concern. Sometimes he looked just like my mum.

"This is it," I confirmed.

He peered at me through the bars of the cage, chewing the inside of his cheek, one hand still on the steering wheel as if he might simply restart the engine and drive me away, as if he was fighting every instinct to do exactly that.

"Right," he said. He shook his head slightly, snapping himself out of the moment, then plastered a smile on his face that didn't reach his eyes. "Let's get you moved in. You got the keys, babe?"

I nodded and patted my top pocket, the keys clinking against my already cracked phone screen. I had picked them up from the estate agent last week and paid £50 for the pleasure.

I'd never actually been inside the flat, but I had done a virtual tour that was like viewing a dollhouse in a fishbowl, which is to say, unhelpful. I went and stood outside last week though and looked in from across the street like a creep. I may as well have been holding a pair of binoculars. I'd clutched the keys in my hand but couldn't quite bring myself to use them. It wasn't my life yet.

Now, I pushed the front door open and called out a tentative hello into the hallway, but all was quiet. It was eleven o'clock on a Saturday morning—I guess everyone was out making the most of the sunny day. My new housemates had moved in the previous weekend, but Uncle Pete didn't have time to drive me last week, or perhaps he had taken pity on me and given me another week at home.

On a normal Saturday, I would have been halfway through my morning at Glazed, the pottery café I'd worked at for the past decade, nodding while mothers told me to be careful because their toddlers' "work" was really "very advanced."

I led Uncle Pete up two flights of narrow stairs. On the first floor there were two bedrooms, a kitchen, a cupboard-size living room (probably genuinely once a cupboard) with two pleather sofas wedged in it, and a bathroom. We peered through the open doors of the communal spaces, and Uncle Pete made a series of noises that suggested he was not impressed. On the second floor, the loft extension, there were two bedrooms: one was big with double doors leading onto a roof terrace (we were explicitly told it was not a roof terrace, it was just a roof, but all the photos showed it decked out with furniture), and the other, for the next year, belonged to me.

My room was the smallest one in the house, with a single bed pushed up against the wall next to the narrow window looking out over the downstairs' garden. I suspected that it might once have been an en suite bathroom for the much bigger bedroom next door, mostly because three of the four walls were tiled. There was a mosaic accent border somewhere just off-center, and every third one of those tiles was a turquoise fish. I would be sleeping where a bathtub should be.

The existence of the single bed was something that was made very clear to me before I accepted the room—that it was small, for one person; that it was nonnegotiable; that it would under no circumstances be replaced; *did I understand?* I had a single bed at home, I said, and the estate agent had frowned and checked my paperwork again as if to make sure he wasn't accidentally leasing the room to a child on stilts rather than an adult. I had always had a single bed. I wasn't really sure what the big deal was. Plus it made the room £200 cheaper a month than the other three in the flat. I jumped at the chance to sleep in the bathroom-bedroom if I'm being honest.

By the time we'd finished lugging my things up the narrow staircase, my bedroom floor had pretty much disappeared under piles of boxes. I brought the cage up last and placed it carefully next to the chest of drawers in the corner of the room. It looked even bigger in this small space. I'm not sure I'd ever noticed before that it came up to my waist.

Uncle Pete stood with his hands on his hips, his cheeks bright pink, trying to get his breath back. He pulled the papery blind up and down, opened and closed the window, shook the bedframe a little as if to test that it wouldn't simply collapse under me. He ran a finger over one of the tile fish and paused, seemingly lost in thought. I tried to remember if I had warned him about the room's past life or not.

Once he'd finished his inspections and nodded to himself, he turned to me and said decisively, "I'd better head off or I'll hit the lunchtime traffic."

I nodded. His voice sounded strange.

"Now," he said, covering his mouth with his hand, clearing his throat, "I've put some money into your bank account."

"No, Uncle Pete, I . . ."

"I know you've been saving, I know, but I had some money put away for if you ever went to, you know, uni or anything like that, and I want you to have it now. It's not much, but it should help with your rent. Buy the odd pint for your new mates."

I opened my mouth again to protest.

"Issy," he said, before I got a chance. He shook his head slightly; this conversation was as hard for him as it was for me.

"Thank you," I said. "Really. Thank you."

Uncle Pete cleared his throat again and pretended to inspect the doorframe.

I followed him back down the stairs and out the front door. I walked him all the way to the van. Neither of us said anything.

"Will you tell Mum I'm all right?" I said eventually, not quite to him, more to my feet, to the scorched grass beneath them.

I felt Uncle Pete glaring at me until I was forced to look up and meet his eyes.

"*Are* you all right?" he asked. His voice sounded more normal now, unreasonably loud.

I swallowed.

"Yes," I said.

"Sure?"

"Yes," I repeated, with a confidence I didn't feel. I wondered if he thought my voice sounded strange too, as I concentrated on keeping it steady.

"Then I'll tell her," he said.

He grabbed me and pulled me in for a hug, squeezing me tightly. I would normally have protested, but that day I let him. I squeezed him back, not minding his sweaty T-shirt pressing against mine, ignoring the smell of Lynx and miniature Kit Kats.

"We're very proud of you, Wizzy," he said gruffly into my hair.

"Issy," I mumbled into his chest.

He pushed me back, gripping my shoulders. He looked into my eyes, and I saw that tears were threatening to spill from his.

"You know you can always come home, but . . ." He paused and exhaled slowly, gathering himself. "Your life is really starting now, so you make sure you enjoy every second of it."

I nodded, even though I wasn't really sure exactly what he meant. Or how to do that even if I wanted to.

Uncle Pete got back into the van.

"Remember you're the star of the show," he said to me through the open window.

"What?" I said. "What show?"

"What they were saying earlier," Pete said, "on the radio."

"About being the main character?" I said.

"That's it," Pete said, rummaging around in his glove compartment and producing a pair of wraparound sunglasses that make him look like a fly. "You're Beyoncé; that's what she was saying, wasn't it?"

"I don't know that she was saying that I'm Beyoncé, I suppose it's more . . ."

He grinned at me and wound up the window while I was still talking. He mouthed "Beyoncé" at me and gave me a thumbs-up.

He did a three-point turn without looking at the road, pressed the horn until he was out of sight, and then he was gone. And I was away from home for the first time in my life. Or I was in my new home. Or I was sort of nowhere at all.

"Hey!"

I turned away from watching Uncle Pete disappear down the road to see a woman standing in front of me. She had thick dark hair messily spilling out from underneath a baseball cap. She was wearing jeans and a white T-shirt with the sleeves rolled up. The T-shirt had black fingerprints smeared all over it.

"Oh," I said, "Hi, I'm ..."

I gestured toward the house, to explain why I was standing on the street, staring wistfully after a white van.

"Did you see someone take my bike?" the woman interrupted. She had a Scottish accent; it might have sounded quite nice had she not essentially been barking at me.

"What?" I said. "Oh, no, I ..."

"It was literally just here," the woman said, gesturing at the lamppost we were standing next to. "I was fixing something, and I ran inside quickly, and when I came back out ... How can you not have seen? I don't understand. It was *right here*."

The woman narrowed her eyes at me, and it dawned on me what she was implying.

"I only just came out here to say goodbye to my uncle. . . . I'm sorry, I ..."

I felt like emptying my pockets for some reason, to prove the bike wasn't on my person.

"Jesus," she said, closing her eyes briefly. She pinched the bridge of her nose, clearly employing some kind of anger-management breathing exercise.

I took a step back.

"Do you want me to . . . Do you think we should call the police?" I asked tentatively.

She snorted and ignored me. When she pulled her hand away from her face, she had black fingerprints on her nose.

"You've got um . . ." I gestured to my own nose and nodded at her.

"Fuck!" she said.

To my surprise, and I think to hers, she kicked the lamppost. The bike lock, now that I was properly looking, was still attached but cut in half. Her eyes widened, and I saw her swallow a scream. Her cheeks went bright red. She blinked back tears. It must have really hurt.

"Are you OK?" I asked. I took another step back from her. I really didn't want to meet the same fate as the lamppost.

She ignored me.

I don't know why I didn't go inside at that point, remove myself from the situation, but I felt compelled for some reason to keep talking to this clearly unhinged person.

"Why are you covered in . . . stuff?" I asked. I rummaged around in the pockets of my jeans and produced a tissue.

Good god I was really turning into my mother; perhaps I had left home at exactly the right time.

I offered it to the woman, my arm outstretched as far as it would go, like I was handing food to a wild animal. She hesitated and then took it from me, dabbing ineffectually at her nose.

"It's oil," the woman said, as if I was the stupidest person she'd ever met, "because there was something squeaking on my bike, and it was driving me up the fucking wall. And guess what?"

She actually paused, like I was meant to guess.

"Um," I said, "what?"

"I'd just fucking fixed it after months of fucking squeaking and now some other fucker is going to fucking get to enjoy it."

"I'm sorry I didn't see anything; I wish I could help," I said.

"Yeah, well," the girl said. "You didn't; you can't."

She turned to walk up the path in front of the house next door.

"I'm Issy," I said to her back.

As I should have predicted, she ignored me.

Welcome to the neighborhood, I guess.

I wandered back inside number 47A and closed the front door behind me. The back of the letterbox fell off and landed with a clatter on the plastic, laminate floor. I put my hand through the place where it had been as if to check the impact of the breakage. Yes, confirmed—I waved into the open air—huge gaping hole in the middle of our front door.

I had to admit, as hard as I was trying to be an optimistic kind of person, breaking the front door combined with the bike-theft accusation did not feel like the best omens for life in my new home.

I headed upstairs, taking in the blue sheets drying over the banisters, the framed generic prints on the wall, the faint smell of the kitchen bin, and the threadbare carpet. I closed the door when I reached my bathroom-bedroom and sat cross-legged on the only space left on the floor, my back against the cold tiles. I reached up to open the door to the cage.

"Abigail," I whispered, "you can come out now, it's OK. It's just me."

I waited in silence for a minute. Nothing. I knew she'd punish me for the hair-raising car journey. I wished I could have explained to her that it wasn't my fault that Uncle Pete drives like a maniac and that, if it were up to me, we wouldn't have left her alone in a twenty-four-hour Asda car park.

I reached into my backpack that I'd slung onto the bed behind me and pulled out a packet of salted popcorn. I made a big deal of rustling the bag, opening it slowly. I took out a piece and popped it in my mouth, crunching as loudly as I could.

"Yum," I said out loud, "my favorite, *popcorn*."

I waited another minute, ate another handful of popcorn, and then, finally, a little gray snout poked out of the lovingly decorated shoebox on the second floor of the cage—an area Mum and I had dubbed "the chill-out zone."

Abigail squeezed her ears out of the hole in the side of the box and then wriggled her increasingly round body out. She emerged with a pop, and I made a note that I might need to make the doorway to the chill-out zone a little wider to accommodate her new, larger frame.

I held a piece of popcorn out to her, and she waited a moment before gently taking it from me. Once she'd eaten a couple of pieces, I tentatively put my hand inside the cage. She didn't immediately run away, which I took as a sign that I had permission to gently lift her out. She sat in one hand, a comforting weight, while I stroked her soft bat ears with the other.

I breathed a sigh of relief and passed her another piece of popcorn. Everything was easier with Abigail on my side.

I've been fascinated by chinchillas ever since we learned about them in primary school during a dubious "South America Week" in which we also ate tacos, wore sombreros, and drew pictures of alpacas wearing rainbow-colored ponchos.

Chinchillas are famously pretty frosty creatures until they warm up to you, but when they love you, once they trust you, they're yours. I loved that, the idea of something so fluffy and sweet-looking, with such big ears and soft paws, being picky about who can handle them, about who they liked. Lots of kids wanted puppies and kittens; the less ambitious ones asked for goldfish or hamsters. Mum and I never had any pets when I was growing up, but I knew that one day, I'd take care of a chinchilla and that I would be the person it chose to love the most.

And then ten years ago, on my eighteenth birthday, my mum brought Abigail home. Mum crept into my room, clutching a small cardboard box, and placed it into my hands. I just knew, I knew what it was even before I took off the lid. Abigail was the size of the palm of my hand, fluffier than a bunny rabbit, ears like Dumbo. I might have laughed at how out of proportion they were, how silly she looked, but I wasn't laughing much then.

Her nose twitched frantically, her eyes wide, taking me in.

"The man in the shop said she might be shy at first," my mum said.

She was wiping a tear from her cheek; I remember that because she never cries. But I understand why she was crying then. Abigail was so tiny and strange; she didn't seem real. Like holding magic in my hand.

Mum reached out a tentative finger and touched Abigail's back very gently. "So you need to be patient with her."

I nodded. I had all the time in the world.

When Abigail had had enough popcorn, I placed her in front of her water bottle and watched as she drank. When she finished, she disappeared back into the chill-out zone. She was an older lady now, she took a lot of naps and played less. I sat and listened to her rustling for a moment, but soon there was silence.

I got onto my new bed, a bare mattress. I bounced up and down a little. It wasn't as bad as it looked. No springs digging in, firm enough, no creaking. And when you consider the alternative—an actual bath—I was pretty happy with it.

I rolled over and reached down the side of the bed to rip open the cardboard box nearest to me. I pulled on one end of the tape, and as the box opened, handfuls of tiny Abigails began to spill out. I tore open a second box, and the same thing happened. It was full to the brim. I tipped the chinchillas—knitted, crocheted, felted— out onto the floor until I couldn't see the carpet, only Abigails. I lifted two heavy frames from the bottom of the box. An Abigail sketch and an Abigail watercolor, and leaned them up against the wall.

I lay there for a while, in a tiny room in East London, a hundred miles and a world away from Margate, surrounded by Abigails, and my chest ached. I supposed this was homesickness. I'd never had it before. I'd never left home.

CHAPTER TWO

I'm aware that the hundreds of chinchillas thing is quite weird, believe me. Let me explain. Ultimately, the chinchillas were why I was in number 47A in the first place. And there were a lot more of them than the ones I've just told you about.

Abigail had a lot to answer for.

I began knitting when I was very small, with bright yellow, blunt plastic needles. My mum has always knitted—she's not terribly good at it, but she's always done it. Jumpers with one arm shorter than the other, scarves that dwindle into nothing, and hats that slide off heads are her specialty. But she likes it, it soothes her.

She was a surprisingly patient teacher, my mum, for someone who could barely sit still. It wasn't long before I overtook her, when the teacher became the student. Some of my happiest childhood memories are of us sitting next to each other on our tattered sofa when Mum got home from work at the local library, not having to speak, just the sound of the clock ticking and knitting needles clacking together.

Occasionally my mum would pierce the silence, swearing loudly as she dropped her stitch—the only time I ever heard her swear. I'd take whatever she was making from her, and she'd watch me put it back together. When things felt particularly bleak and I couldn't imagine ever feeling the desire to make something ever again, when I could hear other teenagers shrieking and laughing outside, and the whole world was gray, she still sat beside me, persevering.

I've worked on various projects over the years, some more ambitious than others, ranging from basic stuff—teddy bears, clothes, blankets—to large-scale projects that took me months. Projects so big, buildings and landscapes and skylines—my own miniature universe—that once I'd finished they'd be displayed in our living room for a couple of weeks, taking up so much space that, eventually, I simply unpicked them and made something else. I liked knowing that the creations were temporary, everything could be destroyed and given new life.

A few years ago, I started focusing on making Abigails—the Abigail Project, if you will. And I just never stopped making them—it became habitual, ritualistic even. It started with knitting—giant Abigails, Abigails eating popcorn, Abigails the size of my fist, Abigails the size of a fifty-pence piece. Some are soft and fluffy, some coarse. Some are gray, true to life. Some are brightly colored, multicolored, luminous. Then I started sketching her, and painting her—she lives in tiny notebooks and on huge canvases leaning up against my wall. She is a crude sculpture made of discarded clay from the pottery café; she's a print; she's a watercolor. Abigail is everything.

I don't know exactly what compelled me to keep going long after my shelves were full, windowsills heaving, walls covered. Someone I worked with once asked about it when we were on a quiet morning shift, after I'd handed in my notice, a decision inextricably linked to the Abigails.

"I just don't get it. What's the point?"

I shook my head.

"I suppose," I said, after a moment, "I'm just trying to capture her, and I haven't managed to do that yet, so I'm just going to keep going until I get her right. Maybe I never will. Or maybe I'm just trying to capture how I feel about her and it's too much? There may not ever be a way to express that. So maybe I won't ever stop."

She laughed at me then.

"You're talking about a chinchilla, right?"

I nodded. And then I shook my head again. What was I talking about exactly?

The reason that the Abigail Project was inextricably linked to me handing in my notice at Glazed is because of an act of blind faith by a famous artist, Elizabeth Staggs. And because of a brief moment of uncharacteristic optimism by a not-at-all-famous artist, me.

Elizabeth is originally from Margate, the seaside town where I'm from. It's changed a lot in the past few years, become a tourist destination for Londoners wanting cocktails and small plates by the sea, but parts of it are the same as it's always been—run-down, forgotten, neglected. Bleak and desolate, sad and wanting.

Elizabeth went to the same high school as me, although she'd left a few years before I started. A beacon and an icon in the field of failing schools. We had pretty much nothing going for us: the whole place was in a state of desperate disrepair; the classrooms were damp and cold and filled with restless students with various unmet needs. Depressed teachers watched the clock until they could take a break to smoke in their cars and think about their life choices.

And yet, the bleak corridors were adorned with Elizabeth's work. Worth a small fortune probably, now that I think about it, commissioned by the school and gifted with the idea that it might inspire the pupils, inject some hope into an otherwise rather hopeless place.

There were a lot of her trademark abstract works that had the effect of not only brightening up the beige walls but also of radiating light somehow. I was drawn to one painting in particular, a canvas in the cold corridor I used to walk down to get to double maths. Splashes of every shade of red and pink you could imagine.

To me, it was like the sun.

It reminded me there was a world outside. A world bigger than double maths. Bigger than me and high school and my mum and the persistent ache I carried with me.

When I left school, three years earlier than everybody else, I thought of that painting often. Of the sun that hung in the dark, radiating light. I would close my eyes and try to feel the warmth of it on my skin. Elizabeth had always taken an interest in the community in Margate. She still lives there half the time, in a huge town house. Tourists take selfies with the mural painted outside.

She sometimes does workshops there for locals, in schools and in community groups—what one might call "giving back"—although I'm not sure I've ever heard her describe it like that herself. Occasionally she films segments of her TV show—*Artistic License*—there. Shots of her walking on the beach with her greyhound, Walter. So when I say that my work "attracted the interest of" Elizabeth Staggs I mean that, on a whim, I entered the Abigail Project via a series of photographs and a long personal essay to a competition she was running. Every year there is a weekend where locals can open their houses to members of the public, almost like every home is its own gallery, and Elizabeth always takes part. She ran a contest last year for a local amateur artist to display a piece of their own work in her home, and by some miracle, I got through several rounds and the project landed in front of Elizabeth herself.

The piece that actually won was a lovely painting of the lido reimagined on a sunny day, bright and gleaming, with all kinds of people dressed both in contemporary and in 1920s swimwear lounging around in it. It was the perfect smushing together (an artistic term) of past and present, and I loved it. I bought a postcard with the print on it in fact and pinned it to the noticeboard in my bedroom.

I still don't know what possessed me to submit my own work, to reach so far outside my little bubble and invite somebody else in. But I'm glad I did, truly thank god I did, because it led Elizabeth to send me an email which I, of course, ignored.

In that email, Elizabeth asked me for my details, gave me her personal phone number, and asked me to call her. She said she wanted to speak to me about something and that it was important.

She rang me, but I ignored the calls too. I didn't think I had very much to say about the Abigails, they were, to my mind, pretty much self-explanatory.

By that time, the flash of optimism that had inspired me to enter the contest had well and truly disappeared. I was embarrassed, exhausted, terrified by the prospect of any kind of disruption to the careful routine that was my life. I was furious with myself for inviting it in.

Elizabeth tried to call me every day for a week, and every day I watched the screen light up and dim again. I never even saved her number.

One day my mum saw me rejecting a phone call while we were watching *Pointless*, and when she asked me who it was, I made the mistake of telling her the truth. Her eyes widened. I wished I hadn't said anything, but I guess the flash of optimism must have still been in there somewhere, a little bit of dormant hope.

"Oh, Isobel," Mum said. "You must answer. You have to."

"Why?" I said. "I shouldn't have entered the competition in the first place; it was a moment of madness."

Mum tutted; she hated it when I called myself mad.

"Well," she said, in a particularly annoying voice that she reserved for when she knew she was about to have a mic drop moment, "I think it's madness to pass up this opportunity, Issy. So, yes, if that's what you're doing, then I agree, it is . . . it is *madness*."

I could tell she was angry or frustrated, or something indecipherable that she was finding deeply galvanizing. She could barely sit still.

I should have predicted what would happen next.

A couple of nights later, I got home from work, a particularly rough Saturday, two kids' parties—screaming, crying, someone throwing up in a Postman Pat bowl. And there she was, sitting in the living room. A flash of offensively bright orange jumper against our beige sofa. I stood in the doorway and blinked stupidly a couple of times, trying to place her.

It takes a moment when you see something unexpected like that, like a bird inside the house—so familiar but by virtue of its location, briefly, totally disarming.

"You're a hard person to pin down, Isobel," Elizabeth said to me. Her face remained impassive; it might have felt like I was being chastised were it not for the unmistakable hint of playfulness in her eyes, bright blue and outlined in black kohl behind huge cat-eye glasses. "I decided to book an appointment with your manager instead. She suggested you might be easier to speak to in person."

Elizabeth jerked her head toward my mum, who was sitting on the edge of the armchair where no one ever sits. Mum smiled nervously; she'd been gnawing on a hangnail, and I could see that she'd drawn blood.

"I really think you should talk to her, love," Mum said to me, quietly, as if the stranger two feet away might not be able to hear. "In fact, I'll leave you to it. Let me know if you need anything."

Mum brushed past me in the doorway and squeezed my arm gently. An apology for the ambush and a pinch to wake me up.

I gingerly walked into the living room, and after hovering in front of Elizabeth for a moment, I perched on the opposite end of the sofa to her, depositing my backpack with a thump on the floor.

I was acutely aware that I smelled like pottery glaze but, more pressingly, of sweat and of the cheap prosecco one of the parents had accidentally poured on my trainers earlier in the day. I'd said "Don't worry" before realizing she'd actually not said sorry. I'd been on my feet for nine hours, and my body ached. Elizabeth Staggs was serene, as if this were her living room that I was visiting, as if I had requested the meeting with her myself.

"Your mum tells me you've always been an artist," Elizabeth said.

Ah, no small talk, then. It was a relief, I suppose, to not have to go through the ordeal of telling her about my day. My eyes fixed on a small hole on the shoulder of her jumper. It looked hand-knitted, and I wondered if the hole had always been there. If it was someone's mistake once.

"Yeah, she would say that," I said. "That's mums, isn't it? They think their kids are good at everything."

Elizabeth just looked at me curiously, ignoring my glib answer. It made me feel silly, although I don't think that was her intention. I sat up straighter.

"But you've never studied art or textiles formally?" she said.

I shook my head.

"No, I've never studied . . . anything really."

Elizabeth sat back on the sofa as if to get a better look at me.

"And you said in your essay when you entered the contest that you never finished school? It sounds like you've had a pretty tough time. You dropped out after . . ."

I focused on the hole in the jumper again, imagining poking my finger and thumb through it and stretching it until the threads snapped.

"Right," I said, before she could finish her sentence, my fingernails digging into the palms of my hands. "Yes."

She tilted her head to catch my eye. I reluctantly looked up.

"I didn't finish school either," she said. "Did you know that?"

I shook my head, surprised. Elizabeth not finishing is not part of the narrative my high school liked to tell about her.

"I left when I was fifteen," Elizabeth said. "Things were very hard at home." She paused. "You know what that's like."

She did not say it with pity. She said it as a matter of fact.

I nodded again and swallowed hard. There was normally a cacophony of unwanted sound in my and Mum's flat—pipes clanging and neighbors' TVs and dogs barking—but in that moment it felt as though the world had gone silent. It was just us.

"And I was utterly miserable," Elizabeth said.

"At school?" I said.

"Everywhere," Elizabeth replied softly, "all the time. You know what that's like too."

I inhaled sharply.

"But," Elizabeth carried on, "leaving school, not having qualifications, all of that stuff, it doesn't have to mean it's the end."

"The end of what?" I said.

She smiled then, a warm smile that lit up her whole face, as if my answer had taken her by surprise and delighted her. We were both quiet for a moment—me, waiting for her answer; her looking around the room slowly, curiously, her eyes finally landing on the cage in the corner.

"The famous Abigail?" she asked.

I nodded.

"I suppose she won't come out to meet me?"

"No," I said, "she won't come out until later. And she doesn't really like strangers; she's a bit shy."

She hadn't actually met any strangers, it occurred to me. Abigail's world consisted entirely of me and my mum and occasionally my uncle Pete if she was too slow to hide before he came into the room bellowing "You all right, Annabel, my darling?"

"Of course," Elizabeth said.

We sat in silence again, both looking at the cage as if waiting for something to happen.

"So," she said, after a moment, "if I can't see the real thing, can I at least see the other Abigails?"

I hesitated, although I'm not sure why. She was clearly here to see them; the guided tour was inevitable.

"I'm amazed Mum hasn't already shown you," I said, getting to my feet, sharp pains shooting up through the soles.

Elizabeth laughed, and I felt a flush of warmth in my chest. She had effectively forced her way into my life and yet still, despite my protestations, there was a part of me that came alive sitting next to her—I wanted to impress her.

"Oh, she tried. But I wanted to see them with you, the artist."

It felt absurd being referred to as "the artist," but I already knew better than to correct her or say something self-deprecating. I instinctively knew that when she'd said it, she'd meant it, and that she was probably not the kind of person who said things she didn't mean.

I led her up to my bedroom. We stood for a while in silence very close together because my room was tiny. Cupboard tiny. Elizabeth was wearing a perfume unlike any that I'd smelled before, different to anything my mum would wear. It was heady and rich and like something, I suppose, I'd imagine a man might wear.

Elizabeth inspected the Abigails carefully, as if she were in a gallery and it was a real exhibition. She stepped toward them and bent her head as if she were reading little plaques explaining them, explaining me.

I wondered if she expected me to say something, to tell her something new or interesting or impressive about them, but I couldn't think of anything to say, so I just watched her instead. She snapped her head back after a while and turned away from the Abigails and back to me. It was decisive, like she'd seen all she needed to see.

"Do you paint other things too?" Elizabeth asked.

"Sometimes," I said, surprised by the question. I hoped she wouldn't ask to see my paintings—mostly crinkled, faded water-colors of the beach, discarded because my cheap paint was never going to be able to capture the colors of the sky.

"Sculpture?" she asked, politely ignoring the attempts at sculpted Abigails on top of my chest of drawers.

"No."

"Ceramics? Do you often work with clay?"

"I mean I work at Glazed, the pottery café in town. I make flat whites and put tiles with babies' handprints on them into a kiln."

She laughed again and nodded to herself. She shook her head from side to side a little as if weighing everything.

"Why do you do it? What got you making this stuff?"

"It gives me a purpose, I suppose," I said. "If I feel directionless, I can make something that didn't exist before, that wouldn't have existed if I didn't exist. It makes me feel less like everything is . . . insignificant."

My cheeks were burning again. I felt quite sure these were not the answers she was looking for, although at this point I still couldn't quite imagine what she *was* looking for.

I scanned my shelves, packed with well-thumbed charity-shop copies of books about great artists, history, women breaking glass ceilings, and racked my brain for what exactly had inspired me.

I'd missed out on most of the school trips to the galleries in London. Mum and I had never been. I could only think of Elizabeth's work in my school corridors making the dead space alive, but I couldn't say that.

So I stayed quiet, and so did she for a moment, before she sat on my bed and patted the spot next to her. I hesitated before sitting down beside her. I felt the mattress springs creak beneath the weight of us both.

"I've got something I want to talk to you about. And I want you to seriously consider it—I don't want you to dismiss this because, let me tell you, I don't do this often. In fact," she said, and she nodded at me until I nodded back, confirming I was listening, "I never do this. But there's something about . . ." She paused, looking around the room again. "There's something about you that's really got to me. You remind me of me, I think that's what it is. And of someone very special who works for me. It's uncanny."

I felt like I was dreaming. I realized she was waiting for me to say something, to assure her I understood that something big was happening.

"Yes," I whispered, "OK."

"Will you promise to take on board what I've got to say? To consider what I'm offering you?"

I looked down at her feet dangling over the side of my bed. This stranger.

Her socks were mismatched. I think about that a lot when I remember that moment, which, even while it was happening, I knew was life-changing. One of those moments when you can almost feel the shift, the world adjusting in real time to a new reality. This is what I think of: one pink foot and one blue.

"Yes," I said again. I looked up at her. "I promise."

So here I am. About to start working for Elizabeth Staggs, an intern in her London office, an assistant in her studio, a student of hers there to soak in everything I can. And make a lot of coffee, presumably.

A whole year away from home. A whole year of not working at Glazed. A whole year of not living with my mum. It turns my stomach every time I think about it.

My plan for the afternoon was to make my room feel more like my own, but actually what happened was, after I had put the real Abigail back in her cage, I curled up on top of my unmade bed and fell asleep. The strange sounds of my new home crept into my dreams, distorting familiar images into something more vivid, darker. I twitched and started and eventually woke up with a jolt when the front door slammed shut and someone yelled, "What the fuck happened to the fucking letterbox?"

Shit.

I crept down the first flight of stairs and stood at the top of the second, looking down at the front door, filled with dread. The woman in the hallway didn't notice me for a moment; she had her back turned, doing exactly what I had done—sticking her arm through the hole in the door.

I took another step down, and hearing the creak of the floorboards beneath my feet made the woman spin around. She glared at me, and I braced myself for a telling-off. I opened my mouth to begin apologizing, to offer some kind of explanation for the letterbox on the floor, but before I could, her expression shifted, and she smiled at me.

"Isobel," she said, pointing at me. "Get down here right now!"

She said it with such feeling, with the kind of enthusiasm you might normally reserve for greeting an old friend, that I found myself grinning back. When I reached the bottom of the stairs, I hovered awkwardly, unsure of my next move, but she pulled me in for a hug. She was wearing so much sweet perfume that it caught in the back of my throat.

"All four," she said, when she pulled away.

"Sorry?" I said.

"All four of us are here!" she said. "You, Robin, Mo, and me."

She slapped her hand to her forehead.

"I haven't even introduced myself—I'm Alyssa, obviously."

She stuck her hand out, and I shook it, even though we'd just hugged. I guessed we were doing the business side of things now.

"I'm Isobel," I said, "obviously."

I did, of course, know it was Alyssa because I'd never been in so much and such intense communication with anyone in my life before her, apart from, perhaps, my mother. But honestly, they might be neck and neck.

Alyssa posted the SpareRoom advert that I replied to. There was something about her vibe that I responded to—a sort of no-nonsense, take-charge attitude combined with an element of being quite unapologetically strange. It felt a little like I might be moving in with a particularly strict schoolteacher or a Brownie pack leader with a wild side, and I was surprised by how drawn to it I was.

3 spare rooms in a gorgeous flat WITH A ROOF TERRACE in ZONE TWO. I am a 33-year-old woman (SHE/HER) retraining to be a midwife and I'm looking for 3 MATURE people, preferably other older students or professionals to share this flat with from SEPTEMBER. The contract is for ONE YEAR NONNEGOTIABLE.

Must like spending time together, RESPECTING each other, having fun, being quiet, enjoying life, being clean and tidy.

I don't smoke but I don't mind if you want to smoke on the ROOF TERRACE. I drink MODERATELY and it would be nice to share a bottle of wine sometimes or a NONALCOHOLIC beverage, no discrimination, I respect all choices and all people from all walks of life.

Absolutely no musicians or people who play musical instruments under any circumstances. NO DJS. DO NOT APPLY.

LGBTQIA + friendly household, actually preferred (I am straight).

Contact Alyssa for more information.

"Have you met anyone else yet?" Alyssa asked, walking through to the kitchen. I assumed I was expected to follow her. "Or are they still out?"

"No, not yet," I said. "You're the first one back."

"Wait a sec," she said, holding up one finger to stop me, as if she hadn't just asked me a question. She frowned at her phone, rolled her eyes, and then started yelling at the top of her voice into it, telling someone that they "must be joking" and that "they're going to live to regret it."

"Voice note," she mouthed to me, as if I might not have figured that out.

I watched her as she moved around the kitchen; she held a mug up to me, and I nodded. She switched the kettle on and got tea bags out of the cupboard without pausing her monologue about whoever was on the receiving end of the phone's terrible boyfriend. The volume of the monologue was truly deafening.

Alyssa was much smaller than I thought she would be, I don't know why I expected her to be tall. I suppose because she was *a lot* via email—she really gave tall-person energy, but I'd say she was at least a head shorter than my five foot seven. She was slight too and had dark brown skin. Her black hair was knotted in a bun at the nape of her neck. She was wearing pink scrubs, and when she turned around to shake a carton of oat milk at me (I nodded), I noticed how tired she looked. She put her phone down on the counter and sighed as she stirred milk into our mugs and the kitchen fell into silence. She lifted the front of her scrubs and sniffed, then wrinkled her nose slightly. I didn't know how she could smell anything other than her perfume, but then again, perhaps that was the point—to mask the smell of her day, of the hospital. I don't even really want to think about what learning to be a midwife actually entails. I've seen *One Born Every Minute*, a horror show essentially, and that is more than enough information for me.

"I'm going to go and take a shower," Alyssa said, wrapping her hands around her mug as if to warm herself up, even though it was uncomfortably hot in the kitchen. She shuddered slightly.

"I'm so tired," she said. "I've been at work for like . . . thirteen hours or something, I think all I've eaten is biscuits for about three days." She closed her eyes and then snapped them open again, shaking her head slightly, refusing to give in to sleep. "A shower will be good though, I think it'll wake me up."

If she were someone else, I might have suggested she try a nap or even a full night's sleep, but I got the impression that Alyssa probably didn't accept advice, and so instead I nodded and gratefully took the mug of tea from her.

"But," Alyssa said, "I really want to catch up with you properly. I'm so excited that we're all here. I've said to the others that we should hang out on the roof later, about eight p.m.? A little get-to-know-you sort of thing?"

She posed this as a question, but I felt instinctively, in my bones, that attendance was mandatory.

"I'll be there," I said.

"Yes," Alyssa replied, as if I was stating the obvious.

I drank my tea in the kitchen, the open window letting in the slightest of breezes and the sounds of the street below. There were kids screeching and parents yelling. The road was on a bus route, and so every few minutes the kitchen was plunged into relative darkness as the number 69 pulled into the stop across the road and blocked the sun. When the bus pulled away, I took my mug over to the sink and washed it carefully. As I was drying it, I looked out onto the park across the road and something pulsed through me. It was so close to homesickness that I felt tears prick in my eyes again, but it wasn't quite that. Somewhere in me, deep down, was a flicker of excitement. Uncle Pete's words had struck a chord (something I have never said before and probably will never say again)—maybe life really was just beginning.

CHAPTER THREE

The roof terrace was accessed via the big bedroom next to my own bathroom-bedroom. I was meeting everyone in ten minutes, and I was stressed because I wasn't well-versed on the etiquette of accessing a communal area via a private one. Was it like a public thoroughfare? Did I have the right-of-way any time of the day or night?

I knew that if I hadn't been specifically invited, I would never venture onto that roof terrace.

I didn't have a full-length mirror in my room yet, so I just had to guess what I looked like. It wasn't difficult to imagine: I have had the same two or three outfits on rotation for the past few years. That night was black jeans with a black belt, a faded gray T-shirt tucked in, with a navy-blue corduroy shirt on top in case I got cold.

I wear a thin gold chain around my neck, once my grandmother's and then my mum's. When I'm nervous I tend to fiddle with it, place it on my bottom lip and taste the sharp metal on my tongue.

The previous tenant of the bathroom-bedroom had left one of those small round mirrors on top of the chest of drawers, so I peered into that, my pores comically enlarged. It was like a funhouse mirror for your face, only not fun, just a terrifying peek at the evidence of your own slow but inevitable decay.

That was the kind of thing my mum hated me saying.

Oh stop, she'd say, *you're so maudlin, you look like a baby, you'll always look like a baby.*

She meant it as a compliment—not the maudlin thing, the baby thing. And I do, I suppose, look a bit like a baby. I'm pretty skinny but still have the chubby rosy cheeks I've had since, I don't know, birth? I have pale skin that never tans and green eyes and sort of sand-colored hair that my mum says is dirty blond, but I'm not sure about that. I don't mind it, I just don't think too much about it. It's cut short because one time in primary school when my hair was long past my shoulders, I let Michael Simmons (class clown, whose mum gave him two chocolate biscuits in his lunch box) paint it blue with that thick paint you squeeze out of a bottle. The real problem though was that just in case it didn't stick, we made sure to cover my hair in a thick layer of PVA glue first—we were real smart guys, me and Michael Simmons.

My mum cut my hair in the kitchen that night with blunt scissors, an old, scratchy bleach-stained towel wrapped around my shoulders. She was cross at first, and silent, but as she cut huge, stiff blue chunks out of my hair, she couldn't help laughing. She began to pass each bit for me to snap satisfyingly between my fingers. She washed whatever blue was left out of my hair while I leaned over the side of the bathtub, my throat pressed uncomfortably into the side as she scrubbed. Cold water trickled down my back and into the waistband of my shorts, but I didn't dare complain.

Once she had finished violently attacking my damp head with a towel, we both stood in front of the big mirror in her bedroom. She carefully arranged my new hair with her fingers so that I almost had the most-coveted boy band hairstyle at that time—curtains.

"You know," she said, "it really suits you like this—although, people might end up thinking you're a boy, especially if you're wearing this."

She tugged gently at the hem of my gym shorts that I had paired with a lime-green Ninja Turtles T-shirt, which was, in my and Michael Simmons's opinion, *very* chic.

And I knew, even then, that she didn't mean this in a good way. But still, something lit up inside me.

I suppose what I'm saying is, I've never looked back since that blue-hair day. And I still think Ninja Turtles are chic. People don't often think I'm a boy these days. But sometimes a girl will do a double take when she sees me just to make sure, and something about that lights me up the very same way.

I waited to leave my room until 8:00 p.m. on the dot, not wanting to hang about on the rooftop alone, or more specifically without Alyssa, who, despite only having met her for a few minutes, was already occupying the space of "social comfort blanket" in my mind.

I closed the door very gently behind me so as not to disturb the sleeping Abigail. She seemed to be as tired out from her long day as I was. A fresh wave of nausea washed over me at the idea that I'd caused her any kind of stress. I couldn't bear to think about what we'd normally be doing at home if I hadn't wrenched us out of our life. I couldn't bear to think about what Mum was doing without us there. Was she going through the motions of our familiar routine? An image of her sitting on the sofa alone popped into my mind, and I immediately banished it, swallowing the lump in my throat. If I let myself think about it, I knew it would be paralyzing. So, instead, I squeezed my eyes shut to block it all out and then knocked softly on the bedroom door next to mine. There was no answer, but when I pressed my ear up against it, I could hear talking, the sound of music on a tinny speaker. I took a deep breath and tentatively opened the door—the French windows on the far side of the room were open, and outside there were three people sitting on camping chairs facing one another.

It's funny to think of them now, like that. Just three strangers on a rooftop, when I had no idea what they would end up becoming.

In front of them was a table that seemed way too low and was scattered with the ends of candles and mugs and saucers acting as makeshift ashtrays. There was a fourth chair, empty, waiting for me.

"Here she is!" Alyssa said. "Come on through, Isobel."

She waved at me with her free hand; the other was clutching a full glass of pink wine. She'd changed out of her scrubs and into a black tracksuit. She seemed infinitely more relaxed than, based on her messages, I ever imagined she could be, and she somehow looked completely revived. That shower really did work.

I lifted my hand in greeting and made my way through the bedroom.

"Everyone," Alyssa said. It looked like she was about to try and get up, but the chair wobbled precariously when she shifted in it, so in the end she gave up and leaned forward instead. "This is Isobel, pronouns she/her, she moved into the tiny bedroom today, she's an artist, and she has a guinea pig called Andrew."

"Oh," I said, "I mean, hi, um she's actually not a . . ."

Alyssa held up her hand to stop me; she shook her head slightly as if to say, *Wait your turn.*

"Isobel, this is Mo, pronouns he/him, he has a very boring job doing marketing for fruit or for juice or something like that, and he actually earns loads of money, but he's moved in here because he got dumped."

Alyssa paused for a moment and then added, "by his *boyfriend.*"

Mo frowned deeply and opened his mouth, presumably to correct her on the litany of mistakes she'd just spouted at me, but she didn't give him the chance. Alyssa was on a roll.

"And," she said, shaking her head as if she couldn't believe what she was about to say, "he's *forty.*"

"Hi, Mo," I said, "it's very nice to meet you. I'm Isobel."

"Hi," forty-year-old Mo said. "Good to meet you too, Isobel."

Mo looked like he could have been my age. He had thick black hair, light brown skin, big round glasses, and the same baby face thing that I've got going on, round with chubby cheeks. I couldn't quite place his accent. Somewhere in the north of England, Yorkshire maybe.

"And this," Alyssa said, "is Robin."

And that was the moment when everything slipped slightly out of focus.

Robin smiled at me, perfect teeth behind full lips. Tanned skin and bleached-blond hair tied up at the nape of her neck. She was wearing a white vest top and gym shorts not dissimilar to the ones I was wearing on the fateful blue-hair day all those years ago. It is not an exaggeration to say that she was the best-looking person I'd ever seen in real life. In fact, she was the best-looking person I'd ever seen, full stop.

Robin did actually get out of her chair to greet me, bounced up, in fact, seemingly effortlessly, placing her own glass of pink wine down on the very low table. She went to shake my hand and then laughed and leaned over to give me a one-armed hug instead—it was a practiced awkwardness, affected but still entirely charming. She was slightly taller than me, so when my arm reached around her waist, I touched the bare skin on her back between her waistband and the hem of her vest top. I pulled my hand back as if I'd been electrocuted. She didn't appear to notice.

I felt it happening again. That thing. I felt the earth shift when my nose brushed Robin's ear as we hugged, when I smelled her hair, a mixture of sweet shampoo and cigarette smoke. When she pulled back and met my eyes and looked at me as if she was both mildly amused and like I was the best thing she'd ever seen.

The way in which I charted the course of my life changed again in that single second—before and after Robin.

"Great to meet you, Isobel," Robin said, apparently completely unaware that she'd just irrevocably altered my life forever. She was posh; that was the second thing I noticed. Her voice was low and a bit husky, as though she was getting over a cold. When she said my name, it was like a bolt of lightning hit me squarely in the chest.

"Robin, pronouns she/her," Alyssa continued loudly and steadily, clearly irritated at her prepared introduction being interrupted. "She used to be a doctor, but she dropped out because she auditioned for drama school on a whim earlier this year and actually got in. She's going to be a star."

Robin smiled at me and, oh no, I could feel my heartbeat in my fingertips.

"All true, unfortunately," she said, smiling. "Well, I don't know about being a star, but I just thought, I've got to stop chasing this crazy NHS dream at some point, the world needs more actors, you know?"

I laughed and gratefully accepted the glass of wine Alyssa passed to me. Mum and I never really drank much at home, but when we did, it was usually something pink like this. I took a sip, and it was sharp and vinegary and familiar. I sat down very carefully in the fourth camping chair, in between Robin and Mo. Robin had one leg resting on the other, jiggling up and down slightly. She had bare feet, and there were discarded Birkenstocks by the side of her chair next to a packet of rolling tobacco. I was very aware of how close her toes were to my knee, and I surprised myself with how badly I wanted them to touch.

"Isobel," Alyssa was saying. My head snapped up from staring at Robin's foot, willing it closer to my leg.

"Sorry," I said. I could feel color rising in my cheeks.

Alyssa smiled at me kindly, although not without some measure of exasperation.

"I was just saying, you're actually impossible to stalk online. Believe me, I tried. And I am *very* good at stalking people online. Usually I don't even need a name. Not even initials."

"Sorry," I said again. "Um, yes. Impossible to stalk online. I just never really got into all that stuff. I never feel like I've got anything very interesting to say. Not that someone else hasn't already said. And it feels weird to post photos of stuff just, like, into the void? Not that I think there's much that people would want to see."

"Wait," Mo said, frowning, "so you don't even have Instagram?"

I shook my head and took another sip of wine. I could feel it going straight to my head. Sharing that popcorn with Abigail felt like a long time ago.

"No TikTok?" Mo said. I shook my head, and his eyes widened with shock. "But how do you get your news?"

"I, um, I just read the news," I said.

Robin snorted with laughter, but Mo nodded slowly, like he'd never heard anything like it in his life.

"I think it's very cool to have no online presence," Robin said, leaning forward to roll a cigarette, using her knee instead of the table.

"Being, like, *very online* is just inherently tragic," she carried on. "When people are sharing every single aspect of their lives, I just think, *Fuck*, you know? You're giving so much of yourself away. And for what? To be consumed by strangers in seconds. It's actually really fucked-up when you think about it."

"Robin," Alyssa said, "you have Instagram. You're on it all the time. You posted literally ten minutes ago."

"I know," Robin said, "but I don't have a choice, I have to have a presence for my work."

For a moment I thought she might really be annoyed with Alyssa for pulling her up, but then she lit her cigarette, took a long drag, and broke out into a broad grin. "Plus," she said, blowing smoke away from the group, "I'm a *massive* hypocrite."

Alyssa rolled her eyes, but she couldn't help but smile—I wondered if Robin was having the same effect on all of us, whether it wasn't just me sitting there slowly losing my mind.

We chatted like that for an hour or so, about everything and nothing. The wine was being poured liberally. We got louder, less inhibited. We told each other about where we'd been before. Where we were going, or where we hoped to go. It was exciting to be among these beautiful, worldly people. It made me feel beautiful and worldly too. I was buoyed by their infectious enthusiasm and, of course, by alcohol.

"So this is like a fresh start for us all." Alyssa paused, a wave of inspiration passing over her face. "Like our Freshers Week, isn't it, really? One last taste of freedom before the hard work starts, or the . . . whatever you guys do." She pointed in between me and Robin. "I mean, I've already started my hard work. But, you know, I can still try and have some fun in between shifts."

"I guess it is a bit like Freshers Week," Robin said. "Christ, I never thought I'd go through that again. As long as I don't have to go to any foam parties, I'm in."

She glanced at me, and I laughed a little bit too hard. I'd obviously never been to a foam party in my life.

"No, but you know what we should do? We should play 'never have I ever,'" Alyssa said. She said it in a way that suggested the idea had just spontaneously occurred to her, but clearly it had been in the cards for weeks. I bet she had a document on the go with all our Freshers Week activities scheduled in; she'd probably email it round as soon as we got back inside.

Mo groaned and leaned back in his chair, covering his face with his free hand. He glanced at his wrist, which was bare, but I shared the sentiment. I was tired suddenly; it felt like we'd been up there for hours. I was torn though between wanting to be in my bed but also wanting to carry on sitting next to Robin—possibly forever.

"No," Mo said, "we shouldn't play 'never have I ever,' Alyssa. Because we're not fifteen."

"Yeah, we should," Robin said, a glint of mischief in her eyes, her face lit up at the idea. She turned to me and raised her eyebrows. "What do you think, Isobel? You want to play?"

My stomach flipped when she said my name. I didn't want to

play the game, but I did want to hear about everything Robin had ever done in her life, to absorb every little thing about her that I possibly could. It was a tricky spot to be in. The idea of her finding out how sheltered a life I'd had, how quiet it was, and how little I'd done, was unbearable.

"I don't know," I said after a moment's hesitation. "Can't we just . . . ask each other questions in a normal way? To, um, to get to know each other? Sort of like we have been doing already? Like . . . a conversation?"

"Like a *what?*" Alyssa said incredulously.

Just as Mo said, "Thank you, yes."

"OK," Robin said, immediately abandoning "never have I ever" and jumping on the new plan. "Yes, good idea, it's like truth or dare but just truths, the best bit."

I frowned slightly at this interpretation of what I'd said and glanced at Mo, who just shook his head at me, defeated.

"Alyssa," Robin said, "your turn first." She screwed up her eyes, pretending to think about a question and then immediately saying, "Tell us all about your last relationship, and, most important, why did it end?"

Alyssa groaned.

"This was your idea," Robin said. "You wanted to get to know each other better, so let's start with you. Go on, let's hear all about it."

"OK," Alyssa said. She took a couple of large gulps of her wine and grimaced. "Fine. So his name was Daniel."

"Oh god, I've got an ex called Daniel," Mo said.

"Ugh," Alyssa said, shaking her head.

"I know," Mo said.

I had so much to learn about life. I had no idea about Daniels.

"So anyway," Alyssa continued, "we only broke up at the beginning of this year. In February." She took a big gulp of her wine. "On Valentine's Day actually. We were together for seven years."

"Sorry," Robin said, leaning forward and frowning exaggeratedly, "I must have misheard you because that sounded like you just said *seven* years."

"Yes," Alyssa said. "Seven."

"But you are a child," Robin said. "You are eighteen years old, maximum."

"It's very normal to have been with someone for seven years. I'm thirty-two, Robin."

"Shut up," Robin said, sitting back in her chair, continuing to study Alyssa closely. "You don't look a day over eleven."

"Thank you," Alyssa said, refusing to let her flow be interrupted. "So, we met at a house party. I thought he was fit; he claims I was very rude to him and that he knew I was *the One* immediately."

Now, that I could absolutely believe.

"It was a total whirlwind, but I just knew it was right. I felt all the things you're meant to feel. We moved in together; we spent every Christmas together, you know? All the stuff. All the stuff you're meant to do when it's right."

Alyssa was quiet for a moment. She looked as though she might raise her glass to her lips, but she didn't. She just held it suspended in midair as if she'd forgotten about it entirely.

"What happened?" I asked quietly.

"Basically, I was really unhappy at work and usually he was so supportive about that kind of thing, and he was at first. He was the one who encouraged me to retrain; he said I should do everything it takes to be happy. But then, and I can't really pinpoint when this started to happen, it just felt like he was getting further and further away from me. You know when people do that? And you try to cling on, but whatever you do they just seem to be harder to reach?"

The others nodded, and after a moment I did too. Because I did know what that's like, even if it's not quite in the same way as Alyssa means. What it's like to be sat next to someone and also, somehow, nowhere even close.

"Anyway," Alyssa continued with a sigh, "Valentine's Day was kind of our anniversary. We always said it was. It was a stupid joke because of when this party was. And he came home from work, and I'd made an effort. I cooked dinner, and I dressed up in this black dress he liked that I couldn't really breathe in. And I'd bought these chocolates in a heart-shaped box—it was sort of a joke but it sort of wasn't, and when he saw what I'd done, he just froze in the doorway, and then he started crying."

"Oh god," Robin said. "Alyssa, it's OK if you don't want to tell us any more. Don't tell us if you don't want to."

"No, it's OK; it's OK," Alyssa said. "It's actually good to talk about it, no one ever asks me about it. We all just sort of pretend it didn't happen the way it did. Like people think I'm embarrassed or ashamed or something, but I'm not; I'm really not."

Alyssa took another deep breath and exhaled slowly.

"So he starts crying, and he can't really look directly at me. And then he says he can't do this to me anymore. That he's met someone at work and that he swears nothing's happened between them but that they've been talking a lot and they both have feelings for each other. He made it sound like I should be grateful, but it's kind of worse, I think, the feelings."

"That is worse," Mo said decisively. "I really think that's worse, you're right. You don't have to be grateful that someone didn't fuck somebody else when they've been telling them they want to."

Alyssa looked momentarily stunned and then nodded at him gratefully. You could almost see the cogs turning—clearly no one had ever said that to her before, confirmed to her that her feelings about it were right.

"So he moved out for a little bit. But he earned more than me, and I couldn't afford the rent by myself so he ended up moving back in, and I left instead. Back in with my mum and my stepdad for a few months. I saved some money and got my shit together. And now I'm here, and I really like this place. I have a good feeling about it. I think I might be really happy here."

Alyssa gestured around the rooftop, flinging her arm out in the direction of the park.

"It feels like a new start. It's something that's just my own. It's still sad sometimes, and I miss him, and I think about what he's doing and whether he's with her and whether he thinks about me at all anymore, but that's OK." She paused for a second and then said, more quietly this time, "Isn't it?"

"Yes," we all said at once, loudly and with conviction.

"It's OK to be sad," I said. "I always try to remember, if you're never sad, then you're also never really happy. You're just sort of . . . nothing."

Alyssa looked at me for a moment, and I worried that I'd said the wrong thing, but then she smiled.

"Exactly," she said. "That's exactly it. You're right, I'd rather feel something than nothing, even if it's fucking painful."

"It goes without saying that it's his loss," Robin said. "What an idiot. He'll do the same thing to her. People don't change; I really believe that."

"Thanks, mate," Alyssa said, and then, without pausing, "OK, now your turn." The joyful glint at the prospect of gossip returned to her eyes. "Robin, what was your *first* relationship, and why did it end?"

I watched as Robin tipped her head back and screwed up her eyes, mock deep thinking.

I knew then that, unfortunately, I was going to find every single little thing she did devastatingly charming.

"So, that would be Jonathan Fleming, and I was, I'm going to say, six years old . . ."

"No, stop," Alyssa said.

"Stop?" Robin said. "Why? Do you know him? Is this bringing something up for you?"

"I didn't mean that; you *know* what I meant. I meant your first proper relationship, not when you were six, obviously."

"Oh!" Robin said. "Fine, but I don't know how Jonathan would feel about being so quickly dismissed; he's a legitimate part of my rich dating history actually. I think of him often."

"He'll cope," Alyssa said.

Robin was quiet for a moment as she began rolling another cigarette, the filter between her lips. No one spoke while we waited for her.

"OK," she said, looking up, "so, then, I guess my first proper relationship was with a girl called Sadie, and I was fifteen years old and she was, get this . . . sixteen years old."

"Whoa," Mo said, "an older woman."

"Right?" Robin said. "She was a full four months older than me, and, oh man, people warned us about that age gap. They said, 'Listen, when you're seventeen, she'll also be seventeen for most of that time,' but did we listen? No. Love is love, I guess."

"Get on with it," Alyssa said. She was still trying to be serious, but the corners of her mouth were twitching.

"So, we both played field hockey, which is, famously, a very gay sport."

Robin looked at me and smiled as if we were in on a joke, and I smiled back knowingly having never picked up a hockey stick in my life.

"We didn't really know each other at all. We'd just see each other in the changing rooms, maybe a nod in the corridor. She was in a different house; we were in different classes; we could have gone through our whole school lives without ever knowing each other, I reckon. But then one day in hockey practice she accidentally hit my hand with her stick and it caught my thumb in such a way that the nail came off. The whole nail just gone."

"Oh Jesus Christ," Alyssa said. She brought her hand up to her mouth. "That's so disgusting, ugh, I can't even bear to think about it."

"Are you kidding?" Robin said. "You're going to be pulling babies out of vaginas? Rips and tears and literal blood and guts."

"Stop talking about it," Alyssa said. "Move on from the thumb thing. I'm not joking, Robin. I'll be sick."

Robin rolled her eyes.

"OK, so she felt awful, obviously, and our PE teacher was raging at her, which was really unfair, but she made Sadie take me to Matron."

"Matron!" Alyssa scoffed.

"I know, I know," Robin said, "we can get into my ridiculous school another time. So, she took me to Matron, and Matron was *so* mean, she made me sit next to an open window to get some fresh air, and when I asked if I could have a painkiller, she acted like I'd asked for a bump of coke. I had to literally beg her to ring my mum to come and get me. Anyway, Sadie stayed with me the whole time. Just sat next to me on this little bench, both of us shivering in our PE kit because of the open window. And I couldn't really bring myself to look at my hand, but she almost couldn't stop looking at it, inspecting the damage she'd done and apologizing over and over."

Robin sighed then; the rest of the story seemed well rehearsed, but the sigh seemed real, wistful.

"And at one point she really gently reached over and took my hand and said, 'God, it looks so painful, I hope it doesn't leave a scar or anything. You have such lovely hands.' And from then on basically, I loved her and I thought I would love her forever."

"What happened?" Mo asked. He was sitting forward in his chair, transfixed. "I can't believe you had a girlfriend in school, I could never in a million years have had a boyfriend, not even a secret one, which"—he raised his eyebrows—"is where I suspect this story is headed, unfortunately?"

"Oh, of course," Robin said. "Which was fun for a while, for example, being allowed to sleep over at each other's houses and parents being none the wiser."

She grinned, and my stomach flipped.

"But it was also mostly absolute torture and pain and a hotbed for feeling intense and uncontrollable shame?"

Mo nodded sagely, and I watched as Robin downed what was left of the wine in her glass.

"I got to a point after a few months where I felt like I loved her—" She stopped for a second. "No, I did love her. I don't want to disregard those feelings just because I was young; they were very real to me. I got to the point where I loved her and I wanted to tell people even if I thought that would be awful and hard. But you know when you love someone and you just want to shout about it? And show them off? When I told her that, she just went completely silent, which I took to mean she was thinking about it and I know now was actually her completely freaking out."

"So did you tell anyone?" I asked. "What happened?"

"I didn't tell anyone," Robin said, "because there was nothing to say in the end. I got to school the next day, and she just pretended like I didn't exist. She wouldn't even look at me. It made me feel quite mad actually. Like, I started to wonder if I'd invented the whole thing. If she ever felt the same way about me at all."

"Fucking hell," Mo said, "I'm sorry."

"It's OK," Robin said, and then, "thanks."

She smiled at Mo, and they shared a grim look.

"Do you ever speak to her now?" Alyssa said. "Do you know what she's up to?"

"No," Robin said, "I left to go to a different sixth form. And after that I never let myself search for her online or anything. I'm over it." She sighed. "But I think I could quite easily have gone down quite a dark path with her. I wanted something from her she couldn't give me. For all I know, and I think this is quite likely, she's told herself it never happened so many times that she believes that now, you know? So, yeah. That's me."

"God," Alyssa said, "no offense but why are we so tragic?"

"I know," Robin said. "Sorry, I feel like that was even more of a downer than it usually is. I swear I normally manage to get a couple of laughs in."

"OK, you can ask another question, Robin," Alyssa said. "Maybe something a bit fun to make up for that."

"Oh," Robin said, "I was going to ask Mo about whether he has a difficult relationship with his father and then make us all go round the group and say all the different ways we feel we've disappointed our parents. But I guess I could ask something else instead."

Robin lit the cigarette she'd been rolling and grinned at Mo.

"OK, Mo, where's the weirdest place you've ever had sex?"

We all laughed, grateful for the change in tone. The atmosphere shifted easily. However much Alyssa liked to think that she was in charge, it was clear in that moment that Robin was the conductor of us all, bringing us down and lifting us up at her will.

Mo raised his eyebrows and reached over to take Robin's cigarette from her. He inhaled slowly before passing it back. He screwed up his face as he blew out the smoke, like he was remembering why he didn't normally do it. He brought his hand up to his mouth like he was expecting to cough but he didn't, he just held it there for a second while he considered his answer.

"Well, first of all," he said. "I want to make it clear that I reject the central premise of the question. What even is *weird* in this context? Like, do we really want to categorize things into 'normal' and 'weird'? Especially when it comes to sex. We're past that as a society, surely?"

Robin rolled her eyes at him and cocked her head to one side.

"Oh, shut up," she said affectionately, "you know what I mean."

"OK, yeah," Mo said, nodding. He thought for a brief moment before answering, decisively, "Sea kayak."

Alyssa's eyes widened and she opened her mouth, but Mo held up his hand to stop her speaking.

"No further questions at this time."

Alyssa shrieked with laughter, and immediately, like they'd been waiting for their moment, someone in the garden below shushed her, which just made her cackle even more.

"It's early," Alyssa said loudly, "we're just having a nice time."

"Yeah, well I'm just trying to sleep," the voice from below yelled back, a distinct Scottish twang. "Some of us have to get up early tomorrow. So can you maybe stop screaming?"

"Are you sleeping in the garden?" Alyssa yelled back. "Why are you outside? If you go inside the house you won't be able to hear us."

Robin giggled, and Mo shook his head at her.

"Sorry!" he called out. "Don't worry, we'll keep it down."

We heard a door slam and then silence.

"I met her earlier," I whispered. "I met her outside the house, that grumpy neighbor—she thinks I stole her bike."

Alyssa screwed up her face at the very thought. "I hope she never finds her stupid bike."

"Alyssa!" Mo said.

"What?" Alyssa said. "I was just laughing at having sex in a sea kayak like any normal, reasonable person. It's not my fault she's boring."

I was so focused on trying to figure out the logistics of how one might go about having sex in a sea kayak that I briefly forgot to worry about the fact that it was my turn next, so when Mo said my name, quietly, a stage whisper, my stomach flipped.

"Last, but certainly not least, my question is for the lovely Isobel—I want to know, who was your gay awakening?"

I didn't know what question I was expecting, but it certainly wasn't that.

Mo smiled at me; he'd obviously chosen this particular question, like Robin, with the intention of keeping things light.

"Mo," Alyssa said, before I got a chance to speak. "You can't ask that. That's rude."

"It's not rude," Robin said. She stubbed out her cigarette and smiled encouragingly at me. "Everyone's got one."

"Not *everyone*," Alyssa said, glaring at her, "and not everyone wants to talk about it even if they have got one. You don't have to answer that, Isobel. Just think of another question, Mo. Ask about her hamster or something."

Alyssa made us all fill out a form she made herself on Word before we moved in, and so she knew I didn't specify a sexuality when asked. I left that section blank, and she replied to my email within thirty seconds asking, "Did you know you missed this one out, babe xx?"

I said "yes," and she said, "OK hun xx."

"No, it's fine," I found myself saying. "It's OK. I don't mind answering. But, thank you," I said to Alyssa. I nodded at her, and she frowned at me like, *You're sure?*

I could feel that my cheeks were pink from the wine and the proximity of Robin and the outrageously personal question, but I felt excited by it too. No one had ever asked me anything like that before. No one had ever thought of me in that way. It was strangely thrilling as well as, obviously, mortifying.

"So the thing is," I said, sort of to no one, just out across the rooftops, "is that I've never really come out, as such."

"What?" Mo said just as Robin said, "Oh shit."

"No, no, it's OK," I said. I leaned forward and placed my empty wineglass down on the table; Alyssa was refilling it before I'd even moved my hand away. I felt a rush of fondness for her even though I was sure that if I drank any more wine I might not be able to stand up.

"I've never really come out," I continued, "but I've also never not come out; does that make sense?"

I was met with a sea of blank looks. Alyssa opened her mouth, immediately keen to fill even the slightest of silences, so I made sure to get in there first.

"OK," I said, "I mean, I've never said I'm straight, and I've never said I'm not straight. No one has ever asked really. I've always just kind of . . ." As I reached around for the word, I picked up my glass again and took a sip of warm wine, before landing on: "I've always just existed, I suppose."

I thought about the majority of my life. Me and Mum on the sofa. Quietly disassociating at the pottery café. Alone in my room. Existing.

"I'm so sorry," Mo said, "I just assumed because of . . ."

His hand hovered in midair, while he decided what specifically to point out about me. In the end he just waved in my general direction. I wanted to melt into the camping chair, just disintegrate into the fabric forever. It was an odd feeling, to be really seen by someone.

"Because of everything really," he said. "Your whole vibe is very . . ." He shook his head slightly, deciding not to finish his sentence. "But I shouldn't have ever assumed; I'm truly sorry. I've just had some wine and I was being silly."

"But wait though, have you ever had a boyfriend?" Alyssa asked, apparently having forgotten the indignation she felt on my behalf mere moments ago.

"No boyfriend," I said.

"Not even at primary school?"

"Nope. I was perpetually single at primary school, just could not get a date."

Alyssa frowned at me.

"And no girlfriend?" she said.

"No," I said, somewhat wistfully. "No girlfriend."

Alyssa nodded thoughtfully. She looked at me like I was an exhibit in a museum, her eyes narrowed, trying to figure me out.

"And no one at home was ever like, 'Isn't it so weird you've never had a boyfriend or girlfriend?'"

"Alyssa!" Robin exclaimed.

I couldn't even bear to look at her; the idea of her feeling sorry for me was a waking nightmare.

"What?" Alyssa said. "I'm just trying to understand."

I smiled at her. I knew her intentions were good, even if her delivery was what I imagine it's like to be interviewed in police custody.

"No one thought it was weird," I said. "I just was never that kind of person. We never talked about it at home."

I remembered my mum once asking me if I'd danced with any boys at the primary school disco and me saying yes and her face lighting up and how I instinctively realized that I had misunderstood the question. That she didn't mean did I spend all night with the boys skidding all over the floor and running around, she meant did I put my hands on their shoulders and let them put their hands on my waist and slow dance. I don't think she ever asked about boys again after that. Or girls.

"But you're, like, really pretty," Alyssa said, "or, like, good-looking or whatever? Can I say pretty? Sorry I don't know, I don't want to offend you." Alyssa looked to Mo and Robin for backup. "But she is though, isn't she?"

I blushed furiously, still not daring to look up. I would have fainted in my seat if I knew Robin thought I was "pretty or good-looking or whatever."

"It's not really about that though," Mo said, coming to my rescue. "If you don't want a relationship, you don't need one. And you certainly don't need a relationship to define who you are. And you don't even need to define who you are if you don't want to, especially not to a group of drunk people playing a game. You can just be you."

I let Mo's words hang in the air for a moment. I swallowed hard. I've always just been me, I suppose, but the way he said it, he meant something different.

"It's not that I never wanted a relationship, I don't think. . . . It just never . . . it's never really happened for me. And that's OK. It's not that I haven't ever been happy."

There were murmurs of agreement from everyone, although I could tell that they were finding it hard to believe that I'd been happy with twenty-eight years of singledom.

"One more question," Robin said, "if I may? And you don't have to answer it, obviously, seeing as you have, without a shadow of a doubt, been the most thoroughly grilled housemate this evening."

I finally looked up at her. I expected to feel embarrassed, but surprisingly I didn't. She wasn't looking at me with the sympathy I was dreading; she was looking at me with interest.

"Sure," I said. "Go for it."

"Do you fancy people? Or, like, not really?"

"I fancy people," I said, "all the time."

I'm amazed there weren't love hearts shooting out of my eyes at that moment, a huge arrow pointing from my heart to hers.

Robin broke out into a grin.

"Same," she said. "I love having a crush; I think it's healthy to always fancy someone. Adds a bit of pep to your day, keeps you on your toes."

"I never fancy anyone," Alyssa said. "Because men are disgusting."

"Tell me about it," Mo said.

"So, Isobel," Robin said, ignoring the others, keeping her focus on me, "since this year is all about a fresh start, it could be the time to finally meet someone."

"Maybe," I said.

"Definitely," Alyssa said. "I can feel it, you're going to have sex ASAP."

"Alyssa," Mo groaned.

"What?" Alyssa said. "I mean only if you want to, obviously. Do you want to, Isobel?"

Thankfully before I could even think of an answer, and before Alyssa inevitably asked if I'd ever had sex before—I could basically see the question written all over her face—Robin rescued me.

"Time for bed," she said. "I think we've interrogated Isobel enough for one night. Enough forever probably. I wouldn't be surprised if we wake up in the morning and she's moved out to escape us. I wouldn't blame you for a second."

"Oh, no," I said, before I'd even thought about what I was saying, "I'm not going anywhere."

"Hmm," Mo said, slowly pulling himself up out of the camping chair and stretching, "let's see how you feel after your first night in the tiny bedroom. Yeah, come on, let's go. Before we get in any more trouble."

"True, I've never slept in a bathroom-bedroom before," I said, and Mo honked with laughter.

"I didn't want to say"—he shook his head—"but it's still got ..."

"Tiles?" I said. "One of the main things a person can want from a bedroom?"

The others headed down to the kitchen, and while they were chatting, I brushed my teeth in the unfamiliar actual bathroom. My stomach rumbled, but I was too tired to eat, or too wired, I couldn't figure out which. I gathered up armfuls of Abigails and swept them onto the floor so I could climb into my unmade bed. My head was spinning, but it wasn't unpleasant. A combination of the wine and an entire mental reset. My thoughts were racing so fast, I could barely keep up with them. A cocktail of exhilaration and, somewhere in there, panic. And sadness, I wasn't surprised that when I squeezed my eyes shut, tears began to roll down my cheeks. What a lot of time I had spent unexamined.

As I drifted in and out of sleep, I was jolted awake by my phone vibrating under the pillow next to me. My first thought was that it was Mum. I grabbed it and breathed a sigh of relief when I saw what it was.

47A Girlies!! <3

Alyssa: *We need a house WhatsApp group, obviously! Wanted to wait to set this up until you were with us, Isobel. I'm so glad the gang is all together, we're gonna have so much fun!! :) xx*

Alyssa: *We can talk about all house things on here and make our plans for freshers week and share goss and all the good stuff but also if something needs cleaning you know where you'll hear about it lol!!! xx*

Robin: *Looking forward to being told off on here 24/7, Al. Thanks, mate*

Mo: *Just so you know, I'm muting this immediately*

Mo: *(Thanks for a lovely evening though, 47A girlies)*

I smiled dopily at the screen, too tired to add anything but happy to be involved. Just as I'd switched my phone off the vibrate setting and was about to put it face down for the night, one more message popped up on the screen. It was a number I didn't yet have saved, but I recognized the photo.

Robin: *So fun to get to meet you tonight, Isobel! Hope this isn't an overstep but i did just want to say if you ever want to chat about anything, i am next door—i'm aware tonight might have been a bit overwhelming*

Robin: *And after all that you never even got the chance to answer who your gay awakening was*

Robin: *Maybe next time*

CHAPTER FOUR

I woke up the following morning with a banging headache and four missed calls from my mother. When I called her back, she answered the phone before I even heard a single ring. I opened my mouth to say hello, but nothing came out.

"Isobel? Isobel, are you OK?" She sounded, not uncharacteristically, frantic. "What happened? I couldn't get hold of you."

I cleared my throat and tried to speak again, my mouth so dry that my tongue was sticking. There was no water by the side of my bed like there usually was. I found myself gazing longingly across the room at the water bottle in Abigail's cage. Truly desperate.

"Mum," I croaked, several octaves lower than usual, "I'm fine, I just wasn't really on my phone. I ended up having a few drinks last night."

"Where?"

"At home," I said, and then corrected myself quickly, "here, I mean. At the house."

She was silent for a moment. My mother doesn't need to speak sometimes—her thoughts are loud enough.

"I couldn't get ahold of you," she said again, and she sighed heavily. "I was worried about you. I thought something might have happened."

She didn't sound angry or disappointed even, she sounded exhausted. I had no doubt that she had been awake all night. I didn't even want to think about all the grim ends I had met in her mind.

"I'm sorry," I said, attempting to sit up—a huge mistake; the spinning room made my stomach lurch. I gently nestled back into my pillows again and closed my eyes. "I got carried away getting to know everyone. I should have messaged you."

"No," she said, "no, it's OK, don't be sorry. You should be getting to know people, making friends. That's a good thing, I was just . . . Have you taken your . . ."

"Mum," I said. "I woke up thirty seconds ago."

"Right," she said, "yes, of course."

There was a pause, which I filled with trying not to throw up.

"What will you do today?" Mum said, after a moment.

"Well," I said, swallowing hard, closing my eyes, placing my hand on my head like a damsel in distress, "I need to drink some water."

"And?" she said.

"I can't really see past that right now, to be honest."

"Isobel."

"Mum."

"Do you promise me that you're OK?"

"Yes. I promise," I said as my eyes throbbed. My skull felt as though it was about to split in two. I wondered if I'd even be able to make it down to the kitchen alive. I wished that the bathroom-bedroom was still just a bathroom and I could simply turn my head and drink from the tap.

"All right," she said, "well, will you at least message me later on so I know you're safe? You don't need to call. I know you're busy."

"Yes," I said. "I will. I promise. And, Mum, what will you do today?"

"Oh, you know," she said, brushing the question away, "the usual."

We were both quiet for a moment as we silently acknowledged that neither of us knew what that was anymore. Mum had no work on Sundays; the library was closed. The usual was both of us together. My stomach lurched again, a different kind of nausea.

"I love you, Mum," I said.

"Take your pills," she said.

I bit my lip and nodded silently into the phone. I know that she heard me anyway.

When I eventually managed to make it downstairs to shakily fill somebody else's pint glass with water, there was a mug on the draining board and the scent of sickly, sweet perfume in the air. Alyssa had been up already and gone to work; she was probably delivering babies that very second—a miracle if she felt anything like I did. That woman truly was a force of nature. I sat at the strange kitchen table with my head in my hands.

I opened one eye when I heard footsteps approaching the kitchen.

"How's the patient doing?"

Robin leaned against the doorframe and grinned at me. She was wearing pretty much the same outfit as yesterday—white vest top, shorts—and I noticed for the first time, she had a small tattoo on her thigh, which of course made me blush. It was two short lines of text, and I'd never wanted to read anything more in my life.

"Huh?" I said articulately, charmingly.

Robin laughed and came to sit down next to me, resting her feet on the bottom of my chair. She lifted the back of her hand to my forehead and gently pressed against it as if taking my temperature. She smelled like sun cream and cigarette smoke, a combination I'd never previously thought could have the power to make me lightheaded. I found myself involuntarily leaning into her hand.

"Hmmm." Robin removed it after a moment and sat back in her chair. She looked at me and shook her head. "I'm afraid it's a rather bad case of what we refer to medically as Way Too Much Wine."

"Will I ever recover, Doctor?" I said.

I wrapped both hands around my glass just for something to do with them. I suddenly felt deeply self-conscious in my shorts that were technically swimming trunks and my old Glazed T-shirt, long retired and living out its twilight years as pajamas.

"It's touch and go," Robin said. "I've seen miraculous recoveries, but I'm afraid to say, I've also seen people take devastating nosedives. Let me ask you this, miss . . . I'm terribly sorry, remind me of your surname again?"

The corners of my mouth were twitching, but I resisted the urge to break into a grin. I wanted to play her game.

"It's Bailey, *Ms.* Bailey, if you don't mind, actually."

Robin raised her eyebrows then, a glint of something in her eyes. I wondered gleefully if she was repressing her own smile.

"Ms. Bailey, of course. Apologies. My question to you, as it is to all my patients suffering from your particular condition, is have you eaten yet?"

I shook my head and then very quickly stopped: the movement made me dizzy enough that I thought I might fall off my chair.

"Water only," I said, nodding at my glass.

"Right," Robin said, tapping my bare knee gently with her index finger. It was so quick I could have missed it apart from the fact it sent shock waves shooting through my entire body. "Then my prescription for you is this—finish your water, take two paracetamol, quick prayer to all gods to cover your bases, and then you come to breakfast with me. It will make or break you, but I have a feeling you're strong; you're going to rally. What do you think?"

I nodded in a way I hoped suggested I was reluctantly agreeing rather than suggested I would have jumped off a cliff with her had she asked me to.

"I'll do whatever it takes, Doctor."

"Go and get dressed," she said. "I'm afraid it's a time-sensitive cure; we need to hurry." She swung her legs away from my chair to let me out, and I slid past her; our knees touched briefly. I flinched away, but Robin didn't move; she just sat back watching me.

"I hope this works," I said from the doorway. I pointed at her, and she raised her eyebrows at me. "You know I'm putting my life in your hands."

"I'm a professional, Ms. Bailey," Robin said, taking a sip from my abandoned glass of water. "You can trust me."

Fifteen minutes later we were strolling down the street, blinking into the sunshine. Well, I was blinking, Robin was wearing sunglasses and rolling a cigarette as she walked. This was the first time I'd ventured out into my new neighborhood. I tried to take it all in—the noise, the people speeding past on bikes, the fruit and veg piled up outside, the coffee shops with no names and the people standing outside them with anxious-looking sight hounds—but it all faded. I was singularly focused on the person walking next to me.

"We've not got far to go," Robin said, "don't worry. Are you hanging in there? Not going to faint on me, are you?"

"I'll survive, I think," I said. "I'm very brave."

I didn't want to reveal that proximity to Robin appeared to have cured me of my hangover entirely—I didn't just feel better, I felt wonderful, on top of the world even.

"Are you really not feeling it at all?" I asked. I glanced at her; she was concentrating on her cigarette.

"Oh, I've definitely felt better," Robin said, "don't get me wrong. But fortunately I've built up a rather strong tolerance for rosé over the course of the summer. Or unfortunately I suppose, if you're my liver or my bank balance."

We stopped outside a café on the edge of the park that looked like the kind of place I might have been taken to when I was a child—my mum carefully watching me eat pieces of toast while she nursed a single cup of milky tea.

"Do you mind if we sit outside?" Robin asked, pulling a chair out from under a table on the street and making a move to sit down. "It's not too hot yet, is it?"

It was 11:00 a.m. and sweltering. Even the backs of my knees were sweating.

"No, of course not," I said. "I'm fine, plus it's good for people watching out here."

Robin lit her cigarette, inhaled deeply, and slid a laminated menu toward me. I watched as she blew the smoke up in the air, away from me.

"I don't need to look," Robin said, nodding toward the menu. "I always get the same thing here. I recommend salt and grease and caffeine consumed slowly. I guarantee in an hour you're going to be a brand-new person. Better than you were yesterday even."

Robin ordered a bacon sandwich and a cup of black coffee. I very nearly ordered the same before I remembered that I was meant to be a vegan.

"I try to tell myself that the smell is better than the taste," I said. "But I'm lying to myself, aren't I?"

"I'm afraid so," Robin said. "I feel terrible about it, to be honest. I do keep meaning to go veggie, it's one of the many things I like to flagellate myself over and then, ultimately, do nothing about."

We both looked at the nearly finished cigarette between her fingers, and she grinned, took one final drag, and, in the absence of an ashtray, stubbed it out beneath her foot.

Robin gestured to my coffee and then pointed at me.

"Drink up, Ms. Bailey, you're looking a bit peaky."

I did as I was told, my heart pounding extra hard, thunder in my ears. The coffee, thick and tar-like, slid down my throat, and I shuddered. It tasted like medicine.

Our sandwiches arrived quickly—Robin's bacon and my vegan substitute. I drowned it in ketchup and took a tentative bite. I chewed slowly and carefully and allowed a couple of minutes between bites. Robin was right—grease and salt and caffeine consumed slowly really did bring me back to life.

Robin ate her food quickly and enthusiastically and ordered another coffee to drink while she watched me eat. I apologized for my speed, or lack of it.

"Oh please," Robin said. "I don't have anywhere to be, it's a pleasure to sit here and watch you try to survive eating a sandwich."

"So, when does your course start?" I asked, licking some stray ketchup from my thumb, beginning to relish the sharp vinegar, the acid on my tongue. The nausea was passing.

"Tomorrow," Robin said. She lit the cigarette she'd been rolling and blew the smoke out slowly. "I'm really nervous about it to be honest."

I raised my eyebrows—it was hard to imagine Robin being nervous about anything.

"Why?"

Robin's phone lit up between us. She glanced at it but instead of picking it up, she turned it over so she couldn't see the screen.

She could have just given me a generic answer: that it's always nerve-racking starting anything new, that she was sure she'd be fine once she got there. But she didn't; she sat for a moment and considered it.

"I suppose," she said, after a moment, "I rarely do anything I don't know for sure that I'm good at. And I even more rarely do anything where other people have the opportunity to witness me being vulnerable or to judge me. I worked very hard at medical school, and I worked very hard as a doctor, and people see that as an achievement and a vocation. But this . . ." She shook her head. "The way I've had to back myself to make this decision. To recognize that I was really unhappy and I needed to do something else—basically it feels like a lot of people are waiting for me to fail, you know? A lot of 'I told you so' and 'What were you thinking?' right on the tip of everyone's tongues. My parents think I've lost the plot, that I'm having some kind of nervous breakdown."

"Are you?" I asked.

"Not right now," she said.

"But you must be good," I said, "or you wouldn't have got into drama school in the first place, right? You had to audition, didn't you?"

Robin nodded, tapped ash onto the floor.

"I did. I guess I know that I'm good enough to get to this stage. I'm good enough to get in. And then it's like, OK, you can leave that at the door because so are all these other people who are younger than you or more experienced than you or, I don't know, whose parents are on prime-time TV. It will be starting from scratch on Monday. I'm going to be a small fish in a big pond and I've worked very hard to make sure I haven't felt like that in a long time. I know this is hardly the biggest sob story—will the white middle-class doctor survive drama school? It's such a hard life!"

"It's your life though," I said. "It's OK to be stressed about it. You don't have to be flippant about it, or apologetic for caring. It's frightening to start something new. You're just acknowledging that."

Robin frowned at me, in mock confusion. She sat back in her chair, studying me.

"I thought you were brutally hungover and could barely string a sentence together. Where did that come from?"

"What?" I said. "I blacked out."

Robin threw her head back and laughed.

"I'm highly therapized," I said. "Sometimes I feel like I don't retain anything, and then something comes over me and I am momentarily very wise."

Robin nodded, still studying me, smiling now.

"You had it all mapped out," I continued, "and now you're taking a risk. That's huge."

"It does feel like that, a risk," Robin said.

"Are you a risk-taker, do you think?" I asked.

I genuinely didn't intend for it to be a flirty question, but somehow it came out that way. I blushed, and Robin grinned. She leaned forward again in her chair, pushed her sunglasses back down.

"I can be, about some things. Why? Are you?"

"No," I said. "I'm not. Ever."

"I disagree," Robin said. "I mean, based on what I know about you so far, which admittedly isn't much. But haven't you dropped everything you've ever known to move to London and pursue your dreams?"

I picked up my paper napkin, wiped ketchup and grease from the corners of my mouth.

"I suppose, then," I said, after a moment's consideration, "I've taken precisely one risk."

"Just one risk might be all you need," Robin said. "Are you nervous?"

"Oh, constantly," I said.

"I mean about starting your new job."

"I know," I said. "Yes, those particular nerves have been incorporated into the general feelings of dread."

We walked home slowly. Robin stopped to buy some sparkling water at a newsagent and then handed it to me, telling me it was the final stage of my recovery. She was right. By the time we got back to the house and the bottle was empty, I did feel like a brand-new person. The kind of person who walks around in the sunshine getting breakfast with their gorgeous housemate. It was hard to believe that I'd ever been anybody else. I'd been at home in Margate just the day before, but in that moment it felt worlds away.

Mo was sitting with his laptop at the kitchen table when we got in, wearing a white cotton dressing gown with the sleeves rolled up.

"Hi, lads," he said, "sorry, I hope you don't mind me hanging out down here in this"—he gestured at his dangerously short robe—"but my room is a thousand degrees, and this is the only place in the house that feels remotely bearable."

He looked us up and down.

"How are you wearing clothes? How have you even been outside when it's like this?"

Robin pushed herself up so she was sitting on the kitchen counter, legs dangling. She picked an apple from the bowl and bit into it.

"We've been eating bacon sandwiches in the sun, haven't we, Isobel?" she said, crunching, her mouth full. "Curing our hangovers."

She winked at me conspiratorially, and my cheeks reddened. I caught Mo's eye.

"Vegan bacon," I said. "From vegan pigs."

"Well," he said, "I think you're both mad."

I looked around the kitchen, at the bare walls and the chipped, grubby magnolia paint.

"It's a bit bleak in here, isn't it?" I said.

I thought of our kitchen at home, the jumble of trinkets we'd acquired over the years, the bright yellow walls and the low-level hum of Radio 4 my mum played constantly—she could never stand the quiet.

"Beyond bleak," Mo said. "I asked the letting agent if the landlord might paint the kitchen, and he fully laughed in my face."

"There's a hook," Robin said, pointing to the space on the wall above Mo's head, "we could hang something up."

"We could put an Issy Original up there," I said.

I froze, instantly flooded with embarrassment, Issy Originals was something Mum and I said. I braced myself for them to laugh at me, but they didn't.

"Yes!" Mo said. "Go and get it! These walls are crying out for an Issy Original."

I returned from my room with a large framed sketch—Abigail in dark gray and neon pink and blue, one of my favorites. I stood on a chair and hung it on the wall while the others watched.

"Fuck off," Mo said.

I glowed at the compliment, the highest praise.

"Thanks, Mo."

"Aha," Robin said, "so you're like, really, really good, then."

"I mean, I don't want to toot my own horn," I said.

"But yeah," Robin said.

"But yeah," I agreed, "I like to think I'm number one in the field of chinchilla fan art."

"So she's a chinchilla," Robin said, "not a guinea pig called Andrew."

"Not Andrew," I say. "Abigail."

"I love it," Mo said. "I feel like she's watching over us."

"Our fairy godmother, Abigail," Robin said.

I left Robin and Mo chatting in the kitchen and started the painful journey up to my room. I needed to lie completely still with my eyes closed. I didn't feel sick anymore, just deeply bone-tired and sort of not really in my own body.

"Oh, Isobel." I heard Mo's voice from the bottom of the stairs.

I looked down to see that he was holding a brown cardboard package.

"This came for you earlier."

He must have read my mind that going back down and up the

stairs felt impossible because he ran up, taking them two at a time, and handed it to me.

"Thank you," I said.

"Useful to have a massive hole in the door," Mo said. "They can just chuck parcels in. Let's maybe leave it how it is. Landlord doesn't have to know, eh?"

When I finally made it to my bathroom-bedroom, I chucked the package down on the bed and knelt down next to Abigail's cage. I poked my finger through the bars.

"Hey," I whispered, "are you awake? Are you doing OK, little one?"

I listened carefully. Not even a rustle. She was clearly fast asleep.

I looked around me. I was in the only space that wasn't covered in boxes, some ripped open, most still closed. It added to the feeling of slightly disassociating. I was all packed away still; I hadn't quite landed anywhere yet. I resolved to do something about it soon. But not then, then I needed sleep.

I climbed up onto the bed and took my phone out of my pocket to set an alarm. I knew from bitter experience that a nap longer than an hour is dangerous. I had two new messages, which I read through bleary eyes.

Mum: *Hi Isobel, I just wanted to check again that you're taking your medication at the same time every day, it really does make a difference. I know you know that. It's just if you could confirm to me that you know that, that would be good. Also please wear sun cream. Factor 50. Do you have some? I'm sure you have some. OK. Speak to you later. I hope you're having a nice day. Remember to stay in the shade. And to drink plenty of water. And to get an early night. Big day tomorrow. Let me know when you've seen this. Mum.*

Elizabeth Staggs: *Looking forward to tomorrow, Isobel. I know you're moving this weekend. I hope you've settled into your new place OK. I'm just around the corner if you need anything—when I said you could ring me anytime, I meant it. And remember to have some proper fun this weekend before the hard work starts. Elizabeth.*

I sent my mum a thumbs-up and placed my phone face down on my bedside table, unable to cope with writing coherent messages right now. I opened my bedside drawer, popped a small white pill from a packet, and swallowed it. She was right, I did know I had to take it at the same time every day. And she was right again: I'd forgotten.

I lay flat on my back and ripped open the cardboard package, holding it above my head.

Inside was a small wooden sign with a piece of string attached so it could be hung on the wall. It read: *Normal Gets You Nowhere* and it also featured, inexplicably, an illustration of what appeared to be an Aperol spritz.

I stared at it for a moment before shaking the box, refusing to believe that was it. A printed note fluttered out, landing on my face.

Always proud of you, Iz. Normal or not. Go get 'em. Love Uncle Pete and Auntie Jan xxx

Incredible. I rolled my eyes. But still I set it down on my bedside table, leaning it up against the wall so I could see it from my bed and remind myself every day that even though I'm abnormal, that's OK! And of course, crucially, to remind myself: Aperol spritz.

Beautiful.

———

That evening, I sat in bed with my sketchbook and doodled absentmindedly, trying to soothe my Sunday night nerves, to make my eyes heavy enough to sleep. I drew the fish on my bathroom-bedroom tiles, the Abigails spilling from boxes on my floor, next door's giant tree looming outside the window. Objects in isolation, floating around the page.

CHAPTER FIVE

I woke up with a start on the first day of my new job. I checked the time on my alarm clock and groaned when I saw that it was not due to wake me with fake birds and a synthetic dawn for another hour.

In the whirlwind of the previous couple of days it had almost been possible to forget that I was actually there, living that strange, new life away from home for a reason. That I hadn't just been transplanted to that house in East London to play "never have I ever" with strangers and spend extraordinary amounts of money on ordinary things. I was actually there to work. I was there to make art for a living. Well, I was there to be around art for a living, which was more than I'd ever thought was possible. Despite the insistence of some of the more enthusiastic parents who came into Glazed—Thomas the Tank Engine plates are not high art.

I rolled over and considered trying to go back to sleep, but I already knew it would be impossible. My thoughts were racing, skin tingling, legs restless—my body was raring to go, even if my mind wasn't quite there yet.

I wondered if my mum was awake too, sitting upright at the kitchen table in our flat, thinking about me. I thought about messaging her—I even opened our chat, my fingers hovering—but I didn't. I placed my phone face down on my bedside table instead, and I felt the guilt immediately. It was quiet though, and I knew she'd interrupt that, in all the ways possible. I wanted to savor that morning where I felt like the only soul awake in London, and keep it just for myself.

I crept down to the kitchen to make myself a cup of tea and wasn't surprised to see that Alyssa had already been there before me. I washed her mug, bucket-size and bright pink with a glittery *A* on it, while I waited for the kettle to boil. I stared out absent-mindedly over the park, the sky turning pink over the trees, and noticed that I was already becoming accustomed to it, that view, the fact of being there in that house. It no longer made my stomach flip. It no longer felt like a dream. My feet were touching the ground for the first time in days.

I had already picked out an outfit to wear on my first day. I decided to go for all black, which felt like the kind of thing serious creative people wear so as not to distract from the business of being serious creatives. Straight-legged trousers with a belt, a crisp new T-shirt with the sleeves cuffed (obviously), Doc Martens shoes, a flash of white sock to show some personality. I wore my usual jewelry— Grandmother's gold chain, two tiny gold hoops in each ear.

When I looked at myself in the mirror, I couldn't tell if instead of looking like an important artist, I actually just looked like I was going to a funeral or to my job as a puppeteer.

As I frantically rooted through my still-packed boxes searching for something, anything else to wear—although I had no idea what—there was a gentle knock on my bedroom door.

"Come in," I said, without looking up. I had stumbled across an old pajama top with Garfield on it and in my state of panic was trying to decide if I could make that work. Was Garfield chic?

"I've not got any hands, let me in," a muffled voice said from the other side of the door.

Mo was standing in the doorway wearing his tiny robe and clutching two large cups of coffee. His hair, even though he'd clearly just woken up, was immaculate.

"I thought you might be in need of a caffeine boost and a pep talk," he said, a sleepy smile on his face. I could have kissed him.

He looked around my room, at the floor covered entirely with discarded clothes and endless Abigails and then took in my manic expression, my pink cheeks, the beads of sweat forming on my upper lip.

"And," he said, "it looks like I was right."

"I look like a mime," I said, turning back to face the mirror, pulling at my T-shirt.

"No," Mo said calmly, sitting down on the edge of my bed and handing me one of the cups, "you look lovely. A lovely mime."

He leaned back onto my bed, assessing me. I took a sip of coffee and almost grimaced at the strength of it, although the warmth was comforting. I would deal with the heart palpitations later. I mean, I was already having heart palpitations.

"Do you ever wear glasses?" Mo asked, after a moment.

"No," I said. "I have twenty-twenty vision."

"Shame," he said, chewing his lip and continuing to evaluate me.

"And do you have any tattoos?"

He asked this as if I might be able to produce some out of one of the boxes and try them on for him.

I looked down at my arms as if expecting some to magically appear, as if I might have one that I'd forgotten about.

"Um, no," I said, folding my arms across my chest, starting to become self-conscious about the unsolicited full-body appraisal I was being given.

Mo took a sip of his coffee, placed his mug down on my bedside table, and then pointed at me like he'd just landed on the solution.

"You've absolutely got to get tattoos, Issy. You'd look fucking great. And you've got good arms actually, strong. All that knitting and using the potter's wheel and stuff probably. Very sexy."

"Do you think?" I said, looking at my sexy knitter's arms with fresh eyes. "I'm worried I'm not really a tattoo person, I'm a bit too . . ."

"What?" Mo said, frowning.

"I don't know. I'm not very cool."

Mo laughed, shaking his head at me.

"Tattoos aren't cool," he said, "everyone's got them. What even is 'cool' anyway? Nothing's cool. Everything's cool. You're a tattoo person, if you want to be! Don't ever let anyone tell you you're not. You've got to just do whatever you want. Get that tattoo, baby!"

I decided not to point out that it was actually Mo who wanted me to get a tattoo, but I did stare at myself in the mirror, imagining what I might look like. Pretty good actually, I thought. I knew what I'd get immediately, obviously.

Elizabeth Staggs's studio was a thirty-minute walk from my new house and so, full of nerves and dread and excitement, I decided to go in on foot. I left myself over an hour and then walked so quickly that when I arrived, I had plenty of time to spare. I bought myself an iced coffee and sat on a bench on the little green opposite, sweating profusely.

I put my phone away for a few minutes to watch the world go by, let my brain suffer a moment of peace and quiet. I have a complicated relationship with watching the world go by. Sometimes it's a good place for me, to watch dogs run around and people chatting and the trees being nudged by the breeze. But sometimes, without the company of a podcast or the same upbeat song over and over again, my raw thoughts creep in, like parasites looking for a host.

At 9:00 a.m. exactly, I approached the gates and was buzzed in immediately, silently—no one replied to my tentative hello, which felt ominous. I made my way down the cobbled mews street, passing multicolored doors and windows adorned with blooming flower boxes. It was an entirely different world to the bustling road on the other side. There was no one else around, and I couldn't help but feel like I'd stepped into a parallel universe. I looked over my shoulder, half expecting the gates I'd just walked through to have disappeared.

I stopped outside one of the houses, the door painted a dark racing green with matching window frames. There were two expensive-looking bikes with baskets on them chained up outside. I not only knew this was the right house because Elizabeth had texted me the address but, thrillingly, because I recognized it from seeing it on TV.

I took a photo for my mum; I knew she'd be anxiously watching her phone, and I wanted to appease my guilt from not messaging her earlier.

Isobel: *Look! I'm really here—it's real! Wish me luck. x*

I saw her typing, and before she could get a chance to finish, I quickly fired off another message.

Isobel: *Yes, Mum. I've taken them. :)*

The typing stopped momentarily and then started up again.

Mum: *Good luck, sweetheart. We're rooting for you.*

I pictured her and Uncle Pete sitting together, wondering what I was up to. I swallowed hard, trying not to let myself think about that too much.

Before I could even lift my hand to the large brass knocker, the front door swung open and Elizabeth stepped outside, pulled me toward her, and hugged me tightly, all in one quick motion. I was engulfed in her perfume. It took me right back to that day where she sat on my bed and told me she was going to change my life. There was a dog panting and running circles around our feet. Walter the black greyhound—he had only one eye, and he wore a pink bandanna tied around his neck. He seemed delighted to see me, and I felt myself relax, just a little.

"Isobel," Elizabeth said, pushing me back so she could get a better look at me. She kept her hands gripped tightly on my shoulders. She gave them a gentle shake, as though she were trying to wake me up. "I am *so* thrilled that you're here. This day feels like it's been *such* a long time coming, doesn't it?"

I opened my mouth to reply, but she didn't wait for me to answer, just ushered me inside and carried on talking. Walter rushed past my feet, his paws clattering on the bare floorboards, leading the way. The hallway walls were painted a different shade of dark green to the front door, like a forest. The floorboards were dark and glossy. There was a scented candle burning on the table by the front door—it smelled like woodsmoke and tobacco, heavy and heady. It was a stark contrast to the bright, white light and the summer's day outside, but it felt appropriate; it matched up to my internal feeling that I'd climbed through the wardrobe and stepped into Narnia.

"Did you get here OK in the end?" Elizabeth said. "Easy journey?"

I nodded, but she didn't turn around, just gestured for me to carry on following her. She looked different from the last time I'd seen her but still as brightly colored and striking. She was wearing baggy white linen trousers with splotches of paint on them and a baby blue shirt with the sleeves rolled up. Her hair, which I'm sure the last time I'd seen her had been mousy brown, was now bleached blond and streaked with pastel pink. I found myself lifting my hand to my own hair, wondering if I could get away with something like that. I'd never dyed my hair before—well, apart from with the blue paint.

"I'm so excited for you to meet everyone, Issy," Elizabeth continued. "I thought I'd introduce you to the team, and then you and I can get a coffee and make a plan. We're going to figure out how you can best use your time with us. What do you think?"

She said everything in a rush, barely pausing for breath, as though she was so excited, she had to get the words out as quickly as possible.

Elizabeth turned around to face me then, stopping in front of a wooden door with a latch on it, the type you might expect to see in a cottage or a farmhouse. You could open it halfway if you wanted to, hang over it like a horse in a stable. She smiled at me expectantly.

"Yes," I said. I could feel a blush rising in my cheeks. "Sorry, yes, that sounds good. Great! I'm just trying to take everything in, I think. I'm, um, I really can't believe I'm here, to be honest, I just wanted to say thank you again, I—"

Elizabeth held up her hand to stop me. She looked at me sternly, her brow furrowed. I noticed she also had paint in her left eyebrow.

"Isobel, you're here today because you deserve to be. I wouldn't have asked you to come and work with me if I didn't think you should be here. I'm not doing you a favor. I'm not ever going to waste my time on somebody I don't think is worth it. So that's the last time you thank me for this, OK? You take your place on this team, and you remember why you're here, yes?"

I swallowed hard again. I nodded.

"OK," I said. "Yes. I'll remember why I'm here."

"Good," Elizabeth said.

She fiddled with the latches on the door for a moment, almost as if she'd never done it before, until the door swung open, not because she'd successfully opened it but because someone had pulled it from the other side.

We stepped into a huge, bright white room—the floorboards were white, the walls were white, the beams painted white. All the furniture was white too, apart from one long, rustic-looking wooden table that ran down the center of the room. It looked like it could have seated about thirty people. There were canvases everywhere, sinks filled with paint, materials in seemingly random piles. But despite the appearance of chaos, I still got the impression there was order here. Everything had its place.

"Hi, Lizzie," said the person who had opened the door, a tall white woman with long red hair wearing an oversize stone-colored suit and massive white trainers.

When she smiled, I noticed she had a gap between her two front teeth.

"And you," she continued, "must be Isobel Bailey. We've heard so much about you."

She closed the door behind me.

"Oh," I said, "really?"

"Really," she said, looking me up and down as she spoke. "I *adore* the Abigails. What a wonderful thing. Oh my god." She shook her head dramatically. "I'm so rude—I've not even introduced myself, have I? I'm Olivia."

She held out her hand, and I shook it. Her grip was loose, and when she let go, she took out a tiny bottle of hand sanitizer from her top pocket and applied it liberally to her palms. She did not offer it to me.

"Issy," Elizabeth called from the other side of the room, "come and meet everyone else; don't let Olivia hog you. She'll never stop talking your ear off."

"She's not wrong; you go and get on," Olivia said. "I'll talk your ear off later instead."

I turned to Elizabeth, who was sitting at one end of a long wooden table with Walter and two other people, waiting for me.

One of those people, it turned out, did not need an introduction. I blinked a couple of times as though she might be a mirage, as though she might disappear. But no, unbelievably, there she was, right in front of me.

She looked different from the last time I'd seen her. Her dark hair came down past her shoulders, even longer and stragglier than I'd realized. The kind of hair that would prompt my mum to whisper to me, "That girl needs a good haircut." She had a septum piercing and ridiculously long eyelashes, and she was wearing an outfit almost identical to mine—black T-shirt, black trousers, black Doc Martens—except she had the tattoos that Mo suggested I might look into getting. The olive skin on her arms was covered in thin black-line illustrations. They were so intricate they almost looked like sketches. Had she been friendlier I might have asked if I could look more closely, but as it was, I got the impression that if I got too close, she might have snarled at me.

Oh yeah, and this time, she was not covered in oil.

"Issy, this is Aubrey," Elizabeth said, "my right-hand woman. I honestly don't know what I'd do without her."

"Hi, Aubrey," I said, "um, we've obviously already met."

I held out my hand to shake hers, and for one sickening moment I really thought she wasn't going to take it. After way too long, Aubrey reached out gingerly, as though I might be poisonous.

She dropped my hand as quickly as she could and continued to look at me blankly.

"Outside my house?" I said, worried then that I was going mad, that this was a total stranger who had a doppelgänger.

"It was literally just the other day . . . the bike?" I said. "You— you thought I might have stolen your—"

"I remember," Aubrey said steadily.

I swear she looked like she was about to jump across the table and deck me. I tried to remember that one self-defense lesson we'd had in primary school—something, something, elbow?

"What?" Elizabeth said, looking between us, her eyes wide. "Oh my god, what have I missed? Tell me. I'm dying."

"Aubrey is my next-door neighbor," I said. "We met over the weekend."

"No," Elizabeth said, clapping her hands together excitedly.

"Well, will you look at that? Fate really does sometimes put us in people's way."

The other person at the table snorted, and I turned to look at them properly. They were wearing pink linen shorts with a matching pink linen blazer and a white vest top and huge bright green plastic glasses. They had dark brown skin and jet-black hair that they wore clipped short. Their lips were glossy and tinted red, and I noticed that their hands were covered in tiny tattoos.

"Sorry," they said, standing up to give me a one-armed hug, a takeaway coffee in one hand, a vape in the other, "I just think you've got rubbish luck if fate is putting you in the way of Aubrey Kerr."

They winked at Aubrey, and she rolled her eyes, but I noticed a smile playing on her lips.

"P," Elizabeth chastised gently, as if she were a mother despairing of her arguing children, "really."

When P pulled away from hugging me, they grinned. They had one of those faces, one of those smiles that just demanded you smile back—infectious—and a glint in their eye that I couldn't quite work out the meaning of. I immediately felt more at ease though, and less like I'd murdered Aubrey's entire family and forgotten about it. Clearly she was just difficult with everyone.

"So you're the famous Isobel. Or Issy, is it? *The* Issy," P said, sitting back down at the table and shaking their head.

They gestured for me to sit in the chair next to them. I was aware of Aubrey watching us.

"That's me," I said. "Not sure about 'the famous' Isobel. But yes, that's me."

"I'm P," they said.

"P," I repeated, "like the letter?"

"Exactly like the letter," P said.

"That's very cool," I said. "It suits you. I've never met a 'P' before."

"Thank you. I just *love* your accent," they said. "So cute."

"Oh," I said. "Thank you?"

I'd genuinely never thought about my accent before. Everyone I know sounds like me. Even Elizabeth, whose accent has been ironed out from years of living in London, still occasionally sounds like someone who grew up in a rough seaside town on the Kent coast.

Olivia came bounding back to the table. I noticed the socks peeking out over the top of her bright white high-tops had frills on them.

"So," Olivia said, clapping her hands together decisively, "what can I get everyone? Coffees? Teas? Breakfast?"

"Oh," I said, immediately panicking that I'd already gone wrong. "Should I be . . . I should be the one who . . ."

"No, no," Elizabeth said, rising to her feet. "I'm taking Issy out of the office this morning."

"Lovely," Olivia said, her smile not faltering although I noticed her glance at P, the briefest widening of her eyes. "OK. Have fun. Do you want me to take Walter?"

"No, thanks," Elizabeth said, "we'll take him with us. Come on, baby dog."

Walter yawned and slowly started making his way toward the stable door, his tail wagging.

"See you later," I said, lifting a hand to the rest of the team. "Do you want me to . . . I could bring you something . . ."

"No, you relax," P said, "it's your first day. Just worry about yourself."

I nodded and glanced over at Aubrey. She did not look up from her iPad, just frowned into it, waiting for me to go away.

I walked next to Elizabeth while she spoke on the phone, her voice carrying up the quiet street. Something I'd already noticed about her and liked a lot was that she laughed loudly and often. Walter walked just in front of us; he wasn't on a lead, but he also walked exceptionally slowly, looking up every few seconds to check we were still with him.

Elizabeth pressed a code into the keypad beside the gate, and when it swung open and we stepped outside onto the street, it was an assault on the senses. Everything was louder and brighter and grimier than I'd remembered from the time before I knew about life behind the gate. It honestly felt like weeks had passed since I'd been sitting on the bench thinking my raw thoughts.

We ambled across the road, dodging cyclists and people on scooters. Elizabeth hung up the phone as we entered a small coffee shop. The staff inside all knew her, waving and shouting good morning over the grinding of the coffee machine—I stopped by the counter to order, but they waved us through, indicating they'd be with us soon. So I followed Elizabeth and Walter through the bustling café, past the staff entrance, and out the back door. We entered a little courtyard, an oasis of calm filled with green plants creeping up the high, white-painted brick walls. There was just one small, rickety wooden table and two chairs, and when I sat down I stared at myself in a huge, cracked dirty mirror leaning up against the wall opposite. I lifted my hand slightly, as if just to check it was real, to see if the girl in the mirror moved with me.

Elizabeth sat down, pulled a packet of cigarettes from the top pocket of her shirt, and offered it to me. I had never seen cigarettes like those before, pastel colored with gold tips. I shook my head, but I must have looked tempted because she left the packet open on the table like a box of sweets, and I couldn't take my eyes off them.

"Fun, aren't they?" Elizabeth said, popping a pink cigarette between her lips. "I've been trying to quit for years and never quite managed it, so my concession is that I can have one a day with my morning coffee."

As if by magic a young guy with a handlebar mustache, wearing what looked like a butcher's apron, appeared at our table carrying two tiny cups of coffee with hearts drawn in the foam. He placed them carefully on the table in front of us and reached down to pat Walter on the head. He produced a treat from the pocket of his apron.

"Thank you, darling," Elizabeth said, beaming at him and lighting her cigarette with a heavy silver lighter, "and then," she continued explaining to me, "I have one in the evening, standing in my garden. A little moment to myself at the end of each day. I find it very peaceful, and I am loath to give up anything at all which brings me peace these days, Isobel."

I nodded, watching the smoke curl from her mouth as she spoke.

"My mum says living in London and breathing in all that pollution is the same as smoking ten cigarettes a day anyway," I said, picking up a tiny teaspoon and running it straight down the middle of the foam heart in my coffee. "She says she read that getting on the Northern line every day takes years off your life."

Elizabeth laughed and raised her eyebrows.

"Well, there you go," she said. "I never get the Northern line, so actually, probably"—she inhaled deeply—"I'm making the healthier choice here."

The young guy with the mustache appeared again to place a saucer in front of Elizabeth just as she needed to tap the ash from the end of her cigarette.

She exhaled, closing her eyes.

"Right," Elizabeth said, "sorry, I always find it so difficult to kick into gear on a Monday morning. Shall we get one of the boys to bring us some lovely breakfast and we can get started?"

I hadn't realized exactly how much I wanted some lovely breakfast until two plates of pastries appeared in front of us. My stomach rumbled, and I remembered that I hadn't eaten yet that morning. The caffeine on an empty stomach was by then having the effect of making my jaw shake.

"Tuck in," Elizabeth said, tearing into a croissant, "it's impossible to get anything at all done on an empty stomach."

I gratefully took a large, shiny pain au chocolat (bad vegan) from the plate and took a bite into it, crumbs flying everywhere. Walter was having a field day under the table.

The second I had my mouth full, Elizabeth wiped her hands on a napkin and said, "So, Issy, what do you most want to get out of the next year with me?"

She leaned back in her chair and waited patiently for me to finish frantically chewing.

"I suppose," I said, after a moment, wiping my mouth with a paper napkin, "I want to learn everything I can about being a real artist."

"You are a real artist," Elizabeth said immediately. "Anyone who creates art is an artist."

"Right," I said, "of course, I suppose I mean a professional artist, as a job. What you do."

Elizabeth nodded but didn't say anything, she smiled at me, encouraging me to keep talking. I realized how rarely this happened. That I was given space to talk. And not just to talk, but to say what I wanted and for someone to listen to me. Normally I just listened to my mum. And now mostly to Alyssa, I guess.

"The way you found me," I said, "the way I just was living my ordinary life and making the Abigails, and everything was so . . ."

I reached around for the word. I nearly said *dull*, but that wasn't quite right. My life didn't feel dull at the time, even though it had dulled in comparison to this.

"Quiet," I landed on. "My life was very quiet, and small. And . . ."

Walter nudged my elbow. I reached down to place my hand on his velvety head.

"Sad," I said. "My life wasn't always sad, or it was, I suppose, but that's because I was."

I swallowed hard, surprised to feel a lump in my throat.

"Am," I said, correcting myself after a moment, "Quite a lot of the time."

Sad is a nice word, isn't it? It's gentle. Like *blue*. Inoffensive.

I thought Elizabeth might jump in and say something, tell me how sorry she was or ask me how I was feeling, but she didn't. I caught her eye, and she was just looking at me steadily. She nodded slightly. She wasn't going to interrupt me or comfort me or save me. She wanted to keep hearing what I had to say. Walter licked the palm of my hand, which was both very sweet and very disgusting.

"So when you came to see me," I continued, "it felt like a dream. I didn't even really know that what I was doing was special— I was just doing it, you know? For me. I always have done. It's like a compulsion. And I just know there are loads of other people like me. Who are out there living small lives, or sad lives, and making something to try to make sense of it all, or get something out of their head that feels too massive to stay inside. And I suppose that's what I'd like to do. To find more people like me. To work with more people like me. To find art that hasn't been found yet, that people don't even know counts. Even though"—I smiled at Elizabeth—"I know it all counts."

"Well," Elizabeth said, "if that isn't a wonderful goal, I don't know what is."

She picked up her cup and drained the last of her coffee, wiping foam from her top lip.

"You know, I have a different person come and work for me in this capacity every year—as my intern, my assistant, whatever you want to call it—and usually they're fresh out of art school and highly ambitious, which is fantastic in its own way—like P and Olivia, that's how they both came to work for me. But they always say the same thing when we have this chat—'I want to learn about the business side of things' or 'I want to pick up the skills I didn't learn at school' or 'I want to make a particular project I've been thinking about for a while and reach a new audience.'"

Elizabeth paused while Handlebar Mustache came back to place two glasses of water with lemon and ice cubes on the table and to whisk away our empty cups.

"You are the first person," she said, once he'd gone back inside, "to ever say you want to reach out to creatives we don't know about yet, and you are the first person not to talk about expanding your own project. Which is very interesting to me."

"I mean, I want to learn about all that other . . . ," I started, but she waved away the end of my sentence with her hand.

She shook her head.

"You naturally will," she said, "just from being in the office and being around the team, but as a goal? As an intention for your year? No."

"OK," I said, twirling the paper straw around in my water. The ice was melting rapidly. I wasn't sure what I was meant to say next. Although it did feel like I'd managed to pass some kind of test I didn't even know I was taking. I watched as Elizabeth reached into her glass, took out an ice cube, and passed it to Walter, who took it very gently from her and then trotted to the other side of the courtyard to munch noisily.

"So," Elizabeth said, "with all that in mind, I have a proposal for you. It's something I'd been thinking about anyway, but everything you've just said to me confirms I was right."

I nodded. I could not imagine what she was going to say next.

"I want you to set up a group, reaching out to people who have been working on their own projects. And I want you to bring them together every week to work and talk about their art and their lives and to encourage one another."

"Like a support group," I said.

Elizabeth laughed.

"I guess," she said. "I was thinking more like an art class but one with no structure, just free-form, people can work on whatever they want, but we provide the space and materials and the exposure."

"Exposure?" I said, frowning.

"Sure," Elizabeth said, "we'd film some of it, for the TV show."

"Right," I said, "to actually be broadcast on actual TV?"

"Yes," Elizabeth said patiently.

"For your TV show, that's on the TV that I would also be on?" I said.

"Yes, Issy, that's exactly it."

"Wow," I said, "fuck." And then, immediately: "Sorry."

Elizabeth laughed again.

"We've got five episodes next season, each an hour long, plus a summer special, so we're looking for the group segment to be ten to twelve minutes per episode—enough for our audience to get to know them. But you'll meet them more regularly than that if you want; I'd like this to be ongoing, a commitment, not just about getting content for the telly. And we'll do an exhibition at the end. A friends-and-family thing."

I nodded, trying to take it all in.

"How will I find these people?" I said.

"You write the brief," Elizabeth said. "The production team will reach out and find them; you don't need to worry about that."

"This is mad," I said after a moment. "I kind of thought I'd just be making coffees and stuff, like, going out to fetch everybody's lunch, that sort of thing."

"Oh, darling," Elizabeth said, "you absolutely will. So many emergency Pret trips you wouldn't believe."

"OK, great," I said. "I know I can do that at least."

Elizabeth smiled. She ran her fingers over the still-open packet of cigarettes on the table as if she was contemplating another and then stopped abruptly, snapping it shut, taking it off the table and putting it in the top pocket of her shirt.

"You can do it all, Isobel. I have no doubt about that."

Toward the end of the day, Elizabeth called an impromptu team meeting.

We gathered around one end of the long wooden table. Elizabeth was sitting at the head, and Walter scrambled up on the end of the bench to sit next to her. If Aubrey was her right-hand woman, then he was her right-hand man. I don't know how I'd missed it before but hanging on the wall behind where Elizabeth was sitting was an enormous canvas with a life-size Walter sketched onto it with thick charcoal.

The team of producers that she'd spent the afternoon with in one of the meeting rooms joined us—two men and a woman, all wearing black and looking very tired. They inhaled deeply on their disposable vapes near constantly and murmured "Fuck" at their phone screens every few minutes.

"So," Elizabeth said, "my beautiful team, I wanted to gather us all together to make sure that everyone is staying hydrated in this dreadful heat."

She gestured toward the glass jugs I'd just decanted two-liter bottles of sparkling water. One of the producers picked two chocolate chip cookies off a plate in the middle of the table, pressed them together, and started eating both at once.

"And, of course," Elizabeth continued, "I wanted to update everyone on our upcoming plans because, as we all know, filming resumes next week for season five of *Artistic License*."

P whooped, and Elizabeth paused while we all dutifully did a little round of applause. Walter barked until we stopped.

"I can't even believe I'm saying that sentence. I can't believe we've come this far." Elizabeth shook her head. "And it's only happening because of you."

Olivia placed her hand on her chest and nodded, as if Elizabeth were speaking to her specifically. Aubrey glared at her, crushing her biscuit between her thumb and forefinger.

"So, I was just chatting to the guys here." Elizabeth gestured toward the producers, who did not look up from their phones. The biscuit guy was now methodically working his way through the plate; I don't know how he was swallowing or even breathing really—it was mesmerizing. "And they have loads of ideas for the direction we want to take the show this season. Obviously we love all of your ideas too, but there's one thing that we'd love to really hone in on this year, which is the theme of creativity as a lifeline."

Elizabeth looked at me then and smiled encouragingly. I froze, chocolate chips in my teeth, as I felt the eyes of everyone else on me all at once.

"We want the message that our audience takes away from the show to be that creative expression can be a way to untangle feelings, expand them, shrink them, for them to evolve and shift and mutate outside of your body. A way to physically observe something that feels intangible or inexplicable. Something you can hold in your hand and say, '*Look*, this is what I'm feeling, and I want to scream or cry or punch something but I can't; so let me show you, let me show you what it's like.'"

Elizabeth paused. The room was completely silent. The producers weren't looking at their phones any longer; they were all watching Elizabeth intently.

"But it's also an opportunity to create hope, for ourselves, for others. To show how art is not just about galleries and shows and prizes and prestige. Art is not those things. Art is being human; it's expression and feeling and meaning beyond skill or criticism or this industry."

I glanced across the table and saw that Aubrey was watching Elizabeth, utterly transfixed. I hadn't seen her face so open before. She was even more beautiful without her brows knitted together, without the scowl.

"I *love* this show," Elizabeth continued, "don't get me wrong. It's my baby; it's my dream come true. And I love what we've created together as a team. But I don't want to move too far away from where we started, and I don't want to forget where I started either. And sometimes it feels like . . . it feels like I forget myself. And I don't want to forget myself, even if it's difficult to remember."

I thought of her then, sitting on my bed in my mum's flat surrounded by the Abigails. One pink sock and one blue.

"*Amazing,*" Olivia said. "So what's the plan, then?" She opened the brand-new hardback notebook in front of her, cracking the spine.

"You know, now that I think about it," P said, "something I've done a lot within my own work is sort of visual storytelling via the medium of—"

"Me too," Olivia chimed in before P could finish what they were saying. "Oh, sorry, P, were you done? It sounded like you were done."

They smiled at her, and she smiled back. I noticed that they were both showing a lot of teeth and not really blinking.

"Me too," Olivia repeated, before P had a chance to confirm or deny if they were finished speaking. "I'm also really up for taking on this kind of work, and with my experience of working with communities . . ."

Aubrey snorted. "What communities?"

Olivia spun around to look at her, eyes wide and nostrils flared, furious at being interrupted.

"Um, I don't know if you recall, Aubrey, that last year I actually went to that *gay* weekender at Butlin's as an *ally* and got everybody I met to write down a word that summed up their experience of the weekend on my literal *skin,* and then I turned those words into a very unique aural experience in which people were immersed in—"

"Yes," Aubrey said, "I remember now. How could I possibly forget how important aural experiences within the gay community are to you."

P raised their eyebrows. They didn't look up from doodling in their notebook, but they couldn't disguise a little grin on their face.

"*And,*" Olivia continued, turning her attention back to Elizabeth, "there's the fact that we've spoken about me maybe having the opportunity to get in front of the camera at some point this season? This feels like the perfect time to explore that. . . ."

"Right," Elizabeth said before Olivia could finish her thought, clapping her hands together, indicating she was ready for everyone to shut up.

"I so appreciate the ideas, as always. That's why you're here. But actually I do know which direction this season is going to take. I was speaking with Issy this morning about it."

Elizabeth paused to beam at me.

"And she's going to run a group for people who are making art at home, the kind of people who didn't even really know that that's what they were doing. A group for people who are making art that helps them to live in this world."

"Right," Olivia said, nodding. "OK. I see. So, like, an art class with a sob story, like a competition element even, like *Pottery Throwdown* or *Bake Off* or *X Factor* or—"

"Jesus fucking Christ," Aubrey said, cutting her off.

"I suppose I would describe it as a group for people who aren't fitting in anywhere else," Elizabeth said. "For people who have slipped under the radar somehow or have got lost or left behind in some way."

"We could call it Outside the Lines," Aubrey said quietly. She was practically rolling her eyes at herself as she said it, furious that she was saying something sincere.

"Outside the Lines," Elizabeth repeated. She looked at me. "What do you think?" she said.

"Perfect," I said.

I tried to catch Aubrey's eye, but she was looking resolutely at the wall directly behind my head.

"Well, that's decided, then," Elizabeth said, "and this leads me nicely on to my next point, which is that Aubrey, I've decided that you're going to lead this project and Isobel is going to assist you. I just know the two of you are going to love working together, and it's perfect given that you're already friends."

I might have been wrong, maybe it was a trick of the light, but I'm sure that I spotted a hint of mischief in Elizabeth's eyes.

I thought Aubrey might try to catch me after the meeting, that we'd discuss some of the finer points together, but instead she walked straight over to Elizabeth, and the two of them immediately started fervently whispering, their heads close together. P and Olivia tried to maintain a conversation on the other side of the table while clearly straining to hear what they were saying.

I returned to my desk and began to gather my stuff away into my backpack. I picked up my phone after a day of barely even glancing at it and could see that my new housemates had been very busy in the group chat. It also looked like my mum had been messaging me every hour on the hour. If I didn't reply soon, I imagined a helicopter would be sent out searching for me. I half expected to see a missing persons poster taped to the lamppost outside. I smiled as I sent her a holding message, a thumbs-up and a heart.

"Hey, babe," Olivia said.

I looked up from my phone to see her and P standing in front of me.

"Congrats," she said. "Looks like you're coming in strong. Was that your idea? Or did Elizabeth come up with it, you know, based on you and your . . . life."

They both looked at me with something bordering on pity. I

worried then for the first time that day what Elizabeth might have told them about me. It hadn't occurred to me she would have told them about how she'd found me, but of course she had. Of course. My sad reputation preceded me.

"Oh," I said, "the group was Elizabeth's idea, but I broached the idea of reaching out to the wider community. I just really love the idea of working with—"

"Totally," Olivia said, "I'm one hundred percent the same. Listen, we should all go out for drinks soon—me, you, and P, I mean." She jerked her head toward Aubrey, who was clearly in earshot, and shook her head as if to mean, *Not her*.

Aubrey looked over as she slid her iPad into her bag; she looked amused for some reason.

"I know the three of us are going to be *great* friends. We're going to have the best time working on the show together this year."

"Yes," I said, "yes, that would be so . . . Thank you, that's so nice of you."

"Gorgeous," P said, "perfect, can't wait."

They both finally stepped aside and let me pass.

It was 6:00 p.m. and as bright as it had been at midday—it felt like I still had an entire day ahead of me, limitless possibility. I stopped outside the studio to finally reply properly to my mum and call off the search party. I heard a door slam, and then Aubrey was standing in front of me, wearing a blue bike helmet.

"Hi," I said. I smiled at her, what I considered to be my best, most winning smile.

"Hello," Aubrey said, without even looking at me. She bent down next to one of the bikes chained to the lamppost—the bike was lilac with a wicker basket attached to the front.

"You got a new bike, then?" I said.

She looked at me incredulously. As if she couldn't tell if I was joking or not.

"This is obviously not my bike," she said. "This was my sister's bike."

"Right," I said, "is that why it's . . ."

I gestured toward the basket.

"She used to put her dog in it," Aubrey said, and then she sighed heavily, "it was actually very cute. But if it was up to me, I would not be riding a bike with a basket on the front of it."

"No, of course," I said, "understood; you hate baskets. Awful. Listen, I'm really looking forward to—"

She got on the lilac bike and cycled off halfway through my sentence. I don't know what else I was expecting.

"We'll talk about it tomorrow," I shouted to the back of her head as she disappeared down the street and out of sight.

47A Girlies!! <3

Issy: *GUYS, you won't believe who works at my office*

Alyssa: *OMG, who, someone famous? Is it Alison Hammond?*

Issy: *Aubrey from next door*

Alyssa: *Ew, only famous for being a PAIN IN THE ARSE*

Mo: *What?? That's mad, is she a grouch in the office too?*

Issy: *Yes! She definitely thinks I stole her bike!*

Alyssa: *Ohhh, did you?*

Issy: *NO*

Alyssa: *It's ok if you did xxx*

Robin: *Yeah it's ok if you did, hunny xoxoxo*

Alyssa: *Shut up, Robin*

Alyssa: *Xoxo*

CHAPTER SIX

On my second day in the office and after getting to grips with the new email system, a notification popped up in the corner of my screen to tell me that a meeting I didn't know was happening had already started. There were just two participants.

I looked up from my laptop to see Aubrey sitting directly opposite me at a desk in the back of the room, her arms folded. She looked me dead in the eye and tapped her watch.

I ran over, which took all of seven seconds.

"You're late."

"I'm sorry," I said. When I sat down, the chair screeched across the floor, like nails on a chalkboard; I winced, but Aubrey didn't react at all. "Although Aubrey, I was just sitting over there, you could have . . ."

"Let's just get straight to it, shall we?" Aubrey unfolded her arms and opened her laptop. She had her hair pulled into a ponytail; it made her look younger somehow. She wasn't wearing any makeup either, and I noticed she had a smattering of freckles across her nose.

"Yes," I said. "OK, let's do that."

I waited for her to say something else, but she stayed silent, watching me. She raised her eyebrows as if to say *I'm waiting.*

"Sorry," I said, "if you could just remind me . . ."

"The brief," Aubrey said, cutting across me.

"The brief for Outside the Lines?"

Aubrey's eyes opened wide like she simply could not believe someone could be so incompetent.

"Right," I said, "yes, obviously. I've come up with a few ideas. I did it last night."

I had written it by hand, and when I passed my notebook to Aubrey, I honestly felt like I may as well have handed her a wax tablet that I'd scratched into with a stick.

She read for a long time, frowning at my handwriting, exaggeratedly turning the pages over as if looking for more, and when she looked up at me, she simply said, "This needs a lot of work."

"I know I literally just started on it . . ."

"And ideally we need to get it out by the end of the week."

"OK, I can—"

"I'll send you some thoughts, and you can come back to me tomorrow with a finished draft, and we'll take it from there."

"Thank you," I said, "that would be . . ."

"You need to get better at checking your emails because I did already send you some ideas yesterday in this meeting agenda, we could have avoided all this time wasting."

"I will," I said. I fought the childish urge to cry.

"Right," Aubrey said. "Cool."

She looked back down at her laptop.

Clearly dismissed, I stood up to leave, but something was making my feet stick to the floor. I watched Aubrey as she tapped away on her keyboard, waiting for me to leave her alone. I took a deep breath.

"Aubrey, have I done something to upset you?"

"Excuse me?" Aubrey said.

"Have I done something to upset you? Because it seems like you're very . . . You don't seem to . . ."

I couldn't quite bring myself to say, *You don't seem to like me*; it was simply too pathetic.

Aubrey stared at me, her expression utterly inscrutable.

"We're fine," she said after a moment.

I nodded and turned away, and then I don't know what possessed me to say it; I don't know what possessed me to turn back around. It came out of nowhere.

"Aubrey, I didn't steal your bike; I really didn't!"

Her head shot up from her laptop screen. Her expression no longer inscrutable; she was shocked and then, maddeningly, she looked like she might laugh.

"Well," she said after a moment, "I'm afraid that's a matter for the police now, isn't it?"

The following day her demeanor toward me noticeably softened. I no longer felt like the prime suspect in her bike-theft investigation. Instead, it was like working with a pleasant robot—detached, polite, and efficient.

"Good morning," Aubrey said on her way in, her voice light and pleasant. On her, it sounded unnatural.

Olivia was vaping inside the office before Elizabeth got in to tell her off. Her face disappeared behind a cloud for a moment, and when it dissipated, I saw that she was frowning.

"Why are you saying good morning?" Olivia said.

"Can't I wish my colleagues a good morning?" Aubrey said. "Isn't that a nice thing to do?"

"But why though?"

P walked through the door, sipping an iced coffee; they pulled an AirPod out of one ear and raised their eyebrows as if to ask what was going on.

"P," Olivia said, taking the coffee they'd bought for her. "Aubrey just said 'Good morning.'"

P frowned in Aubrey's direction.

"Why?" they said warily. "What's going on?"

Aubrey rolled her eyes.

"Issy," she said. "Are you OK to kick off in about ten minutes? I've blocked out both our days to try to get this thing done."

"I saw," I said.

"I wasn't sure if you'd check your calendar because you don't look at your emails," Aubrey said. And then she remembered to smile. "But that's great!"

Aubrey and I settled in a small room at the back of the studio. I think it might once have been a pantry or a utility room, but it fit a small wooden desk and two chairs perfectly. We sat opposite each other. This time I had come prepared.

"So," I said, sliding my laptop in front of Aubrey before she could say anything, "I wrote this last night, what do you think?"

"Wow, no small talk, then," Aubrey said, adjusting the screen so she could see better.

"Oh," I said, "sorry. How was your evening?"

"No," she said.

"No . . . evening?"

"No small talk is good," she said. "Shh, now, I'm reading."

She remembered to smile again just in time to counteract the rudeness of her shushing me.

"This is better," she said, after a few minutes of tutting and typing. "I think you just need to land on exactly why it is we're doing this and what people can hope to get out of it. I'm worried at the moment it feels a bit blah."

"Blah?"

"Blah," she confirmed with no further explanation.

"Right."

"We'll do it together," she said. And she carried her chair around the table so she could sit next to me.

"Budge up," she said, and then, "please."

We sat like that, our heads close together, me watching Aubrey type, exchanging ideas for a couple of hours. At one point Olivia poked her head around the door.

"What are you doing?" she said.

"Working," Aubrey said, without looking up. "You won't be familiar with it."

"But why are you sitting on top of each other?"

I felt my cheeks turning pink, I didn't look up either.

"This is *next to*, Olivia, we're sitting *next to* each other. But good try," Aubrey said. "Now go away, please, you're being very distracting, and I'm sure your schedule is packed—so much coffee to drink, so much vape to vape."

"Good luck, Issy," Olivia said. "It is probably illegal to trap you in here with her; let me know if you want to speak to HR."

Olivia stalked off.

"Why are you two so . . ."

"This sentence isn't right," Aubrey said, jabbing at the screen.

Still no small talk, then.

Eventually, Aubrey sat back in her chair and stretched her arms above her head. I heard her shoulders click.

"I think we're done," she said. She turned the laptop back toward me. "Have a read through, I'm going to message Elizabeth, tell her to come have a look."

ARTISTIC LICENSE WITH ELIZABETH STAGGS is starting a new community project for season five, and we need you, artists at home.

OUTSIDE THE LINES will be a place for like-minded people to regularly meet to work on their individual projects without judgment, without time pressures. We will provide a safe space for people to share their work, to speak honestly, to be themselves, to thrive—whatever that means for you.

OUTSIDE THE LINES is looking for members of our artistic community who have struggled with their mental health and who have found making art to be a lifeline and a way to express themselves when nothing else seems to work. We will not ask you to share your story if you don't want to, but we will ask that you share your art, and through that, we might all know one another a little better at the end of the process.

Filming will be between October and February, with a special one-off event in May to share whatever you wish to with friends, families, and our wider colleagues on the Artistic License team.

I looked up from reading and nodded at Aubrey.
"I think so too. I think this is it."

Elizabeth poked her head around the door. She was wearing a huge sun hat, and bejeweled sunflowers were sparkling in her ears. I was reminded of her painting that hung in my maths corridor, warm like the sun.

"Done?" she said. She had a huge smile on her face, but she still looked a bit frazzled.

"Sorry," Aubrey said, "I know I could have just emailed it to you but . . ."

"No, no," Elizabeth said, picking up the laptop and sitting on the edge of the desk. "I want to be here with you two while I read it. How exciting!

"Oh," she said, after a couple of minutes, "yes, this is perfect. But you need to add your names. I'll be in and out, but I don't want everyone to think I'm going to be there the whole time."

Aubrey nodded, took the laptop back from her and started typing.

Project led by Aubrey Kerr and Isobel Bailey.

Excitement burst through me. How was this my life? I really couldn't believe I wasn't just filing and picking up people's dry cleaning and—

"Issy," Elizabeth interrupted my thoughts, "you couldn't nip out and get me a coffee, could you?"

The brief was sent to the production team for them to do their thing, to find our group of people, and I spent the rest of the week shadowing Elizabeth in meetings, picking up lunches, organizing a ton of parcels that had arrived at the studio—stuff people sent hoping it would be featured on the show.

I didn't see much of Aubrey, but when I did, she was pleasant to me. A smile, a nod, a polite request to run out and buy some particular type of pencil when I got the chance. And yet, I found myself getting increasingly frustrated. I couldn't shake the feeling that however civil she was, there was something else going on just below the surface. It might have been nothing, or it might have been that she hated me and wanted me dead. I was desperate to get to the bottom of it.

I had promised the housemates a knitting lesson on Thursday night. I had actually never taught anyone to knit before. I had never even had a lesson myself, apart from Mum teaching me the basics, but I assumed it would be pretty easy in the way that you do when something is second nature to you.

I cast on for everybody and did the first row to get them started. I used leftover balls of wool from past projects—one pink, one blue, one yellow—and explained we would be making ten-centimeter squares.

"I want to make fingerless gloves," Mo said, pointing his knitting needle at me, "can I make gloves instead?"

We were gathered on the roof terrace, sitting cross-legged on a blanket on the ground. I had angled myself so I had my back to them and they could watch what I was doing over my shoulder.

"Um," I said, "how about we start off with a square and see how we get on."

It took a few goes to get up and running, although Robin learned surprisingly quickly.

"My grandma used to show me all the time, but I wasn't interested," she explained as she started her second row, "but I guess some of it must have gone in."

"I don't know that this is right, babe," Alyssa said, as she essentially just wound a piece of wool around the needle. She didn't mean that she wasn't right, she was suggesting that I had taught her incorrectly or perhaps even that knitting as a concept was flawed.

"Try again," I said, "but this time, um . . . knit? Instead of . . . not knitting?"

"Right," she said, frowning.

But after a while of sitting in silence, concentrating, the clicking of needles began to fall into a rhythm, brows unfurrowed, and importantly, once everyone had gotten the hang of it, chat resumed.

"So," Mo said, sitting back down, "are any of you around this weekend? Shall we do something—tomorrow night?"

"Yep," I said instantly, "no plans."

What else would I be doing on a Friday night in London? Hanging out in a bathroom with Abigail is what.

"Yes," Robin said. "I think we should go out."

"Agree," Mo said. "I am keen to spend Saturday lying in bed, preferably not alone."

"Same," Alyssa said, "but preferably alone."

"Gorgeous," Robin said. "We can absolutely make that happen."

"We could all head to the pub at the end of the road," Mo said. "Looks cute, has that rainbow flag that I think is probably gay rather than NHS."

"You never know," Robin said.

"You never know," Mo agreed. "And then we could head out from there? See where the night takes us?"

"Sounds perfect," Robin said.

"Issy," Mo said, frowning at the woolen mess in his hands, "how did you get so good at this?"

"Well," I said, gently taking it from him, "I spent a lot of time doing it; it's just practice."

And because my fingers were busy and my mind half-focused on unpicking, I found that I kept talking.

"I had a lot of time when I was a teenager especially," I said, "because I was ill and spent a lot of time at home."

"Ill how?" Mo said, watching me fixing his square, mesmerized.

I didn't look up; I sensed the others were listening too.

"Well," I said. "I was very depressed. And for ages I couldn't work out what was wrong with me; no one could. I was tested for everything under the sun to explain why I felt so shit all the time. And in the end I went to this one doctor who asked different questions and was like, 'Oh, you're mentally ill.'"

"And it was making you feel normal ill?" Alyssa said.

"Oh my god," Robin said. "Alyssa."

"You know what I mean! You do, don't you, Issy? Like physically ill?"

"Yeah," I said, "exactly. I could barely keep my eyes open at some points, and it was just my brain shutting everything down."

"I'm sorry, mate," Mo said, "that sounds shit."

"Thanks," I said, "yeah it wasn't the best."

"So did you leave school?" he asked.

"Yeah," I said. "In my GCSE year. I was meant to go in for the exams, but I just never did. I am, technically, very unqualified."

I passed Mo's square back, intact and ready to be attacked by him again.

"Well," he said, "you might not have a certificate, but I'd say you're very bloody good at what you do."

I nodded, squeezed his knee gently by way of reply because I didn't know what to say.

"Someone dropped out of my school before GCSEs," Robin said, after a moment.

"Oh yeah?" I said. "Why's that?"

"Well," Robin said, "her dad sold luxury yachts, and it turned out it was a front for money laundering and they went on the run to South America, and no one ever saw them again."

"Right," I said. "So a similar thing, then."

"Exactly," Robin said, grinning at me. "I thought you might relate."

We sat on the roof for a while longer, until people started complaining of tired eyes, of aching hands, of repeatedly stabbing themselves with knitting needles. I was happy to go to bed: I was drained, my social battery running on reserves. I couldn't remember a day where I'd spent so much time speaking to so many people.

"Issy," Robin said, catching me before I went next door to the bathroom-bedroom, "what do you think?"

She showed me her finished pink square, kind of wonky with a few significant gaps—perhaps she had not taken in as much from her grandmother as she thought.

"Perfect," I said. "It's beautiful."

She beamed and squeezed my shoulder.

"Thank you for tonight," she said. "It was fun. Whenever I think of acute shoulder pain and getting a rash from scratchy wool, I'll think of you."

"I love that," I said, "I've been waiting to hear that my entire life."

She handed the square to me.

"For you," she said.

"Don't you want it?"

She waved her knitting needles at me, and the rest of the ball of wool.

"I can make another one now that I've got these mad skills."

I shut my bedroom door and went to sit on the edge of my bed. I closed my eyes, decompressing, clutching the pink square in my hand, and then I placed it carefully on my bedside table, next to my inspirational Aperol spritz.

I fed Abigail, who was snuffling about looking for treats, and then I swear I went to sleep before my head hit the pillow. Even though my mind had been swarming with thoughts, I didn't dream at all.

CHAPTER SEVEN

For most of my life, Friday was my least favorite day of the week. I couldn't put my finger on exactly why, or what it was about that day that stuck out as especially bad among the maelstrom of other bad days, but now I realize it was the sense of anticipation for the weekend that I no longer shared with other people—yet another feeling that should have been easy and enjoyable that I was disconnected from.

I had memories of Fridays that I would dwell on from when I was a child. I'd try to conjure that giddy feeling in my chest as the clock inched toward 3:15 p.m., my eyes drawn to the classroom windows—freedom. Knowing there was no early alarm the next morning, that I would be allowed to stay up just a little later that evening, maybe someone's birthday party on the Sunday afternoon in the bowling alley or a Pizza Hut. The excitement about the fish and chips from Peter's Fish Factory to come that evening, eaten from soggy paper, knees crossed in front of the telly.

That's one Friday routine that remained in the years I spent feeling especially bleak—the "blackout years" as Uncle Pete sometimes calls them, as if I'm in the light now, as if we've closed the door on that particular room and forgotten all about it—the fish and chips. Even when I would not eat them, even when it would hurt my skin and bones and I would sob as I climbed out of bed, I would sit opposite Mum at the fully laid kitchen table, a plate of fish and chips in front of me. The portion size became smaller and smaller each week, until it became clear Mum was just giving me a little of hers—half a portion of chips, a handful, three even. Maybe I would just eat one?

"You need to eat," my mum would say, "to live."

Exactly, I would think.

I would sit there, silently, barely occupying my body at all until Mum was finished, and then I'd go back to bed and keep on living all the same.

My Fridays got better as I did, which is to say, sometimes they were pretty decent, as good as anyone else's, and sometimes for absolutely no discernible reason they were hell on earth. I couldn't speak to anyone. I could not open my eyes. Drinking a glass of water would take me ten minutes because the effort of doing something that felt so pointless was exhausting. The world was burning, and I wished to be set on fire. My soul was crushed—if it ever existed. That sort of thing.

I got my job at Glazed when I was eighteen. I'd been recovering for a while by then, slowly returning to myself—a combination of the right medication and therapy and whatever alchemy that exists inside the human brain created a random chemical reaction that allowed me to feel human again. When I blinked, my eyes no longer hurt. I laughed sometimes. I walked on the beach and looked at the waves appreciatively. I didn't long for them. Some days they brought me peace.

I spent weeks handing around my pretty much blank CV until the manager at Glazed, newly hired and inexperienced, took pity on me. I guess I was lucky enough to be eighteen at a time when jobs were available to people like me—by which I mean, on paper: uneducated and with no discernible skills. The manager asked me if I could make coffee and keep my hands out of a fire, and I confidently said yes, those were both things I could do.

She was understanding when there were "blackout" weeks and slowly but surely my life became different. A routine set in where I left my bed and took my meds and worked at the café and came home. I leveled out, is what it felt like.

And I started eating my fish and chips. And sometimes I felt alive.

That Friday at work in Elizabeth's studio, for the first time in years, I felt that giddy anticipation. It's not that I didn't enjoy my working day, it's more that I knew that at the end of it, there was more fun to be had. More people and stories and laughter. Everything had been so quiet for such a long time, I couldn't get enough of the sound being turned up.

"Right," Elizabeth said, clapping her hands at 6:00 p.m. on the dot. "That's it, kids."

"Woo!" Olivia snapped her clutch bag shut and stood up. She'd been on the phone for most of the afternoon by the sounds of it, trying to persuade someone with a private art collection to come and let us film at his house, but she'd also taken the opportunity to do her hair and makeup (actual curling iron plugged in under the desk) so that by the time she got up to leave, she looked like she was going to a movie premiere.

"We're going to a movie premiere," she announced.

P went and stood beside her, looking at the time on their phone anxiously. They tapped Olivia's elbow as if trying to get her to hurry up.

"My friend has made a short film about these gay marmots at London Zoo. It's very moving," P said, "and we need to go now if we want to watch it."

"Gay marmots," Aubrey repeated. She had her bike helmet on and was already waiting by the door.

"Yes," P said, "they've had this really turbulent relationship."

"God," Aubrey said. "Well, it is hard to keep the romance alive, isn't it? Cost-of-living crisis and the pressure to have kids and everything."

The door slammed behind them as they all made their way outside with a chorus of byes.

Elizabeth looked at me and smiled.

"One thing I can guarantee you working here, Issy. No late Friday nights, and we don't work weekends, which might be obvious by the way my staff have disappeared within about thirty seconds."

I slid my new laptop into my backpack.

"You got any fun weekend plans?" Elizabeth said. She asked casually, but I wondered if she was checking in on me, concerned that I too wasn't dashing out of the door.

"Oh, yes," I said proudly, as if announcing some huge news, "I do. I'm actually going to the pub right now!"

Alyssa was already there waiting for us when we arrived. She was wearing a black crop top and high-waisted jeans, and there was a bag containing her pink scrubs by her feet. She'd told us she was always early to everything—which was surprising to no one.

Mo, Robin, and I had met outside and walked through the near-empty pub and into the small garden, which was packed with people standing, resting their sweating pint glasses on whatever free surfaces they could find. Alyssa had secured a picnic table in a patch of shade. She was sitting at it by herself, scrolling on her phone, apparently entirely unaware of the hubbub around her.

"Yes, Alyssa!" Robin said as she sat down opposite her. "It's completely rammed out here, how on earth did you manage this?"

"Manage what?" Alyssa said, looking up from her phone and frowning.

Robin paused for a moment to see if Alyssa was joking, and when it became clear she genuinely had no idea what she was talking about, Robin burst out laughing. Mo, opposite me, caught my eye, and we shared a smile. My heart leaped at it, this small moment of connection. I loved the feeling of being in on something.

"Never mind," Robin said. "It doesn't matter. What's everyone drinking? I'll get the first round."

Robin came back to the table a few minutes later carefully carrying our drinks, and two bags of salt and vinegar crisps in her teeth. She placed the glasses down on the table to a chorus of congratulations from the rest of us.

"I used to work in a pub when I was a teenager," Robin said. "I can carry armfuls of pints, charm old gross men, and wow, you should see me washing up."

"I'd *love* to see you do some washing up," Alyssa said, taking a sip of her Aperol spritz.

"What?" Robin said, although she'd obviously heard her perfectly clearly.

"Nothing," Alyssa said. "So, I need to get a gorgeous photo of me sitting out here because the light's amazing and I look really good today."

Robin nodded and held out her hand to take Alyssa's phone. Alyssa ignored her and wordlessly passed it to Mo.

"OK, so make me look nineteen but not in a creepy way, in a hot way, in like *I know she's not nineteen but she* could *be nineteen because her skin is so soft and glowy, like a child's skin*, do you know what I mean?"

"Yep," Mo said, standing up from the picnic bench and then crouching down beside the table, holding the phone at a ridiculous angle. He made a face as if his knees were hurting him as he lowered himself, exhaling slowly. "Got it."

Once Mo had taken what seemed to me to be hundreds of the exact same photo of Alyssa, he passed the phone back to her, and she began the process of frowning and deleting. Every few seconds she'd turn the phone around to show the rest of us, inviting the group to share our opinions.

"Mate," Robin said after a few minutes of this, "no offense, but you look identical in all of these."

"Are you joking?" Alyssa said just as Mo said, "No, she doesn't."

"She does," Robin said. "I'm getting that thing like when you see a word written down too many times and it loses all meaning—but with Alyssa's face. Who even are you anymore? You're a blur. I feel like I'm looking at an optical illusion."

"Why do you need a perfect photo? Which all of these are, obviously," I said before Alyssa could snap back at Robin.

I took a sip of my pint of IPA. It tasted sour and bitter and quite disgusting. I savored it.

I didn't want to tell the others but this was, privately, a bit of *a Moment*. I had never had a pint in a pub with a group of friends before.

I'd been to the pub before, obviously. I'm not a full hermit, not most of the time anyway. I'd been with my uncle Pete when I was a kid loads of times to play on the slot machines and drink dangerous quantities of Coca-Cola. A wobbly tooth once came out in the Northern Belle because of a particularly crunchy pork rind. Uncle Pete made me tell my mum it had been because of an apple, which she did not believe for a second. And of course I'd been to the pub occasionally with the people I'd worked with at Glazed—at Christmastime or when someone left, but I often wasn't drinking alcohol for various reasons, or I just had a glass of warm wine from a bottle someone had already bought. And I was never among friends.

"Because," Alyssa said, "I need to post something on Instagram today where I look very stunning and casual as if I'm just casually at the pub having a drink while looking stunning."

"The ex?" Robin said, cigarette hanging out of her mouth, patting herself down for a lighter.

"Yeah," Alyssa said. "He's on holiday with this new . . . ugh, whatever she is, and he's taken her to this place in Spain we always used to go to, that I took him to, in fact. It was actually my place first. And he's plastering it all over his stories like he thinks he's an influencer or something, and it's not like I care but . . ."

"You've got to stop watching his stories, man," Robin said.

"No," Alyssa said, "but I don't want him to think I care, it'll look like I care if I suddenly stop watching them."

"But, you do care," I said.

"But I don't want him to *know* I care," Alyssa said, turning to look at me. She stared for a moment like she was only just taking in the fact that I was there at all.

"Huh, you look nice today, Issy. Very pink and dewy." She gestured to my face.

I was sweating, I think she meant. And sunburned.

"Thank you," I said, putting my hand under my chin and pouting, one of Alyssa's signature poses.

"Yeah," Alyssa continued, nodding to herself, "you should get a nice photo for Instagram too while we're out here, you never know who's watching."

"You literally do know who's watching though," I said. "That's what you just said."

Alyssa ignored me and held out her hand to take my phone. I hesitated.

"Issy doesn't have Instagram," Mo said, "remember? She's cool. She's off-grid. Literally."

"That's me," I said, "off-grid, a nomad, just living off the land like our ancestors."

"Shit," Alyssa said. "That's right. Well, there's no time like the present."

She reached across the table, took my phone out of my hand without asking, and started stabbing at the screen.

"What's your passcode, Iz?"

My birthday, obviously.

"Right," she said after a few moments, "what do you want your username to be?"

"Oh god," I said, "I don't know."

"Don't put numbers in it," Mo said. "I hate that, it just makes me think the person is a robot or old."

"OK, I mean . . . I don't know what it would be apart from Isobel, but I don't want anyone to think I'm an old robot; that's the last thing I want."

Mo nodded seriously.

"What about Issy and Abigail, all one word?" Robin said, stubbing out her cigarette.

"Who the hell is Abigail?" Alyssa said.

"My chinchilla," I said.

Alyssa looked at me blankly.

"My guinea pig," I said.

"Oh shit, yes," Alyssa said. "OK. Yeah, that username is free. That's cute."

Alyssa took a lot of photos of me ranging in vibe, from vaguely uncomfortable to deeply uncomfortable, and then she added heavy filters to them. She uploaded my first post for me—a photo of me staring straight down the camera, the early-evening light a summer haze streaked across the screen, my drink in one hand and the other running through my hair. I liked the photo. It looked like me, and it didn't.

"Gorgeous," Mo said. "Properly gorgeous, Issy."

Alyssa eventually handed me the phone back, and I checked my profile for any rogue behavior.

I had followed just three accounts, and they had all followed me back already.

Mo went inside to get us more drinks, and when he came back, he launched into telling us how he thought the guy behind the bar might have been on this Australian reality show he once watched called *Step Up*, where people married the parent of their best friend. He was halfway through an animated reenactment of his favorite scene (*Don't call me son; I'm older than you!*) complete with the accent, when a woman approached the table. I could see Alyssa opening her mouth to tell her that actually we were using the entire table and no she couldn't borrow the ashtray, but the woman ignored us all and spoke directly to Robin.

"Hi!" she said expectantly, her cheeks flushed. She was pretty, this woman. Forehead slightly sweaty, dark hair falling in curls.

She was wearing a dress that half the people out there were wearing, kind of shapeless but nice in a polka-dot sort of way.

"Hi!" Robin said back, her smile wide, matching the woman's tone.

There were a couple of beats of silence where it became obvious that Robin had no idea who this woman was.

"How have you been?" the woman said.

"So great," Robin said, "so, so great. How have *you* been? God, it's been ages . . . hasn't it?"

"Pretty much a year," the woman said, "since I last saw you in this exact pub."

"Yes," Robin said, "pretty much a year."

And then it was like a light bulb switched on above her head. For someone who wanted to be an actor, I have to say she did a horrible job of masking the moment she actually figured out who this person was.

"Milly!" Robin said. "Exactly a year ago. Wow, time flies."

"Molly," the woman said.

"No, *of course*," Robin said. "Obviously Molly."

There was another silence. Alyssa and Mo were visibly thrilled, leaning into each other and popping crisps in their mouths like they were at the cinema.

"So, I really only came over to . . ."

"Yeah!" Robin said. "For sure, for sure."

"I'd better get back to . . ." The woman waved in the general direction of a group of people—it was easy to pick out who her friends were because they were all staring at us.

"So good to see you," Robin said, and Molly-Milly lit up.

"Yeah," she said, "so good. Well I'll hopefully see you . . ."

"Yes. One hundred percent," Robin said. "Have a great night."

We all murmured our goodbyes as Molly shuffled off.

"Um, who was *that*?" Alyssa said.

"Molly," Mo said, "obviously."

"I went on *one* date with her a year ago in this exact pub," Robin said, downing the rest of her pint.

"She loves you," Alyssa said matter-of-factly. "The girl is literally obsessed with you. I bet she's saying to all her friends right now that she's just bumped into the love of her life. She's probably working up the courage to come back over here and ask you out."

"Shut up," Robin said, before worriedly turning to look at the gaggle of women the person had returned to. "No, she's not, is she?"

"Probably," Alyssa said, "the way she was looking at you. Did you sleep together?"

"Yeah," Robin said. "But it was just one time."

She paused.

"Well, I suppose technically, two times. Three times max."

"Once is all it takes," Alyssa said sagely. "That's why I never sleep with anyone on a first date."

"Why?" Robin said. "So people don't fall in love with you?"

"No," Alyssa said, "so I don't fall in love with them. I've never been any good at having casual sex. It's so annoying. Something kicks in, just like hormones or something; it's got nothing to do with my brain."

"I can be the same," Mo said. "Sometimes it's fine if I'm in the right headspace or something, but if I'm not, I can get accidentally attached. Doesn't that ever happen to you, Robin?"

Robin thought about it for a moment. Waited for the person clearing glasses to leave before answering.

"I mean, if I really like someone?" Robin said. "Maybe? But on a first date I rarely really like someone, but I really like having sex."

"Babe," Mo said, "that's fine. You don't need to worry about her, I'm sure she's not spent the past year pining over you."

Robin immediately looked hurt.

"Probably a bit of pining," Mo conceded. "Obviously. A healthy amount."

"Thank you," she said.

"What about you, Issy?" Alyssa said. "Sex feelings?" She pointed at Mo. "Or no sex feelings?" She pointed at Robin.

"Well," I said. I took a deep breath. "I don't know."

I was prepared to answer a barrage of questions, but Alyssa just nodded; she reached across the table and patted my hand like I was perhaps an elderly relative.

"You're not missing anything, babes," she said. "You take your time."

"Arguably I've taken enough time," I said. "Like, a really long time."

Mo shrugged.

"What's a long time when it comes to this stuff?" he said. "There's no time limit."

I nodded.

"It's not that I haven't wanted to. . . . It's just that I've never . . ."

How hard it was to explain exactly how small my life had been. How utterly out of my comfort zone I was. The idea of me going on a first date at home was laughable, so the idea of sleeping with someone on a first date? Entirely unimaginable.

"Guys," I found myself saying, the beer, combined with a healthy amount of sunstroke, definitely having gone straight to my head. "I've never even *kissed* anyone."

Well, unless you count that time Ryan Dingle caught me during kiss chase in year four. Which I absolutely do not.

There was quiet for a moment as my housemates took in this information. Alyssa lifted her spritz to her mouth and sipped slowly through her straw without taking her eyes off me.

"You will," Alyssa said, "if you want to."

"Yeah," Mo said. "Exactly."

"Maybe tonight even," Alyssa said.

"Or not," Robin said quickly. "Maybe just whenever she's ready."

"Maybe she's ready tonight though," Alyssa said.

"OK, thanks, guys," I said, before they got into a full-blown argument about whether I was or wasn't ready to kiss anybody, which there was no way to win because I had no idea myself. "Maybe tonight, yes. What exactly are we doing again?"

The club was surprisingly small. Once we'd been scrutinized by the bouncer and squeezed our way in, we were immediately wedged between bodies tightly packed together. I felt like a sardine. A gay sardine.

I had been to a gay bar before, believe it or not, although it was treated by locals and tourists alike as simply the bar with the best view over the beach in Margate. This meant you got groups of boys from London having Big Gay Weekends and drinking blue drinks out of fishbowls called subtle things like "cocksucker" next to Uncle Pete and Auntie Jan eating scampi and chips.

I thought I might feel claustrophobic surrounded by all those people, or anxious. But I didn't. It was oddly comforting. The heat and the music and the energy. The wonderful proximity to queerness, being immersed in it.

"You OK?" Robin yelled at me, reaching out to pull me through the crowd. I looked down at her slender fingers intertwined with mine.

I nodded.

"Yes," I yelled back. "I'm good."

Alyssa was in front of Robin, attached to her other hand. I saw her head pop up above the melee as she stood on tiptoes.

"Drink?" she shouted. "Mo is at the bar. Shall I tell him four porn-star martinis?"

"No," Robin said, "I'll have a . . ."

But Alyssa had already turned her head back to the bar, holding up four fingers at Mo. He gave her a thumbs-up.

We stayed upstairs for a while, sipping our sweet drinks. I was feeling more than a little tipsy by this point, but it was a nice feeling, everything was slowed down. It felt easy. I listened as the others chatted, and took in the people around me. Everyone was beautiful—that was the thing that struck me the most. There was beauty in all these people and the way they wore their clothes on their different kinds of bodies and the way they cut their hair and held themselves and each other.

We went downstairs after a while to dance, clutching fresh porn-star martinis, which I bought and nearly fainted at the price. Truly thank god for Uncle Pete and the big shop. It wasn't as rammed downstairs—there was room to move about, and I quickly lost all notions of self-consciousness dancing with my friends.

After what might have been two minutes or three hours, I went to put Alyssa's and my empty glasses down on a table in the corner of the room. I took a moment to have a breather, took my phone out to check the time, thought about water, thought about how surreal my life was. Just as it was all about to get a bit existential, I became aware of someone looking at me—a woman standing close by with a group of people. Before I could even think about it, she'd broken away from her friends and was standing directly in front of me.

She was taller than me by a couple of inches and had long dark hair. When she tucked it behind her ear, even in the dark I could see that she had a tattoo behind it. A delicate heart.

"What's your name?" The girl leaned into me so I could hear her over the music. I could feel her lips vibrating against my earlobe.

"It's Issy," I managed to say. I was glad to have my phone to hold, just for something to do with my hands. This girl didn't have any such problem though, because instead of telling me her name, she hooked two fingers through my belt loop at the front of my jeans and pulled me toward her.

"Can I kiss you, Issy?" she said.

I nodded, in disbelief.

And then she did it. She kissed me. The things I remember most are these: she tasted like something sweet I didn't recognize, and her lips were soft. She parted mine gently with hers, and my head started to spin. Thank god I was leaning against the wall, otherwise I might have actually keeled over.

Twenty-eight years of not being kissed and here I finally was. I'd pictured it before: I suppose I always thought it would be with someone I was madly in love with, or at least with someone whose name I knew. I'd never thought it would be like this—my back pressed against a wall, a stranger's hand behind my neck, fingers gently tugging on my hair. It was even more thrilling than I could have imagined.

I really would have loved to have gotten properly carried away in the kiss, but I was far too aware of everything around me, the proximity of other people, the lights, the mechanics of someone else's mouth on mine. I felt, as I often do, like an observer rather than a participant. And yet, there I was. The one that something

was actually happening to for once. Just as I vowed to stop thinking and start enjoying it, the woman with no name and her hands
roaming all over me pulled away. She looked at me and smiled,
licking her lips.

"You're hot," she said, "find me later." And then she walked away,
melting into the mass of people on the dance floor.

I made my way into the toilets and into the only free cubicle. I
sat down heavily on the closed toilet seat, aware that the cubicles
around me seemed to be filled with people, the chatter in there
almost as loud as the music outside. I closed my eyes and put one
hand on the wall to steady myself. This was top-level drunk, the
most drunk I could be and still have a nice time. I pressed my fingers to my lips. Everything felt sort of numb, or sort of tingly. I was
acutely aware of every single sensation. I was reeling and kind of
freaking out and yet also, I distinctly remember, utterly exhilarated.

I pulled my phone out of my pocket to check the time, it was
2:00 a.m. Like any grown adult who has just had their first kiss
on a sweaty dance floor with a stranger, I did the obvious thing, I
messaged my mum.

Isobel: *I'm out with my new friends, you don't need to worry about
me though. We're all going home together:)*

I stood up carefully, my head still spinning slightly, and brought
my fingers to my lips again. I had expected the post-kiss tingling
I'd felt to fade, but if anything it was becoming more intense. Perhaps, I thought, I was drunker than I realized. I left the cubicle
and tried to take a look at myself in the mirror, but the sinks were
crowded with people gossiping, applying makeup, crying. I gave up
in the end and went to find my new friends.

When I found them, a tight group of three dancing in the corner of the room, I had expected they might greet me with excitement, questions, at the bare minimum a pat on the back for getting my first kiss out of the way. What I didn't anticipate is what they actually did, which was, collectively, gasp in horror.

"Oh my god, babe," Alyssa said, her voice naturally so loud, she barely had to strain to be heard over the music. She stepped forward and grabbed my face. The second woman to do that tonight, and, indeed, ever. "What the hell happened?"

"What do you mean?" I said, not sure where to look as she inspected me in wildly intimate proximity with my jaw in her vise-like grip.

"What I mean is, why is your mouth swelling up, Issy? Can you not feel it?"

I managed to wriggle away from her and pressed the back of my hand to my lips. They felt slightly too hot, and now that I thought about it, now that I was really examining what was going on in my mouth, my tongue felt slightly too big behind my teeth. I don't know how I hadn't noticed that before.

"I mean, I can feel it." I paused, unable to decide if my voice sounded strange because of my newly enormous tongue. "But I kind of just thought . . . I kissed someone, did you see?"

I felt a bit like a child who'd just done a handstand and their mother had missed it. Like, what's the point if no one knows about it?

Everyone ignored me.

"It looks like you've been stung by a bee, on your lips," Alyssa said. "Have you been stung by a bee, do you think?"

For the thousandth time in the past couple of days, Robin rolled her eyes at Alyssa. She stepped forward and gently nudged her out of the way. Mo stood back, his eyes still wide with horror. The straw from his vodka soda had not left his lips.

"Of course she hasn't been stung by a bee," Robin said. "Issy, are you allergic to anything?"

"No. Well, yeah, I mean I'm allergic to strawberries, but I haven't eaten any strawberries, I can't because everything swells up."

I realized that I could no longer pronounce *s*—the situation was significantly worsening. Try saying that with a swollen tongue.

Robin frowned. "Could it have been in your drink?"

"No, I always check because I . . ."

And then it dawned on me.

"The girl, the girl I kissed. She tasted like something sweet."

"Something sweet like?" Robin said.

"Strawberries," I said. "Oh no, I'm so stupid."

I suddenly only knew words that began with an *s*.

"What do you need?" Robin said. "Like how bad is this? Are we OK to just get an Uber now to A and E or do we need to get you an ambulance?"

Robin, in the space of just a few moments, appeared to have entirely sobered up. She'd gone into full doctor mode, utterly serious. I realized I'd never spoken to her before when she hadn't been somewhat playful, somewhat in charm mode. Instead of answering her question, I became preoccupied with how much I fancied this serious, doctor version of Robin. I started to picture her in a white coat, holding a clipboard, standing above my bed . . .

"Isobel," Robin said, interrupting the fantasy. "What do we need to do?"

"I just need antihistamines," I said. I took a deep breath. Or I tried to. It wasn't as easy as it should have been. "I have them at home."

Robin frowned.

"You're struggling to breathe," she said. Not even a question.

She glanced at the watch on her wrist and seemed to be making a calculation.

"It will probably be quicker to get an Uber now than an ambulance." She turned to Mo and Alyssa. "I'm going to take Issy to the hospital, I think, to be on the safe side."

Mo took one long final sip of his drink and put his glass down on the ledge behind him.

"We're obviously coming," he said.

"Obviously," Alyssa said. "I've already ordered an Uber, he's outside."

She answered her phone and yelled, "We're coming, we're having a *medical emergency*, so you need to calm down."

"Come on," she said to us, her hand over the mouthpiece.

We emerged onto the street, still packed with people even at this time, and clambered into a white Prius that had pulled up right outside the club. Alyssa got in the front with the driver, and I found myself sitting in the middle seat in the back like a child, wedged between Robin and Mo. The car was small, and both their heads were turned to face me. I had never felt so intimately observed. In other circumstances I might have felt self-conscious, but as it was, I couldn't even enjoy Robin's thigh pressed up against mine because I was mostly trying to decide whether I could breathe or not.

"Wait," Robin said after a few minutes, "can you pull over here quickly, please?"

The driver started to object, but before he really got a chance Alyssa turned to him and said, "Do you want this girl to die in the back of your car, sir? Because she will if you don't pull over."

My eyes widened. Did I really look that bad? Alyssa turned around to me and winked.

Robin hopped out of the car and into the twenty-four-hour pharmacy we'd just passed. While she was gone, Alyssa interrogated our driver about his night, where he lived, his family. He seemed to respond pretty well to her aggressive line of questioning, and by the time Robin returned a couple of minutes later, he was showing Alyssa photos of his daughter on her first day of school.

Robin slid in next to me and ripped into a packet of antihistamines. She handed me two tablets.

"I know these are going to be hard to swallow without water right now," she said, "but they'll help."

I pushed the tiny white pills to the back of my tongue and swallowed as hard as I could. Increasingly difficult. I decided I couldn't even muster up the energy at that point to thank her.

We pulled up at Homerton hospital, and I have to say, the mood as we got out of the car had certainly shifted from somber and stressed to, without a doubt, pretty excited. This was a thrilling end to the evening that absolutely no one had expected. I think I probably would have been more thrilled had I been able to speak or, for example, breathe through my mouth.

The receptionist was entirely unmoved by my situation. I have a feeling if I'd have walked in with my own head tucked under my arm and blood spurting out of my neck, she'd have rolled her eyes and told me to get in line.

We found four seats opposite one another surrounded by two people with bleeding heads and someone so drunk they were passed out, their head lolling back over the seat. The fluorescent lights made everyone look even sicker.

Mo and Alyssa, who were sitting next to each other across from me and Robin, started to play a game of "snog, marry, avoid" involving all the people in the waiting room while I sat back and listened. I realized after a few minutes that my tongue was sitting more comfortably in my mouth. I still did not want to risk speaking, so I messaged Robin instead.

Isobel: *My tongue feels more normal I think the antihistamines are working, thank you*

Robin pulled her phone out of her pocket and smiled as she read the message. I expected her to reply to me out loud but instead she nudged me gently with her elbow and began typing.

Robin: *Glad to hear it*

Isobel: *Does this mean we can go home?*

Robin: *No, I want you to get checked out, we don't want any anaphylactic shock, do we?*

Isobel: *I suppose not, no. But I feel fine now. And I'm tired.*

Robin: *I'm sorry, I'm putting my foot down. Go to sleep, I'll wake you when it's your turn.*

She turned to me then and grinned. She patted her bare shoulder, gesturing for me to rest my head on it. I considered it for a moment and then shook my head. She raised her eyebrows at me as if to say *Your loss*, and for some reason, I felt dangerously breathless again.

After what felt like eternity but was probably only an hour or two, Alyssa went and spoke to the receptionist we'd seen earlier who didn't care if I lived or died, and soon after that, miraculously, I was seen by a doctor. Mo, Alyssa, and Robin all came with me, and after a brief moment of looking like she was going to protest, the doctor simply rolled her eyes and gestured for me to sit down.

"Allergy?" the doctor said, barely looking at me. She pushed her glasses up her nose and sighed heavily.

"To strawberries," I said.

"So why did you eat a strawberry?" the doctor said wearily, prodding my bottom lip with her finger and then peering into my mouth, pressing down on my swollen tongue. I truly don't know how she expected me to answer her.

"She didn't," Alyssa piped up, indignantly. "She kissed someone who had been drinking a strawberry cocktail, *actually*."

"Right," the doctor said, "naturally. Are you taking any medications at the moment?"

I paused.

"Just tell me whatever it is," the doctor said, "I don't care what you've taken, I just don't want to kill you."

"I take . . ."

And I told her the list of medications I take. I didn't look at the others. I guess this is why you don't normally invite a group of essentially strangers into consulting rooms with you.

When I did chance a look up at them, they were all, without exception, on their phones, barely listening. I felt a rush of affection for them.

The doctor checked that I was alive by looking into my eyes and asking me if I was still alive. When I confirmed that to the best of my knowledge I was, she prescribed me some steroids and sent me on my way, shooing us out of the room.

"Next time," the doctor said, as we filed out, "be a bit more careful when you're kissing strangers in nightclubs. Probably not worth dying for, eh?"

I looked back at her, and I could have sworn, even though she was already focused on something else, looking at the massive, ancient computer in front of her, she was smiling to herself.

By the time we left the hospital, the sky was starting to turn pink and the sun was close to coming up. Over the sound of sirens and traffic, if you listened carefully, you could hear the birds singing. It was warm already, and because we hadn't been to sleep and had no concept of the time, everything took on a sort of dreamlike quality.

We walked home along the now-deserted streets, the four of us taking up the entire pavement. We mostly walked in contented silence; one of us would occasionally point out the color of the sky and we'd all murmur appreciatively. At one point we came across a newsagent that was still open, and Mo went inside to buy water, which I sipped carefully. It slid more easily over my tongue as the minutes passed until eventually I felt sure I could swallow properly. My lips stopped feeling as though they were going to burst, and they finally stopped tingling. I concentrated less on my breathing and more on the feeling of walking alongside these people I barely knew who already felt like friends. Like everything from that night, it didn't quite feel like real life.

When we got home, instead of going straight to bed, we headed up to the roof terrace and sat in our mismatched chairs watching the sun rise over the park. At one point Mo went to make us coffee and Robin rolled a cigarette. I watched the smoke waft out over the rooftops, and it felt like, at that moment, I could have happily stayed in that exact spot forever.

At around 7 a.m., we started making our way inside to try to get some sleep. My entire body ached by that point, but it wasn't unpleasant; it was satisfying almost. I'd imagine it might be how your body would feel after you'd run a marathon or climbed a mountain—some impressive feat of stamina and peak physical performance, which, to my mind, that evening had been.

We walked through the pathway in Robin's room, among the clothes and piles of books, and stopped on the landing outside her door.

"Well," Mo said, "safe to say, that was not the night I expected but weirdly"—he rubbed his eyes, bloodshot now, and heavy—"it was kind of perfect too, wasn't it? Sorry, Issy. I mean I'm glad you're alive, obviously. Huge bonus."

"No," I say, "I get what you mean. Thank you all for being so nice to me. And sorry for nearly dying. I really will be far more diligent about who I kiss in the future."

I literally blushed when I said the word *kiss*, which suggested to me I might actually be waiting quite a long time for the next one.

"Never apologize for nearly dying," Alyssa said, pulling me in for a one-armed hug and squeezing me gently. "And you got to have your first kiss, and that's what this whole night was about, wasn't it?"

"Was it?" I said, but it was pointless because she was already on her way downstairs, lifting a hand behind her, waving good night. Mo followed her, yawning loudly.

"Good night, babies," he said when he reached the bottom, "or good morning. Ugh, fuck. I'm too old for this."

"OK," I said to Robin, feeling shy suddenly and not sure why, "I'll leave you to it. Thank you again, for everything."

I turned to head to my room. Despite my aching body, I knew I was too wired to sleep. I wondered if this was going to be a theme in my new life—what if it was all so exciting, I never slept again?

Robin reached out, grabbed my hand and tugged it gently so that I turned back around to face her.

"No need to thank me," Robin said. "Do you promise that you feel better though? You can breathe normally? You're not feeling dizzy? Lightheaded?"

I shook my head, and she frowned.

"I mean yes, sorry," I said. "I can breathe. No, I'm not dizzy. I feel fine, much better."

"Fantastic," Robin said, shifting so she was leaning against her doorframe, her arms folded in front of her, a smile playing on her lips. "Then I'm confident you'll live, Ms. Bailey."

I did feel slightly lightheaded then but not in a way that I thought Robin needed to know about. I smiled back at her, and maybe it was because I was exhausted, or delirious by that point, but I could have sworn I felt something pass between us. Some undefinable, fleeting spark.

"Good night, Doc," I said, after a beat. I don't know what exactly I was waiting for.

"Good night, Issy," Robin said, her voice softer than I'd heard it before.

I guess she was just tired.

When I got to my room, I drew the thin curtains, which made no difference whatsoever to the sunlight pouring in. I had left the window open overnight, but the air was completely still. I knew that in a couple of hours, the heat was going to be unbearable.

I crept over to Abigail's cage, located in the shadiest corner of my room, and opened the door. I could hear rustling, and when I opened up a new bag of popcorn, she wriggled out of her little house and waddled over to sit on my lap so I could feed her. I watched her as she ate and stroked her soft, gray head with one finger. I bent down to sniff her, to bury my nose in her warm fur.

She allowed it because she was preoccupied. She smelled like she always did—earthy and comforting, like warm beds and sawdust.

Eventually, she had enough of eating, but instead of going back inside her cage, she started pottering around the room, exploring. I watched her sniffing about for a little while until she made her way back to me. She rarely allowed me to cuddle her, but sometimes, when she was sleepy, I could scoop her up with one arm and she'd fall asleep across it. This was one of those rare times. Even after my arm started to ache from holding it in the same position, I couldn't bear to put her back, so instead I leaned against the cold, tiled wall and closed my eyes, drifting in and out of sleep, my thoughts racing, clutching a little piece of home tightly to my chest.

CHAPTER EIGHT

The next couple of weeks flew by in a flurry of meeting new people, taking notes, trying to remember everything, and trying to stay sane. Easy!

I woke up early and went to bed early, just about managing to eat a piece of toast or whatever leftovers my housemates had kindly left me, before feeding Abigail and collapsing in a heap on my bed.

I was a different kind of tired than when I worked at Glazed—that was a pure physical exhaustion, aches and pains and a strain behind my eyes from the bright lights and the children screaming. This was something else entirely, it reached bone level. It was a tiredness borne of smiling all day and constant new information and trying to figure out exactly how to behave. A tiredness borne of worrying I wasn't doing it right, that someone was going to catch me out for something I hadn't even remembered to worry about. Every day that I got through without someone unmasking me as an imposter, a fraud, as stupid, I breathed a sigh of relief before the knot began curling in my stomach again, wrapping around all my internal organs preparing for the next day. I had not, however, been poisoned by any more rogue strawberry women, so all things considered, it was going really well!

One morning toward the beginning of October, I woke up and, despite what Elizabeth kept saying about work-life balance, checked my emails. It had become habit. Partly because I was terrified of slipping up and missing something and partly because it gave me a genuine thrill that I had something to check, there was something exciting to wake up to. I never knew what I was going to find.

> *To: Isobel Bailey*
> *From: Aubrey Kerr*
> *Subject: Hope you see this in time . . .*

> *. . . to meet me at the Beaton Gallery this morning instead of at the office. I asked Elizabeth yesterday if I could take the newbie out on a field trip but forgot to tell you, so that's my bad.*
> *If you're reading this and panicking in the office—chop chop!*

I beat Aubrey there. She found me leaning up against the wall outside the gallery and raised her eyebrows.

"Very good," Aubrey said, as she chained her sister's bike to a fence outside that had a sign on it saying not to chain your bike up.

"I'm a consummate professional," I replied.

She took off her helmet and shoved it in the top of her back-pack. She shook out her helmet hair.

"OK, consummate professional, shall we go inside?"

"What are we here for?" I said, walking in ahead of her as she held the door open for me.

"Well, this is called a gallery, it's where you see . . ."

"I mean, what are we here to see?" I said, rolling my eyes.

Aubrey pointed at the sign ahead of us.

Radical Craft: Eighties and Nineties

This exhibition looks at craft and queerness over the span of two turbulent decades for the LGBTQ+ community. Craft—textiles, pottery, collage, knitting, embroidery—is something that has been long over-looked and undervalued by the arts world. Here, we celebrate it. Pieces made for the community by a com-munity that has also consistently been overlooked and undervalued.

Aubrey and I hadn't spoken about queerness. As we walked around the quiet room together, just us and the work, it felt as though we were saying a thousand things, all the conversation we could ever need to have.

I looked at intricate quilts made for sick friends, at badges and buttons, at handmade drag costumes and pieces made of glass, delicate and powerful all at once. A colorful collage made up of thousands of pieces of paper with people's names on them. Mes-sages for all of them. It covered an entire wall.

I stopped in front of a large piece that from far away looked like a painting. A figure with their back turned, their head down, in motion, a dog by their side looking up at them. On closer inspection, it was a knitted print, so intricate that the lines could be mistaken for brush strokes. My eyes filled with tears because I recognized this person instantly—I recognized myself; I recognized what the artist was trying to say. It was what I was trying to say too, what I couldn't articulate. What I tried to channel through a thousand Abigails, what those Abigails were screaming.

It was dark all around them, and they moved regardless.

Aubrey and I didn't say a word until we walked into the lobby, the daylight was confusing; it was like time had stopped for a while.

"This is what we're doing," Aubrey said.

I nodded.

"I wanted you to see the impact of amplifying voices other than our own."

"Thank you," I said.

"And that you should lift your own voice too," Aubrey said.

"What do you mean?"

"I've seen your work," Aubrey said. "You're weird. It's good. I feel like you think Elizabeth's taken pity on you, but she hasn't."

"Oh," I said, "thank you, I . . ."

"It's not a compliment," Aubrey said, "it's a fact."

"Right," I said.

"Come on, we can't hang out here all day, some of us have got work to do," Aubrey said, striding out of the gallery and going to unchain her bike.

"Listen," she continued, "I heard from the producers, they've got a group of people whittled down, they just need to finesse and find the first filming date—they're thinking end of October."

"That's so exciting," I said, "I can't believe we actually get to—"

And halfway through my sentence, Aubrey cycled off.

———————

"Are you coming out for drinks tonight?" I asked Aubrey that evening as we were packing up.

P and Olivia were already outside waiting for me, vaping and talking animatedly. I could hear them through the open window.

"I don't think so," Aubrey said. She stretched and ran her hand through her hair. She had nice arms, I thought fleetingly, watching her closely. Is that what my sexy knitter's arms looked like? I looked down at my own arm, tried to do a surreptitious flex.

Aubrey put her bike helmet on, and I felt something strangely close to panic.

"I think we're going to a pub around the corner," I said, "just for a couple of drinks."

It was out of character for me to push on anything, but I didn't want to let Aubrey go. I wanted more time with her, more opportunities to get her to crack, to get past pleasant robot and into human being, whatever that might mean.

"I'm good," Aubrey said, "you have fun though."

She pulled her backpack onto her shoulders, and for a moment, she looked like she might be about to say something else, but then she walked out without saying goodbye—another thing I'd quickly got used to. Something tugged in my chest. I did not know what. I packed up my things and went for drinks without her.

P and Olivia had been sweet to me since I'd started. They'd taken me with them for lunch and asked me lots of questions and wanted to hear all about Abigail even though Olivia did say, when I showed her a photo on my new Instagram, that Abigail looked like "a rat in a fur coat."

Chinchillas aren't for everyone.

"So," P said. They were wearing a pale pink knitted vest that day with lots of gold jewelry, matching pink eyeshadow, and a long pink-and-baby-blue kilt. Kind of like Androgynous Barbie. I was enthralled. What I wouldn't have done for Androgynous Barbie. "How are you getting on with the group project, it starts soon, right?"

"Ugh," Olivia said, taking a sip of her vodka soda, "poor thing. Working with Aubrey every day."

"Oh," I said, "no, it's not so bad."

We were sitting in a booth in a pub, the two of them on one side and me on the other. It felt a little like an interview panel.

"Really?" Olivia said. She didn't look convinced.

"Really," I said. "Well, I mean, mostly. Sometimes she's a bit, you know, absolutely terrifying to be around. Sometimes she's nice, and then sometimes it feels like she hates me and wishes I'd never been born."

"Oh she does," Olivia said lightly.

I noticed P chewing the inside of their cheek, and they suddenly seemed pretty focused on stirring their drink with their straw.

"Sorry," I said, confused. "She does hate me and wishes I'd never been born? Did she . . . did she tell you that?"

"Well," Olivia said, "not in so many words."

"No," P said. They shook their head at Olivia, but she wasn't looking. "She didn't tell her that, she hasn't said anything of the sort."

"She didn't have to," Olivia said, "she just hates everyone, doesn't she?"

"Right," I said. "Why though?"

"Jealousy," Olivia said confidently, "probably."

"What on earth has she got to be . . ."

"Anyway," Olivia said, "enough about Aubrey," as if she hadn't been the one who'd brought her up in the first place. "Let's not bring the mood down."

For the next thirty minutes, Olivia spoke at length about someone from the production team she'd been sexting while P nodded and ummed and aahed in all the right places. Meanwhile I was mulling over the fact that Aubrey hated me, turning over each of our interactions, worrying that I'd never get past pleasant robot because she might kill me first.

When Olivia got up to go to the bar, P leaned forward and said, "Olivia is just being dramatic—don't worry about Aubrey; she's not so bad."

"OK," I said dubiously. "So then why does Olivia think that?"

"She's got her own . . ." P trailed off, watching behind my head in case Olivia reappeared. "Don't worry about it basically. Of course Aubrey doesn't hate you."

I nodded, although I wasn't sure I believed them.

"I like your vest," I said. "You look like Barbie. I hope you don't mind me saying that."

"I don't mind in the slightest," P said. "You know who made me this vest . . ."

Olivia came back to the table with another round at that very moment. As she was settling back down in the booth, P grinned and mouthed at me, "Aubrey."

A few days later, the production company finally approved our first session, the first time we'd meet the Outside the Lines group and film the entire thing—it was going to be on Halloween.

"Do you love Halloween, Aubrey?" I said.

"Why would you think that?"

"No reason."

"No," she said. "I don't."

"What do you love?"

I'd taken to asking her goading questions like this. She brought out this side of me, like a little kid on the playground trying to provoke a reaction. I began to treat her grouchiness like a joke we were both in on, and I enjoyed the rapport it created, even though my role was of mild irritant, like a persistent dog begging under the table for scraps.

"Nothing," Aubrey said.

"You love nothing?" I asked.

"I love peace and quiet," Aubrey said. "I love being left alone."

I mostly think she enjoyed the rapport too. So I carried on my important work of trying to get her to crack, to show me something real.

She did. Once.

After work, on a whim, I walked to a hairdresser I'd found on the brand-new, cutting-edge app—Instagram. I didn't have an appointment, but the salon was quiet and I asked if there was any chance they could fit me in. The person behind the counter smiled and gestured for me to sit in the chair.

"Are you happy facing the mirror?" they said.

"Oh," I said, not understanding, "I don't . . ."

"Because you don't have to, if you find it stressful. I can spin you round the other way."

They grinned and twisted my chair a little side to side as if to demonstrate.

"Wow," I said, "I didn't know that was an option. Um, it's OK; I can look in the mirror."

I wanted to watch it happen.

"So what are we doing today?" they asked.

"I've had this same haircut forever," I said.

My mum's hairdresser who came to the flat had been replicating my mum's "get the blue paint out" emergency haircut for the past twenty years.

"And I want a change, something to make me look a bit more . . ."

I realized I didn't really know what the end of that sentence was.

"Got it," the person said confidently.

And they did get it. I looked in the mirror and over the course of an hour, I transformed.

When I walked into the office the next morning, my hair was shorter at the sides, longer and curly on top, styled instead of floppy and incidental. I loved it. Aubrey was the only person there, hunched over her laptop, clutching a coffee, already scowling.

She looked up from her screen and raised her eyebrows. Thrillingly, she smiled. I sat down without saying anything and slid a coffee across the table toward her.

"Looks good, Bailey," she said.

It did look good. I looked good. I walked on air all day.

CHAPTER NINE

"It's not that I ever really intended to do it, it's just that I started one day and never really stopped."

I was looking over the shoulder of an elderly gentleman called William. He looked tiny in his beige chinos, his blue-striped shirt tucked into them. His clothes were far too big for him, like a child starting school, meant to grow into his uniform. He walked slowly and with a stick, which was decorated with bolts of lightning.

He had light brown skin and patchy gray hair—a little on top of his head and a little on his chin, which he stroked often. His hair was thinning, but he had combed it so that it covered more of his head, a detail that endeared him to me immediately. The great care he had taken to try to obscure something that could not be obscured. It was something I understood profoundly.

"And now," he said, "six years later, I am in a bit of a situation with my landlord."

I wasn't at all surprised to hear that William was in a bit of a situation with his landlord because what I was looking at over William's shoulder was a slideshow of photographs of his small terraced house in Birmingham. Every wall had been painted with a beautiful, elaborate mural from top to bottom. Vivid colors covering every single inch. His bathroom, for example, was a seascape— pink coral and dreamy pearl on one wall, deep blues and greens on another. The living room was covered in portraits, men with beards and women wearing bright colors and smiling. Some of the photographs were of the ceilings, more complicated and intricate than any I had ever seen.

"How did you . . ."

I poked Aubrey's iPad screen with my forefinger, traced his kitchen ceiling with my fingertip.

"Stepladder, cricked neck, quite bad vertigo," he said. "And some good luck."

He chuckled.

"Right," I said, marveling at the detail, trying not to think too hard about William wobbling about on a ladder.

"So, William, as incredible as these are, I have to ask—what is it exactly you're wanting to do with us? In this group? It's just I'm pretty sure we can't . . ."

I looked around me, helplessly, at the spotless white walls.

"I don't think we can let you do that here."

"I know," he said. "I can't do it at home anymore either. They really are going to kick me out. They've been threatening to evict me for a while now. I'm going to have to paint over it. Paint it all white. Make it like it didn't exist. Like erasing a whiteboard."

"I'm sorry," I said. "You've really created something so beautiful. I hate the thought of it disappearing, being buried like that."

"That's why I want to re-create it," William said, impatiently almost, like he didn't have time for platitudes. "In miniature. So that I can keep it. And remember it exactly as it is now. And . . ."

He stopped, as if reaching around for the right words.

"Control it?" I suggested gently.

He nodded.

"Exactly," he said. "Control it. It's my world, to do what I like with. I can invite people to look, and I can tear it all down, or I can preserve it. But it's mine."

I thought of my own childhood creations, built in miniature and then painstakingly deconstructed to be woven into the next world I wanted to inhabit.

"We can do that," I said. "Can't we?"

I looked up at Aubrey then, standing on the other side of William's workbench. She was already watching me, ready to catch my eye. I couldn't read her expression, as usual, and she didn't say anything, but she nodded at me.

"We can do that," she confirmed. "Yes, we can definitely do that, William. It sounds like a wonderful project. We'd love to help you."

"Really?" William said, his eyes lighting up. He sat back in his chair, relieved. I hadn't even noticed he was nervous until just then—he seemed even smaller somehow. "Thank you. I could never have believed that I would find myself in London and be in this kind of place, surrounded by all of you . . ."

William gestured at the three other group members, Elizabeth, and then at Aubrey and me.

"It feels like a dream," he said. "A total dream.

"Although," he continued, shaking his head, "it's not at all what

I expected. When you think of being on the telly, you think of the glitz and glamour not the um . . ." He gestured to the room around him. "Well . . . this."

The first session with the Outside the Lines group wasn't held in Elizabeth's studio but instead in a huge loft in a warehouse in Hackney Wick. From the outside the building looked derelict—when I first arrived I thought I'd got lost. The buildings surrounding the warehouse had broken windows and chain-link fencing with huge holes in the middle, as if people had cut into them and climbed through. There were empty cans and cigarette ends and silver laughing gas cylinders all over the floor. Someone had left a *Scream* Halloween mask impaled on a spike on the fence.

I had been about to ring Elizabeth to double-check I'd got the right address when I noticed that Aubrey's bike, well, Aubrey's sister's bike, was chained to the corrugated metal fence across the street.

I turned back to the door and pressed the buzzer. Aubrey answered immediately, her voice crackly over the intercom.

"Hello?" she said.

"Hi," I said, expecting her to buzz me up.

I was met with silence. The door did not open.

"Who is this, please?"

"Aubrey," I said. "You know who it is."

More silence.

"It's Isobel," I said. "You're expecting me, I believe."

"Isobel," she said, as if she were mulling it over. "OK."

I could have sworn I could hear the smile on her face; she was amusing herself at least.

"You'd better come in, then."

She finally buzzed me into the building, and I made my way up to the loft via a stairwell exactly as grotty as you might expect from the outside—gray concrete and dubious smells and slightly sticky banisters.

I pushed the doors to the loft open and gasped. Actually gasped, like someone who had never seen exposed brick or large indoor plants and lovely Scandinavian furniture before. Of course, I had seen all those things, but I am not sure I'd seen them all together. Or in real life. And certainly not in a converted warehouse in East London. Aubrey raised her eyebrows at me.

"You all right there, Bailey?" she said.

"I just . . . wow," I said, turning around slowly, taking it all in, "it's really nice in here, isn't it?"

"You're late," she said by way of reply.

Aubrey, as usual, looked effortlessly cool in loose-fitted black jeans and a crisp white T-shirt. Her long hair had been cut and sat just below her shoulders in waves. She had gold rings on her fingers and fingernails that were bitten down to stubs. She was wearing glasses that I hadn't seen before, round with gold frames. She looked like a very chic owl. I didn't dare tell her that, of course. I valued my life.

"I was actually on time," I said, "I just didn't know if I had come to the right place; it's weird around here. It doesn't feel like the kind of place where you'd have a nice meeting; it feels like the kind of place you might come to get murdered."

"We use this place for filming," Aubrey said. "Spacious, quiet, great light. It's worth a little murder every now and again."

I nodded.

"Sure," I said, "we suffer for our art."

Aubrey, predictably, ignored me.

"So, we're filming today, right?" I said nervously.

Aubrey looked around her, exaggeratedly making a show of the fact that there was equipment all around us, two guys from the production team setting up, signs ready to go up that read, "Quiet: Filming in Progress."

I rolled my eyes.

"All right, all right. I just mean, like, this is really happening, isn't it? Like, Elizabeth is going to come here and meet everyone and we're eventually going to put this whole thing on actual TV?"

"You're going to be a star, Bailey," Aubrey said, deadpan.

She glanced at her watch, a delicate brown leather strap with a small gold face. It was intriguing to me, this watch—it was exactly the kind of thing that didn't fit with her general vibe. I half expected her to look up and tell me it was her sister's watch or her sister's dog's watch or whatever it was to explain it away. I promised myself I'd ask her about it at some point.

"We've got about thirty minutes until everyone arrives, including Elizabeth," Aubrey said, and I snapped my head up from staring at her wrist. "I've got tea, coffee, soft drinks, snacks"—she ticked her mental list off one by one on her fingers—"and I've bought some pencils, paper, that kind of thing—so people can sketch out or write down whatever it is they want to work on, and then when we get a sense of the scale of the projects we can figure out what they need accordingly."

"Great," I said. "Sounds perfect. Thanks."

She had everything covered. Of course she did, she was Elizabeth's right-hand woman, after all. I felt, as usual around Aubrey, deeply inadequate and, reluctantly, in awe.

"Now," Aubrey said. "Elizabeth has been quite clear that even though I'm technically in charge here, this is your project and that I am to oversee in a hands-off kind of way."

She held her hands up as if to surrender to me. I don't know how, but she even managed to do that sarcastically.

"And I'm happy to do that," she said. "If you're confident that you know what you're doing and you think you can do a good job for the people we've got coming in today."

She paused as if waiting for me to say something, but I sensed that her little speech wasn't finished. I nodded for her to go on.

"But." She put her hands on her hips, a classic power pose, I had recently learned from Alyssa. "It's important that you tell me if you're feeling overwhelmed or you don't know what you're doing, because these people are very graciously giving up their time . . ."

"I know that," I said indignantly.

Aubrey carried on speaking as if she hadn't heard me.

"And they're being hugely vulnerable by allowing us an insight into their lives like this. We have to remember that this is work that for most of them nobody has ever seen before, so we need to treat it all with the utmost care and respect."

"Aubrey," I said. "I'm not stupid."

She looked at me dubiously.

"There's a reason Elizabeth assigned me to this project," I said calmly, refusing to give in to the irritation bubbling away inside me; I would not give her the satisfaction. "I know what it's like to be invisible one minute and to be seen the next; I could very easily have been in this group. It is only by a series of wild coincidences—miracles even—that I'm on this side of the table."

"What table?"

"Shut up," I said, "you know what I mean."

We both froze. I'd never told Aubrey to shut up before. Aubrey went completely still. She didn't say anything for a moment, just chewed the inside of her cheek and stared at me. I saw my life flash before my eyes. I hoped someone would feed Abigail for me.

"OK," Aubrey said eventually.

"OK?" I said, standing my ground. I placed my slightly shaking hands on my hips too.

"Yeah, OK," she said briskly. "I'm going to check in with everybody that they're finding their way here all right. Even in a cab it's a fucking nightmare. Once you've stopped power posing perhaps you could put those chairs in a circle before everyone gets here."

She turned on her heel and walked out of the loft.

For fuck's sake.

I stood with my hands on my hips for a moment longer, in useless defiance, before grabbing the chair in front of me and doing exactly what Aubrey told me to do.

One by one the members of our group arrived. William had been the first, then we had Leah, a young trans woman who did self-portraits like I'd never seen before—looking at them was like looking into someone's soul. Then Aisha arrived, a slightly flustered middle-aged woman from a small town in the Midlands; she was a graphic artist and made comic books. Last to arrive was Stella, who simply dominated the room. She had spiky short hair, and was big in every way, tall and broad. Her age though was indeterminate. She might have been the same age as William, or she might have been thirty, or she might have been one hundred. I didn't dare ask. Stella did pottery, working with huge slabs of clay. She made all kinds of things, but, from the photos, mainly seemed to enjoy wearing goggles and working with medieval-looking tools and fire.

"I like your tattoos, Stella," I said. We were both by the coffee urns, and I was watching her pile several brown sugar cubes into her cup. Her arms were covered, every inch of skin bright and colorful. My eyes fixed on an electric pink Cadillac driving down her forearm.

"Thanks," Stella said, "you got any?"

"No," I said. "I want one though."

She pointed her sugar spoon at me.

"I see it," she said. "Let's get it done."

She walked off, and I honestly wasn't sure if I should follow her. If I had, she might have whipped a needle out of her bag and done it then and there.

Finally, Elizabeth walked in with Walter, wearing a see-through white chiffon dress over jeans and a vest top and pink leather cowboy boots that matched her hair. Walter's bandanna was pink too. He trotted up to me and gave me the customary hand lick.

"He loves you, Issy," Elizabeth said, giving me a warm hug.

"I love him," I said. "He's so chill; I find him very soothing."

"I often say," she said, "that if he wasn't so lazy, he could be a therapy dog, but honestly, I don't think he could be bothered."

Once Elizabeth had greeted everyone with a kiss on the cheek, she threw herself down on the sofa and slapped her hands on her knees.

"Come on," she said, "shall we all sit down and have a cup of tea, get to know one another?"

We gathered around her—Aubrey and I sat on the floor cross-legged because we'd run out of chairs. That's when the cameras started rolling.

"I want to tell you how happy I am that you're joining us," Elizabeth said. "I already know that this is going to be the best part of the show this year. Now I'm not going to make you sit here and go around in a circle introducing yourselves because I just think that's awful, instead we've set up workstations for you to go and get cracking whenever you feel like it, and then you can chat us through whatever you're working on. I know from reading about you that some of you are working on something very specific." She glanced at William and smiled; he lit up.

"And others are just going with the flow, seeing where it takes you. You do whatever you want. This space is yours. You can work on something new each week and chuck it out at the end of every session if you want. Although," she said, "we'd love it if you had *something* to share at the friends-and-family event when we finish. We'll film that too, for part of our summer special, so it would be great exposure for those of you who care about that sort of thing.

"Any questions?"

Everyone was quiet. I was feeling overwhelmed, I couldn't imagine how they all felt.

"If you need anything, I'm here for the next hour or so—I'd love to say I'm doing something glamorous afterward, but actually Walter is going to the groomers for a B-A-T-H."

More giggles when she covered the dog's ears.

"But Aubrey and Isobel will be here with you all day, and they'll be able to help you with whatever you need. And just before we get started," Elizabeth continued, "please don't worry about the cameras, you'll get used to them in no time."

In reality, we were all a bit awkward for the first hour or so, staring directly down the camera lens, stumbling over our words, saying strange things. But we got into a rhythm—we managed to find one another amid the nerves and the chaos, and it all started making sense, we started having fun even.

It was all down to Aubrey, of course, the silent conductor of our ramshackle orchestra, working her magic. It helped that everybody else was a little bit scared of her too—crew included—so we all just did what we were told. And she was always right. To be honest, I was more than happy to run around being her assistant all day.

It turned out that Stella, our potter, was a natural on camera and was obviously going to make great TV. We'd set up a workstation for her in one corner of the loft: a wheel, a bench, and her terrifying-looking tools. I found myself having flashbacks to my days working at Glazed—I prayed she would not be making Thomas the Tank Engine plates.

Stella laughed and joked with the producers, and told great stories. She'd had a difficult life, I knew that from when we were briefed by production. She referenced it all when she was speaking about her work, and she made it so funny—things that shouldn't have been funny at all. It was magic to watch.

William started work on sketching out the perfectly scaled-down model of his house. He worked with a magnifying glass taped to a headband so he could see what he was doing up close. When Aubrey saw him slip his homemade device onto his head, she and a few of the crew members hurried over, trying to figure out what he needed, what they could send out for that he could use instead, but he waved them away. He said he was perfectly fine and actually, very pleased with his invention.

I gave him a thumbs-up.

"Looking good, William," I called out across the loft.

Aubrey rolled her eyes at me and threw up her hands in defeat, but I'm certain she was smiling as she walked away.

Aisha and Leah decided, even though there was ample space, even though we'd set up four separate workstations, that they wanted to work side by side. We didn't say anything about it, just silently facilitated it, moving equipment, changing lighting. They leaned over at points, checking in with each other, asking questions quietly. They were the slowest to warm up to the cameras, to answer questions about themselves, to share details about their projects. That was until we started asking them together rather than separately. Then they started to open up, laughing at one another's answers, listening closely, comparing utterly different experiences and finding profound similarities.

"No one at home understands what I'm doing at all," Aisha said. "They think I'm fully mad. That it's all just a complete waste of time. An expensive waste of time."

"Oh, same," Leah said. "My family look at my paintings and are just like, 'These look nothing like you, what are they meant to be?'"

Stella cropped up in between them at that point, her head poking through to peer over Leah's shoulder at the canvas they were working on.

"To be fair, love," Stella said, "they're not wrong, are they?"

Leah squealed and slapped Stella on the arm.

"That's just my hair," she exclaimed. "Shut up, it'll all make sense when it's finished."

"If you say so," Stella said, before looking straight down the camera and raising her eyebrows, prompting more giggles from Leah.

Aubrey kept sending me out to buy more and more food and then a couple of bottles of wine after we passed 5:00 p.m. She did it all without interrupting the natural flow of the day. She somehow managed to orchestrate breaks and boss me around without bursting the bubble we'd created together.

"So what's the aim here, really?" Leah asked just as we were wrapping up—cameras had stopped rolling; the crew had gone home.

"The aim?" Aubrey said. "Good question. I'd say the aim is to help you create work that you're proud of, to elevate your voice as artists, and to introduce your work to a wider audience. We'll showcase the work at a gallery event attended by industry professionals and host a big celebration that will be filmed for the finale of the TV series."

These were lines lifted straight from the original brief we'd distributed to find the artists in the first place. This was not lost on Leah.

"Yes," they said, "I appreciate that. That's why I'm here. I suppose I mean, why? What's in it for you?"

Aubrey smiled, apparently completely unfazed by the challenge, which was just as well because my heart was thumping in my ears at even the merest potential of the mildest confrontation.

"Sure," Aubrey said. "OK. Well, as a team we've really been looking to focus on getting back to our roots and making sure that we're giving back to the community in terms of . . ."

She tailed off, it was clear we were losing Leah's interest with the well-rehearsed spiel. They slumped back in their chair. The look on their face was clear—disappointment.

"For real?" Aubrey said. "This is Issy's project."

Aubrey pointed me out, as if I hadn't been there the entire time.

"But it could easily have been my project."

I stared at her, but she looked away, concentrating on Leah. Was this it? Were P and Olivia right? Was she about to admit to hating me because I'd stepped on her toes? Did she think I'd stolen her ideas as well as her bike?

"Or," Aubrey continued, "it could have been Elizabeth's project. It's because we came to this job in different ways, or perhaps at a disadvantage. We spent our lives thinking we weren't good enough or not believing our work was 'real.'" She put *real* in air quotes, screwing up her face to show her distaste. "Whatever that means. Never believing that anyone would take us seriously."

Aubrey took a deep breath.

"I can't speak for Issy, but when Elizabeth gave me this job it was like a lifeline. And I knew she understood what it meant because it was her lifeline too. And I suppose that's what's in it for us. To offer a lifeline, whatever that looks like to you. In whatever way we can. And to hope that this work reaches others outside of this tiny group and they see themselves in you and your work too."

We were all quiet for a moment. I watched as Aubrey sat back in her chair, ran her hand through her hair, exhaled slowly.

"Thank you," Leah said eventually, breaking the silence, "that answers my question."

"Great," Aubrey said; she smiled. "Who wants another drink before we finish up?" She did a round with the wine bottle and topped me up without looking at me at all.

Most of the group left at around 7:00 p.m., but William's taxi didn't arrive for a little while after that. We hung out with him, chatting about not much—the weather, how much London had changed, how few crisps you get in a packet these days. I got the sense that he didn't get much of a chance to speak about these things with people. That he didn't get the chance to speak to people about anything much at all.

When he finally got up to leave, it was with a packet of crisps and a compostable cup of white wine for the road; he took his time packing his bag, making his way slowly across the loft like he didn't actually want to leave.

Aubrey was perched on the countertop in the kitchenette, grimacing at her phone, and I was leaning next to her, trying to decide, despite the rumbling in my stomach, whether I could be bothered to eat a real meal when I got home or whether to do a William myself and pinch some snacks from the loft.

"Thank you for today," William said, as he made his way toward the door.

"Let me come down with you," Aubrey said. "I want to make sure you get off OK."

"No, no, dear. I'm fine," William said, shaking his head, taking a sip from his very full cup.

"I'm coming," Aubrey said.

"Right, yes," William said.

He hesitated for a moment by the door while Aubrey slid off the countertop and put her phone into her back pocket. She downed the last of her sauvignon blanc.

"Isobel?" he said, glancing back at me as Aubrey held the door open for him.

"Yes," I said.

"You understand why I did it, don't you? Why I painted my house like that, I mean. Even when I knew I was going to be thrown out because of it. Even when I didn't have enough money for the paint and I couldn't pay my bills?"

He took a deep breath, and for a horrible moment I thought he might burst into tears, but he didn't, he kept going.

"Even when I was exhausted and my back hurt and my knees hurt and my eyes hurt and I couldn't even really see it properly anymore. Do you understand it?"

I glanced at Aubrey, but she was looking at the floor, her knuckles white on the door handle.

"Yes," I said quietly. "I understand."

"I had to," he said.

"I know," I said.

"Good," he said. His face flooded with relief at knowing he was not alone in his brain chaos spilling out in wild and unexpected ways. "Good."

Aubrey placed her hand gently on William's shoulder then.

"Your cab's here, darling," she said.

I'd only ever heard Aubrey calling people pricks and bellends before, so I was surprised to hear *darling* come out of her mouth just as naturally.

"Yes," he said. "Right. I'll see you soon."

"I'm really looking forward to it," I said, my voice wobbling. I put my hand over my mouth and coughed slightly, trying to mask it.

Aubrey rolled her eyes at me and guided William out the door.

I packed my bag so that I'd be ready to leave when Aubrey got back upstairs with the keys to lock up. I didn't want to hold her up. But when she reappeared, she sighed heavily and threw herself down on one of the sofas.

"What a long fucking day," she said. "I'm exhausted, aren't you? Hey, pour me another glass while you're up, will you?"

I wasn't up, I was perching on the edge of my chair, but I put my backpack down and did as I was told, of course. I got her wine and went to sit down next to her, at the opposite end of the sofa—a safe distance. I stared at her. This was the last thing I had expected. I watched her drinking her wine, waiting for her to speak, and when she didn't, I took a deep breath and took a chance.

"I had a really good time today," I said. "The best time, actually. Thank you."

I didn't want to admit that I couldn't have done it without her, but I really couldn't have.

"They're a good group," Aubrey said, refusing to acknowledge the fact that I was clearly getting emotional again, which I was very grateful for. "I think this is going to be a really interesting project. I've been waiting for Elizabeth to do something like this, it's been a long time coming."

I didn't know what to say, so I just sat there reveling in Aubrey talking to me like an equal, telling me my project was good, that she was happy to be working on it.

"Earlier on," I said, "you said this could have been your project."

"I did," Aubrey said. "Great memory, Bailey."

I rolled my eyes.

"I just wanted to ask what you meant."

"I meant exactly what I said. I've been bugging Elizabeth to do something like this, but whatever you said to her must have got through. You've got a way of getting through to her."

She eyed me closely.

"You've got a way of getting through to people in general."

"Really?" I said.

"Mm," she said, "it's very charming, this whole *thing* you've got going on."

I bristled. Of course she wasn't actually being nice to me. How silly of me to think she was treating me like an equal.

"What *thing*?"

"You don't need to get defensive, Bailey. I'm complimenting you."

"It doesn't sound like it."

She nodded, like she was accepting the feedback. And then she turned to face me, leaned toward me a little, closing the gap between us on the sofa.

"I'm telling you that you're very charming. Whether you mean to be or not."

Everything went completely still again. Sort of like earlier when I'd accidentally told her to shut up, but also somehow not like earlier at all. I realized I was holding my breath.

"We should head off," Aubrey said, breaking the silence, glancing at her watch before leaning back into her side of the sofa again. Her voice was light—I had imagined the moment. It was the wine. It was the emotions of the day. "It's gotten really late."

"Yes," I said. "Do you want to share an Uber with me? I don't really fancy walking around here alone at this time of night."

We both looked toward the huge window in front of us and at the dark sky beyond. It was, now I thought about it, very romantic in the loft. The window looking out onto the stars (light pollution and planes), the dim lights, and the wine.

"I would actually love to share an Uber," Aubrey said, "but I have my bike. Well, I do if it's still there."

"You can't blame me this time if it's not," I said, holding my hands up, trying to inject some lightness back after our weird moment, real or imagined. "You can check the CCTV."

Aubrey nodded, trying to keep her face looking serious, but then she cracked into peals of laughter in spite of herself. Aubrey's laugh was great, deep and real. There's something extra special about a laugh heard rarely.

"You know I obviously never actually thought you'd stolen my bike," she said.

"Aubrey. You did."

"Yeah, I did," she conceded.

"Maybe I did steal it," I said, "and I just squirreled it away and in a year's time when I'm moving out of the house, you'll see me riding down the street and off into the sunset."

Aubrey looked at me, some indecipherable look. Her specialty.

"Nothing would surprise me about you, Bailey."

I didn't know what to say to that.

"Right, so I'm off," Aubrey said, heaving herself up from the sofa. For a moment it looked like she might reach out, give me a hand up too, but then she appeared to think better of it.

"Are you coming? I can't leave you to lock up, I'm afraid, insurance and all that. Plus you're famously, deeply untrustworthy."

I followed her down the dark stairwell, out onto the empty street, and ordered my Uber as I watched her unchain her bike.

"I can give you a lift home in the basket," Aubrey said. "If you fancy it?"

"Oh, sure," I said, "actually that would be great."

"Wonderful," she said, deadpan, "climb in."

She gestured at the basket, maybe big enough to fit Abigail.

"Actually," I said, "on second thought, maybe next time. It's pretty windy, and I've *just* done my hair."

"Of course," she said, "I understand."

She put her helmet on and started pedaling away.

"Get home safe, Bailey."

And I could have sworn, although she was cycling pretty fast in the opposite direction, that I heard her say, "Good job today."

47A Girlies!! <3

Alyssa: *Who is in tonight and does anyone wanna share some pasta with me, I've made loads xx*

Robin: *Sorry baby girl I'm on a date good luck finding a pasta friend though*

Mo: *None for me I am eating a sad sandwich at my desk and doing some screaming*

Alyssa: *OK hun xx*

Mo: *Robin, give us date goss, let us live vicariously through you*

Issy: *Al, if there is still pasta going, I'll have some. I'm just in an Uber on my way home from work now. Guess what, guys, I just had a lovely day . . . with Aubrey?? Of evil next door neighbor fame. I think underneath it all she might be . . . secretly nice??*

Alyssa: *She was prob not being nice she was being sarcastic and you couldn't tell, babes. Pasta in the fridge, it tastes weird but nice xx*

Robin: *Looking forward to hearing the goss at dinner this week— both about Aubrey and the weird but nice pasta. Date is going OK although she did just tell me she's "addicted to water" so let's see*

When I got home, Aubrey's sister's bike was already chained up outside her house—one of the wheels had been removed, and I really hoped she'd done that herself and it wasn't the work of a wheel thief. I couldn't go down for this too.

I let myself into the silent house. All I could hear was the sound of the fridge humming. Alyssa was probably asleep already because of her weird shift pattern. Mo must still have been at work. And I guessed Robin's date with the girl who was addicted to water was going well enough that they were still out together, which made me feel, if I was being honest, a little bit sick.

I sat at the kitchen table, picked up my phone and I saw that I had a message.

Aubrey: *Hello, it's me Aubrey, your boss. I just wanted to check for insurance and good people management reasons that you got home alive. Please confirm.*

Was this . . . flirting? Surely not. She was so inscrutable I genuinely couldn't tell. Why would she flirt with me though? Up until this afternoon I thought she fully hated me. Or at the least, she thought I was a bit stupid. She definitely thought I was a thief.

I wished Mo or Alyssa were here to guide me through this. They'd know just what to say. I ate weird pasta in the dark for a while, deciding how best to respond.

Issy: *Hello Aubrey, it's me Issy, your colleague, next door neighbor, and local bike thief. I am home but not alive unfortunately. Let me know if you need any more information for your records.*

Aubrey: *No, that's perfect. Thanks. Got all I need.*

Issy: *Great. Good night then.*

Aubrey: *Rest in peace, Bailey.*

I heard Robin get home a couple of hours after I'd climbed into bed. One set of footsteps followed by another. Hushed voices and giggling. Someone tripping at the top of the stairs and being shushed.

I took a pair of foam earplugs from my bedside table and jammed them hard into my ears. They expanded slowly.

I lay awake for a long time after that, listening to the sound of my own blood rushing in my ears.

CHAPTER TEN

"I'm sorry, no," Alyssa said. She was spooning dal onto her plate and speaking with a mouth full of homemade naan. "I don't trust her. No offense, but you're not good at this kind of thing."

Right.

I was relaying to the housemates how well the first session with the group had gone and how Aubrey was seemingly warming up to me, that she'd messaged me, flirted with me even, potentially . . .

I'd thought about it a lot in the past couple of days, even when she'd ignored me in the office. Even when, in our debrief with Elizabeth, Aubrey had been so businesslike—talking about risk assessments, budgets, what we needed to do going forward to make the project work—that I wondered if I'd imagined the whole thing. Whether I'd experienced that brief hiatus in her coldness at all.

"I'm not good at what kind of thing?" I said, chasing around a stray lentil with my fork. Robin poured me a glass of red wine, and I smiled at her gratefully.

"Reading people's vibes," Alyssa said, holding her own glass out for Robin to fill. "I think the main problem with you, Issy, is that you're always seeing the good in people."

"Is that not . . . a positive thing?" I said.

"Oh, babe," Alyssa said. She made a *Bless her* face at Mo, who rolled his eyes in response.

We were sitting around the table for a house dinner on Bonfire Night.

It was Mo's turn to cook, and he'd outdone himself: the small kitchen table was groaning with food, enough to feed us for about six weeks by the looks of it—although our heroic efforts at previous house dinners meant I was quite sure we'd manage to bravely struggle through it in one evening.

"Well," I said, "I really do think we've had a bit of a breakthrough. We're not *friends* exactly, it's just that maybe she's starting to see me as more of an equal at work. More of a colleague rather than someone she's babysitting, you know?"

"Why do you care what she thinks of you?" Alyssa said. "It sounds like Elizabeth loves you, and that's what matters, right?"

"Yeah," I said, "I suppose it's just . . ."

Why exactly did I care so much about what Aubrey thought of me?

"Free yourself, babe," Alyssa said, pointing her fork at me. "The only opinion that should matter is your own."

"And yours too, apparently," Mo said.

"What?" Alyssa said.

"What?" Mo said.

"Anyway," he continued, "Robin, we have been waiting for the goss for literally *years*. Please tell us everything. I can't remember the last time I went on a good date."

I took another gulp of wine and smiled encouragingly at her through wine-stained, slightly gritted teeth.

"Oh man," Robin said. She ran her hand through her hair and sighed heavily.

"Well, we went to a really nice wine bar," she said, taking quite a pointed sip of the wine we were drinking, which someone who ran a wine bar probably would have described as "rough."

"Which one?" Mo said.

"The one run by the lovely lesbian," Robin said.

"Ah," Mo said, clicking his fingers in recognition. "Ring of keys."

"Exactly," Robin said, nodding. "Ring of keys."

I had absolutely no idea what they were talking about, which wasn't unusual.

"So you went to the wine bar and what?" Mo said.

"Well, we drank some wine. Very nice, very expensive," Robin said. "We ate some cheese."

"Cheese on a first date?" Alyssa said. "Wow."

"I know," Robin said.

"What?" I said. "Would you not normally eat cheese on a first date?"

"No," Alyssa and Mo said in unison.

I was always learning so much. I shook my head in wonder.

Robin rolled her eyes at us all.

"There are no hard-and-fast cheese rules," Robin said to me. She placed her hand on my knee, so briefly I might have missed it. "Don't listen to those two. I'll take you sometime. We can have the vegan equivalent of a cheese plate, whatever that might be. Bowl of crisps. A peanut."

Robin popped a piece of naan in her mouth with the hand that just seconds ago had been on my knee, and we watched her chew, waiting for the rest of the story. She pointed at her mouth, taking ages to swallow. She loved having everyone's rapt attention. For me though, time had stopped still because it sounded like . . . it sounded like Robin just invited me to her date spot, didn't it? To romantically share a bowl of crisps and a peanut?

"So anyway," Robin continued, "we had a nice time together, if a little bit of an . . . I don't know . . . an average time?"

Mo winced.

"Not average," Robin said quickly, "not average, I take that back, maybe that's the wrong word. I just mean, I feel like that kind of night could have been with anyone."

"Mate," Mo said, shaking his head.

"OK," Robin said, "OK, maybe that's even worse. I don't know. I'm just saying that she didn't stand out to me. There wasn't a spark. There wasn't that *thing*, you know. I'm sure she's at home right now telling her friends the same thing about me."

I found that hard to believe—that anyone could think that Robin was average, that she didn't stand out to them as, I don't know, the hottest human on earth to ever exist, for example.

"But you brought her home, didn't you?" Alyssa said, frowning.

I shoveled a large forkful of food into my mouth, so much that I could barely chew.

"Yeah," Robin said, her tone light, refusing to accept Alyssa's judgment. "We had a nice time!"

"Good?" Mo said, he gestured toward Robin's room with his head.

"Nice!" Robin repeated. "We continued having a nice time, that's all I'll say about that."

I was retrospectively grateful for my earplugs.

"Anyway," Robin said, "we're not going to see each other again.

I'm trying out this new thing where I don't continue to date people I'm not one hundred percent interested in."

"Why? Do you typically do that?" Mo asked.

"Yeah, for some reason I always give everyone a minimum of two dates. But not anymore. I don't have the energy."

"Well you don't need to, do you? Not if now you just cram loads of dates into one long one," Mo said. "Wine, cheese, sex, breakfast."

"Exactly," Robin said, grinning. "What else is there?"

We all had second and third helpings and then picked at whatever was left in the bowls on the table until we started to feel physically unwell.

"I've been talking to someone on Hinge," Alyssa said, sitting back in her chair and unbuttoning her jeans.

"Name?" Mo said.

"Jaden," Alyssa said.

"Age?"

"Thirty-seven."

"Occupation?"

"Optician," Alyssa said. "Is that a red flag?"

"Why would that be a red flag?" I asked.

Alyssa shrugged. "I don't know," she said. "But why would you want to be all up in people's eyes all day? Maybe he's got an eye thing? Like he wants to have sex with eyes."

"Mmm, could be a creep hiding in plain sight," Mo said.

"Something to keep an eye on," Robin said.

Alyssa nodded seriously.

"You chatting to anyone, Mo?" Robin asked.

"Nope," he said. "Well, my ex."

"No!" we all said at once.

"I know, I know," Mo said.

He rubbed his eyes and sighed.

"He wants to be my friend. And like it's not that I don't want to be his friend, one day."

Mo got up from the table and plonked two tubs of Ben & Jerry's in the middle of the table—four spoons. One of them was vegan, which, of course, the others dug into first.

"But it's more that I don't want to be receiving links to TikToks all day long, when I know he's going home and shagging Brandon while I'm coming back here to you guys, no offense."

He looked around the table.

"None taken, babe," Alyssa said.

Mo sighed heavily.

"His Instagram is just filled with *Brandon* and that tiny fucking dog."

He paused.

"I take that back," he said, "the dog seems lovely. I would genuinely like to be friends with the dog one day. Pretend I didn't say anything about the dog."

"Stop looking at his Instagram," Alyssa said, her mouth full of ice cream. "No good can come from that."

"Um, I'm not taking advice from you on not stalking exes on Instagram," Mo said, reaching forward with his spoon to dig out a piece of cookie dough.

"Well, you should take advice from me because I stalk my ex on Instagram all the time and I'm telling you from experience that no good comes from it," Alyssa said, knocking his spoon out of the way with hers and taking the ice cream he was just about to scoop up.

"Fair enough," Mo said. "I don't want to end up like you."

She kicked him under the table.

The three of us cleared the table while Mo, the chef, sat back with his glass of wine, relaxing.

"Shall we retire to the roof, pals?" he asked when we were finished. "It's not too freezing tonight, is it? We could wrap up and watch the fireworks? I bought some sparklers for our after-dinner entertainment."

"You're a sweetheart," Robin said, "yes, let's do that." She held up the last of a tub of ice cream. "I'm just going to finish this if no one objects. It won't fit in the freezer."

"Go for it," Mo said. "I'll explode if I eat another thing." He picked up a packet of chocolate buttons from the counter to take to the roof with him. "Enjoy!"

I hung back in the kitchen while Mo and Alyssa headed upstairs, bickering amicably about whether we should buy a patio heater or "tough it out" for the winter with blankets. I was very unsuccessfully trying to slam the heaving freezer drawer shut.

"Issy," Robin said, "just eat the rest of that tub, for the sake of our freezer. And for my sake. Watching this is torture."

By that point I had been eating for several hours like a Roman at a banquet, but I would have done anything to stay hanging out in the kitchen with Robin for a bit longer, forever in fact.

"Fine," I said, "to tackle the scourge that is food waste and freezer drawer breakage, I'll do it. And for you."

"The planet is very grateful, I'm sure," Robin said seriously. "And, of course, our landlord."

She pulled herself up to sit on the countertop and I did the same. On opposite sides of the stove, we ate our ice cream. Someone let off a firework in the park, and we both watched as the sky lit up with pink diamonds before they dripped away.

"So," Robin said, "when are we going to the lesbian wine bar, Issy?"

"Do you really want to?" I said. "Won't there be too many memories of . . . um . . ."

"Bea," she said, helping me out.

"Right, too many memories of your date with Bea."

Robin grinned at me and put the empty tub of ice cream down next to her. She placed a hand on her stomach and rubbed it gently.

"I'll let you in on a little secret, my friend. I've probably been to that wine bar with twenty different people. I'm not very sentimental, I'm afraid. All it reminds me of is spending way too much money."

"Twenty people," I repeated.

"I mean, maybe not twenty, maybe like . . . nineteen," she said.

"All dates?" I said.

"To my knowledge."

"Wow."

"So, will you be number twenty, possibly twenty-one?" Robin said, grinning.

I nearly tumbled off the countertop.

"Yes," I said, quickly. Too quickly probably. Embarrassingly keen. "I'd be honored to be number twenty, possibly twenty-one. Shall we see when Mo and Alyssa are free? We could always go there instead of a house dinner one time?"

"Yeah, we could," Robin said, nodding her head slowly. "Or we could go just the two of us? I feel like we haven't had a chance to get to know each other properly yet, without the others."

Just us. Like . . . a date. I'd never felt more special than when Robin asked me to be one of an untold number of women she had taken to the lesbian-ring-of-keys wine bar. I glowed.

"OK," I said. "Let's do it. I'd love to."

Robin smiled at me as I licked the ice cream that had dripped down my forearm. Sexy? Maybe. I felt sexy under Robin's gaze, like all my senses were unusually alive. I was more aware of my body, conscious of the sensation of being seen by her, like wading into the freezing ocean on a hot day—a relief and a shock all at once.

"Great. I'll sort it," Robin said. "I'll send you some dates, I know you're in high demand."

Was I in demand? I don't think I'd ever considered myself in demand before, apart from perhaps by my mum, who, I remembered, I owed a phone call to. I immediately tried to banish all thoughts of my mum from my mind. Not now, for god's sake! Sexy! I was being sexy!

It felt good to know that Robin didn't consider me available to her constantly, even though privately, I was at her beck and call.

Robin slid off the countertop. She pulled a hair tie off her wrist and tied back her short blond hair into a scruffy ponytail. A few loose strands fell down at the back of her neck. Soft baby hairs that I longed to touch, I just wanted to reach out my hand and . . .

"Come on, then," Robin said, "let's go and see if Mum and Dad have stopped arguing."

I nodded and followed her upstairs, my head spinning.

There wasn't any wind that evening, and the sky was clear. It was so mild that I unzipped my coat and took off my woolly hat. We stood on the roof together, the four of us, and wrote our names with sparklers, bright lights in the night sky.

At some point Mo and Alyssa sloped off to bed, blankets wrapped around their shoulders like the sweet, elderly couple they were quickly becoming.

"I'm not tired yet," Robin said, leaning back in her chair, one leg resting on the other. "Are you, Issy?"

"No," I said. "Not at all. Wide awake."

I stifled a yawn, my eyes watering.

"Do you want to watch something with me?" Robin said. "Is it too early for a Christmas film?"

"I don't think so," I said.

I did think so. There were still seven weeks until Christmas. I had inherited my mother's sensibility that there is such a thing as too much fun.

"OK," Robin said, standing up and holding out her hand to help me up from my chair, "let's do it."

I took her hand and decided to forget all about work the next day, and sleep, and that it was absolutely, definitely not Christmas.

We settled on the uncomfortable sofa in our living room, cross-legged, knees barely touching, but intermittently brushing against each other. Robin insisted we watch a made-for-TV Christmas movie featuring time-traveling lesbians, telling me it would be the best and worst thing I've ever seen.

"You're going to die," she said. "I'm so excited."

"Robin," I said, "I hate to break it to you, but I've seen this film, obviously."

"What?" she said, genuinely crestfallen. "Have you really?"

I almost felt bad for telling her, she so wanted to be the one to introduce me to this particular genre of gay Christmas chaos.

"I didn't live under a rock before I came here," I said, gently poking her in the knee. "I've seen TVs before. I've even got Netflix, Robin, if you can believe it, on which I have absolutely done a full and thorough search for all gay time-traveling content."

Robin shook her head, trying to suppress a smile.

"You know," she said, "I can't actually believe it, but that's beautiful. Common ground between two people from such different worlds brought together by subpar queer seasonal content."

"A tale as old as time," I said.

We laughed and chatted our way through the movie, our own commentary running over the top of it. I was giddy with delight at making Robin cackle. Robin was naturally more tactile than me, her hand regularly straying over to my leg to squeeze my thigh or rest on my knee during tense or particularly absurd bits. Eventually she settled back on the sofa, her feet resting up against mine, our toes touching. I didn't move long after my foot fell asleep.

When the film finished and the room plunged into darkness, the night was silent around us. It didn't feel as though the night was ending, it felt as though we had barely started.

It was 1:00 a.m.; my eyes were heavy with tiredness, but my body was wide awake.

Neither of us moved.

"I guess we should go to bed," I said after a moment.

Robin sat up and looked at me, her teasing smile gone, her eyes sleepy and sincere. She seemed to be hesitating, but then she nodded.

I stood up, wobbly on my feet, and held out my hand to help her up. She took it, and when she stood right in front of me, inches away in the dark, I can't really explain what happened other than to say that in one moment we weren't kissing and in the next, we were.

My hand wasn't at the back of Robin's head, gently pulling her toward me, and then it was. Fireworks didn't go off. That's the first thing I noticed. No fireworks. Just like my near fatal strawberry kiss. I guessed that fireworks going off when you kissed someone really was a myth, based on my now extensive kissing experience of two whole women and, of course, year four's kiss chase champion, Ryan Dingle.

I didn't even have an out-of-body experience, which I think on balance was probably a good thing. In fact, it was a great thing to be in my body, experiencing Robin's own in such close proximity. Her lips were soft, her breath sweet. I felt her smiling into my mouth as she pulled away.

"I've been thinking about doing that for ages," she said softly.

"Really?" I said.

"Of course," Robin said.

"Me too," I said. "From the moment I met you."

Robin didn't reply, she just kissed me again. Her hands on my waist this time. I ran my hands up her arms, around her neck, played with the strands of her hair that I'd thought about so often, soft and fragile between my fingers.

"Shall we go to bed?" Robin said. And the words I'd uttered only moments ago took on a whole new meaning.

I followed her up the stairs, my hand in hers. Everything felt new and exciting as if this wasn't actually my house too.

Robin didn't even pause when we got to my room, no hint of pretense, she just pushed her own bedroom door open and gestured for me to go inside first.

I expected her to follow me in but she paused in the doorway.

"Actually," she said, "I'm just going to run to the bathroom. Hey—make yourself at home."

She leaned forward and kissed me on the cheek before going back downstairs.

Robin's room was familiar to me by then, from evenings before bed that I'd spent hovering in her doorway chatting. I couldn't even count the number of times I'd walked through on my way to sit on the roof. My feet had kicked her stray socks, I'd taken in the unmade bed—laptop in between her sheets—I'd cast a brief eye over the books on her shelves, trying to figure out what made her tick, what we shared. I knew the smell of her room, the way it made my heart beat a little faster, the blood thick in my ears, the way I could almost taste it.

Tonight felt different though. The vague familiarity blurring once I started interacting with my surroundings. I sat on the edge of her bed; the white sheets were soft, and when I looked at her shelves more closely, I saw that they were dusty, and for some reason that made my stomach lurch. It was real, I suppose that's why. The idea of her was coming to life. The lamp by Robin's bedside table was bright, too bright, and I noticed for the first time that she had placed a pillowcase over the top of it to soften the light.

I desperately wanted her to come back, and I didn't. A part of me wanted to stay suspended in time, in this moment where nothing had happened yet but the possibilities were endless. Once she came back, once we pressed play again, it would be closer to being over.

I wanted to live in the heady anticipation forever.

After a few minutes, Robin pushed the door open, and the room shifted back into sharp focus.

"You know," she said, "no offense, but it would have been so great for me if your bedroom had just stayed a bathroom so I didn't have to keep running up and down the stairs every time I want to go for a wee."

"Sorry," I said, "that really is very inconvenient."

Robin laughed and slid open one of the doors leading onto the roof terrace, letting in a blast of cold air. It looked for a moment like she might suggest we head outside and then she changed her mind, sliding the door shut again. She picked up a pile of clothes from the floor and flung them inside the wardrobe, slamming the door shut before any of them got a chance to fly out. Her eyes darted around her room. I hadn't expected her to care what I thought of it. This was as close as I'd seen to her being flustered.

"It's fine," she said, taking her phone out of her pocket and putting it face down on her dressing table, "I can put up with stairs if it means having you as a next-door neighbor."

She crossed the room to where I was sitting in the bed and kissed me. I responded eagerly, as if each time she did it she might suddenly realize who I was and take it back. Like it was a dream I was just on the verge of waking up from and needed to hold on to for as long as possible.

Robin pulled away after a little while and gestured for me to sit back on her bed. She did the same, her body next to mine, one arm dangled over my stomach. She pushed up my best black jumper gently and traced a line over my skin, dipping her finger into my belly button. I watched her hand as she did it, completely enthralled. Every hair on my body stood on end.

She kissed me again, harder this time, with more intention, and when I kissed back, properly, deciding not to be afraid of doing the wrong thing and just living in the moment for goodness' sake, she made a noise somewhere between a sigh and a moan and started fiddling with the button on my jeans, which, I was pretty sure, meant I was doing something right.

"Is this OK?" Robin said, pulling herself upright and positioning her hands as if she was going to tug my jeans off.

I nodded.

"You sure?" she said.

"Yes," I said, shifting in the bed, tilting my hips upward to make it easier for her. I truly had never consented to anything more in my life.

"I mean," she said, her hands still on the waistband of my jeans, "is it all OK? I know this is, um, significant for you"—she screwed up her face like she couldn't believe what she was saying but she persevered—"which is totally fine as long as we're both clear on what this—"

"It's all OK," I said, refusing to let her finish that sentence. "Yes. Yes. I understand what this is." I remembered everything she'd said at the pub. "Don't worry, I'm not going to fall in love with you, Robin."

An absurd promise. I'd have thought by that point, love hearts were practically shooting from my eyes, but it was enough for her. She nodded, leaned down to kiss me again, and I instantly forgot everything I'd just said.

After that, it was a bit of a blur. I thought I might get in my head about it, but I found that the opposite was true—I inhabited my body more than I ever have. Parts of me came alive that I had barely been aware of. If I had been cold before, now I was burning, flames licking every part of me.

So to speak.

Robin asked me several more times if I was all right, she told me to tell her to stop if I wanted her to. I said "Don't stop" at one point, and based on her enthusiastic response, she really seemed to like that even though I was just answering her question.

After what could have been ten minutes or ten hours, Robin lay beside me in the soft glow of the pillowcased lamp and pushed hair out of my eyes. She kissed me gently on the cheek, and I smiled back dreamily at her. I reached out to touch her necklace, a thin gold chain, similar to my own. I picked it up and dropped it back against her chest. She watched me, amused.

We stayed that way for a moment, just looking at each other, listening to each other breathe. It was blissful then. That space in between the anticipation and the aftermath, waiting for my heart rate to return to normal. That brief window when my life was just the smell of Robin, her skin beneath my fingertips, her gaze solely on me.

Robin fell asleep quickly, her back turned to me, her hand loosely holding mine. She twitched, her fingers pulsing against my palm. I couldn't fathom how she could switch off from what had just happened, find sleep so easily. I lay awake for a while, my nose pressed into her back, breathing her in, and then I untangled myself from her, gathered up my discarded clothes and crept next door to my bathroom-bedroom.

As hard as it was to leave her, I knew instinctively that I didn't want to wake up with her. The magic was already fading. By the morning, it would be gone.

I said I wasn't going to fall in love.

I put some food down for Abigail, though I must have missed her—maybe it was too late, even for nocturnal creatures. I worried about her for a moment, before my mind returned to Robin.

I rummaged in my bedside drawer for my phone charger and my hand landed on a packet of pills.

I had taken them that morning, hadn't I? Or was it yesterday?

It didn't matter really. Because I felt good, great even. I found my charger and closed the drawer. I'd take them tomorrow and it would be fine.

CHAPTER ELEVEN

I woke up early, feeling surprisingly energized despite the lack of sleep. For the first time in a long time, I was excited to be awake, to be in my body. I let the previous few hours play out in my head on repeat. Each time, I would add a new detail or a detail would be taken away until I couldn't tell what was real and what I just wanted to be real. I scrutinized Robin's every word and every movement. Every time she touched me and it felt electric. The way that just for a little while, she and I were the only people in the world.

I stared at my ceiling and let my mind run wild, reveling in the most important detail of the previous night—I had finally had sex! I felt triumphant, like a teenager. I wanted to boast about it, shout it from the rooftops. I, Isobel Bailey, had had sex. And not just sex but sex with Robin. Robin with her long legs and scruffy blond hair and raffish charm and knowing smile. Robin's hands all over me, my hands all over Robin. Her mouth on mine, her mouth, her mouth.

And it turned out, it wasn't as big and scary and life-changing as I thought it would be. It was just a lot of fun and a bit silly.

No one ever tells you that sex is a bit silly.

Mostly I felt exactly the same as I had the day before, only slightly delirious and a bit more pleased with myself. More knowing perhaps, a little more in step with the rest of the world. I was catching up. Kissing? Done it. Sex? Completed. What next?

I got out of bed, feeling light on my feet. An undeniable spring in my step. I was up long before everybody else would be, which meant I was first into the bathroom—I could luxuriate in a long shower without someone hammering on the door. I opened the bathroom window and let in some fresh air. It was cold, but the early-morning sky was blue and bright, the sun was shining. I stood for a moment, naked and shivering slightly, looking out over the gardens below. It was like the resolution had been turned up on the screen of my life—the whole world was in Technicolor.

I was almost moved to tears by the beauty of a red fox standing on a shed, a McDonald's bag in its mouth. We looked at each other, a moment of understanding passing between us. We were not meant to be here but somehow, we were thriving! I see you, Fox!

I felt close to Mother Nature, at one with the earth. I looked at my body in the shower anew, at all the exciting possibilities it held. And when I was brushing my teeth I caught my eye in the mirror and realized I was grinning from ear to ear.

———

I was headed into the loft in Hackney Wick that morning to meet Aubrey and the Outside the Lines gang for filming. Great timing because I felt I looked the best I'd looked in a long time, maybe ever.

I had started, thanks to Alyssa's unsolicited advice, using an eyebrow gel with a little brush, and I have to admit, I liked what it did to my face. How it gave it more structure somehow, I looked a little less like a cherub than usual. Or I at least looked like a cherub with great eyebrows. A cherub who had had sex!

I walked slowly from the station, stopping to pick up coffee and pastries from my favorite, most absurdly expensive bakery. I day-dreamed about taking them back home, climbing into Robin's bed, and surprising her. She'd look at me the way she did last night, like nothing else existed but me and a croissant that cost £4.75.

I smiled at a baby in a pram; I patted a dog on the head; I caught the eye of a pretty woman at the bus stop, and she smiled at me and I didn't blush or look away, I smiled back. I was perfectly in sync with the world. It was a no-headphones kind of morning—let the raw thoughts roll in, baby!

I pulled my phone out of my pocket to see if there was a mes-sage from Robin, but there wasn't anything yet. She must have still been asleep. Plus she wouldn't normally message me in the morn-ing, and I was different from the other girls, chill and casual. Not in love, definitely not in love.

I arrived outside the loft just in time to catch Aubrey locking up her sister's bike on the fence outside.

"Good morning," I chirped as she took her helmet off and shook out her signature helmet hair. She was wearing a worn, vintage-looking black leather jacket with a black wool jumper underneath.

"Here you go." I threw a croissant in a brown paper bag for

her to catch. But she didn't catch it. Instead, it hit her right in the middle of her forehead and fell to the ground by her feet.

We both stared at the paper bag in stunned silence.

"Sorry," I said at the exact same time as she looked up and said, "What the hell is wrong with you?"

"Nothing," I said, stepping forward to rescue the croissant from the ground, thankfully still in its paper bag, "nothing's wrong with me, I'm just in a good mood. It's Friday, the sun is shining."

Before I could get to the croissant though, Aubrey bent down and grabbed it.

She raised her eyebrows at me, as if to say *Too slow*.

"Come on," she said, gesturing with a nod of her head that I should follow her. She opened the door to the warehouse and then leaned her back against it, letting me past her. Aubrey ripped the bag open and took a bite of croissant.

"Next time, Bailey," she said with her mouth full, as I brushed past her, "if you want to assault me with breakfast, at least get me that Marmite one, will you?"

"Noted," I said, as she closed the door behind us. "Aren't you going to ask why I'm in such a good mood?"

"No," Aubrey said. "I assume it's chinchilla related."

I opened my mouth to correct her.

"But, Bailey," she said before I had a chance to speak. She took another bite of croissant and then chewed slowly so I had to wait for her answer. "It's important to me that you know, I truly don't care."

I laughed, refusing to let her bring me down with her.

"I'll tell you later," I said.

———

I don't know if it was just me, living in my good-mood bubble, but it felt like everybody was extra buoyant. There was an added layer of silliness to proceedings, infectious giggles, a giddy restlessness manifesting itself in yelling over each other, showing off for the cameras, egging each other on.

"This is your fault," Aubrey said to me at one point, watching Leah collapse into hysterical giggles as Stella tried to show them how to use the potter's wheel, *Ghost*-style.

"What's my fault?" I said. "Everyone having a lovely time?"

"Mmm," Aubrey said.

"Lean in," I said, "go on. Do you ever just have silly fun?"

"No," Aubrey said.

"Serious fun only?" I said.

"You have paint on your sweatshirt," Aubrey said. She reached out and touched it, right in the middle of my stomach. She was right, there was a big splotch of green from when I'd been helping William mix earlier.

"No problem," I said. I took my jumper off and immediately got goose bumps. I hadn't realized how chilly the loft was.

"Are you cold now?" Aubrey said. "Already?"

"No," I said. "If anything, I'm overheating."

"Have mine."

Aubrey slipped her black jumper off over her head and handed it to me.

"That's very nice of you, are you sure?"

"I'm sure I don't want to hear you complaining about how cold you are."

I pulled the jumper over my head. It was warm and soft, it felt handmade. It smelled sweet and citrusy, like Aubrey.

"How do I look?" I said.

Aubrey closed her eyes and exhaled slowly.

"Are you fantasizing about throwing a croissant at my head?" I said, nudging her.

A cameraman laughed, and I realized that this whole exchange was being filmed.

"This cannot be interesting to you," Aubrey said to him. She rolled her eyes and walked away.

The cameraman shrugged and then he winked at me.

"Let's see," he said.

"All right," Stella said, as she was leaving. She pointed at me. "You ready, mate?"

"Yep," I said. "Wait, no. Maybe. What am I meant to be ready for?"

Stella took my arm and rolled up the sleeve of Aubrey's jumper.

"Right about here," she said, poking her finger into the soft flesh of my upper arm.

"Oh," I said, realization dawning. "Oh, no, I don't think so."

"Yes," Stella said, "it's time. You want to do it at some point, don't you? Why not today?"

I stared at the blue veins and the porcelain-white skin. Why not today?

"I don't . . . where would I even . . ."

I looked at Aubrey for help for some reason. Her eyes were fixed on her phone, but her wry smile gave away the fact she was listening.

"I know a guy," Stella said.

I looked at her dubiously.

"A legit guy!" Stella said. "He's done all of mine."

I looked at the dragon smoking a joint and wearing a top hat on Stella's forearm, and she followed my eyes.

"He's very versatile," she said. "All sorts of styles."

I nodded. I could think of a million reasons to say no. It was on the tip of my tongue.

"Go on, Issy," William said. "I'll come with you."

I looked at his face, lit up at the prospect of a spontaneous excursion, and couldn't bring myself to deny him an extension to his day out.

Why not today?

"Fine," I said. "Yes, OK. I'll do it!"

Aubrey snorted.

"Are you coming too, Aubrey?" William said.

"As much as I would love to see this, and believe me I would," Aubrey said, "I have things to do this afternoon that aren't watching Issy squirm."

"I think you quite enjoy watching Issy squirm," Stella said. She raised her eyebrows at Aubrey. They were both still for a moment, and then Aubrey raised her eyebrows back, a slight nod of her head. I couldn't quite decipher what this coded eyebrow conversation meant.

"Have fun," Aubrey said, walking away, her bike helmet under her arm, "and hey—be safe."

"He's a legit guy!" Stella called after her.

The tattoo studio was a short walk from the warehouse, longer with William in tow, but Stella and I were more than happy to amble along in the sunshine with him. I pulled out my phone while the two of them were chatting. Some messages from my mum, seventy messages on the house group solely about, as far as I could tell, soup for dinner, but nothing from Robin. Although she had replied to the group to tell Mo and Alyssa she would be out and would therefore, tragically, be missing out on soup.

I wondered about messaging Robin first. I wanted to tell her everything about my day and about all my thoughts and feelings and emotions and then also everything about myself that had ever happened, but I sensed that might be a bit much on WhatsApp. I put my phone away.

I ignored the nagging feeling in my chest. Not today. Today was good mood only.

The tattoo studio was painted black on the outside, and on the inside the walls were covered top to bottom in tattoo art. Cases of piercing jewelry were lined up against the back wall. There was no music playing; it was surprisingly peaceful, and it smelled like the dentist's.

"Can you tell Riccardo that Stella's here to see him?" Stella said to the receptionist who was sitting behind a desk, scrolling through her phone.

She had braided blue hair, dark brown skin, and both cheeks pierced. When we walked up to her, she smiled warmly, and the piercings disappeared into deep dimples. I couldn't take my eyes off her.

The blue-haired, dimpled receptionist didn't even have a chance to call Riccardo before we heard the sound of footsteps bounding up the stairs.

A slight man wearing a crop top with the word *Baby* emblazoned across it in diamantés walked up the stairs and straight into Stella's arms.

"More beautiful every day," he said to her in a thick Italian accent.

"You glow," he said, shaking his head as if in disbelief.

"I do glow," Stella said. "Listen, Ricci, can you fit us in?"

"You know how long I have known this angel?" he said to the receptionist. "It is nearly twenty years; it is decades of my life."

"Five years," Stella said, "at most."

Riccardo waved her away. "This maths," he said, "you are breaking my heart."

"Listen, my love," Stella said, "can you fit us in or not?"

Riccardo took a dramatic step back as if he had only just spotted me and William. He tutted. He did not like what he was seeing.

"You all?" he said. He tutted again.

"No, just Issy today. Show him what you want, Issy."

Stella gave me a gentle shove in the back, and I stumbled forward, feeling shy suddenly.

I passed Riccardo my phone, half expecting him to laugh, but he didn't. He studied the picture carefully, zooming in, and after a while, he looked up at me.

"You did this?"

I nodded. "Yes."

"You trust me with it?" he said.

"Yes," I said. And I did, that day in my good-mood bubble, I really did.

"We do this," he said. "I take this with me."

Riccardo disappeared for forty-five minutes with my phone before finally yelling up the stairs to us that he was ready. Stella and William followed me, despite the signs everywhere stating explicitly that you weren't allowed anyone accompanying you.

The others chatted while Riccardo placed the stencil on my upper arm, adjusting it as I watched in the mirror until we'd found the perfect spot. I listened to William asking Riccardo questions about whether any tattoos have ever gone wrong ("No, I am very good") and had he ever tattooed anyone's private parts ("It is non-stop with the private parts"). I listened to Stella asking whether, if she came back another time, he could do a cover-up of someone's name ("Baby, not again").

But when I lay down on my back, and the needle came out, everyone went quiet. Riccardo needed to concentrate.

"You do not need to close your eyes," he said to me quietly, "but it is also better that you do not watch, you will notice the pain too much."

I nodded and for the next hour, I stared at the ceiling, and noticed just the right amount of pain.

I paid the receptionist what didn't seem like the correct amount of money based on my research—it seemed like at least half what I had expected to pay. I wondered what Stella had on Riccardo.

"I really love it," the blue-haired, dimpled receptionist said to me, just as I was leaving.

"Oh," I said, "thank you. Me too."

In all honesty, I hadn't even looked at it yet. It didn't feel real; it had all happened so fast.

"Hey," she said, "I never do this."

People who say they never do things always do them, in my experience.

"But can I get your number?"

"I . . ." I very nearly asked *Why?* before I realized, she wanted my number as in *was asking for my number!* This had never happened to me before, but it made perfect sense on that day, the good-mood bubble was infectious.

"Yes," I said. "Sure, of course."

She handed me her phone, and I put my number in. Simple as that.

I stared at my arm wrapped up in cling film all the way home on the overground, slightly pink and swollen and changed forever. I loved it.

When I got home, I headed straight to the kitchen, where I could hear voices and music playing. My stomach flipped in anticipation of seeing Robin, but when I pushed open the door, it was just Mo and Alyssa, hovering over the stove.

"Guys," I said, all excitable like a kid showing off to their parents what they did in school. "Look."

"Oh my god, Issy," Mo said, practically pushing Alyssa out of the way so he could get a closer look. "You actually did it! Did I not tell you it would suit you?"

"Oh wow," Alyssa said, peering at me closely, "so cute, babe. What is it? A little cat?"

"You're joking," I said.

I looked at Mo, and he just shook his head at me, defeated by Alyssa.

"I can't," he said to himself as he turned back to the stove. "I literally can't."

"No, why?" Alyssa said. "What, then? A horse, is it?"

Alyssa squinted, grabbing my arm and twisting it to get a better look in the light.

"Look behind you, you maniac," I said, pointing at the sketch hanging on the wall.

"Ohhhh," she said then, without even needing to turn around, "of course, of course it is. I see it now. Babe, it's perfect."

And it was perfect. The perfect Abigail. A replica of my own sketch, etched into my skin forever.

"Have either of you seen Robin today?" I asked, sitting down at the table, helping myself to the open bag of crisps, trying to sound as casual as possible.

"Yeah," Mo said, blowing across the top of a wooden spoon coated in the much-discussed soup before he popped it in his mouth, "this morning, briefly. She was in a rush, though. She'd slept in. Why?"

"Oh, no reason," I said.

"Wanna do something tomorrow?" Alyssa asked. "Me and Mo were just saying the four of us could do something cultural, use our brains."

I glanced at my phone—another message from my mum. I vaguely remembered that we'd talked about her coming up to visit at some point—was that tomorrow? I didn't want to see her; I knew on a profound level that she did not fit in the good-mood bubble. I pushed any guilt I felt about that deep, deep down.

"Yes," I said to Alyssa. "Count me in."

I messaged Mum an apology, a let's do it another time, a promise to call her. I meant it. I did.

I ate my soup and took myself to bed. Robin got in late. I heard her gentle footsteps on the stairs, a pause on the landing, and then the closing of her door.

It didn't matter though, I told myself, because I was not like the other girls. I was not going to fall in love with her.

CHAPTER TWELVE

On Saturday morning I picked up my phone and googled "sad after sex."

A low point. Even for me. My good-mood bubble was deflating rapidly, pierced with anxious thoughts like needles, sharp and precise.

The Abigail on my arm hurt.

I learned that being sad after sex was a "common biological condition"—well, if anyone was likely to experience "postcoital dysphoria," then of course it would be me. I could find anything to be sad about. I could be sad on a roller coaster at Disneyland while winning the lottery.

I got the real Abigail out of her cage. She was grumpy and sleepy, but I pulled her onto my chest, felt her wriggle in my hands and then slump against me, resigned to the cuddle. I wanted to stay there all day, my nose buried in her soft ear fluff, but Alyssa had given strict instructions about getting up and out of the house early, so after a few minutes, I kissed Abigail on her head, placed her gently back in her cage, and did as I was told.

I tried not to think about Robin asleep in the room next to me. So close and so completely out of reach.

She had messaged the house WhatsApp group in the early hours of the morning saying she was shattered and very sad to be missing out on Big Cultural Day Out. She demanded photos and a full review. I thought I would feel disappointed that she wasn't coming with us, but I didn't; I felt relieved mostly. I didn't know what our new dynamic was yet, and I wasn't quite ready to find out.

Alyssa and Mo's Big Cultural Day Out involved going to an exhibition at a tiny gallery in Dalston that one of them had seen on TikTok.

"I swear," Mo said, as we walked along the pavement side by side, "that TikTok thinks I'm a lesbian. A lesbian who has somewhere between three and ten Alsatians."

We arrived early but still there was a small queue outside of the gallery door, which we dutifully joined—it was full of other people who looked like us, sleepy, chilly, and pleased with themselves.

It was only when we got inside and paid for our tickets that I realized I had no clue what we were there to see. Mo and Alyssa, our resident scorned lovers, had described it vaguely to me as "a visual graveyard of past relationships"—fun!

It turns out that it wasn't a graveyard of past relationships so much as it was a graveyard of abandoned sex toys. Display cases full of them, shelves heaving, some even attached directly to the wall, which upsettingly, were the only exhibits with barriers around them. I tried not to think about why.

There was everything I could imagine, from giant purple dildos and pink fluffy handcuffs to stuff I literally had never imagined but would likely never get out of my head—frighteningly realistic sex dolls, fleshlights created from molds of real people, clips and clamps that made me wince.

Mo and Alyssa took off at lightning speed. They barely paused to read the descriptions, each written by the person or couples who had contributed the toy to the graveyard or what the gallery was calling: *Sex Toy Amnesty*.

A couple of highlights:

Carmen and I chose this together. She insisted on the glittery one, which was significantly more expensive than the regular one, but I gave in even though it looks like a unicorn horn. She left me three weeks later. I thought about sending it to her, but I didn't want to tell the man in the post office what it was. I have to do my ASOS returns there.

Jess, 36, London

My partner bought this ball gag after we watched Fifty Shades of Grey as a joke. I thought we were both laughing, but apparently not. When we broke up due to irreconcilable differences (they wanted to be together, and I didn't), they left it behind, and for some reason I couldn't bring myself to throw it away. If you see this exhibition, S, know that I think of you often, gagged and not gagged.

Hassan, 29, Manchester

I found Mo and Alyssa in a dark room. There was a projector playing a video of two people enthusiastically grinding on each other, which Mo and Alyssa were ignoring, and staring at their phones instead. A handful of other people were watching the grinding intently, stroking their chins, nodding pensively. The volume was way up; it sort of sounded like a tennis match—mostly grunting with the occasional scream.

"What did you think of the exhibition?" I whispered, sliding into a seat in the row behind them, poking my head between them.

"At first I thought it was funny," Alyssa said, "like obviously all the massive dildos and everything."

Mo nodded thoughtfully.

"But then," she said, "I realized how sad it all was. It was just . . . I suppose it's just a reminder of how temporary it all is, isn't it?"

"Something can be so personal and intimate," I said, "and then just a piece of plastic on display."

We were all quiet for a moment.

"Issy," Mo said, "you seem a bit distracted."

"Do I?" I said, unable to take my eyes off the video on the wall—a third person, a woman, had joined in and was doing a lot of rolling around.

"Yeah," Alyssa said, "are you feeling sad about the sex graveyard? All those abandoned willies?"

A woman at the end of the front row, tutted at us as she made her way out of the room.

"Um," I said. I hadn't planned on telling them what was going on, although when I thought about it, I couldn't see any reason why not. "I am a bit distracted to be honest. It's not the willies. It's um . . . it's Robin."

They both froze.

"Stop," Mo whispered. He motioned for me to carry on.

"So, on Thursday night . . . we sort of . . . well we watched a film."

"And?" Alyssa said.

"And after it finished we ended up kissing," I said.

"And?" Mo said. He placed his hand on Alyssa's forearm for support.

"And, well, we went up to her room."

"You slept together," Alyssa said. "You had full sex with Robin."

I nodded.

"I knew it," she said triumphantly, slapping Mo on the knee.

Someone at the back shushed us.

"You did not," Mo whispered to Alyssa. "You're as shocked as I am."

"No," she said, shaking her head, "I had a feeling about it."

She looked me up and down.

"I sensed the change in you, Issy."

Mo rolled his eyes.

"So now what?" he said. "Are you guys . . . are you going to be a thing?"

I shook my head.

"So the thing is, I haven't actually spoken to her since."

"She hasn't messaged you?" Alyssa said.

"No, but . . ."

"Oh my god," Alyssa said, "she's giving you the Robin treatment. She's Robining you. You're being Robined right now."

"I . . . what?"

"Where she sleeps with people and then phases them out," Alyssa said.

"Oh," I said. "No, I don't think so. Am I? She might be just busy . . ."

Or, you know, dead?

"Did you guys talk about it?" Mo asked.

"We didn't really talk about anything, I mean she asked me to go to the lesbian wine bar with her."

Alyssa shook her head. "Means nothing, what else?"

"And then just before we . . . you know."

"Full sex," Alyssa said.

"Right, well she just checked I was OK because obviously for me, I hadn't . . ."

"You were a virgin," Alyssa said, unnecessarily loudly.

"Thank you, yes," I said. "So yeah, she checked in with me, but she also implied that she didn't want anything else, like for her this was just . . . that one time, I think."

"And what did you say?" Mo asked.

"I said she didn't have to worry about me falling in love with her," I said.

"Oh, babe," Alyssa said. "She even pre-Robined you; she got all bases covered."

"What do you want, Issy? That's the only thing that matters. Do you want it to be more than a one-time thing?" Mo continued.

"I don't know to be honest."

The man on the screen had turned pretty much purple by this point. He, like me, looked like he was utterly exhausted.

"Do you want to be her girlfriend?" Mo asked.

"No," I said, surprising myself. It was true though. I didn't. "No. I'm not ready for a girlfriend."

A vision of my own future sex toy graveyard flashed through my mind.

"This house is so important to me. I care about you all so much, and I don't want anything to ruin that. I do want Robin, in some ways. But I think I mostly want her as"—I gestured around the table—"part of this."

"What you don't want," Mo said, "is to end up in a situationship."

"So true," Alyssa said.

"What's . . ."

"Where you're not technically girlfriend and girlfriend but like, you also kind of are, but there's no rules or commitment or anything."

"Oh no," I said, "I don't want that. That sounds awful."

"So what are you going to do?" Alyssa said.

"I'm going to talk to her," I said. "Is that mad, to like . . . communicate and stuff?"

Alyssa raised her eyebrows and nodded slowly, like she was coming round to a very rogue idea.

"Take charge," she said eventually. "I like that. It's unexpected. It's out there."

"It's more just . . ."

"Girl power," she said. "Yes! *You're* Robining *her*."

On our way out of the gallery, as I was shrugging my coat on, Alyssa tugged at the back of my jumper.

"This is nice, is it new?"

"Oh," I said, looking down as if I hadn't dressed myself that morning, "no, it's actually Aubrey's."

Alyssa screwed up her face.

"What are you wearing Aubrey's jumper for?"

"I don't know," I said. "I like it I guess."

———

When we got home, I saw Robin's battered trainers kicked off by the door, her tote bag was hanging on a hook, and her keys were on the table next to the ornate bowl Alyssa provided for us to keep them in (mandatory).

"Maybe go and talk to her now, Issy," Mo said. "Get it over with."

"I know I should," I said, "but the thing is I don't want to."

"I know," he said. "But you'll feel better afterward, I promise. Rip the Band-Aid off."

"Bleurgh," I said, but I dutifully walked the stairs up to her room. My stomach fizzed with nerves. The last time I'd seen her, I'd been unfurling myself from her naked body and slipping away into the night (my bathroom-bedroom).

I knocked softly on Robin's bedroom door, so softly in fact that I had hoped she wouldn't hear, but she yelled, "Yeah?" in response straightaway.

"It's me," I called, resting my forehead against the door, my eyes closed, psyching myself up.

"Come in then, silly," she said.

I pushed the door open and took it all in, her room, different and exactly the same. The pillowcase was still on the lampshade. The light soft.

Robin was lying on her unmade bed, wearing gym leggings and an oversize gray sweatshirt. She had her glasses on and her laptop resting on her stomach, which she closed and placed beside her when she saw me standing in the doorway. A big grin spread across her tired face. She shuffled over in bed, sat up slightly, and patted the space next to her.

"Hello, you," she said and when I sat down, she squeezed my knee, jiggling it slightly, in the way you might if you were trying to wake someone up. "How was today? It looked like fun from the many, many updates Alyssa sent me."

"Illuminating," I said. "You missed out."

"I know," Robin said, "I was just so shattered today, rehearsals ran super late last night, and we ended up going for a drink after. I just needed a day in bed recuperating."

She took her glasses off and ran her hands through her hair.

"I'm just sort of shattered in general at the moment, to be honest," she said. "Loads on."

I nodded. We were both quiet for a moment. I noticed, in the pile of clothes on her floor, a sock that belonged to me.

I took a deep breath.

"And the late night on Thursday probably didn't help," I said. I found myself smiling awkwardly at my sock, and then at her. My cheeks were hot.

Robin chuckled. If she felt any of the nervousness I was feeling she certainly wasn't giving anything away.

"Right," she said, sitting up straighter still. She smiled back at me. "It probably didn't help."

We sat in silence again for a moment, waiting for the other to speak first. Robin did, in the end.

"I'm glad it happened though, despite the sleep deprivation."

"Me too," I said quickly. Glad was an understatement. "But I do just want to . . . I wanted to talk to you about . . ."

I realized as it was happening that this was an advanced-level conversation. I'd been thrown in at the deep end of the love life pool. I was not ready for a "situationship," I did not want a situation of any kind. I was absolutely, definitely not falling in love.

Thankfully, Robin rescued me.

"Yeah," she said, "ugh, you're right. I'm sorry. I shouldn't have just disappeared. I hope you didn't think that was anything to do with you."

"Of course not," I said, hopefully somewhat convincingly, sweating liberally.

"I like you," Robin said, "obviously. And we just have this sort of natural-chemistry thing."

Natural-chemistry thing!

I nodded seriously, as if I weren't just on the verge of spontaneously combusting at her words.

"But," Robin continued, "obviously we talked about . . . I just don't think we're in a place where we want to . . . I mean I'm not ready for a . . . Um, and you know, you're only just . . ."

It was my turn to rescue her.

"I really like you, Robin," I said. "But I just needed to know that we're still friends. I don't want anything to mess up what we've got in this house. I realized today that I value that more than anything."

"Me too," she said. She looked relieved. "Oh my god, Issy, me too."

Her hand squeezing my knee again.

"I value it so much. And you. I don't want you to think I took anything lightly, like, you're not just anyone. I'm sorry if it was a stupid thing to do."

"No, it's OK," I said. "I knew you wouldn't Robin me."

"What?"

"What?" I said. "Nothing. I just mean, we're good . . . as friends?"

"Very good," Robin said. "The best."

"OK," I said, "great." I leaned forward and plucked my sock from her pile of clothes. "This is very mature, isn't it? Or is it? I've never done this before."

"Very," Robin said, "and very gay. An initiation for you into the lovers-to-friends club."

"Lovers," I said, trying it out. "Robin, my former lover and current friend."

"You're very silly," Robin said.

"You like it."

"I do."

I sat there for a beat, holding my sock.

"Right," I said, "I'm going to take off, I think. I've got a long journey back to mine."

"You're more than welcome to stay here with me and be very lazy and gross, there's plenty of room," Robin said.

I thought about it, how easy it would be to slide into bed next to her and do my best at acting like everything was fine.

"As appealing as that offer is, I'd better go and see to Abigail."

"I can't compete with that chinchilla," Robin said.

"No one can," I said.

I knew that Mo and Alyssa would be waiting for the debrief, but I couldn't face it yet. Instead, I slipped into the bathroom-bedroom to throw myself dramatically onto my bed, face down in my pillows. It hurt to be nothing more than Robin's friend, even if I knew it was for the best, even if it made sense, even though I'd said I wouldn't fall in love.

It was a bittersweet heartbreak. A brand-new pain for my fragile heart, but a simple one, one I could endure. A breakup for beginners.

I was glad even then, with fresh tears on my cheeks, rejection in my stomach that it had happened. That Robin was my first. That she was right next door. That she cared.

I picked up my phone and replied to a message from my mum.

Isobel: *Hi Mum, I'm sorry about today. The exhibition was very interesting. No, perhaps not one for you and Uncle Pete when you next come up.*
I'm tired now but I'm having a lovely time.
Love you. Issy xxx
P.s yes I remembered to take them

And nearly all of it was true.

CHAPTER THIRTEEN

Holiday season arrived early in the office. The theme Elizabeth had chosen was "kitsch Christmas." When I first stepped into the office after it had been decorated, it was like stepping into Narnia. On acid.

The fairy lights strung through the Norwegian fir, and across the ceiling were multicolored—pinks and greens and blues—like the ones we would have on our tree at home except that this tree was real, and so tall that the deranged-looking plastic angel on the top touched the ceiling. Her neck was bent, her head at such an angle that it looked like she was always maniacally staring down at us.

Every surface was covered in what my mum would call "tat" and what Elizabeth would call "wonderful pieces!" A train set with Santa in the driver's seat ran all day. There were snow globes from all around the world and a giant cuckoo clock counting down until December 25, which made us all jump every hour on the hour. Elizabeth commissioned a piece of work from me, my first ever paid commission—a Christmas Abigail. I asked what she had in mind, but she told me to make whatever I liked, that it was just a bit of fun and then laughed when she saw the look of horror on my face.

"She does this every year, commissions work instead of giving Christmas bonuses," P said. They nodded at a naked man with the head of a snowman hanging on the tree. "Mine from last year."

"Blimey," I said.

"I know," they said proudly. "She said it was very striking."

"What was Olivia's?" I asked, intrigued by what she might have produced, I couldn't imagine her filled with Christmas spirit.

"The big Walter!" P said, pointing at the wall behind us, "didn't you know that's hers?"

I shook my head.

"I didn't even know she liked Walter."

"She spent weeks on it," P said. They watched my face trying to match up the perfectly captured angelic Walter with Olivia. "I know you'd never believe it, but she's very sentimental. Like she'd do anything for you if you asked. She might not be nice about it, but she'd do it."

"Ha," I said. "Sure."

"Honestly," P said, "she and Aubrey are not all that different."

P looked like they wished they could take it back the moment they'd said it.

"Do *not* tell her I said that," they said.

"Which one can't I tell?"

P hesitated a moment.

"Either of them."

It took me a while to figure out who Christmas Abigail was and what form she might take—there were many sleepless nights and weird dreams of Abigail climbing down chimneys and cooking giant turkeys. In the end I trawled eBay for a cheap cage, as similar to Abigail's as possible, and then I knitted a tiny stocking and hung it above a knitted fireplace, beside a knitted Christmas tree with some presents underneath it. I filled the cage with sawdust and red and green glitter and one of Abigail's little houses that she could no longer fit inside. I made tiny paper chains and hung them across the top of the cage. I strung lights up on the outside, woven through the bars—there were so many of them that when you switched them on it was so aggressively cheery and bright, you almost had to turn away.

I got into work early one morning and placed the cage on top of a countertop in the corner of the office. Elizabeth got in to work a little after me but before everybody else. She walked in with Walter and was, as usual, on the phone talking animatedly. She smiled at me and gave me a little wave, surprised to see me so early and then she stopped in her tracks and told the person on the phone she'd call them back.

She squealed and ran over to inspect the cage with childlike glee. "It's a bit silly," I said, "but I thought it was funny and, you know, festive."

"Oh, Issy," she said, "this is exactly what I was hoping for."

Elizabeth opened the door of the cage, poked her finger in the sawdust, lifted up the house, looked behind the Christmas tree. She gently unhooked a tiny, painstakingly detailed portrait of Abigail I'd painted, and inspected it carefully. That portrait had given me the kind of headache I thought I'd never recover from, but it was worth it to see the look on Elizabeth's face.

"There's no Abigail in here, is there? I'm not just missing her?"

I shook my head.

"There's no Abigail."

Elizabeth gently closed the cage door.

"It's just an empty cage and a Christmas," she said. "God, Issy. It's sad, isn't it?"

"It's just a silly thing," I said. "I had meant for an Abigail to be in there, but when it came down to it, I realized it was meant to be empty. I didn't mean for it to be so . . ."

Depressing? Bleak? Utterly devoid of Christmas spirit?

Elizabeth put her arm around me, she squeezed my shoulder tightly.

"It *is* silly," she said. "Our very own phantom Abigail. It's silly and beautiful and fun and sad, which is Christmas in a nutshell, isn't it?"

She stepped back then and looked at me properly, her eyes narrowed behind her big cat-eye glasses.

"You doing OK, kid?"

"Yes," I said, on autopilot.

"You'd tell me if you needed anything, wouldn't you?"

"Yes," I said.

"Because you've had a big life change and maybe you're finding it a bit destabilizing? That would be completely understandable."

"I'm not," I said, "I'm the opposite of destabilized, if anything."

"So," Elizabeth said, "stable, then."

"Exactly."

She paused for a moment, like she didn't believe me, but then she smiled.

"Great." She picked up her phone again. "God," she said, "I do love this time of year, Issy."

She disappeared into the little kitchen, and after a moment "Last Christmas" started playing at a deafening volume over the office speakers. Elizabeth flicked a switch, and all the fairy lights came on. It felt like living inside a fever dream.

We were filming with Outside the Lines at the end of November. This was the last time we'd see the group until after Christmas, so the day had a special feel about it even though as far as I could tell, the plan was just business as usual, plus mulled wine.

It still felt surreal walking into the loft and seeing cameras and lights set up. I waved at the harried producers; they greeted me with a nod, dashing around, looking stressed, which seemed like most of what their job entailed.

I was delighted to see Christmas catering, a foldout table laden with gingerbread and Santa doughnuts alongside the urns of tea and coffee. That's where I found William: he'd arrived before everybody else, bright and early and as keen as ever to be more involved than was necessary or, indeed, wanted. He kept stopping members of the crew when they were walking past carrying heavy things and asking them questions, which they'd politely answer, their arms shaking.

"Have you seen these?" William asked, holding one of the Santa doughnuts up to me and marveling at it.

"I know," I said, "they've really pushed the boat out."

I poured myself a coffee into a paper cup from one of the urns and stirred oat milk into it.

"Are you nervous?" I asked.

"About what?" William said, still in awe of the doughnut, unable to take his eyes off it.

"Being on camera," I said. "I'm still not used to it, I have to gear myself up every time."

William shook his head.

"It's hardly like I'm doing *Strictly*, is it? Not many new experiences come my way these days—I'm just trying to make sure I take it all in."

"You're very wise, William," I said, blowing across the top of my coffee.

"I'm just very old, dear," he said cheerfully.

Aubrey appeared over my shoulder out of nowhere just as I'd picked up a gingerbread man from the table and was about to dunk him in my coffee.

"Once you've finished up whatever important business you're doing over here, could you let me know, because we're all ready to get started."

In fact, I noticed, cameras were already rolling. They were filming us. They must have been doing a test, I thought.

"Is the poor girl not allowed a break?" William said.

"A break," Aubrey said, "implies she has been working."

"Where's your Christmas spirit?" I said. I lifted the gingerbread man up to her to show off his elf hat.

"Bah humbug," Aubrey said. "Et cetera."

And then to my absolute delight, before she stalked away to no doubt tell someone else off, she bit the head off my gingerbread man.

Although William continued diligently working on his miniature house with his magnifying glass strapped to his head, the others took a far more laid-back approach to the session—it had a very end-of-term feel about it. I understood why my French teacher would just wheel in a TV and stick on *The Muppet Christmas Carol* for our last few lessons before the holiday. No one could concentrate.

At lunchtime, Elizabeth popped by with Walter and Christmas gifts for everyone. She walked around talking to each group member individually, throwing back her head in laughter every few minutes, which made the bells attached to her massive Christmas earrings jingle. She was, as usual, walking sunshine.

"You two," she said to Aubrey and me, "are doing a fantastic job. Everyone is having such a fabulous time."

"It's all Aubrey," I said.

"Correct," Aubrey said.

Elizabeth laughed. "I hear," she said, with a conspiratorial smile on her face, "we're getting some lovely footage."

"Oh yeah," I say, "everyone's been great on camera; they've warmed up to it so well."

Elizabeth raised her eyebrows at me, and I felt like I was missing something. I turned to Aubrey, who looked as confused as me.

"What?" Aubrey said to Elizabeth, "why are you being weird?"

Elizabeth chuckled, jingling.

"No reason," Elizabeth said. "Or I suppose I should say, *you'll see.*"

"Before you go," I said at the end of the day, once we'd all had an awkward group hug and people were getting their coats on, "I've just got a little something for you."

I passed each person a tiny brown paper package tied up with red string. One for Aubrey too, which I pressed into her hand without looking at her.

I had spent a bit of time over the previous week making presents for everyone—they were, of course, Abigails. I was and continue to be a one-trick pony.

"Save them," I said, "or open them now, I don't care."

I was already blushing.

"Issy," said Aisha, who had already opened hers, "this is the cutest thing I've ever seen, how do you make them so tiny?"

She held hers against Leah's, they were matching exactly. Two peas in a pod.

"Another group hug," Stella demanded. She clapped her hand on my back, briefly winding me. We squeezed each other, Aubrey's hand barely touching my lower back, like I had something contagious she didn't want to catch.

"We're going to FaceTime on Christmas Day," William said on his way out, to nobody in particular, just utterly joyful at the prospect.

"We are if you can remember my instructions," Stella said.

"He'll be fine," Leah said. "I'll talk you through it again, William."

I heard them chatting all the way down the stairwell until the door slammed and the loft fell silent.

I felt like a proud parent of a very strange group of children, some of them quite elderly. I turned away from Aubrey in case it was obvious how close I was to bursting into tears.

"Bailey," she said after a moment, "is this a bike helmet?"

I turned to face her, and between her thumb and forefinger was indeed a tiny, blue helmet, in soft wool. A perfect replica of hers.

"Yes," I said, "so the Abigail can have helmet hair too."

"My favorite," Aubrey said.

"I know," I said.

She poured another cup of mulled wine and passed it to me.

We hadn't discussed it, the staying behind, just us. It just hadn't occurred to me for a moment that we wouldn't.

"I think that went pretty well; we got some good stuff," Aubrey said. "Everyone had fun, didn't they? They seemed like they were having fun. Not too overwhelming? Everyone had what they needed?"

"They did," I said. "Loads of fun. Everything they needed. All thanks to you. It was a great day."

Aubrey shook her head, uncomfortable, refusing the thanks. It might have been the space where someone else would have said, "no need to thank me, it's all you," or "I couldn't have done it without you." But instead Aubrey said:

"So, what are you doing for Christmas, Bailey?"

"I'll be going home," I said. "Spending it with my mum."

"Where's home again?" Aubrey said, sloshing more wine into her glass.

"Margate?" I said, as if I was checking with her. "On the Kent coast."

Aubrey raised her eyebrows at me. "Very trendy."

I laughed. "Not in my mum's flat."

It was her turn to laugh then, a proper one. I lit up.

"Will it be just the two of you?" she asked.

"Yeah," I said. "My uncle Pete and my auntie Jan will come round on Christmas Eve and we'll do a couple of presents, eat a mince pie, that kind of thing. And then the actual day is just me and Mum. And Abigail, of course."

"Of course," Aubrey said. "Do you always do the same thing?"

I nearly laughed. What else was there to do?

"Yeah," I said instead. "Always the same. How about you? Back to Scotland?"

"Back to Scotland," she confirmed.

"And you're from Edin . . ." I hazarded a guess, trying to remember if I'd heard her talk about it before.

"Glasgow," she finished my sentence for me.

"That's what I was going to say," I said.

"Of course," Aubrey said.

"So it's you and your parents?"

"Yeah, my mum and my stepdad, my siblings, stepsiblings, their partners, my nieces and nephews. Some of my family from Greece. It's a madhouse, to be honest."

"How many of you?" I asked.

"Oh Christ," Aubrey said. "Twenty? Thirty? A hundred? It's endless. I just keep being related to people."

"I can't imagine what that's like," I said. "To have that many people in one house."

"Loud," she said. And then added, "I love them. It's just *a lot*."

"Well, I can empathize with it being *a lot*," I said, raising my glass in silent cheers.

She raised hers too.

"Do you like Christmas?" she asked.

"Doesn't everybody like Christmas?"

She didn't answer, just waited for me to reply properly.

"Some bits," I said.

I thought about it for a moment.

"Actually, no," I said. "I don't. Not really."

"Why not?" Aubrey said.

"I suppose, I know that I am meant to be happy at Christmastime. And to be anything other than that makes me feel like even more of a failure than usual. And I really hate mince pies."

"Oh fuck," Aubrey said. "I'm sorry. Really rough season for you, pie-wise."

"Thank you, yeah. People don't talk about it enough, really. I'm out here raising awareness all by myself."

We were both quiet for a moment.

"I get it," she said, not looking at me. Looking into her glass and frowning at its contents.

"Yeah?"

"Yeah," she said. "I think the real meaning of Christmas is managing to get through it."

"Amen to that," I said. We clinked our glasses together properly that time, a real cheers.

"Do you reckon you'll go to the Christmas party at number seven?" I said.

Everyone on the street had been invited weeks ago, apparently number 7 always hosted a Christmas get-together that spilled out into their garden for the neighbors. We, at number 47A, were extremely keen to get the opportunity to snoop around and, crucially, eat some free food.

Aubrey snorted.

"I went the first year I lived on the street, and honestly, it was pretty weird."

"Oh yeah?" I said. "Weird how?"

Aubrey thought about it for a moment.

"OK, so, I'd say the vibe was somewhere between, like, a charity gala and a swingers party."

"Christ," I said.

I simply was not ready for a swingers party. That sounded intermediate level at least, maybe even advanced. I'd have to speak to Mo and Alyssa about it.

"Yeah," Aubrey continued, "I couldn't tell if they were trying to do philanthropy on me or proposition me."

"Both, maybe?" I said.

"Maybe," she said. "No offense to the people at number seven, but they are *deeply* not my type. Well, maybe Mrs. Lawrence. I get the impression she can be a bit wild after a couple of mistletoe martinis or whatever awful thing they've concocted."

She smiled at the look on my face, which I believe was part horrified and part intrigued.

"Have I convinced you to go?"

"Yes," I said. "Absolutely. We're all going, so—safety in numbers."

"Well," Aubrey said, grinning. "Best of luck to you. Or enjoy yourself, I guess. Who am I to assume what you're into?"

"Well, I don't know what a mistletoe martini is exactly, but it does sound like the kind of thing that could make me anyone's."

Aubrey nodded.

"Interesting. I'll bear that in mind."

I blushed from ear to ear, but I didn't look away.

I waited outside for Aubrey to unchain her bike before walking to the station.

"Are you OK to cycle?" I asked, shivering. "You've had a lot of wine."

"I'll be fine," she said. "But thank you, Mother."

She put her helmet on and then she took her tiny Abigail out of her coat pocket and silently, without even looking at me, put her helmet on too. She placed her back in her pocket.

"Good night, Bailey," she said, hauling herself onto the saddle and starting to move away down the dark street.

———

47A Girlies!! <3

Issy: *Guys, Aubrey said the vibe at number 7's Christmas party is like a charity swingers party—do we definitely want to go?*

Mo: *God, YES*

Robin: *More than ever*

Alyssa: *It's free champagne, hun, legally we have to go xx*

CHAPTER FOURTEEN

I hadn't been sleeping well. I'd spend all day exhausted, but when I got into bed, sleep would not come. I'd lie awake listening to Abigail rustling, waiting for the sun to come up, sometimes feeling deeply, gut-wrenchingly nostalgic, daydreaming about the seaside, my mum, my old routine. Sometimes though, I felt numb. There was comfort in feeling pretty much nothing at all.

I was kept busy at work in the couple of weeks leading up to Christmas. My job consisted of the activities I'd been anticipating when I started—running out to buy lunches, emergency Christmas present hunting, sending vast, luxurious hampers out to Elizabeth's friends and acquaintances. There were so many hampers going out that in the end, we'd ordered more than we needed and so, on a whim, I added William's, Aisha's, Leah's, and Stella's addresses to the mail-out list.

Everything I did at work went through Aubrey first, and I watched her across the office when I sent the list through for approval. She raised her eyebrows at her laptop screen, and I watched her typing.

From: Aubrey Kerr
To: Isobel Bailey
Subject: re: Elizabeth Christmas gifts—approval from the boss please

All looks good to me. Nothing untoward here whatsoever.

"You look nice, Aubrey," Olivia said, peering at her over the top of a pair of thick-rimmed bright blue glasses I hadn't seen before. She was wearing an oversize coat like a duvet that she'd refused to take off all week, citing that the studio was so cold it was "inhumane."

I was packing up at the end of a torturously long day just before the office closed for Christmas, but I stopped in my tracks because in the past three months I'd been working for Elizabeth, I genuinely could not recall a time when Olivia had come anywhere close to complimenting Aubrey.

"Yeah," P said, looking as surprised as I did at Olivia's comment, "you do look nice. Where are you off to?"

Aubrey was sitting at her laptop. She showed no signs of heading home any time soon, even though Elizabeth had already left and office hours were technically over.

Aubrey *did* look nice. I mean, I always thought she looked nice. Actually, *nice* is too insipid a word for it. She always looked cool and hot and like she'd just thrown on whatever she was wearing in the best possible way. But that day she was wearing a blazer for goodness' sake. Eyeliner. There was not even any helmet hair. Now that I thought about it, she hadn't ridden her sister's bike to work that day. Unheard of.

My interest was piqued.

"I'm just meeting a friend for a drink," Aubrey said without looking up.

"No you're not," Olivia said, laughing, "what 'friend'?"

"Olivia," P said. They rolled their eyes at her, but they were still smiling.

"I'm joking," Olivia said. "I'm just playing, you know that I'm just playing, don't you, Aubrey?"

Aubrey didn't answer, just kept her head down.

"But you're not meeting a friend," Olivia persisted.

"I can tell. Oooh," she exclaimed, gleefully, "are you going on a date?"

I don't know why, but that thought truly hadn't occurred to me. I frowned, scrutinizing Aubrey. The slight pink tinge to her cheeks, her knee twitching under the table.

"What?" Aubrey snapped, looking up finally, catching my eye.

I couldn't help myself.

"Well," I said, "are you?"

"Yeah!" Olivia said. "Come on, are you?"

She was so delighted at my joining in with interrogating Aubrey that I immediately knew I shouldn't have. That I should have stayed quiet.

No, not stayed quiet. I should have told them to leave her alone.

Aubrey ignored Olivia, she just continued staring at me. There was a flash of something, disappointment maybe, before her face hardened again.

"Why do you care if I'm going on a date?" she said, directing her question solely at me.

"I don't care," I said quietly.

I was aware of Olivia and P watching us with interest.

"No?" Aubrey said.

I swallowed. Waited a beat too long to reply.

"No."

"Fine," she said. "Yes, I'm going on a date. Happy?"

"OK," I said, "no, I mean . . ." Fortunately, Olivia and P started whooping, drowning out my incoherent mumbling. They started asking more probing questions, all of which Aubrey ignored.

I wanted to say something else, but I felt like whatever I said would make it worse.

"OK," Aubrey said, standing up abruptly and slamming her laptop shut. "I'm off."

She didn't look at me on her way out, although I tried to catch her eye. I felt frustrated, like I so often did with her. I wanted to chase after her either to confront her or have her reassure me. Something.

That was the overwhelming urge I was always resisting, I thought—chasing after Aubrey Kerr. Even when she was right in front of me.

"She is literally *so* moody," Olivia said, interrupting my thoughts and holding her hand out for P's vape, which they reluctantly handed over. "Ignore her."

P and Olivia walked away from me arm in arm. They got halfway to the door before stopping and doubling over, seemingly unable to keep walking because they were laughing so much.

I waited until they were gone and then I did what I really wanted to do.

Aubrey hadn't left yet. She was standing in the hallway, leaning against the wall, glaring down at her phone.

"Hi," I said.

She didn't look up.

"Are you OK?"

"I'm fine," she said to her screen, "why wouldn't I be?"

"Well," I said, "because you just stormed out of the office and now you won't even look at me."

She looked up at me then. It was apparent, from the look in her eyes, that she was furious. I started to regret following her. It sort of felt like when humans claim they've tamed wild animals and then the wild animals eat them.

"What do you want me to say, Bailey?"

I stared back at her, just us in the dark hallway, the tobacco-scented candle flickering.

What did I want her to say?

"I don't know, I just don't want to . . . I don't know," I said, frustrated with myself for being so inarticulate. "You're angry with me."

"I'm not," she said.

"You are, and I'm sorry. I—"

"Bailey," she snapped, "I'm not angry with you, OK? I don't care enough. I don't care enough to be angry. You and your friends in there don't bother me. I don't care about them; I don't care about you. Is that what you want to hear?"

I shook my head.

"I've got to go," she said.

I walked home. I'd missed that it had been raining, having been inside all day, but the streets were wet, cars splashing through puddles. The shop windows were illuminated with Christmas lights, and the pubs were heaving, people spilling out onto the streets clutching pints and laughing raucously.

I felt, on that walk down those busy streets, a way that I hadn't felt in a long time. I felt that I couldn't be sure if I was really there at all. I watched myself for a little while, a ghost among the people, before landing back in my body again, resettling. I let the feeling fade away, unexamined. It was a relief, not to think too deeply.

When I got home, I had intended to go straight to my room, but I couldn't help but notice that the carpet on the staircase leading up to the first floor was covered with pine needles.

The living room door was closed, and Christmas music was blaring behind it. I pushed it open tentatively to find Alyssa and Mo decorating a Christmas tree that I can describe only as bald.

"Hi," I said.

They didn't hear me over the music. They didn't have much in the way of Christmas decorations, and Mo was in fact tying a silk scarf around the top of the tree.

"Hi," I tried again, louder this time.

"Oh," Alyssa said, turning around. "Hi, babe, you all right?"

"Yeah," I said. I walked over to the speaker and turned the music down. "What happened to your tree?"

"What do you mean?" Alyssa said.

"I . . . it . . ."

They both looked at me blankly.

"Nothing," I said, "it's lovely."

"Thanks," Mo said, "I got it at the corner shop, they were selling it for a tenner for some reason."

Mo stood back, his hands on his hips, admiring it. "I mean I don't even celebrate Christmas, really. Apart from like, the presents and eating all the food and the time off work and watching the films and the TV and stuff. But you have to admit that is a *nice* tree."

"It's gorgeous," I said. I noticed as well as the silk scarf the tree appeared to be wearing clip-on earrings.

"Do you need any help?" I said.

"No," Alyssa said, "too many cooks."

"Mm," I said, watching as she attached a little hair clip to the end of a branch and the remaining pine needles fell from it, "don't want to ruin it."

Instead of going to my room, I slumped down on the sofa and helped myself to a handful of star-shaped pretzels in a bowl on the coffee table.

At some point, listening to Mo and Alyssa chatting and the soundtrack of the Destiny's Child Christmas album, I fell asleep. My head jerked up at the sound of the front door slamming. I turned to Mo and Alyssa, who were squished together at the end of the sofa next to me, they'd moved my feet so they were on Mo's legs and covered me in a blanket. The room was dark apart from the TV flickering and some blinking LED lights on the tree.

I wiped drool from the corner of my mouth.

"How long was I asleep?" I asked croakily.

"Hours, babe," Mo said. "It's nearly midnight. Are you feeling all right?"

Robin poked her head around the door, she was clearly tipsy and grinning dopily. And I still felt it, despite myself. Happy to see her and sad too, because of that little jolt in my chest, that little wish that she was grinning dopily because of me and not because of the date she'd just come home from.

"Oh, babies altogether!"

She came into the room and lay down on all of us, limbs everywhere, trying to hug us all at once. We protested until she settled, sitting across Mo and Alyssa, her feet up on me.

"Your bum is so bony," Alyssa said.

"What is wrong with that tree?" Robin said.

I shook my head at her.

"What do you mean?" Mo said.

"Um," Robin said, "I mean, why is it tucked away in the corner? We should bring it out more—celebrate it, it's so beautiful."

"Oh," Alyssa said, "yeah, you're right."

Robin grinned at me.

We stayed like that for a while, piled on top of each other, finishing watching the film Alyssa and Mo had been watching. And I felt briefly better in the pile of people, lit up by the worst Christmas tree I'd ever seen.

When I finally went to my bathroom-bedroom, I fed Abigail in the dark.

I climbed under the covers in my clothes, and lay awake for hours.

CHAPTER FIFTEEN

I stayed in bed all morning, which turned into all afternoon. I
didn't get up, not when I was so thirsty my throat burned and so
hungry my stomach ached. Not when I heard Robin get back from
Christmas shopping, bags rustling outside my bedroom door, and
not when my phone lit up beside me, my mum's name flashing,
Uncle Pete's name flashing. Over and over again.

At one point Alyssa banged on my door when I was googling
"cheap therapy near me" and "do I need to go to the doctors or am
I being dramatic?"

(Inconclusive)

"Babe, you all right?"

"Yeah," I said, forcing my voice to sound normal. "I'm just fighting off a cold, I think."

"Want me to bring you a clove of garlic? You're meant to eat it raw."

"No," I said.

"You still coming to the Christmas sex party?"

"Yes," I said. "No to garlic, yes to Christmas sex party."

"Perfect," she said, and I heard her run down the stairs shouting, "Don't worry, she's coming!"

I looked at my motivational Aperol spritz on my bedside table and tried to feel something.

I rallied by 7:00 p.m., long after dark. I forced myself out of bed to drink water directly from the bathroom tap. I took two paracetamol and stuck my head out of my bedroom window, the fresh air hitting me like a slap in the face. It felt good. The harsh cold, the mild nausea from the all-day nap, and the waking from my stupor.

My hunger was gone. I fed Abigail.

I got dressed, a new shirt over old trousers. Fresh white socks and Doc Martens. Gold hoops in my ears. My cool new haircut was growing out, tufts over my ears. I brushed my eyebrows carefully with the clear gel, just as Alyssa had taught me to do. I avoided my own eyes in the tiny mirror. I couldn't bear to look.

Issy: *Hi Mum, I'm really sorry I missed your calls. I've actually had a busy day in the studio. I'm going for some Christmas drinks at a neighbor's house tonight but I promise I'll call tomorrow. Love you!! Xxxxx*

When I went downstairs, into the kitchen, Mo and Alyssa, both wearing sparkly outfits, cheered when they saw me, and I smiled. It was a real smile, their infectious happiness almost penetrating the protective shell around me.

I called it a protective shell, but I'm not sure that's accurate. The shell that was my prison. Occasionally it wrapped around me and I couldn't quite seem to prize it open.

"Issy!" Mo exclaimed. "Oh my god I was convinced you weren't going to come. And you look gorgeous. Do you feel better?"

"Loads better," I said, "and I just couldn't deprive the Christmas sex party of all this, you know?"

I lifted the bottom of my shirt as if it were a flouncy dress and did a little twirl. They both laughed.

The thing about the shell, protector or prison cell, was that no one else could ever see it. We hid each other well.

"Eyebrows looking good, Issy," Alyssa said approvingly. "Didn't I tell you? Like a whole new face."

"Thanks. I think."

My former lover, current friend Robin walked into the kitchen then, carrying a bottle of champagne. She looked incredible, as usual, in a black jumpsuit and black boots. She had her blond hair slicked back and smoky eyes.

"Hello, you," Robin said, grinning at me. She stepped forward and kissed me on the cheek. Out of the corner of my eye, I saw Mo and Alyssa glancing at each other. I was engulfed in her perfume.

"I was under the impression that you were planning to give tonight a miss," Robin said, stepping back and looking me up and down. "What a nice surprise."

I watched as she fiddled with the champagne cork, struggling to ease it out of the bottle.

"I didn't feel great earlier," I said.

"Yeah?" she said, stopping just before she popped the bottle open.

"But I'm feeling much better now," I said.

"You're OK?" she said.

I paused.

"I'm fine."

Robin smiled at me and then twisted the cork out of the bottle. She filled our glasses all the way to the top.

I cannot stress how accurate Aubrey's description of the party at number 7 was. Had I not been grumpy with her, or scared of her, or confused about whatever had happened between us before her date, I might have messaged her, made a joke about it. I wanted to make her laugh. I wanted to feel at peace with her, with everyone—to settle that feeling deep in the pit of my stomach and in every crevice of my mind.

That's my overwhelming sense memory from that night, that yearning, that desperation. I wanted, I wanted, I wanted.

If you are a depressed person, I cannot recommend going to a Christmas sex party more. I can't promise it will make you feel better, but it will certainly be a distraction from the old existential dread.

We were greeted at the door by Mrs. Lawrence, who kissed us all enthusiastically on both cheeks. She must have been in her late forties, maybe even in her fifties—somewhere close to my mum's age, but they couldn't have been more different. Mrs. Lawrence was wearing a low-cut black dress; it had a deep red trim and sleeves that sort of rested on the top of her arms. It was very tight fitted, the kind of thing that would prompt my mum to say something like, "Now that's not a dress you can sit down in." Mrs. Lawrence was a tiny woman, but she was wearing such towering heels that she had to bend down slightly to kiss me. I, of course, blushed.

"Darling," she yelled behind her, champagne precariously swilling about in her shallow glass.

"Yes, darling," Mr. Lawrence appeared behind her. He was wearing a green velvet suit with a waistcoat and, I have to say, looked not unlike a festive Toad from *Wind in the Willows*.

"Will you please get these gorgeous young people a drink and show them through?"

"Drinks for gorgeous young people coming right up," Mr. Lawrence said. And he winked at us.

"Make yourselves at home," Mrs. Lawrence said. "Mingle, have fun. I'll catch up with you all later."

She winked at us too.

"Christ," Mo said as we made our way down the hall and through to the living room, "what *are* we actually going to have to do in return for this free food?"

When we got to the living room and saw the food that was on offer—a table overflowing with every Christmas treat you could imagine: cheese, fruit, mince pies, oysters piled on ice, prawns bigger than my hand, chocolate truffles, bottles and bottles of champagne, and a huge bowl of festive punch with oranges and cranberries swimming inside—Mo turned back to us wide-eyed.

"Yeah, forget I said anything, I'll do whatever they want. Lawrences? I'm yours."

We ignored the rest of our neighbors and took turns going back and forth to the best buffet we'd ever seen. I ate a handful of grapes, some crackers, trying to stimulate my appetite. I bit down on a dark chocolate truffle, letting it melt over my tongue, trying to just enjoy the sensation of it. I let the chatter wash over me, laughing when I needed to laugh, nodding when I needed to nod. I drank my champagne slowly and listened to a bored-looking man playing Christmas classics on a white piano.

When we started getting judgmental looks from other neighbors at the party who I suppose wanted to access the buffet too but were behaving like civilized human beings, we took ourselves on a tour of the house. An unofficial tour—we had not been invited to do so. Mr. and Mrs. Lawrence weren't around though, in our defense. They kept disappearing from the throng of the party and then would come back giggling and merrier than ever. Mr. Lawrence was never without a bottle of champagne, topping people up without asking.

Their house was beautiful, the same layout as ours but decorated with the utmost taste and care. The walls were painted in dark colors—reds and greens and blues—and there were heavy drapes everywhere. No drafts, no creaking windows, no scratched laminate flooring. I brushed my fingers along a thick velvet curtain wistfully.

We crept upstairs and opened the door to the main bathroom. We gasped when we saw what was inside. The walls were painted black, the floor covered in gleaming black and white tiles illuminated only by an expensive-looking candle burning next to the sink. It smelled like woodsmoke. One of the walls, opposite the enormous sunken bath, was covered in antique mirrors and what we discovered, on closer inspection, was framed vintage pornography.

"Fucking hell," Alyssa said, squinting into one of the gold gilded mirrors, pouting at herself. She leaned in to inspect one of the framed pictures of a woman who wasn't wearing any clothes but was brandishing a whip, "This really is a Christmas sex party, isn't it? I thought you were all just messing about, taking the piss out of me."

"This one's even wearing a Santa hat," Robin said, taking a sip of her champagne, nodding at another picture on the wall.

"Really?" Alyssa said.

"No," Robin said, "but she is sporting a *very* festive gimp mask."

After a comprehensive look in their bathroom cabinets (nothing—Mo hypothesized that the good stuff must be locked away elsewhere), we made our way to the end of the corridor, poking our head into the bedrooms on the way—they were surprisingly tame, like something out of a chain hotel or a show home. We finally reached a door right at the end that we couldn't open. We shook the handle a couple of times, each of us testing to see if our magic touch could get it to open.

"That one is always locked." A voice came from behind us. "It won't open, believe me. I've tried."

Aubrey was leaning against the wall, a glass of festive punch in her hand. My surprise at seeing her at the Christmas sex party was overshadowed by my being momentarily floored by her outfit. By her Christmas jumper specifically—which looked hand-knitted, ill fitting, and featured what I can only describe as a 3D Christmas tree, which was flashing sporadically.

"Christ," Mo said. He looked in horror at Aubrey's jumper and then actually shielded his eyes. "You scared me."

"Sorry," Aubrey said, "I'm just heading to the loo." She nodded past us. "But, like, everyone here has tried that door, and it's always locked every year."

"Maybe it's just a cupboard or something," Alyssa said. She pressed her ear up against the door and then shook her head, nothing.

"Nope," Aubrey said, "that's just off the bathroom. No, it's another bedroom or, um, something similar."

"A sex dungeon?" Alyssa whispered. "Like in *Fifty Shades of Grey?*"

"Could well be," Aubrey said, nodding seriously, taking a pensive sip of her festive punch. "Could well be."

"Come on, guys," Robin said, shaking her head at Aubrey, "let's head back downstairs. I reckon I could fit another oyster in."

We shuffled out past Aubrey one by one—Robin looked up and grinned at her, and Aubrey slapped her on the top of her arm. It was surprisingly matey given that I thought the others knew her only as "mean neighbor."

"Hey," Aubrey said, as I moved past her, "can I talk to you for a sec?"

I think she meant to catch my hand, but she ended up grabbing the sleeve of my shirt and tugging me. I looked up at her, surprised, expecting her to apologize, to let it go, but she didn't, she just loosened her grip and looked back at me, waiting for me to answer.

The lights on her ridiculous jumper began to pulse alarmingly quickly, and I couldn't help but laugh. She looked down.

"I should probably be handing out sunglasses, shouldn't I? Or at least have warned people before I got here. It's a health-and-safety issue for sure."

"For sure," I said. I looked at the others, lurking on the stairs. "Guys, I'll be with you in a minute."

"You sure?" Alyssa said. "We can wait for you."

"I think she'll be OK," Aubrey said. "I'll take very good care of her. The sex dungeon is locked, after all."

She rattled the door handle to emphasize her point.

Alyssa stared for a long time at Aubrey's jumper and then looked back at me, her eyes narrowed.

"Don't look directly at it."

They all walked down the stairs loudly talking about their pudding strategy, specifically how they could get away with transporting as much as possible home without getting caught.

Aubrey and I waited to speak until they were gone.

"Sorry about them," I said. "They're very protective of me. They have this idea that I'm this tiny, helpless baby they need to look after."

"I get it," Aubrey said, "I have been known to rub people up the wrong way."

"No," I said. "Really?"

"Bailey," she said, ignoring me. "I don't do this very often. But I wanted to apologize to you. For the way I acted in the office. I overstepped. I shouldn't have spoken to you like that." She paused as if she was choosing her next words carefully.

"I do care about you. Obviously. I'm your boss."

"Sort of," I said.

"Not sort of," Aubrey said. "Actually. Your full-on boss."

I stayed quiet. I wanted her to say more things. For her to stay on the back foot for once, just for a little bit longer. For her to chase me for once. But I knew I had an apology to make too.

"I'm sorry too," I said.

"For what?" Aubrey said.

"Joining in."

Aubrey cocked her head on one side, observing me as she often did. Like a curiosity. She shook her head slightly.

"Anyway," she continued, as if I hadn't spoken, "I have something for you. I actually came to this mad horny party just to give it to you."

"Wow," I said, blushing at the word *horny* like a teenager, "some career advice maybe, *boss?*"

"No advice. I'm happy just watching you lurch around life like a human Bambi and keeping my mouth shut."

"Thank you," I said. "I appreciate that."

Aubrey reached into her back pocket and produced a slightly

crumpled brown envelope with my name written on the front of it. My full name, *Isobel Bailey*, which struck me as weirdly formal and perfectly Aubrey.

"Don't open it now," she said, handing it over, "because that will be torture for me. Save it for Christmas Day. No one ever saves things for Christmas Day anymore. It's all now now now, more more more. Instant-gratification culture."

"You sound like a grumpy old man," I said, sliding the card into the top pocket of my shirt. "I will; I'll save it for Christmas Day. Thank you, old man. I mean, boss."

"You're welcome, Bambi."

She opened her mouth to say something else and then, uncharacteristically, appeared to change her mind.

"What?"

"No, nothing," she said, "I literally just said I wasn't going to give you any advice, didn't I?"

"Say it," I said. "Otherwise I'm going to think it's worse than it is."

"Robin," she said.

My stomach lurched, a fresh burst of adrenaline at hearing her name.

"What about Robin?"

I thought of the way they'd been with each other, the smile, the hand on the shoulder.

"I mean, are you guys, you're not . . . anything?"

"No," I said. "We're just friends."

She nodded.

"What?" I said.

"OK," she said, "cool."

She lifted the glass of festive punch to her mouth, draining it.

"The thing you wanted to say about Robin was, 'OK, cool'?"

"Yes," she said.

We were both quiet for a moment. I couldn't quite identify what exactly it was about this conversation that made me feel so bad. What exactly it was that was making my veins run with dread. Of course Aubrey fancied Robin. Of course she did; everyone did.

Instead of looking up and meeting Aubrey's eyes, I stared at the flashing jumper. It was really quite impossible not to.

"I made it myself," she said, "if you're thinking, 'where can I get one of those gorgeous jumpers?'"

She tugged at the Christmas tree at the front a little bit and then pulled her hand away quickly. "Fuck, it's quite hot."

"Oh god, Aubrey," I said. "Are you going to catch on fire?"

"It would be worth it," she said, "to die for fashion."

My mouth began twitching at the corners. I loved when she was in this kind of playful mood. I realized that other than the gallery trip and the time she thought I'd stolen her bike, we'd never actually spent any time together outside of work. Unless you counted our informal post art-group loft debriefs.

"Did you really make it yourself?" I said.

"Yes," she said and then she leaned forward faux conspiratorially. "Knitting is one of my many talents, Bailey."

"Ah," I said, my eyes widening.

"Ah," she repeated.

It made sense, everything P and Olivia said.

"So that's why you hate me," I said.

Aubrey frowned.

"What are you talking about?"

"You hate me because I stole your thing. Your work. P and Olivia said it was because you're . . ."

I realized I didn't know how to finish that sentence.

"Go on," Aubrey said.

"I'm sorry," I said. "I had no idea."

"I don't want to burst your bubble, Bailey, but we are not the only two people in the world who knit."

"No, I know but . . ."

"There are like five million grandmothers we're in competition with," she said, standing up straighter now. "Plus, as you can see"— she looked down at the burning-hot, tatty jumper—"I'm not as good as you."

"I know, that was a silly thing to say. I guess I just . . ."

"Do you really think I hate you, Bailey?"

I looked up at her properly then, not at the flashing, dangerous jumper.

"Sometimes," I said.

Aubrey nodded.

"Do you think I hate you right now?"

I was suddenly aware of how alone we were up there, how quiet it was and dark away from the party. How close we were standing.

"No," I said.

"No," Aubrey repeated.

We stood for a moment like that, the air crackling between us.

And then Aubrey jerked her head toward the stairs. "You'd better get back to your friends; they'll think I picked the lock to the sex dungeon and trapped you inside. And I'd better go to the loo; I've had about three pints of festive punch. I do not recommend."

"OK," I said. "Thank you for . . ."

I patted my top pocket.

Aubrey pointed at me and looked at me seriously.

"Christmas Day," she said.

I nodded.

"Christmas Day."

I turned to walk back downstairs, and when I reached the top step, Aubrey called out to me.

"Bailey." I looked up at her, her head poking out from behind the door of the sexy bathroom. "You OK?"

"Yes," I said, on autopilot. "Why?"

She hesitated, choosing her words carefully.

"It's like you're behind glass," she said after a moment.

It was so unexpected and said so matter-of-factly that I stood completely still for a moment on that step, stunned to have been seen like that. And by Aubrey of all people.

"Have a good Christmas, Aubrey," I said quietly.

She looked at me, waiting for me to say something else, and when I didn't, she nodded.

"You too, Bailey," she said.

CHAPTER SIXTEEN

When Uncle Pete came up to London in his van to take me and Abigail back to Margate for Christmas, it felt like no time had passed since he'd first dropped me off at 47A. And it also felt like a lifetime ago. I was a different person than the one who'd sat up front with a cage wedged on my lap, and yet I settled back into the seat comfortably, as if I'd been there the whole time.

I closed my eyes, breathed in the familiar smell. My shoulders relaxed sitting next to Uncle Pete. I listened to him swearing at other drivers, singing along to Christmas songs on the radio, slurping the dregs of a McDonald's milkshake. Sounds of home.

"You all right, Iz?" he said, rattling ice cubes at the bottom of his cup, perhaps finally admitting defeat.

I peeled my eyes open, looked at him blearily.

"Yes," I said. "Fine."

"You been going a bit hard on the Christmas parties, have ya? Bit too much eggnog last night, was it?"

"No one drinks eggnog, Uncle Pete."

I closed my eyes again. And then sat up, wriggling out of my jumper. It was too hot in the van. I felt clammy, my skin sensitive and tingling.

"Rubbish," Pete said, "it's the UK's favorite drink."

"It is not."

"It is, Issy. I read it in the newspaper."

We fell into silence. I screamed "Facebook is not the newspaper!" in my head instead of saying it out loud, not wanting to get into an argument before we'd even hit the motorway. I was busy playing scenes from the past few days in my head: falling out with Aubrey, making up with Aubrey.

Aubrey seeing me behind glass.

"And our little Abbie is doing all right as well, is she?"

"Who?" I said.

"Who?" Pete repeated incredulously. "Who? Your bloody chinchilla? The reason I'm picking you up? Madam needs to be chauffeured home because her *abode*"—he gestured at the cage—"is too big to be taken on the train."

"Right," I said. "Yes, yes, Abigail's fine, thanks."

I poked my finger through the bars of the cage as if to stroke her, even though she was nowhere to be seen. I tried to remember when I had last seen her, and suddenly, it felt like ice was trickling through my veins.

Yesterday, wasn't it? Surely. Or was it the day before? Had I put food out for her that morning? Or was it yesterday's food untouched in her bowl? I couldn't remember. The days had all blurred into one. When did that start to happen?

I felt immediately very sure that I was going to be sick.

I opened the cage door and stuck my hand directly into the shoebox, feeling around for Abigail. I expected a bite, I expected to lose the tip of my finger even. I couldn't find her. I lifted the box out entirely.

"Oi," Uncle Pete said, "no loose rodents in my car."

I ignored him, his voice faint against the cacophony inside my head.

"Issy, I'm serious, stop messing about with that thing."

I lifted the shoebox to peer inside.

Abigail was curled up into a ball right at the back. I wrapped my hand easily around her. She was getting smaller. She'd ballooned over the past couple of years and now the air was slowly leaking out.

I felt her heartbeat beneath my fingers. She wriggled, and I loosened my grip on her.

"Sorry," I said. "I'm sorry for waking you, I'm sorry."

I put her back down gently and placed the shoebox back in the cage. I shut the door carefully, double-checking I'd locked it as per Uncle Pete's instructions, lest she ruin the pile of plastic bags and chocolate bar wrappers he'd carefully curated in his van.

I kept my eyes open for the rest of the journey, straining to stay awake, to stay alert. I wasn't going to let things slip. I was fine. I was fine and Abigail was fine. It was all absolutely *fine*.

When I walked through the front door of the flat, my mother screamed.

"Hi, Mum," I said. "Merry Christmas."

I deposited Abigail in the living room and waited for her to calm down. She was right behind me though, flapping.

"Isobel, is that a real tattoo?"

I'd forgotten to put my jumper back on before I came inside, although I didn't have any real intention of hiding it from her. I'd forgotten about it entirely to be honest.

"Yeah, Uncle Pete did it for me in the car."

"Isobel!"

"Yes, it's a real tattoo, obviously. It's lovely, isn't it?"

I held my arm out for her to inspect it properly, and she hurried off to get her glasses so she could be accurately horrified.

"Hmmm," she said, after a while of twisting my arm about, moving me under various living room lamps. "This is one of your drawings."

"Yes."

"Did it hurt?"

"Not too badly."

She nodded.

"It's quite nice, isn't it, actually," she said.

She touched it and pulled her hand away quickly as though it might sting her.

"I think so," I said. "I'd say it's not worth screaming over."

"I was in shock, Issy."

"Right."

"Shall I get the kettle on?" Mum said, taking off her glasses again. "And will you have a piece of Christmas cake?"

And just like that, it was like I'd never been away.

When I went to my room that night and got into my single bed, with my mum pottering about next door, I lay awake for hours. I tried to practice mindfulness, a thing I read about from time to time. A thing that a forgotten app on my phone sent me sporadic notifications about. I tried to root myself in my surroundings, the sounds, the smells, what I could feel beneath my fingertips. But my brain was already somewhere else entirely, floating away from me, out of reach. I had no control over my nerve endings in overdrive, my chest tightening, my breath shortening.

I was home and not home, all at once.

The run up to Christmas Day was quiet. Well, it was the same as usual, I suppose. It just felt quiet compared to the past few months. It was a relief, the quiet, in some ways, and stressful in others. I found myself feeling twitchier and more restless than usual. I was either flooded with adrenaline, on a knife's edge, or exhausted, barely able to string a sentence together. I tried to disguise all of this under a veneer of "fineness," so that Mum would worry less. She asked a lot of questions about London and I answered most of them truthfully. When we sat next to each other in the evenings watching television, I could feel her eyes on me, trying to see me in the darkness.

I became obsessed with checking on Abigail. She got up less, she ate less. I rang the emergency out-of-hours vet; he sighed and in a very bored voice told me it sounded like she was elderly and that's what elderly animals do. I should make her comfortable, is what he said. Make her comfortable. I didn't understand what he meant really—she was always comfortable. I'd always made her comfortable.

I woke up early on Christmas morning, it was still dark outside. I found Mum already up in the kitchen, drinking a cup of tea, doing the crossword on her iPad. There were so many neatly chopped vegetables on the countertop, it looked like feeding time at a petting zoo.

I wrapped my arms around her shoulders and kissed her on the top of her head, her hair still messy from sleep, even though she must have been up for hours.

"Merry Christmas, Mum."

"Merry Christmas, Issy," she said, without looking up from her screen.

I made myself a cup of tea and sat down with her, the light changing in the kitchen as the sun came up, a stream of sunshine flickering across the table. There was a chocolate orange in the fruit bowl, unboxed, the orange foil shining. I took it from the bowl, thumped it on the table to break it up, and unwrapped it. I silently handed Mum a segment, and she took it from me and popped it in her mouth. I did the same thing, and we smiled at each other.

Mum was never silly really, never did frivolous things, but when I was little, every Christmas Eve, she'd leave a chocolate orange in the fruit bowl hidden among the satsumas. And on Christmas morning, I'd come into the kitchen and rummage through them until I landed on it, lifting it out and raising it above my head like a prize. I found it hysterically funny, I'd shriek with glee every year. A brilliant private joke between me and Father Christmas. Mum would stand in the doorway in her dressing gown and watch me.

"Wow," she'd say when I showed her, "aren't you lucky?"

I'd nod, my eyes wide, giddy at the thought of my magic fruit and my good luck.

"Since it's such a lovely morning," I said, once we'd finished our tea and our chocolate orange, "should we go for a walk on the beach?"

Mum raised her eyebrows. We didn't do walks on the beach on

Christmas Day until after lunch, that was the routine. How we'd always done it.

"Just because it's so sunny," I said. I desperately wanted to get out of the flat. Feel the cold on my face, look out at the sea.

"Why not?" my mum said after a moment. "Yes, why not. Let's do it."

It was bitingly cold, but there were plenty of people out walking on the beach. We waved at dog walkers, wished a merry Christmas to a couple out on their morning run. We laughed and winced as we watched mad people run into the freezing cold sea and scream.

There was one place open, serving hot drinks from a hatch, so we bought a coffee to share and passed it back and forth between us.

"Don't get cross with me, Issy," Mum said, taking off the plastic lid to blow across the top of our cappuccino, "but I've just been thinking, perhaps it would be nice if you found someone to talk to in London."

"I have plenty of people to talk to in London," I said, and I immediately screwed up my face, annoyed with myself for being so childish.

"Sorry," I said, quickly, "I know what you mean."

"Maybe a doctor could help you find someone, and just, you know, have a checkup or something."

She said it as casually as she could, which was, of course, very intensely.

I didn't tell her I'd been trying and failing to make an appointment for weeks. I just couldn't quite find the time or the energy or something. I got as far as being told about a talk therapy waitlist. Someone emailed me something about fresh air, moving my body, eating more vegetables, and getting more sleep.

"OK, Mum," I said. "I will."

She nodded, and we carried on walking, passing the paper cup silently between us.

"Mum," I said. I don't know what possessed me to do it, even now I don't know what it was about that moment that compelled me to open my mouth and say something.

"Yes," she said, distracted, watching a Labrador bounding around ahead of us.

"I'm not, I'm um . . . in the past few weeks I've been . . . it's been a really eye-opening . . ."

I took a deep breath and tried not to look directly at my mum, who I knew would be fully panicking.

"I'm gay," I said to the sea. "Or queer or . . . something. I'm not straight."

"Oh," my mum said.

We were both quiet for a moment. My mum passed the coffee cup back to me.

"Have the last sip," she said.

"Thanks."

We walked for a while longer. I realized I had never said the words "I'm gay" out loud before.

"I thought you were just depressed," Mum said.

"I'm both," I said. "Equally."

"Equally gay and depressed?"

"Yes."

She nodded, taking it all in.

"Right. Well, if you're happy, I'm happy."

I laughed.

"You know what I mean," she said, nudging me in the side, a rare moment of playfulness. I put my arm around her shoulder and kissed her on the top of her head.

"This was a lovely idea, Issy," Mum said, looping her arm through mine. "A nice change."

"It is a nice change," I said. "I should tell you I'm gay on the beach more often."

The rest of the day was exactly the same as it always was.

47A Girlies!! <3

Alyssa: *Happy Christmas, babes! Hope you're all having a stunning time. My auntie has brought round this prosecco with glitter in it and it's disgusting but we've all had loads of it and now my mum's annoyed that we're all gonna be too pissed to enjoy dinner. ANYWAY love you!!!! xx*

Mo: *Happy Christmas, girlies. Wish I was getting on that glitter prosecco. Our neighbors have invited us all round for Christmas dinner which is so nice bless them but it means my mum has been cooking for about a week. These poor people do not know what's about to hit them.*

Robin: *Wow god bless us every one, especially you Mo. I have just volunteered as tribute to take the dogs out to get some fresh air (secret ciggie) loads of love to you all*

Issy: *Happy Christmas 47A. My mum bought me some eye cream because I "look very tired"—great stuff!*

Alyssa: *You do to be fair, hun xxx*

Robin: *To be fair*

Mo: *To be fair to Issy's mum, hun*

Alyssa: *You guys are annoying*

Alyssa: *Even on Christmas*

Robin: <3 <3 <3

Mo: <3 <3 <3

Mum and I watched hours of mind-numbing Christmas TV and I ate my way through most of a box of chocolates given to us by our next-door neighbor, Mira. Mum was quite annoyed that I broke into the chocolates because they've been passing that same box back and forth for birthdays, Christmases, watering each other's plants, for a long time. Mum tutted.

"No, it's fine, I'll just have to buy another box now."

"Merry Christmas," I said through a mouth full of praline.

She rolled her eyes and held out her hand.

"Give us one, then," she said, "before Pete comes round tomorrow and hoovers them all up."

I waited until I got into bed to open the brown paper envelope from Aubrey, packed carefully in my backpack between the pages of a book so that it didn't crease.

It was a handmade card on thick white paper, and on the front was a perfect pencil sketch of Abigail, sitting up, her arms reaching out, looking at something off in the distance, just off the page. It was signed with initials: *AK*.

Bailey,

God knows you have enough pictures of that chinchilla, but you really seem to like them, so I thought I'd add to your collection.

I know you think I'm a Scrooge but I'm about to say something nice here. Strap in, here we go:

You've done a great job these past few months. Keep it up.

And Merry Christmas.

Your boss, Aubrey

I read and reread the card. And then I propped it up on my bedside table so that it looked like Aubrey's Abigail was looking directly at me.

I switched out the light, my phone clutched to my chest. My eyes still wide open.

Issy: *Thank you for the card, you really captured her—should I be concerned you're about to start the Abigail Project 2.0?*

Issy: *Ps. Merry Christmas*

Aubrey: *You're welcome, and no need to be concerned, you've got the chinchilla market cornered*

Aubrey: *Thanks for my card too it's really . . . oh wait*

Issy: *Hahaha sorry, I didn't know we were doing cards. Plus this was an apology card wasn't it really?*

Aubrey: *And now you should apologize—for not getting me a card*

Issy: *Fuck*

Aubrey: *Get going*

Issy: *You'll get your card*

Issy: *When you least expect it*

Issy: *That wasn't meant to sound so threatening*

Aubrey: *Terrifying*

Aubrey: *Looking forward to it*

CHAPTER SEVENTEEN

I spent New Year's Eve as usual with Mum and Uncle Pete. Auntie Jan was going to her sister's house, and Pete said he couldn't think of a worse start to the year, so she'd gone in a huff without him, which was exactly what he'd hoped she'd do.

We played card games and ate small versions of normal food that we bought frozen and heated up in the oven. We watched Jools Holland on television, and at midnight, just before he left to face the wrath of Auntie Jan, Uncle Pete asked if we had any New Year's resolutions.

"I'll start," he said, popping one final mini sausage roll in his mouth and clapping his hands together so the crumbs went all over the carpet. "I want to finally get an air fryer. And one of those blenders. I want to make smoothies every morning."

"That's not a resolution," Mum said. She was right on the edge of her seat, itching to get the hoover to deal with the pastry all over her floor.

"'Course it is," Uncle Pete said. "What would you call it, then?"

"A shopping list," Mum said. "A resolution is about yourself, as a person. It's about self-improvement or your goals and aspirations."

Uncle Pete rolled his eyes at me. I ignored him, not wanting to wind her up more.

"What about you, Isobel?" Mum said.

"Same," I said. "I just want to make more smoothies."

"And keep on looking after yourself," Mum said, completely missing my sarcasm.

"Oh, no," I said, "I'm hoping to take much worse care of myself next year."

"Issy," she said.

"Mum," I said.

"Right," Uncle Pete said. "I'm off. Happy New Year, my darlings, I've got a good feeling about this one."

Just before Mum and I went to bed, Abigail came out of her shoebox. We watched her for a little while, pottering about slowly, drinking her water.

"She looks tiny," Mum said. "She wasn't always this tiny, was she?"

"She's getting old," I said, parroting the vet, even though I still didn't really believe it was true that enough time could have passed for Abigail to become old.

"I suppose she is," Mum said.

We both carried on watching in silence as Abigail took herself back to bed, ignoring the popcorn we'd left out for her.

"I've been thinking that maybe she should stay here, Iz?" Mum said quietly. "To save her another long journey. To save you from ..."

I was grateful she didn't finish that sentence. We let it hang in the air for a moment.

"And it would give you more of an excuse to visit us too," Mum said. "You'll come and see her all the time, won't you?"

"No," I said, before she had even finished speaking. "Abigail lives with me."

"I know she does, love. It's just ..."

"Mum," I said. I tried to keep my voice steady, to not betray the panic, the flood of fear rising in my chest because the idea of being without her was impossible. Abigail was the thing I could not leave behind.

"She needs me," I said.

Eventually, Mum nodded.

"OK," she said. "OK."

We both stared at the cage again, quiet and still.

I was the first one back at the house in London. The others weren't due home for a few more days, but Uncle Pete was going away on January 3 to get some winter sun, so if I wanted a lift, I had to go early on the Friday morning even though there was no work until Tuesday. I didn't mind. Margate felt strange and claustrophobic, and although I knew I'd be alone in London, that felt better somehow. I thought I might be able to relax.

However, once Uncle Pete had left, promising to bring me back a souvenir from Tenerife despite my protests, I immediately knew I had been wrong—I did not magically relax. Perhaps it was not Margate that was strange and claustrophobic after all.

I put Abigail's cage down carefully on top of the kitchen table and walked over to the window to let some air in even though it was freezing cold—the air inside was stale or there wasn't enough of it. That's when I saw Aubrey's sister's bike chained to the lamp-post outside, and without even making the decision to do it, I was out of the front door again.

A man opened Aubrey's front door. He had a big, bushy beard and was wearing flip-flops. He looked at me expectantly, and I realized I was meant to say something. Knocking on people's doors is just not very "done," is it?

"Um," I said, "I'm so sorry to bother you, but I just wondered if Aubrey was in?"

"Aubrey?" the man yelled up the stairs; he had a Scottish accent too. I wondered if this was Aubrey's Scottish flip-flop-wearing boyfriend that she'd just failed to mention. My heart sank, it was a reminder that I knew basically nothing about her life.

"She'll be down in a minute," the man said.

I heard thundering down the stairs, and Aubrey appeared at the door. She was wearing gray joggers and a white cable-knit jumper; she had her hair pulled back and her glasses on, and she looked a little bit like she'd just got out of bed. She rolled her sleeves up, folded her arms, and leaned against the doorframe, effortlessly cool despite being caught off guard.

"You moving in, Bailey?"

She nodded at the massive backpack I realized I still had on my back.

"Um," I said, "yes. Is that all right with you?"

"Yep," she said. "I'm sure my brother will be fine with it."

"Oh, is that your brother, then?" I said.

"No, no," she said, deadpan, "my husband."

I hesitated for the briefest moment, but she was already rolling her eyes at me. She could never let me get away with anything.

"Right," I said. "No. Obviously not your husband."

"So other than moving in with me and my brother-husband, what can I do for you?" Aubrey said.

"Well I just got home . . ."

I gestured next door, to my own house.

"And I saw your bike chained up outside, and I sort of . . . I wondered if you wanted to get a drink with me?"

Oh god, this was it. I had gone Full Mad.

Aubrey raised her eyebrows.

"Or not," I said. "No, not. Not a drink. I don't know what possessed me to . . . I literally just got back so . . ."

"Right," Aubrey said, "I'll meet you at the pub at the top of the road in fifteen minutes. Let me change out of my goblin-mode clothes."

"I like them," I said. "I think you look lovely."

Lovely! Oh my god.

"All right. Calm down, Bailey," Aubrey said, starting to close the door in my face. "Or I'll have to report you to HR."

"No, I just . . ."

Too late, she was gone. I ran back to mine, dropped off my backpack in the hallway and didn't think about the empty house. I didn't think about Abigail, or my mum, miles away. I ran upstairs to comb my eyebrows Alyssa-style and headed straight back out of the door.

"So how was your mad Christmas with hundreds of people?" I said.

We were sitting in the corner of the pub on a sofa next to a dwindling fire. I was acutely aware that the last time I'd seen her, we had been standing alone in a dark hallway, the air crackling between us. But it didn't feel strange, it felt natural to be sitting at opposite ends of a sofa, sipping pints.

"Yeah," Aubrey said, "pretty decent actually. My auntie brought Yia-Yia over from Greece, which was nice even though she basically couldn't hear or see anything. She still managed to put away a lot of wine. Brave soldier. Got given loads of socks, loads of chocolate oranges."

I smiled.

"What?" she said.

"Nothing," I said, "just, same. I mean, present-wise, not drunk Yia-Yia-wise."

"Count yourself lucky," Aubrey said.

"I don't know," I said, "she sounds fun."

"What did you do for New Year's?" Aubrey asked. She picked up a beer mat and flipped it, maintaining eye contact with me the whole time.

"Let me see," I said. "Well, it was a pretty mental one."

"Sure," Aubrey said. "Can you even remember any of it?"

"I'm pretty sure at one point I was playing charades with my uncle Pete, and it's hazy but . . . my mum put some mini pizzas in the oven and burned them at around eight p.m. That was a real talking point."

"Whoa," Aubrey said. "I just can't handle nights like that anymore. Getting too old."

"How about you?" I said. "Same kind of thing?"

"Almost, to be honest," she said. "I went to a friend's house party, played board games, held a baby."

"Huh," I said.

"What?"

"It's hard to imagine."

"Me having friends? Holding a baby?"

"I mean, sort of."

Someone else might have been offended, but Aubrey snorted with laughter.

"I'm very good with babies," Aubrey said, "they always stop crying for me."

"It's because you're terrifying," I said.

"Maybe," Aubrey said. She took a sip of her beer and picked up the poker to mess about with the fire.

"You don't think I'm terrifying, do you? Not still, I mean?"

She said it to the fire, the embers flying, rather than to me.

"Kind of," I said. "I like it though, or I'm getting used to it."

She nodded.

"I've been told that before," she said. "I think it just takes me a while to warm up, that's all. I don't actually mean to frighten people, believe it or not."

"Mmm," I said, not believing her for a second, "of course not."

She turned to me then, still holding the poker.

"And I have a rule that I don't get too close to colleagues, I like to keep things professional, you know? Otherwise it can get complicated."

"Has it got complicated before?" I said.

Aubrey cocked her head to one side as if she was trying to weigh what to tell me.

"So Olivia," she said, "one half of the evil twins."

Even as she said it, she couldn't stop a little smile spreading on her face. She lived to wind me up. I rolled my eyes.

"She's not evil," I said.

"Well," Aubrey said, ignoring me, "we started working for Elizabeth around the same time, and we became super close."

I made a face.

"I know," Aubrey said, "she used to be really cool, like properly sweet and shy and nerdy. Although she had this amazing cutting streak in her. You could see the fire, you know? She used to work on all these weird little projects and animations and stuff just for fun. Elizabeth hired her straight out of art college, where she'd had a shitty few years . . ."

Aubrey stopped suddenly, changing her mind about telling me whatever had happened to Olivia.

"So anyway, we did everything together, we'd both moved to London at the same time. We were even planning to live together at one point. We were inseparable basically. It was this really intense friendship, codependent even, now that I look back at it. It was unsustainable."

She took a deep breath.

"Then I got promoted a year later and things just got complicated between us, and our friendship just broke down in this way that I don't think either of us expected. She's genuinely not a bad person or anything, but it's a really competitive business and we are all trying our best, and I haven't been an angel by any means . . . I've changed, she's changed."

I sipped my drink and listened. I'd never heard her speak so openly before.

"So, I suppose," she said, "I've just become very wary of getting too close to anyone at work, because having to see someone every day. That's rough. It's easier to maintain a professional distance, you know?"

"Pleasant robot," I said, nodding.

"What?"

"Nothing. I'm sorry, I had no idea any of that happened."

"Why would you?" Aubrey said. "Listen, it's fine. It's just . . . sometimes I feel like everyone thinks I'm this rude monster and sure, I can be a bit . . ."

She said "Abrupt" just as I was saying "Mean."

She laughed.

"Is this a professional distance?" I asked.

We both looked at the space between us on the sofa, the cracked leather and our knees nearly touching.

"It'll do," Aubrey said. "Plus you're my next-door neighbor. I don't have a rule for that. This is unfamiliar territory."

She lifted her drink, and I did the same, tapping the edge of my glass to hers.

"I like your watch; I was admiring it recently," I said, nodding toward the gold face on her wrist. "Although, no offense, it doesn't seem very you. It doesn't fit with your whole . . . vibe."

Aubrey looked down at the watch, like she was seeing it for the first time.

"It was my sister's watch," she said, after a moment.

"Ah," I said, "bike sister? Dog-in-a-basket sister?"

"That's the one," she said. She put her glass back down on the table and then spoke at it, instead of me. "Issy, you know I told you that I thought the point of Christmas was just getting through it?"

"Yes," I said. "I remember."

"So my sister, whose stupid girly bike I've been riding and whose ugly watch this is, she died a couple of years ago."

"Oh shit," I said. "Oh no, Aubrey, I'm so sorry."

"No it's OK," she said, "it's not your fault. Wait—is it your fault?"

I laughed. I couldn't believe she was telling me about her dead sister and making me laugh.

"I don't think so," I said. "To the best of my knowledge, no."

"Then that's fine," Aubrey said, "no need to apologize."

"That's fucking awful though, Aubrey. Awful."

"Yeah," she said. "It is fucking awful to be honest. But at least I got this disgusting watch out of it."

She smiled at me, and I smiled back because that's what she needed me to do. I didn't ask any questions; I didn't want her to clam up. I liked her with her guard down. Instead, I edged closer to her on the sofa and put my hand on her shoulder briefly.

"HR, Bailey," she said, "I was serious about reporting you."

"Right," I said, removing my hand. I stayed where I was though, and she stayed too, and we sat like that for a long time.

Being home alone with Abigail for the next couple of days wasn't as bad as I had initially feared. The air in the house was not stale. There was enough of it. I went for walks and watched TV and ate toast almost exclusively. I slept a lot.

It was almost as if my time with Aubrey sustained me. Just enough social interaction to keep me going but not overwhelm me. I eked it out until the others got home.

Alyssa was first, slamming the door behind her and yelling, "Honey, I'm home!"

She thundered upstairs and found me lying on my back on the uncomfortable living room sofa. I was half watching *The Great British Bake Off* Christmas special and half crocheting a tiny Abigail; it was easy, repetitive, I could do it with my eyes closed. I had done it a thousand times, but not as much since I'd moved to London. The Abigails were smaller and fewer and further in between. I used to make things to feel better, or to express something unsayable but these days, I wasn't feeling very much at all. I didn't know what I wanted to say. I made the Abigails like a ritual, without thought, a muscle memory. A piece of me I was trying to keep going.

"Babe! I missed you!" Alyssa threw herself at me, and the half-formed Abigail became squished between us.

"I missed you too," I said, squeezing her back tightly.

"What's the goss?" she said. Alyssa asked "What's the goss?" like other people asked "How are you?"

"No goss," I said, lying through my teeth. I knew that me going for a drink with Aubrey was the kind of scandal she lived for.

"Oh," she said, disappointed. "Me neither. I feel like I've been released from food prison, I swear my mum just sat me down and fed me for a week. I've literally brought back a suitcase full of chocolate."

Mo was next; his mum had sent him home with a Tupperware of samosas and a Tupperware overflowing with vegetable biryani for us, which he'd eaten half of on the train home.

"It's a long journey," he said. "God"—he sat next to me on the sofa and stuck his feet up on the coffee table—"it feels good to be home to this crap, freezing house."

"Goss?" I said, speaking for Alyssa, who had her mouth full of samosa.

She nodded at me approvingly.

"Went for a walk with the ex-boyfriend and his dog yesterday, didn't I? They were home for Christmas too."

"Oh god," I said. "What happened?"

"No, nothing happened, that's the thing. I mean, don't get me wrong, for like ten minutes walking along with him and Sprout I was like *Oh god, this could have been my life*. But then, I was like, maybe I don't want that to be my life. Like, that dog looks cute, but is actually really annoying? I miss him but I don't know." He shrugged. "I feel OK."

I leaned my head on his shoulder.

"I'm glad you're here with us," I said, "it's where you're meant to be."

"No, shut up," Mo said, kissing me on the top of my head. "Eat a samosa for god's sake."

Robin got home later that evening with loads of luggage and a huge smile on her face. She'd been skiing since before New Year and looked all healthy and happy despite her insisting that at this point her "organs were pickled by Jägermeister."

She came into the living room with a burst of cold air and a glow about her, kissed us all on the cheek, and handed us each a chocolate Santa wrapped in foil that she'd brought back from Austria.

"How was skiing?" Mo said. "I've never been. I'd be rubbish."

"I once went on a school trip," Alyssa said. "Terrifying. It's unnatural."

"Fun!" Robin said. "I mean I've been going since I was born basically."

"Of course you have," Alyssa said.

"I know," Robin said, "I'm awful. But it was good, to answer your question. I kind of . . . I kind of met someone."

"Oooh," Mo said, "details, please!"

"Yes," I said, resolutely ignoring Alyssa's eyes burning into me. "Details!"

"Well," Robin said, "her name's Kate and she's a ski instructor, she was out there doing a season, but she's from London originally, and she'll be home soon. I don't know . . ." She had a big smile on her face. "It's early days. We'll see."

We sat and watched some more Christmas TV for a while,

an Agatha Christie whodunnit, one about dogs left in a shelter at Christmas that made us all cry until eventually we could handle no more. We watched a program where an elderly white man talked slowly about the great walks of Britain.

"That's what I want to do," Alyssa said.

"What?" Mo said, "walk up and down Britain?"

"Not *Britain*, but I was reading about walking the route of the Victoria line."

"Not reading," Mo said.

"I read it on TikTok," Alyssa said, "there were captions."

"We should," Robin said, "that would be so fun, we can do it together."

"Where did this *we* come from?" Mo said.

"Yeah!" Alyssa said. "OK, perfect, we're doing it. I think it'll only take like minimum ten hours."

"Maximum ten hours," I said. "You mean maximum, right?"

"Sure," she said.

One by one we sloped off to bed. It felt good having the house full again—it had been brought back to life. On my way upstairs, I heard Alyssa and Robin talking in the kitchen.

"I don't know what's happened to me," Robin said. "But I've just never felt like this before; she's changed me. It was like *bam*."

"Love at first sight," Alyssa said.

"Exactly," Robin said. "I never thought it existed until now."

I expected it to hurt, and it did a little but not a lot—a manageable pain. My beginner's heartbreak had healed for the most part. As much, I guessed, as it ever does.

CHAPTER EIGHTEEN

January, usually the longest month of the year, flew by. It felt like I didn't have a moment to myself. I was always rushing onto the next thing. It seemed that way for everyone at 47A, like we'd all hit the New Year with a running start. We were never in the house at the same time. Instead, we left each other notes saying whether people could or couldn't eat things and communicated entirely via the WhatsApp chat.

47A Girlies!! <3

Mo: *Hi girlies, as you know, my 41st (!!) birthday is coming up soon (Valentine's Day) which is mad because I only look 25. I want to do a big dinner at the house for all my friends and treat this like*

*my 40th because my actual 40th was spent in bed crying because
my boyfriend had left me. Oh, life!! What do you think?*

Alyssa: *Of course, hun!! Tell us what you need us to do. I'll be party
planner xx*

Issy: *This sounds perfect, do we need a cake with 41 candles?*

Alyssa: *I'll sort it I know a cake guy don't ask how xx*

Robin: *Beautiful, I'll be there—is it OK if I bring Kate?*

Elizabeth called a meeting in the first week back. The invite was
just to the core group—Aubrey, Olivia, P, and me. And Walter was
invited too, of course, his nose resting gently on the table next to
me, hopeful and longing.

Everyone had brought in their leftover Christmas goodies.
Surplus chocolate coins from stockings and unwanted Turkish
delight. I stroked Walter's silky head, but he was transfixed, his
eyes on the prize.

"Welcome back," Elizabeth said, beaming at us. "It feels good,
doesn't it? I love the New Year. The opportunity for a new start, we
can harness all this fresh energy and turn it into something magic."

I'm not sure what fresh energy she was referring to. We all murmured something that sounded like agreement. The weather was
bleak, the sky gray and heavy with rain. It was hard to match her
enthusiasm. She was wearing tie-dyed jeans and a pink jumper
with "ho ho ho" emblazoned on it—perhaps she was still riding
high on Christmas spirit.

"I wanted to bring you all together to talk about all the exciting things coming up. I'm afraid I'm not going to be here very much—I'm traveling to Athens at the end of the week to interview an artist there who is ninety-seven years old. They live in this beautiful old building, and I'm going to stay for a couple of nights, really get a feel for the place. And then I'm going to be back and forth to Paris for a few weeks."

I noticed Olivia and P glance at each other.

"So, Olivia and P," Elizabeth continued, "speaking of traveling, I'd love you to . . ."

They both sat up straighter, their eyes wide.

"Head to Grimsby to get some footage of this incredible street art project."

To be fair to them both, they did an incredible job of masking their disappointment with enthusiasm for Grimsby.

"Aubrey and Issy, am I right in thinking we're only filming two more sessions with Outside the Lines?"

"Yep," Aubrey said, "two more and then obviously the friends-and-family exhibition, which will be featured in our summer special."

"How is that possible?" Elizabeth said. "It's flown by. And is everyone having fun?"

I loved that she asked that instead of "Is everyone making progress?"

"The most fun," I said, "even Aubrey."

Elizabeth threw her head back and laughed.

"Is that true, Aubrey?"

"Absolutely, categorically not," she said. She shook her head at me, unable to disguise her smile.

"And the friends-and-family exhibition will be at the end of May?" Elizabeth said.

"Yes," Aubrey said.

"And that's when we'll have Issy make a speech," Elizabeth said.

"Yes," Aubrey confirmed.

"No," I said, and then so as not to appear ungrateful, "no, thank you."

"Oh, you must," Elizabeth said, "I can tell you'll be a great public speaker and we all want to hear from you."

I looked across the table, and Olivia was glowering at me. I wondered if she hated me now as much as she hated Aubrey. Could she sense somehow that Aubrey told me about what had happened? It felt like if anyone could read minds, Olivia could.

Elizabeth moved on from talking about the show to talking about an opportunity she had in Paris or was it Prague or Porto? I couldn't concentrate because I was too busy panicking about potentially making a speech in five months' time.

I knew, in my guts, in the deepest, darkest part of my soul, that it absolutely was not going to happen.

We met Outside the Lines for our penultimate filming session in the middle of the month. The loft was bitterly cold because the heating was broken and we shivered our way through the day. Christmas had been a rough one for a few of the group members, I had gathered, but I was delighted to find out that they'd created a WhatsApp group (without me and Aubrey; I guess we were like teachers to them) to keep in touch with one another in between sessions. I found out by walking into the loft and William calling me over to his bench to shove his phone in my face. The group chat photo was a selfie of him, squinting into his camera, looking quite confused.

"Great stuff," I said. I was out of breath; I pulled my scarf from around my neck, sweaty and red underneath. I ducked a little, not wanting any of this to be on camera—as if anyone was interested in filming me stripping down to my sexy high-necked fleece.

My phone buzzed in my hand. My mum was ringing me again. I couldn't bring myself to speak to her. I didn't want to tell her I'd missed the GP appointment I'd finally managed to make. I didn't want to have to tell her anything at all.

I knew, I think, on a subconscious level, that if she heard my voice, she'd know.

"Nice of you to join us, Issy," Aubrey said, and I shoved my phone back in my pocket.

I was late. Again. I kept being late for some reason. However early I got up, however organized I tried to be, everything just seemed to move incredibly slowly. I put it down to a self-diagnosed vitamin D deficiency and had resolved to buy some supplements although I couldn't quite get round to doing that either.

"You're welcome," I said back.

William snorted, and Aubrey shook her head at me. She beckoned me toward her as if I was really in trouble.

"So," Aubrey said, "now that you've graced us with your presence . . ."

I did a little bow, which she ignored.

"I wanted to talk to you about the fact that I haven't heard back from anyone about coming to the final showcase event— I know it's a little while away, but I'm surprised to have heard from no one at all."

I looked at her with a blank expression.

"Issy," Aubrey said.

"One hundred percent," I said. "I'll chase them up."

We were both silent for a beat, staring each other down, waiting for the other one to break. She looked really nice; she was wearing a white T-shirt under a navy-blue sweater-vest, which looked like an Aubrey original.

Of course it was me that broke first.

"Super quick question," I said, "who am I chasing up exactly?"

"The people who you invited," Aubrey said, her eyes narrowing.

"Absolutely," I said.

"Issy."

"I'm really sorry."

"Issy! I emailed you about it weeks ago. You replied! You said you were on it." Aubrey started scrolling rapidly through her phone like she was going to provide evidence.

"I know, I know," I said. "I'm sorry, I think I got distracted by something else and I forgot completely. I'll do it right now, this second."

"Yes," Aubrey said. "Right now. And please apologize for the late notice."

"I will."

"Is there anything else you've forgotten to do?"

"Um, not that I can remember," I said, "but that's the problem, isn't it?"

I smiled weakly. Did she still find me charming? I didn't dare ask.

I don't know if it was me or if it was real, but the group session felt like it had a frenetic energy that day. Like everyone was hyper-aware that the end was nigh and they wanted to have something to show for it, even though that was categorically not the point.

"It is categorically not the point," I said to Stella, who was throwing what was set to be, at that point, *hundreds* of enormous, elaborate plant pots, like bodies with green spidery life spilling out of them.

"If it's not the point to have something to show," she said, out of breath and squinting her eyes at me, "then why are we doing an exhibit and inviting all those people to it?"

"Well," I said, "to be honest, no one's been invited yet. My bad."

"Maybe you could just keep forgetting to do it," Leah said, piping up from their position of being hunched over a canvas. Every time someone tried to look at what they were doing, they covered the edges like someone was trying to copy their answers on a school exam.

"I can't," I said, "Aubrey's too scary to ignore. But, guys, it's not like we're expecting you to have a finished product or anything, you just need to show us bits and pieces of what you've been working on, or nothing at all! Put up a sign that says, 'None of your business' for all I care."

Leah sat back from their painting.

"God," they said, "that's not a bad idea."

William was uncharacteristically quiet, concentrating on his little house, which was nearly finished. It was one of the most beautiful things I'd ever seen. Aisha was sitting next to him, drawing it, incorporating it into her comic strip.

"Meta," Stella said, walking over to have a look over her shoulder, covered in clay.

"Just all keep enjoying whatever you're doing today," I said. "That's the point; that's the whole point."

I look back now and realize I sounded quite manic. Nothing more encouraging than someone yelling in your face to *just enjoy yourself for god's sake!*

When the session was over, with a promise that we'd see one another soon, I spent the afternoon and most of the evening on the phone and fielding emails, sending invites.

"You don't have to stay all night, Bailey," Aubrey said, once she'd packed up. "It's urgent, but it's not life-and-death stuff."

"It's fine," I said, barely looking up.

Aubrey stood there for a moment watching me. I silently begged her not to say anything else, and she didn't; she just quietly left, closing the door behind her.

My brain was completely frazzled. I tried to remember if I'd eaten anything but couldn't. There was a full bottle of water in my backpack. I felt caffeinated, like I'd had one too many coffees, but I was quite sure I hadn't had any.

My phone lit up for what seemed like the thousandth time that day, and I felt something inside me snap.

"Mum," I said, when I picked up, through gritted teeth, "I've not been answering because I'm busy. I have a job. I'm at work. Don't just keep calling and calling."

"Hi, Issy," she said, somehow still not sensing my tone, "I just wanted to . . ."

"Check if I've taken my meds? Check if I've called the doctor? Check if I've read the article you sent me on plastic particles in London water or whatever it is?"

"Well, it's not plastic particles per se, and you'll be fine if you're using the water filter that I—"

"I need a break," I said, my head pounding. I barely recognized my own voice, strained and distant.

"From what?" Mum said. "From work? Do you need to come home, because I can . . ."

"From you," I said. "I need a break from you. I can't do this; I can't keep doing this."

"What are you? Issy . . . what are you talking about?"

"I can't keep placating you. I can't. I can't keep being OK for you. I can't keep telling you everything's fine because you need me to be fine. Every single thing I do worries you. Every single thing I say. Everything in the world scares you. I can't keep thinking about it, I can't. It's too much."

Silence on the end of the phone.

"It isn't everything in the world that scares me, Issy," she said. I expected her to sound upset, but she didn't, she sounded cold and far away.

"What, then?" I said. "What is it?"

"You," she said. "You scare me."

We were both quiet. I listened to her breathing. I knew she'd never hang up first.

"Is Abigail OK?" she asked eventually.

"Yes," I said. "Well, she's still . . . she's OK. We both are."

"Right," she said.

Mum didn't call me again after that. I got the peace I wanted, although it didn't feel like peace at all.

CHAPTER NINETEEN

The day had arrived when we were to complete one of the great walks of Britain—Brixton to Walthamstow Central. That's right, we were walking the Victoria line.

Despite my protests about being dragged out of bed at 7 a.m. on a Sunday morning to get to Brixton so we could start our expedition, the whole thing was actually very appealing to me. I thought there was a chance the shock of so much physical activity might jolt me out of the stupor I was in, might breathe some life back into me. The internet was always telling me I'd feel better if I just started getting some fresh air, and what air in the world is fresher than that of the streets of London?

The four of us stood outside Brixton station being fogged by incense and deafened by someone with a megaphone and a message from God as we contemplated the enormity of our mission.

"All right," Alyssa said, "everyone ready? Got your water? Your snacks? Do you think we need a buddy system? What do we do if we get lost?"

"I'd say, we just ring each other?" I said.

"Yeah," Alyssa said, "or we could buy whistles?"

"Actually," Mo said, ignoring her, "before we set off, shall we just get a quick Pret?"

An hour later we were back outside Brixton station, contemplating our mission once again. This time, we successfully set off in the direction of Stockwell, where Robin used to live and knew the best Portuguese bakery. We stopped for a pastel de nata before continuing on to Vauxhall, walking past the Royal Vauxhall Tavern, where Mo insisted he felt the spirit of Princess Diana, and then over Vauxhall Bridge toward Pimlico, where, less than an hour after we'd set off, we stopped for a coffee and a sit-down. This really set the tone for the day.

By lunchtime, we had made it only as far as Oxford Circus. We bought some sandwiches and some cans of gin and tonic and sat in a row on a bench in Soho Square. It had started to drizzle by then. We grimly pulled up the hoods on our waterproof jackets.

"Right," Alyssa said, "no offense, but this is taking much longer than I thought it would."

"It's thirteen miles," Robin said. "How long did you think that would be?"

"Shorter than this," Alyssa said. "This feels like a hundred miles, already."

"Well, we're not giving up now," Robin said. "We're halfway there. Sort of."

It did feel like a hundred miles, but that's because we were walking at the kind of pace toddlers do when they just learn to walk and because we were stopping every few minutes to look in a shop.

I actually didn't mind though. I didn't mind walking in the rain; I didn't mind my feet beginning to ache or listening to Mo moan about his blisters because he'd insisted on wearing new shoes. I didn't mind any of it. It was a welcome distraction from myself. I was being drowned out.

The second half of the day was tougher than the first because the tube stations are very far apart and there are no landmarks to see unless you count, for example, a really big Tesco or a Wetherspoons. Although, to be fair, sometimes there was also a nice tree or a patch of grass and one of us would point it out, a reminder that we were on a Great Walk of Britain!

The stretch between Highbury and Islington and then Blackhorse Road was particularly grim but we became revived as we turned onto Walthamstow High Street and made our way up toward the station. We had made it! We were athletes and champions, and when we got to the station we took photos together and hugged and cheered, and because we were in London, everyone totally ignored us apart from one woman with a ferret on a lead who told us to "get out of the fucking way, you bunch of fucking hipsters," which was more than fair.

We were actually feeling like such athletes, powered by adrenaline by that point, that we carried on walking, past the station and into the village, to a pink pub called the Nags Head. We went upstairs and collapsed onto cozy red sofas with poodles emblazoned on them. A tabby cat followed us and settled on my lap. I stroked her head absentmindedly as she waited for my pizza to arrive so she could steal it from me.

"Guys," Alyssa said, "well done. See, it wasn't that hard, was it?"

"You were the one who . . ." I started, but I didn't bother finishing because she was ignoring me, looking at her phone, already making a reel of the day for her Instagram.

"We should do more things like that," Robin said. "It's nice to do something different."

"We should run the London Marathon next," Alyssa said, looking up. "Basically the same as what we did today, isn't it?"

"Basically," Robin said. She and I looked at each other and smiled.

"So, Mo," I said, feeding vegan cheese to the cat on my lap. I had ordered a pizza alongside the others despite not feeling hungry. Well, I did feel hungry, that's the thing, but every time I tried to eat, something strange happened in my throat, like I'd kissed another dangerous strawberry woman. "Are you looking forward to your big party next week?"

"Yes and no," he said. "Yes, in that it has to happen because I've invited everyone now and bought loads of food and stuff, and no, in that I don't want to do it anymore."

"Oh no," Alyssa said, "why? We've got all those cute little cookies with your name on."

Mo sighed.

"Obviously I'm looking forward to the cute little cookies with my name on them. It's just a lot of pressure, isn't it? No one likes their own party."

I hadn't had my own party since I was in primary school, when I somehow managed to break my arm during a game of musical chairs, so I fully agreed with him, it sounded like a nightmare.

"Did you invite the ex and Sprout?" Robin said.

"No," Mo said. "I very nearly did. And it sort of felt mad not to, but, like, I'd just spend the whole party focused on him, and I want to focus on myself."

He stuffed a piece of pizza in his mouth.

"Well, I don't," he said. "But I should want to focus on myself, and the only way to do that is just to bloody do it, you know?"

"Will there be anyone there for me?" Alyssa said.

"Sure! If you're interested in a fortysomething raging homo-sexual," Mo said.

Alyssa shrugged.

"Got to be better than Jaden the creepy optician," she said.

Robin threw her head back in frustration.

"He did not want to have sex with your eyes, Alyssa!"

"He said they were beautiful, he kept staring at them!"

"That's a normal thing on a date!"

"Yeah, but not from an eye doctor, Robin. It's unprofessional."

"You were on a date!"

I tuned them out and concentrated on feeding the cat, knowing this could go on for some time.

We got an Uber all the way home because once we'd eaten and had a pint of IPA and liters and liters of water, we crashed. By the time we got to 47A, we weren't even speaking anymore, just purely concentrating on staying awake.

When the car pulled up outside the house and we all piled out, I saw that Aubrey was on the pavement, chaining up her sister's bike.

"Ugh," Alyssa said, fumbling in her bag for her keys. "Just what we need."

"Alyssa," I said, "don't, she's my . . ."

Friend was on the tip of my tongue, but was she my friend? That didn't feel quite right.

"My boss," I landed on, although that didn't feel quite right either.

"Hey," Aubrey said, looking up at us.

"Hey," we all murmured.

"Why do you all look like you're dying?"

"We just walked the Victoria line," I said.

"Why?" Aubrey said.

"Why not?" Alyssa said indignantly. "We're doing all the Great Walks of Britain."

Aubrey smiled.

"Wow," she said, "well, best of luck with that."

The others strode off up the path, but I hung around, and so did she, making no move to go home.

"Big week," Aubrey said.

"Big week," I agreed.

"Glad to see you getting prepared by exhausting yourself for no good reason."

"There was a good reason, I got to walk past like . . . three retail parks."

"Oh!" Aubrey said, "that's beautiful."

"I feel inspired."

"Forget chinchillas," Aubrey said.

We were both quiet for a moment, just looking at each other. It started to rain again, but still neither of us moved.

"Remember when you kicked that lamppost," I said.

"I do remember," Aubrey said. "Christ, that hurt so much."

"You went purple."

"I know, Bailey."

"You were so mean to me," I said. I couldn't help but smile, it felt good—this playfulness Aubrey brought to the surface.

"In my defense," Aubrey said, "you had stolen my bike."

"Oh yeah," I said, "fair enough."

"Plus," Aubrey said, "I've made it up to you a little since then, I'd say."

She leaned against the lamppost, her arms folded.

I nodded.

"You're getting there," I said.

"Issy!"

Alyssa was hanging out of the kitchen window, yelling at me.

"What?" I yelled back.

"We're gonna watch that TV show that's *Love Island* but for dogs, are you coming?"

"Yes," I said, "give me one minute!"

"Do you guys just spend all your time together?" Aubrey said.

"Pretty much," I said. "We're a little family."

I had expected Aubrey to roll her eyes or laugh, but she didn't. She said, "That's nice."

"It is nice," I said.

"Well," she said, "enjoy dog *Love Island.*"

"How could I not?"

She looked at me like she was expecting me to say something. Or like she wanted to say something. In the end she just chucked her keys up in the air, caught them again. Grinned at me.

"See you tomorrow, Bailey."

I stood in the rain and watched her walk up the path to her house like I had on that very first day.

CHAPTER TWENTY

"Issy. Are you listening to me?"

The world slipped back into focus. I forced myself out of my head and back into the room.

"Sorry," I said, "yes, of course I'm listening."

"Don't make me be a teacher," Aubrey said. "Don't make me ask you to repeat what I just said."

"No need," I said, "you were saying that you're going to take me out for lunch to thank me for all my hard work."

"What hard work?" Aubrey said. "Showing up late and gazing off into the distance?"

"OK, fine," I said. "What was it, then?"

"It was that I need you at the loft tomorrow at seven a.m. latest, ideally before that. We want everything to be perfect for the final day, and there's loads to set up. In fact . . ." She rummaged in her pockets and produced a set of keys. "Take these, in case you get there first."

I took them from her and put them in the front pocket of my backpack.

"I know," I said, "you've told me this a million times."

"I'm just trying to make sure it goes in."

"It's in," I said. "I promise."

We were sitting in the office with the doors open, even though it was still freezing cold outside, because the sky was blue for the first time in weeks and the sun was shining.

My mind was actually not with Abigail or with Mum or swimming with existential dread or even entirely blank for once. The reason I wasn't listening to Aubrey was because I was thinking about Mo's birthday dinner that evening. I had been assigned the job of "crisps," which I considered getting off lightly, given what other people had been tasked with, but I still had not actually bought any. And I had not bought Mo a birthday card, or a present. Even though I'd been thinking of doing those things every day for the past couple of weeks. I wished I could show him that, the thought.

When Aubrey went out to buy lunch, P and Olivia sidled over. They'd definitely cooled off with me ever since we'd come back from our Christmas break. Ever since Aubrey had been more friendly toward me in the office—in her own way. Ever since I'd stopped agreeing with them when they said unkind things about her. But when they approached me that afternoon, they were smiling.

"Babe," Olivia said, perching on the table in front of me. She was wearing lime-green flared trousers, which sound awful but looked great on her. "You've got to come to this party with us tonight. Everyone's going."

"Who's everyone?" I said. I already knew she didn't mean Aubrey.

"Everyone," P said emphatically. "Literally everyone. It's for Valentine's Day, Marcus throws a party every year. It's an anti-Valentine's thing, but it's like ironic."

"Anti-Valentine's but ironic?" I said. "So ... it just ... *is* for Valentine's, then?"

They looked at me blankly.

"Sorry, who's Marcus again?" I said.

They turned to each other and laughed.

"Oh my god, you're literally so funny," Olivia said. "Marcus, my best friend." I noticed that P's smile became a little stiffer. "He's an artist too. You've heard of him, you know, *Marcus*."

"Right," I said, "yes, of course. Now you say it like that I know exactly who you mean."

"So, you're coming?" P said.

"No," I said, "I can't; it's my friend Mo's birthday dinner. And I've got an early start tomorrow, as Aubrey keeps reminding me."

I didn't mean it the way it sounded. I felt bad instantly witnessing their reaction, rolling their eyes about her, like we were in on something together.

"OK, so come after the dinner," Olivia said. "It'll be so fun, and there are loads of people we want you to meet. People who you should meet, to be honest. You know, if you want to progress."

"I can't," I said firmly. "But thanks."

"I'll message you the address now," P said, "just in case."

"And, Issy," Olivia said, as she was leaving, "you're looking *so* thin."

"Oh," I said. I realized she was waiting for me to say thank you. I looked down at myself, my belt on the tightest notch.

"What's your secret?" she said, her eyes narrowed. "Go on, tell me. Keto, is it? Fasting?"

"No secret," I said, "I just keep forgetting to eat."

"Ozempic?" Olivia said. She winked. "Say no more."

I didn't know what Ozempic meant.

"Looks good on you," Olivia said.

I nodded, and when I caught a glimpse of myself in the mirror opposite, I didn't know the person who was drowning in my clothes, staring back at me.

As I was dashing out the door at the end of the day, Elizabeth called me back.

"Issy!" she said. "Sorry I've been so busy, but I just wanted to catch you and say good luck for tomorrow."

"Thank you," I said.

"Maybe we can catch up properly soon?" Elizabeth said.

"Yes," I said, "I'd like that."

I was desperately trying to get away, but Elizabeth didn't seem to sense that. She leaned against the wall and smiled at me, like she had all the time in the world.

"What are you working on at the moment?" she asked.

"Well," I said, "mostly with Outside the Lines, we've just been . . ."

"No," she said, "you. What are *you* working on? Are you still making the Abigail Project, have you moved on to something else?"

"Yep," I said. "To both. Loads going on, loads in the old . . ."

I tapped the side of my head.

Elizabeth frowned, opened her mouth as if she was about to say something else, but I stopped her.

"I'm so sorry," I said, "I'm so, so sorry, I don't mean to be rude, but I've got to go and buy some crisps."

"Right," she said.

"Bye!" I called behind me. "Sorry."

When I got home, arms laden with an excellent international crisp selection from the corner shop, there were already a few early guests in the kitchen. Some of Mo's friends from work, I gathered from the brief introductions, and someone he went to school with whose name was either John or Tom.

"Is this enough, do you think?" I said to Alyssa, who was staring into the open fridge, holding two bottles of prosecco, about to play fridge Tetris to find room for them.

She eyed what must have been ten bags of crisps that I'd thrown down on the countertop.

"We can always run out for more," she said, "and listen, hun, put them in bowls; we can't serve them in bags—we're not animals."

Mo came over to us, looking gorgeous if a little sweaty in his birthday suit. An actual birthday suit, I mean, mint green and high-waisted with a frilly white shirt tucked in.

"Sorry to be a pain," he said, "but can we put those in bowls rather than in the . . ."

"On it," Alyssa said.

"Thanks," Mo said. "We're not animals, you know?"

The kitchen filled up rapidly, so much so that people actually spilled out into the living room, which is obviously where they were meant to be in the first place. I poured myself a glass of fizz and sipped it slowly. I tried to stay in the room, to listen to the people who were introducing themselves to me, but none of it really registered. I felt like the wrong kind of magnet, repelling everyone.

I opened the window at one point to let some air into the sweaty kitchen and looked down at the street. There was Aubrey's sister's bike. I thought about what it would be like to be next door with Aubrey instead.

I thought, as I often did, about her seeing me behind the glass, and I wondered if she'd be able to see me now.

"You all right, babe?" Alyssa said. "Bit hot?"

"Yeah," I said.

"You do look tired, you know," she said, as if we were picking up a conversation we'd just been having.

"I know," I said. "I haven't really been sleeping."

Alyssa frowned, lifted her hand, and brushed a bit of my too-long hair out of my face, pressing the back of her hand to my forehead. She looked like she was about to say something, but then Mo called her over, an emergency—someone had an empty glass!—and she hurried away.

Robin arrived late, as usual. And she was with someone who I knew must have been Kate.

I waited for a pang of jealousy, but it didn't arrive. I watched with a detached interest as Robin introduced Mo to Kate, took her jacket from her, handed her a glass of prosecco, and kissed her gently. The quickest, most casual kiss. Like they did it all the time. Which, of course, they did.

Alyssa kept grabbing me and asking me to do an endless stream of jobs. There was always a coat to be put in a bedroom, a plate to be filled with food, a song to be changed. I liked it; I was happy to be told what to do, to flit around from room to room with purpose.

"Hey," Robin said, catching me on my way to the bathroom to check on the loo roll situation as per Alyssa's instructions, "can I chat to you for two minutes?"

"Of course," I said. "Have you checked with my supervisor?"

Kate popped up behind Robin before she could reply.

"Sorry to interrupt," she said, smiling, "but are you Issy?"

"Yes," I said. "That's me."

"I'm Kate," she said, "and I've heard so much about you I just had to come over and say hello. Robin showed me some of your work on Instagram, and I love it."

"That's so nice of you," I said, "thank you."

"We'll be five minutes, babe," Robin said to Kate.

She kissed her quickly, on the cheek this time, which I hoped desperately was not for my benefit, and then she followed me upstairs and out onto the roof.

We each pulled a fleece throw around our shoulders and sat down side by side. Robin tapped her fingers agitatedly on the side of her chair.

"You're not smoking?" I said.

"No," Robin said. "I'm finally quitting, which I've been meaning to do for ages. Kate hates it."

"Wow," I said. "You'll be telling me you're a vegetarian next."

"Issy," Robin said. She leaned forward, her expression suddenly so earnest that I thought she might burst into tears. "I just wanted to check we're all right."

"Yes," I said, without even thinking about it, "of course we are."

"Issy," Robin said.

"What?"

"I know we said we were just going to be friends, but, I don't know, things feel different between us since . . . everything happened."

I didn't know what to say. When I'd first met Robin, if you'd told me we'd be sitting on the rooftop alone on Valentine's Day, I would hardly have dared to believe it.

"You have to understand," I say, "that for me this is all . . . new."

I meant sleeping with people. I meant being infatuated with

someone and having them look at me that way too. But I also meant . . . everything. I was starting from scratch all the time.

"OK," Robin said, clapping her hands together as if she understood. "Yes, it's all new for you, and I didn't take that into consideration. I want to be a good friend to you, and I feel like you deserve better than the friend I've been."

"Why now?" I said. "What's making you think about this stuff?"

"I guess it's just I feel like I've been behaving in a way that isn't really me, and I really care about you, and I was so looking forward to introducing you to Kate, but it's been hanging over me, this *thing*. It's because I was careless, I think. With a lot of people, but with you it's different, and it feels like you're maybe a bit stressed or you're not doing that great, and I want you to know that—"

"I really care about you too," I said, interrupting her. I took her cold hand and squeezed it. "I like you because you're so . . . you're so yourself. You're so sure of who you are, or something. I think I was so into you and I wanted to be around you so much partly because I wanted to be that way too."

"Oh man," Robin said. She rubbed her temples. "That is just not true. That is so mad that that's how you see me. I feel like I don't know who I am at all, that's why I'm such a . . . why I've been so chaotic really."

"It has been this past few months, hasn't it?" I said. "Chaos, I mean."

Robin shook her head, not in disagreement but as if she just couldn't even find the words to articulate it.

"I'm glad we're really OK though," she said, almost like a question.

"We are," I confirmed. "More than OK. And Kate seems lovely."

"She is," Robin said emphatically, "so great. You two will really get along."

We both got up to go back downstairs, into the warm to rejoin the party. I felt a bit lighter, even though I hadn't realized any of that stuff had been weighing on me.

"Hey," Robin said, "I have to ask because I'm so intrigued." She dropped her voice to a whisper. "Is something going on with you and Aubrey?" She jerked her head in the direction of next door.

"Aubrey? Aubrey who I work with? No, no. I mean . . . no. We spend a lot of time together and stuff but . . . she's my boss."

Robin nodded slowly, an annoying smile on her face.

"Ah, the small world of lesbians in London, eh?"

"I know," I said, stepping into Robin's bedroom behind her, closing the sliding door. "As if she lives next door."

"Well, that," Robin said, "but I meant because we went on that date before Christmas."

I froze.

"We?" I said. "As in you and Aubrey?"

"Yeah!" Robin said. "The night before the Christmas sex party. Wait, I thought you knew that? I thought she would have told you that night when you were having your little chat upstairs."

She frowned, watching my reaction.

"Shit, I'm sorry I didn't . . ."

"No," I said, "no, you don't need to be sorry. Nothing's happening with Aubrey. She's just my boss; she's just my colleague."

That was true, wasn't it? I meant the words in my head, but my body was screaming something else entirely. I wanted to cry. I wanted to cry over Aubrey Kerr! No. I wanted to cry over Robin. Or I was just tired. I didn't feel well, that was all.

"OK," Robin said, "it's just you seem a bit . . . it was ages ago, and we only met up one time after that, and it never went anywhere, and then I met Kate. I don't think Aubrey was ever really into *me*, to be honest; I'm bringing it up because I got the impression that she was actually really into—"

"You don't need to explain yourself to me," I said, cutting her off. I smiled, and it felt insane, I couldn't really tell what my face was doing.

"Listen, I'm going to go downstairs and see Mo," I said. I patted her in a matey way on the top of the arm, but it was harder than I expected. I let myself out of her room and ran down the stairs, to where I'd left my phone on the kitchen counter.

"Mo," I said, interrupting his conversation with a group of people I didn't recognize, "I have to go."

"What?" he said, frowning. "But we're only just getting started, we haven't even done the cake yet."

"I'm sorry," I said, "I'm really sorry."

I couldn't stay in the house anymore with all those people. I needed to get out so I could think straight. But I didn't want to think, I didn't want to feel. I wanted my head to stop banging. I wanted to stop feeling sick. I wanted to be able to sit down and eat something and not feel like my heart was going to jump out of my throat. I wanted, I wanted, I wanted.

I walked out of the house without looking Mo in the eye, got in the back of an Uber, and messaged P.

Issy: *Changed my mind. On my way.*

Marcus's ironic anti-Valentine's party or whatever it was, was in a club not too far from the house. I don't remember the car ride there, but I do remember walking down the stairs into the basement and yelling my name at a bored-looking doorman. There were people walking around with trays of shots; I took two and knocked them back. They didn't taste of anything. I took another one.

"Issy!"

I turned around, and there was P, wearing wide-legged black trousers and a mesh top. They had black tape over their nipples.

"You came!"

They gave me a little hug, patting me on the back awkwardly.

"What made you change your mind?"

"I . . ."

I looked around the club, the room spinning slightly.

"Issy?"

"I . . . I don't know," I said.

Suddenly, I desperately didn't want to be there either. P was looking at me, frowning slightly.

"Where's Olivia?" I said. I wanted to shift their focus away from me.

"Oh," P said, pointing in the direction of a throng of people dancing. "She's been dancing all over Marcus all night. Marking her territory."

I spotted her, silver sequins, long red hair tumbling over her shoulders, arms wrapped around a tall man's neck.

"God," P said, "I feel wasted. Thank god I'm off tomorrow. Are you?"

"No," I said, "I've got—"

Someone tapped P on the shoulder before I could finish my sentence, and they turned away from me to speak to them instead. I stood there for a moment longer, the thud of bass in my chest, the vodka in my empty stomach, an ache in my bones, and then I walked away, straight back up the stairs I'd just come down.

"Hey," someone said, passing me on the stairs. They touched my arm, and I flinched.

I looked up, and the blue-haired, dimpled receptionist from the tattoo studio was there. She smiled at me like it was so easy.

"Don't I know you?" she said.

I shook my head.

"No," I said. "No. I don't think so."

I walked home in the dark. It took longer than I thought it would, and when I let myself into number 47A, the party sounded like it was pretty much over apart from a few people still laughing in the kitchen. I crept up both flights of stairs to the bathroom-bedroom and knelt on the floor next to Abigail's cage. She wasn't awake, even though this was peak Abigail time. I reached inside to stroke her, to feel for her faint heartbeat with my fingertips.

She was still there, like she always was.

CHAPTER TWENTY-ONE

I was certain that I had set my alarm clock. And I had. Of course I had.

It had been going off for over two hours when I woke up. The gentle sounds of birds chirruping and the slow synthetic dawn.

Nine a.m., thirty minutes after filming started on our final group session. Two hours after I was meant to meet Aubrey and the production team at the loft.

I grabbed my phone from my bedside table and squinted at the screen, my eyes swimming, head pounding. My tongue was stuck to the roof of my mouth. I had so many missed calls that I gave up on trying to scroll through them all. There were reams of messages from Aubrey, production, even from Elizabeth—starting off concerned in tone and then gradually getting shorter and shorter, angrier and angrier. The vibe changed from "I hope you're OK" to

"You'd better not be OK" and finally "You won't be OK once I've finished with you."

I took a deep breath and, with shaking hands, called Aubrey back, silently hoping she wouldn't pick up. Of course she did, on the first ring.

"Hi, Aubrey," I said, before she could start yelling at me, "I'm so sorry I . . . I don't know what happened but I . . ."

"Isobel." The voice coming through the phone, clear and clipped, was not Aubrey's, but it was familiar.

"Olivia?" I said. I sat up straighter in bed, pushed the duvet off me.

"Speaking," she said. "I'm afraid Aubrey can't come to the phone right now; she's filming. She's given her phone to me in case there's anything urgent that needs attending to in her absence."

I frowned, my already hazy brain trying desperately to process this information. That Olivia was there. That I was not.

"Why are you . . . are you at the loft with her?" A stupid question.

"Yes," Olivia said briskly, "when you didn't show up, she called P and me to help out, she needed all hands on deck, obviously. It's extremely stressful, a huge day for the project. Really important for the show."

She was talking to me like I was a stranger. Like someone who wasn't involved at all.

"Right," she said, "I'd better go, we've actually got a lot of work to do."

I didn't know what to say; I sat frozen, the phone held to my ear with a shaking hand. Olivia was quiet, I thought she'd hung up, and then she sighed heavily.

"Issy," she said softly, in a tone I hadn't heard her use before, "I don't know what's happened, but just get down here now, OK?"

She took a deep breath, not giving me a chance to answer.

"Listen to me," she said, "it's not the end of the world. Even if it feels like it is."

She really did hang up then.

I sat completely still for a moment, my legs dangling over the side of the bed. I wished, on a deep level, that I had not woken up, that I had slept through that day and the next day and the week and the rest of the year. That I could just keep on sleeping.

Instead of getting back into bed though, I dragged myself up. I knew what to do. One step at a time. I knew I had to wear clothes, so I put some on. I knew I had to wear shoes, so I put some on. I knew I had to drink water, so I forced myself to drink a glass. And I knew I should brush my teeth, so I did that too, trying not to gag at the taste of the toothpaste, the way it stuck to my gums.

It was like moving through deep water, slow and heavy, but I did it. I walked out of the house without checking to see who was in, without saying goodbye to whoever was pottering about in the kitchen, and headed off toward the overground station.

It was ten minutes before I noticed it was raining. I hadn't brought a jacket. Water started seeping in through the soles of my shoes.

I made it to the loft nearly an hour later. I didn't need to press the intercom because someone rushed out of the door just as I arrived, an unlit cigarette dangling from his mouth. It was a member of the production team I vaguely recognized. He must have known who I was, because he stared at me for what felt like a long time.

"Are they filming right now?" I said to him as I caught the door to go inside.

"Break," he said, lighting his cigarette. "For fifteen."

I walked slowly up the stairs, not sure what I was hoping for. Not sure, now that I was actually there, what my plan was.

I opened the door to the loft, and a few heads turned to look at me. I spotted Olivia and P huddled in a corner with William, and I thought, not for the first time that morning, that I was going to throw up. William looked up at the sound of the door closing behind me, and his face lit up; he waved enthusiastically. I hoped that P and Olivia were being kind to him.

Before I could go over, apologize to them, try to redeem myself, Aubrey appeared out of nowhere. She grabbed me and pulled me back out into the stairwell.

She dropped my arm as soon as we stopped at the top of a second flight of stairs, and when she looked at me, I could see that she was incandescent with rage. Her cheeks pink, eyes bloodshot, her hair dragged back into a messy ponytail. She looked exhausted.

"What the hell are you doing?" she said.

"I'm so sorry, Aubrey," I started, but she wasn't finished speaking yet. I wasn't actually meant to answer her question.

"This is supposed to be *your* project," she said. "These people trusted you to be here for them; this is a huge day. This is a huge fucking day. They've given up their time and been vulnerable and open and given so much of themselves, and you couldn't be bothered to even show up, and when you do show up it's over three hours late and you look like hell—where have you even been?"

"I'm sorry, I don't know what to . . ."

"I had to call Olivia and P of all fucking people, but at least they're here, at least they had their phones on, at least they're professional, serious people."

"I'm a professional person," I said. "This is just one time and I . . ."

"This is not just one time," Aubrey said. "No, it's not just one time. This is over and over. Because when you've been here, you've been absent, thinking about one fucking thing or another instead of this. You've got a huge opportunity here, and you've had it absolutely fucking *handed* to you, Bailey. Absolutely fucking *handed* to you. And I can't work out what the hell is wrong with you to be fucking it up so badly."

"I don't know what to ... Aubrey. I'm sorry you're so angry with me." My brain felt muddled, I needed to sit down, but I couldn't sit down, I was standing at the top of the stairs, I tried to focus on where I was. "Is this about Robin?"

A look of utter shock crossed her face before, horrifyingly, she burst out laughing—incredulous, awful laughter—and I knew immediately that it wasn't. And I wished I hadn't said it.

"Robin!" she said. "Jesus Christ, Issy, no it's not about Robin. I couldn't give a fuck about Robin. It's about you. Although the fact you're bringing her up even now, even in this moment, speaks absolute volumes about where your head is at. What your priorities are."

"You're my priority," I said. "I mean, no. I mean, this is my priority."

My words were getting mixed up.

"Bailey," Aubrey said, and then she frowned, like she was really seeing me properly. I looked down at myself. My too thin T-shirt and my overshirt, soaked to the skin. I was shivering. "Your priority at this point needs to be yourself."

"No," I said, "I'm fine."

"You're not fine, stop insisting you're fine, it's pissing me off. You're not fine, and I can tell you from experience that the way you're acting now is not taking you anywhere good. You should go home."

"No," I said, "I just need to dry off, I can work the rest of the day ..."

"No," Aubrey said, "we've done it. There's nothing more I need you to do today. I'll wrap it up. Go home, I mean it."

"No, Aubrey, I'm fine, I just need to . . . I want to see everyone and . . ."

"I think you need some time off," Aubrey said. "I'll speak to Elizabeth."

"But I . . . I don't know what I'll do if . . . if I'm not . . ."

"Figure it out, Bailey. You need to stop for a second and figure it out. No one is going to do that for you. I can't do that for you."

Aubrey was being kind. I knew she was being kind. She was furious with me, and she was still being kind. All I wanted, for some reason, even though she'd never done it before, was for her to put her arms around me. But she was standing far away, her arms folded. I'd ruined it. I didn't realize there had been something to ruin, but I'd ruined it nonetheless.

"Get a cab," she said. "Expense it. Tell me when you're home safe."

"Aubrey, I really want to . . ."

"I've got to go," she said. "It's a huge day."

"I know," I said to her back as she walked into the loft, the door slamming behind her. "I know."

I went home because Aubrey told me to, and by that point I had gotten used to doing whatever Aubrey told me to do. And when I got there, I resisted crawling back into bed for the second time that day.

The phone rang once before Uncle Pete answered, and when he did, I found that, actually, I couldn't speak.

"Hello?" he said. "Issy? Are you there, babe?"

I took a couple of deep breaths.

"Iz?" he said gently. "You all right, baby?"

And then I opened my mouth to say yes or no, or anything

really, but instead what escaped was a guttural wail. It sounded like it was coming from somewhere else, it didn't sound human, although by that point I didn't feel human, whatever that is.

"OK," Uncle Pete said. "I'm coming. I'll be there soon. You stay where you are, yeah? Are you somewhere safe?"

I took a ragged breath. I slumped on the side of the bed, all the fight to keep trying to be fine had left me. I had handed the baton to Uncle Pete, and it was a relief. *You keep me going now.*

"Just tell me you're going to stay where you are for the next hour or so, Iz."

"Yes," I said. My voice sounded small and far away.

"Is anyone else there with you?" Uncle Pete asked.

I could hear him scrabbling around, looking for his keys, no doubt. I could hear Auntie Jan in the background asking what was going on.

"I don't know," I said.

"OK, I'm coming. Do you want to stay on the phone with me? Or I can get your auntie to ring or your mum?"

"No," I said quickly. "No, no."

"Right, see you soon, then. I love you, OK? You're fine. It's fine. Nothing we can't sort."

I appreciated his optimism. All I wanted was for him to tell me off for being a bloody grump and to feed me a miniature Kit Kat and for it all to be sorted.

When I hung up, there was a knock on my door, and Alyssa came into my bathroom-bedroom before I could answer. She was wearing a pink fluffy dressing gown and a matching pink satin bonnet. My human comfort blanket.

"I heard you, babe," she said. "I'm at home today. I'm on the night shift later."

I didn't say anything, and Alyssa was quiet for the first time since I'd met her. She wordlessly handed me a jumper and some joggers from the clothes mountain on my bedroom floor. I was still soaking wet, but I couldn't feel it. I changed in front of her, forgetting to be self-conscious. And then, once I was in dry clothes, she lay down on top of my duvet next to me and wrapped her arms around me. She held me like that, in her pink fluffy dressing gown—my shoulders tensed up by my ears, my jaw clenched—without saying a thing, until Uncle Pete arrived to pack me up and take me home.

CHAPTER TWENTY-TWO

Mum opened the door before we could knock, before we'd even made it to the front door of the flat. She walked halfway down the corridor to meet us, and I fell into her arms like a rag doll.

"Let's get you into the bath," she said briskly, as if my problem was that I was just very grubby and needed a wash. Her hands gripped the tops of my arms until it hurt as she guided me inside.

"I don't want to have a . . ."

"Bath," Mum said again firmly. "A nice bath."

I guess I was having a bath, then.

Uncle Pete left but not before giving me a tight hug and telling me it would all be over soon. I'm pretty sure he didn't mean it in the way it sounded.

My mum walked into the bathroom and started running the taps. I watched the bathtub fill up. Just stood there and watched it. I kept expecting for my mum to leave me to it, but she didn't. She stood next to me, watching it too. Occasionally she tested the water as if she were running a bath for a baby.

I wanted to say sorry, but I didn't know how.

When she switched off the taps, the bubbles all the way to the top, threatening to spill over, she said, "OK, get in."

"Mum," I said.

"Isobel," she said.

"Are you really going to stay in here with me?"

Mum carefully closed the toilet seat and perched on the edge of it, gathering her skirt up underneath her, always so neat.

"Yes," she said. "I really am."

For the second time that day, I unselfconsciously got undressed. As I kicked my joggers off, it occurred to me for the first time since I'd left number 47A that Uncle Pete and Alyssa had packed for me while I had been in a crumpled heap on my bed. Christ knows what I'd come home with.

I glanced at my mum as I lowered myself into the bath full of what felt like lava. Her lips were pursed. I was thinner than she would have liked me to be, which is very round like a toddler. I ran my fingers over my ribs.

Mum let me lie there for a moment, under the bubbles, acclimatizing to the water for a second before she started talking.

"I was thinking we could get fish and chips for dinner," she said.

"I'm not very . . ."

"You need to eat, so I was thinking that's what we'd get," she said.

"Right."

"And that maybe we'd watch a film together."

"OK."

I felt like I'd stepped back in time, but everything was slightly off. I closed my eyes and let my head spin. My ears slipped under the water. It was six months ago, and Mum and I were planning our evening together as usual. It was twelve years ago, and Mum was supervising me in the bath.

"Isobel!"

I popped back up.

"I said, I've made an appointment with the doctor, you're going first thing. They're going to see you at eight a.m."

She paused, I could see her chewing her lip; they looked cracked and red and raw.

"Can you wait until first thing?" she asked.

We looked at each other properly for the first time since I'd arrived. *How bad is this?* is what she was asking.

"Yes," I said. "I can wait."

I didn't want to go to the doctor's, but it wasn't in my hands anymore. I had given myself over to Uncle Pete and Mum. I'd do as they said.

We sat for a while in silence. I closed my eyes and popped bubbles with my fingers. That was the only thing I could hear, and the rain against the window. When I opened my eyes, I saw that Mum had closed hers, nodding off to sleep despite sitting bolt upright on the edge of the toilet seat.

Mum jolted awake with a start when she felt my eyes on her.

"Did you fall asleep?" I said.

"Of course I didn't," she said, frowning. "Did you? Don't fall asleep in the bath, Issy, it's very dangerous. I was reading this awful study about how many women aged eighteen to twenty-five fall asleep in the bath and . . ."

"Well, I'm twenty-eight, so . . ."

"Oh, you know what I mean. I'll dig it out—let me go and get my . . ."

"Mum?"

She stopped, just as she was about to get up to retrieve her phone or her iPad to show me her folder marked: *pointless stuff to keep me awake at night* or whatever it was.

"Yes."

"I don't think Abigail is very well."

She sat back down and nodded slowly. She sighed.

"Poor Abigail," my mum said after a moment. "She's very old, sweetheart. She's just tired, I should think."

"Tired," I repeated. It sounded so minor, so fixable. She just needed to go to sleep.

"Do you think she's tired of being alive?"

My mum hesitated a moment and then nodded. "That's a good way to put it. I think she might be, Iz."

I could feel my bottom lip wobbling, and for the first time that awful day, I began to cry. Not wailing or screaming or feeling out of control. Just silent tears pouring down my cheeks. I covered my face with my hands.

Mum didn't try to comfort me, she sat with me and waited for it to be over. And when it was over, and I could breathe normally again, and the bathwater was cold, she said, "I'm glad you're home. I mean, I'm sorry you're home, but I'm glad you're home too."

And looking back, I'm glad too, because I know that in that moment in time, that cold bath with my mother by my side, was exactly where I needed to be.

We spent the evening together on opposite ends of the sofa eating chips and staring at the TV screen blaring in front of us. I have no idea what film my mum put on. I doubt she'd be able to tell you either. I had my phone switched off. My uncle Pete rang the landline, I could hear my mum whispering to him: "Tomorrow"; "a few chips"; "Abigail."

When she came back into the room, I pretended to be engrossed in whatever was happening on the television, my eyes fixed on the blank wall above. Nothing but the clock hanging, slightly wonky. I watched every second go by.

I went to bed at 8:00 p.m. My mum paused the film and got up from the sofa too, as if she was going to come with me.

"You don't need to," I said. "I'm fine."

"You're not fine," Mum said.

"Well, no," I said, "not fine. But you know, fine."

My mum stared at me for a moment, her eyes narrowed as if she had X-ray vision and was doing a quick scan of my brain.

"If you need anything," she said, post-scan, "I'm just out here. You promise you'll come and get me?"

"I promise," I said, and then finally, "I'm really sorry, Mum."

"You don't need to be sorry," she said briskly. "What have you got to be sorry for?"

"I don't know," I said. "I just am. That's how I feel. Sorry for us both."

She unpaused the television. Laughter exploded from the speakers.

"Don't waste your time thinking like that, Issy," she said, as I headed out of the living room. "I certainly don't."

"I love you, Mum," I said.

"I love you too," she said to the screen.

I closed my bedroom door and went over to Abigail's cage for the first time since I'd been home. She wasn't up even though it was nighttime. I wouldn't normally wake her, but nothing felt normal at all.

I opened the cage door and rummaged about for her, speaking softly the whole time.

"It's me.

"I'm sorry for waking you up, baby.

"It's only me.

"I'm sorry, I'm sorry, I'm sorry."

I gently picked up the shoebox that had replaced the well-chewed original chill-out zone and lifted her from her sawdust bed. I shushed her when she wriggled in my hand. I stroked her head with my forefinger.

She was very tiny by then; she had shrunk under her fur, and I ran a finger over her ribs like a xylophone. It was like holding nothing in my hands.

I sat with my back to the wall and held her to my chest, my fingers on her back, until she fell asleep. Eventually, I fell asleep too, intermittently with the kind of restlessness my mum had watching me take a bath. My dreams were vivid, and I woke near constantly. I couldn't tell what was real and what wasn't. My mum came in at one point and brought me a blanket. And then she came back again in the early hours and sat next to me in her nightie, down past her knees. When she crossed her legs, she looked tiny, like a child.

We sat there, the three of us in silence, and when the sun came up, Abigail was gone.

"Remember when you brought her home, Mum?" I whispered, placing Abigail back in her cage. It felt odd, like the wrong thing to do, but I didn't know where else to put her.

"Yes," my mum said, wiping a tear from her cheek. My mum never cried. She paced and twitched and stressed, but she didn't cry. "I said you had to be very patient with her."

"I was, I think," I said.

"You were," my mum said, "and she was very patient with you too. She was magic, wasn't she, really?"

I looked around my room. Abigail was usually everywhere, but now she was filling a bathroom-bedroom back in East London. And she was nowhere at all.

"What am I going to do without her?"

I started at the sound of my own voice. I hadn't meant to speak out loud.

"You're going to keep going," my mum said. "Like you always do."

I got dressed as the sun was coming up. I put on a pair of cargo trousers I'd bought on a whim and hadn't taken the label out of yet because I thought they made me look like a Spice Girl, and my Garfield T-shirt. These were the things Uncle Pete and Alyssa packed for me.

I went to my doctor's appointment.

Mum waited outside the GP's office for me and then bought us each a cup of tea and a slice of cake at the café across the road. We looked at these beautiful, delicious things laid out on the table as if we had no idea what they were or what to do with them.

When the person who worked there asked, after thirty minutes of us not touching a single thing, if everything was OK, we said yes, it was wonderful, thank you.

I hardly remember anything else about that day. It was windy. It was cold. When we got home, Uncle Pete was there and Abigail was gone, really gone.

Uncle Pete had wrapped her up in a towel and placed her in her shoebox, so he could take her home and bury her in his garden. He asked if I wanted to say a few words, and I said no, that I did not have any words.

When I switched my phone on, I had lots of messages I couldn't read, the words dancing across the screen. Elizabeth had tried calling me several times. I listened to a voice note from her. She sounded distant or I was distant. I couldn't tell which one of us was far away.

I couldn't make out most of it, but I remember this.

Elizabeth: *Isobel, just hold on as tightly as you can.*

CHAPTER TWENTY-THREE

For a short period of time directly after Abigail died, the grief adrenaline took over and I felt briefly cured. Sad, don't get me wrong, but cured. I was functioning, laughing; I had energy. I even thought for a moment that I might be able to move back to London, that all of this was a big fuss, a misunderstanding—I had been tired, that's all. Tired and a bit burnt out. I looked at my new meds, still sealed in their pharmacy paper bag, with suspicion. I ignored well-meaning NHS robot messages about finding a therapist. I did not need meds; I did not need to talk. I was a person who was objectively *fine*.

I was not fine, obviously.

After a few days, the adrenaline wore off and the heaviness came back tenfold. One hundredfold. It was an infinite heaviness. I could barely bring myself to open my eyes when the daylight came streaming through the thin curtains in my room. Most nights, I woke myself up crying.

I took my meds. Different from last time, with side effects that I wasn't used to. These meds made me out of time with the rest of the world. Like when the sound is half a second out of sync with the picture when you're watching a film. Almost right, but distinctively lagging behind when it counts.

I was tired all the time, but when I closed my eyes I couldn't sleep. The feeling was similar to when you've been drinking coffee all day, a kind of sweaty, superficial alertness. A hypervigilance on top of exhaustion. When I did sleep, my dreams were vivid and sinister. When Mum asked me how I slept, I pretended I'd slept well, and she pretended to believe me.

I let the battery on my phone get to 10 percent, 5 percent, 1 percent. I let it die. I didn't charge it. I couldn't bear to look at the screen or imagine the people trying to reach me through it.

When I moved my eyes around the room, the exertion made my head spin.

And then, I started to get better.

The acute pain of the adjustment period between no meds to meds, from Abigail to no Abigail, lasted for around two weeks, and after that, miraculously, I began to sleep without waking or sobbing, which was a gift not just to me but also to my mum and my neighbors. Some nights my dreams were so mundane that I didn't even remember them.

A couple of weeks after that, I began getting out of bed in the mornings as a matter of routine, opening my curtains and blinking into the light. I ate cereal, slowly and methodically, like it had been prescribed. It tasted like nothing, but I chewed and I swallowed until it was gone.

Those were two things: curtains and cereal. I was able to do them, and it felt good. Or it felt nothing. It didn't feel bad. I opened my curtains and ate my cereal, and those things didn't make me want to scream or cry or die.

So, I think we can all agree, I was really getting somewhere.

My phone stayed off. I knew people were checking up on me though because my mum would answer the landline in a normal voice and then drop it to a whisper. She never told me who it was on the phone, and I never asked. I guessed Elizabeth, I guessed Alyssa and Mo and maybe even Robin. All three of them huddled around a phone on speaker.

I let myself imagine it was Aubrey on the phone, asking about me. I hoped it was Aubrey. I didn't interrogate that hope too much. I was too busy opening my curtains and eating cereal.

I started going for walks, following the coastal path for miles and miles with no end point in mind. My mum came with me the first couple of times, and then I gently told her that I'd like some time to myself. That I wanted to leave my headphones at home and experience some raw thoughts.

"Raw thoughts?" she said. "Why do you have to make it sound so disturbing, Issy?"

"Well, it is quite disturbing up here," I said, tapping the side of my head. "More often than not."

"Oh dear," my mum said. "Well, perhaps you could try to think some nice thoughts too. Holidays or something. Winning the lottery."

Advice for anyone struggling: try to think nice thoughts.

"I will," I said. "I'll exclusively think about winning the lottery on holiday."

"Lovely," Mum said. "Have a nice time. You can buy milk on the way home."

"Yes, ma'am," I said.

She tutted, but I caught her smiling. And I smiled too.

One day, a few weeks after I came back to Margate, around the end of March, I'd just enjoyed one of my raw-thoughts walks on the beach, culminating at the Turner gallery, where I'd absentmindedly wandered around the Antony Gormley exhibition. The particular raw thought I'd been dwelling on that day was the concept of charging my phone and having some contact with someone other than my mum and Uncle Pete. I was starting to feel ready, instead of feeling numb to it. Thoughts of my other life were creeping in— pangs of yearning for my housemates, dog spotting in the park, even my bathroom-bedroom.

But when I got home, the raw thought went out of the window because for the second time in my life, I walked into my living room and Elizabeth Staggs was there. This time with Walter in tow.

I stopped still in the doorway, and she and my mum stood up. We were all quiet for a moment, and then I walked across the room and wrapped my arms around her.

"Hello, darling," she said, squeezing me tight, kissing me on the top of my head. "What are we going to do with you?"

"Nothing," I said, pulling back so I could pat Walter on his silky head. He pressed his wet nose into my hand like he always did. "I'm a lost cause, I think."

"Oh, Issy," Mum said.

"I'm joking," I said.

"How have you been?" Elizabeth asked.

"*So good*," I said.

"Right," Mum said, "I'm going to make myself scarce. Do you two need anything?"

"We've got everything," Elizabeth said. "Thank you."

Mum went into the kitchen, and Walter followed her. I heard her tell him, "I'm not going to give you a biscuit, you know."

She would of course give him a biscuit.

"Thank you for seeing me," Elizabeth said, sitting back down.

I joined her.

"Well," I said, "no offense, but I didn't know you were coming."

"I know," she said.

"But I'm happy that you're here, obviously."

And I was. I was delighted to see her. A piece of my other life sitting on my mum's sofa.

"We all miss you so much in the office," Elizabeth said.

"That's nice," I said. "I miss you too."

That wasn't really true, but if I'd have been thinking or feeling, I'm certain it would have been.

"Everyone sends their love," Elizabeth said.

"Not *everyone*." I smiled at her.

"Everyone!" Elizabeth said. "I know Olivia can be tricky, but she's not a mean person deep down."

"You know that Aubrey calls P and Olivia . . ."

"The evil twins," Elizabeth said. "I know. Well, the evil twins wanted me to give you this."

She handed me an envelope and inside was a card with my name on the front, beautiful cursive surrounded by hand-painted flowers.

Dear Issy,

We're sorry you've had such a difficult time. The office is weird
without you, when did you become the glue?
  Hope you're back soon. And we hope you feel better.

  Love from, the sexiest ones in the office, Olivia and P xxx

"That's actually lovely," I said. I turned the card back over so I
could admire it. "Please thank them for me. I'm sort of . . . off-grid
at the moment."

"Will you come back?" Elizabeth asked. "When you're ready?"

"To the grid?"

"To work, to London, to your life?"

"Maybe," I said. "I don't know."

I should have known that Elizabeth wasn't the kind of person
to try to persuade me, or placate me with meaningless platitudes.
She just sat still and fixed me with a look.

"Do you want to come back?"

"Yes," I said. "I want for none of this to have happened. I want
everything to go back to how it was."

"No," Elizabeth said. "It can be better than that. You can take
better care of yourself, and we can all take better care of each other."

She shook her head as if correcting herself.

"I can take better care of you."

Elizabeth sighed and sank back into the sofa. She took off her
glasses and wiped them on the bottom of her shirt.

"I've been very absent. I'm sorry."

"Please don't . . . ," I started to say.

"No, Issy. I am sorry. To you and to the others. But to you especially because I came here and plucked you out of your lovely life

and dropped you in the middle of the sea, this little fish, and just expected you to fend for yourself."

"Not a little fish," I said. "Big, strong fish."

Elizabeth laughed.

"I have been absent," she said again, "and it's because I've been dealing with my own things, my own . . . life."

She said *life* like it was the most loaded word in the world.

"I'm moving to Paris, did you know that?"

I shook my head. "I mean I vaguely recall you saying something beginning with P."

Elizabeth smiled. "The *P* was for Paris."

"When?" I asked.

"August this year, so still a few months. Someone I love very much lives there, and I want to take a chance on that. To let myself take a chance."

I nodded.

"That's brave," I said.

"Thank you."

"So, no more show?" I said.

"We'll do the show," Elizabeth said, "I'll just be back and forth. So, no, I suppose it won't be the same as it is."

"Are you excited?"

"Terrified," she said.

"What are you going to do with Walter?" I said. "Is he going to be un French chien?"

I could hear my mum talking to him in the kitchen, she was saying, "OK, just one more, dear."

"I don't know," Elizabeth said. "I don't know."

Elizabeth stayed for a while longer. We drank a cup of tea, I told her about my walks, my meds, my cereal, opening my curtains.

"All of that sounds familiar," Elizabeth said.

"Really?"

"Yes," she said. She didn't elaborate, and I didn't press her. "You're on the right track," she said. "Does it feel like that?"

I nodded on autopilot and then stopped. I wanted to try to do less of that.

"No," I said, "but it doesn't feel like I'm on the wrong track like it did before, I feel sort of ... neutral."

"We can work with neutral," Elizabeth said. "Neutral is a good starting point."

When Elizabeth left, she gave me a hug and told me to call her if I needed anything.

"And the second you're ready to come back," she said, "you come back. There's always a space for you with me."

"Elizabeth," I called after her, as she was walking down the hallway, I couldn't help myself. She turned. "How's Aubrey?"

Elizabeth smiled.

"She's OK," she said. "She's not the same without you."

"Picking on someone else?" I said. "Found someone else to boss around?"

"No," Elizabeth said. "I think you know she doesn't want to pick on anyone else. Don't tell her I said that."

I nodded.

"Does she ... has she ..."

"She's giving you space," Elizabeth said. "I'd say the ball's in your court, Issy."

I went straight to my room and sat on the edge of my bed. I wanted a moment to process what had just happened, but it is quite impossible to get a single moment to process anything in the flat with my mum, who immediately walked into my room without knocking.

"I meant to say," she said, clutching a brown paper parcel, "this came for you earlier."

"Thanks, Mum," I said, taking it from her and placing it down on the bed next to me. My dead phone was there. I picked it up and placed it back in the drawer. A visit from Elizabeth was more than enough contact with my other life for one day.

"Was that . . . nice?" my mum said, hovering in the doorway.

"Yes," I said. "It was. Thank you for inviting her. You were right, I needed to see her."

Mum nodded, and she looked, out of habit, into the corner of my room, expecting to see Abigail's cage there.

Instead, an indented carpet and a gaping hole.

"She's really not here anymore," Mum said quietly before she left, closing the door behind her. And I knew what she meant.

I tore open the brown paper package and out fell what I can only describe as the worst blanket I've ever seen. Lots of different-size knitted squares sewn haphazardly together. Some were the same color—pink, blue, yellow—and others changed halfway down, as whoever had made it had obviously run out of wool. I draped it over my lap.

A note pinned to the top:

Your very own 47A Original. Love you, Iz. Come home soon.
Xxx

I lifted it to my face and breathed it in, and finally I let myself properly think about them, the feelings like a flood.

CHAPTER TWENTY-FOUR

In April, I became a star.

One afternoon I was sitting on the Kings Steps looking out over the beach, eating gelato from Lulu's. It was supposedly cereal-milk flavor, which felt like a safe choice, although like pretty much all food at that time, to me it tasted of nothing. I persevered though, because I *wanted* to taste something and that, my friends, is progress.

"Excuse me?"

I looked up from diligently spooning gelato into my mouth.

There were two young people standing in front of me, both wearing brightly colored overalls and both with short brown hair cut into bobs. One of them was standing back slightly, as if they were embarrassed.

"Are you Issy?"

"Um," I said, "yes?"

"Oh my god," one of them said to the other, "it is." And then much louder this time, to another one, standing a few meters away, also in overalls: "It's her!"

And then, horrifyingly, they both giggled and ran off.

I had assumed it was a case of mistaken identity and tried not to think too much about it. Although I could have sworn there were times when I was on my aimless coastal walks or in the supermarket when people would look at me. But I put it down to paranoia and my hair looking weird.

"Issy." My Uncle Pete poked his head around my bedroom door.

I was fully dressed (joggers instead of pajama bottoms), which meant I was having a good day, and I was knitting, which meant I was having potentially even a *very* good day. I had started to wonder about whether Glazed would have me back, maybe a couple of weekend shifts, or just to cover evening private hires—the hen parties, the corporate team-bonding events.

"Yep," I said, not looking up at him.

The pattern was intricate, it required total concentration. Plus Uncle Pete had gotten in the habit of coming to pester me on the days he wasn't at work. I know that Mum asked him to check up on me, and I really did get it, but also this man, he did not stop talking.

"Have you been watching the show?" he said. "Your mum said you haven't."

I nodded, still not looking up.

"Correct."

Artistic License had been airing for three weeks by then. It was over halfway through the series, and I'd managed to avoid it completely. Despite my recent visit from Elizabeth, I had quite successfully convinced myself it wasn't happening. If I did think about it, it felt more like remembering a strange and distant dream.

Pete, uninvited, came fully into my bedroom. He sat so heavily on the edge of my bed that I bounced up a little. I was forced to put down my knitting and look at him.

"I think you should watch it, Iz," he said.

I expected him to look serious—that he was going to give me a lecture about my hard work and being proud of my achievements or something. But instead, he had a twinkle in his eye, a playful smile on his lips.

"What?" I said, kicking his leg. "Tell me what you're being so annoying about."

"You need to see it for yourself," he said, swatting my foot away like a fly. "Promise me you'll have a look at it, you can fast-forward all the boring bits."

"All the arty bits?" I said.

"Yeah," he said, not picking up on my sarcasm.

"I don't know," I said. "I don't know if I want to watch it. It's going to bring it all back. And I've been . . . you know."

Uncle Pete nodded and got up from my bed. Another bounce. He backed out of my room with his hands in the air.

"I can't make you do anything you don't want to do, Iz. I'm just saying, think about it. That's all I ask, and I shan't say another word about it."

He mimed zipping up his lips. I didn't believe him for a second.

"I'll think about it," I said.

"Good stuff," Uncle Pete said. "And listen, uh, just while we're on the subject, are you on the internet much these days?"

I narrowed my eyes.

"No," I said, "not really, why?"

"No reason," he said, his tone unnaturally light. "Just, um . . . bear in mind that other people are . . . on the internet."

"Why are you talking in code?" I said.

"Not code," he said, "not code, just something to think about. But you know, you might not need to think about it, because you might decide not to watch it. Who knows, eh?"

He left. A maddening little grin on his face.

We both knew I'd watch it.

I carried on as normal for the rest of the day, going through the careful routine I'd established without incident. My whole day was designed to minimize my opportunities to experience any emotional turbulence whatsoever. Life at that point revolved around meals, meds, walking, knitting, my mum, and online therapy with a pretty, dark-haired woman in Brighton who I spoke to for fifty minutes a week. We spoke about the sea. She seemed to get it.

I still had not switched on my now fully charged phone. I did not read books. I did not go on social media or read the news. I lived in a very carefully curated bubble.

It would take something huge to convince me to do anything to upset my microclimate.

I said good night to my mum around 9:00 p.m. I'm pretty sure she didn't suspect a thing, although I'm not sure why I was taking such great pains to keep it from her. She'd obviously been talking to Pete about it.

I took my time brushing my teeth and washing my face. Instead of chucking my clothes onto my clothes mountain on the floor as I normally would, I folded them carefully and put them in my chest of drawers. I even stood in front of my mirror and brushed my hair slowly and methodically like a 1950s housewife. It had gotten long and untamed, a shapeless mass on top of my head.

Finally, once there was nothing else to do in my one-woman show of going to bed, I sat staring blankly at the wall ahead of me, until finally, I picked up my laptop from the floor, found Elizabeth's television program, and pressed play. I turned the volume all the way down in case Mum heard me, like I was watching something illicit. I felt even more like a teenager than usual.

I actually did skip through most of the show, as Uncle Pete had suggested, shots of Elizabeth chatting to artists I hadn't heard of, walking on beaches or in forests, in galleries or schools. Our segment came last. It was surreal to see the loft on the screen, to hear Elizabeth's voice-over explaining what we were doing, to see William perched on the edge of the sofa, his hands clenched together, as he introduced himself to a producer who was sitting just out of shot behind the camera.

"Well, this is really Isobel Bailey's project—our newest recruit."

Suddenly Aubrey's face filled my screen, and a lightning bolt hit my chest. I should have been expecting it, obviously. But still, she took me by surprise.

She looked so serious, her famous resting serious face. I took in her flushed cheeks, her hair pulled up into a messy bun. I'd forgotten how soft her voice was, how it cushioned her often savage words.

Aubrey's face changed on the screen, creasing into a smile at whoever was just out of shot.

"Oh, you're right there. Did you want to talk about it?"

And I found myself smiling dumbly at the screen, remembering.

The camera panned to me, a deer caught in headlights as I shook my head vigorously at her and then looked directly at the camera, my eyes widened in total panic.

Aubrey burst out laughing, and then I burst out laughing too—we dissolved into a fit of giggles. We leaned forward, almost into each other, foreheads bumping together, before we composed ourselves. We apologized to the producer who'd asked the question. Aubrey suggested we start over. I asked for a minute to think about what I wanted to say.

And they'd kept it all in the show. It was all right there on television for everyone to see.

Why would they keep it all in?

Next they showed some more interviews with the group, some clips showing the progress of their projects. There were some messy shots of the loft covered in paint and plaster and wood. A clip of Stella taking something delicate out of the kiln and Aubrey standing close by looking terrified, her hand over her mouth. The moment when Elizabeth met the group for the first time, the way she sat with everyone and enthralled them, listened to them speak, told some of her own story that she hadn't told before.

And then a shot of me and Aubrey by the sink in the loft's kitchen. We're waiting for the kettle to boil, standing side by side, facing away from the camera, just the backs of our heads. At one point I dig my elbow into Aubrey's waist, and she pretends that it hurts. We look at each other then, our side profiles in shot, and we grin at each other.

I had no idea we were being filmed, that us making cups of tea would be of any interest to the camera crew.

Why would they keep this all in?

I switched on the second episode and did the same thing, just skipped straight to our segment. Everyone's projects had begun to take proper shape by that point. William's house was looking wonderful; his eyes were struggling though, and he kept having to go over to the window and take breaks. Stella kept yelling at him that he was going to go blind. When they panned to Leah, they had a cheeky grin on their face watching William do his careful staring into middle distance.

"I think the group is doing so well."

Oh God, my own voice. I sounded different from how I expected. My accent was more pronounced than ever. I was chatting to a producer while perching on the edge of a table, phone in hand. I'd been answering emails, I remembered. They'd caught me off guard, which is why I hadn't frozen, I was talking like a normal person.

"I'm really proud of them all; it's going exactly as I'd hoped, we're all just having so much fun."

"*Ezackly.*"

Aubrey's voice, off camera, interrupted my speaking. The camera panned out to show that she was perched next to me. I turned and rolled my eyes at her.

"Ex-act-ly."

I pronounced the whole word very slowly.

"No, I like the way you say it," Aubrey said. She looked at the producer as if they were sharing a joke, and she did it again—"*ezackly.*"

"Aubrey," I said, unable to stop the smile spreading across my face. "I'm trying to say something very important about our group. I can't concentrate with you sitting here being very rude about me."

"Sorry," she said, "get back to it. Pretend I'm not here."

"I feel like you're there every time I'm trying to say something," I said. "I feel like you're everywhere."

"You wish, Bailey," she said.

The camera lingered on us both sitting there a couple of extra beats before moving on.

I closed my laptop, a relief from the sensory overload. I couldn't face any more just yet. I tried to identify all my feelings as my therapist had been trying to get me to do, rather than simply asserting that I felt "bad."

I didn't feel bad though, although I'd expected to. Not exclusively bad anyway, although I did feel some things that I suppose were bad-adjacent: mild panic, nausea, confusion, overwhelm. I also felt some other things: excited, a bit giddy, the urge to reach out and talk to other people.

Without even really thinking about it, I took my phone out of my bedside drawer and I switched it on. My heart was pounding as I watched the screen flood with messages, missed calls, emails, so fast I couldn't even make out what they said before the next one flashed up. The main thing though, overwhelmingly, and surprisingly, were the Instagram notifications. I had been tagged in what looked like hundreds of photos. I suspected I had more than seven followers now. I clicked through to the app, half thrilled and half dreading what I was about to see.

Oh my god, I am so OBSESSED.

This is the love story we've all been waiting for!!!!!! <3 <3

These two are MEANT TO BE! when are they going to realize it?! Omg DEAD

If they don't get together in the final ep I am going to scream

Why am I watching an art show that my parents watch lololol
I have lost my mind over Aubrey and Isobel

AUBRISSY 4EVA

WE STAN AUBRISSY THEY ARE GIVING ME LIFE!!!

I let these strangers' words sink in. Although I wasn't entirely sure what they all meant, it was impossible to misunderstand *Aubrissy 4eva*. Even though it was silly, even though it made no sense, it made me smile dopily to myself.

All the new tagged photos were stills of Aubrey and me from the TV show. Our heads together, smiling at each other, looking at each other from across the loft. Moments and moments and moments that I didn't realize were happening, but now that they'd been captured, were undeniable.

I scrolled until I couldn't bear to look at my own face anymore. And then I finally opened WhatsApp for the first time in months.

There were quite literally hundreds of unread messages in the *47A Girlies!!* <3 group chat. I had to come to terms with the fact that I would simply never be able to catch up. I had to come to terms with the fact, I suppose, that I no longer had to catch up. I didn't live there anymore.

I ignored the unread chats with everybody else. I ignored the fact that I had thirty unread messages from Robin, which, at one point in the past year, would have left me weak at the knees. I kept on scrolling through my WhatsApp inbox until I got to my chat with Aubrey. My heart leaped when I saw that she'd messaged me two weeks ago. Just one time in the past couple of months.

Aubrey: *I think I'd have gone with Isobrey myself.*

Aubrey: *I really hope you're taking good care of yourself, Bailey. Elizabeth told me about Abigail, I'm sorry. But listen, you can't say you've got nothing to remember her by. Let me know if you ever want a visit from your boss. If not, I really hope we're going to see you at the final showcase for the group. Everyone's asking about you all the time. Everyone wants you there. I want you there too. If you don't want to do it for me, at least do it for our fans. We have to give the people what they want.*

Aubrey: *I hope you want to do it for me though.*

CHAPTER TWENTY-FIVE

I was wearing a suit that was far too big for me. I looked and felt like a sad clown.

I'd bought the suit—black-and-gray pinstriped—in a charity shop in Margate town center a couple of years ago. A mannequin had been wearing it in the window with a pair of shabby black Converse high-tops, and I'd stopped in the street to stare at it. I don't know what came over me when I bought it—a moment of madness, a moment of hope perhaps, a brief flash of optimism where I imagined I might one day be the kind of person who wore a suit to something. I too could be a cool and aspirational mannequin.

Well, this was the something—the occasion worthy of breaking out the suit. When I'd tried it on the day I bought it, the trousers had fit snugly over my hips, strained over my thighs. The blazer was slightly too tight on my upper arms, I couldn't reach above my head or out in front; I moved like a T. rex.

But when I put it on that morning, over the top of a plain white T-shirt, I was surprised to find that it was loose fitting. I ran my hands over my body in a way I hadn't in a long time and felt my hip bones jutting out, although I was pleased to feel they were less pronounced than when I'd arrived back home. I was growing back. I ran my fingers along my jawline, leaned forward to get a closer look in the mirror and pinched my cheeks. My baby face was gone and replaced with, what? I didn't recognize it, the sharpness. But I was growing back. I focused on that.

For the first time in months, I brushed gel through my eyebrows just like Alyssa told me to, and I studied the effect—I looked like myself and not myself at all. I felt like myself though, in the ways that mattered.

The weekend before, I'd had a visit from my housemates. The first time I'd seen them since I'd left. I met them in Margate town, outside an ice cream shop that they all wanted to go to and instead of the screaming I had expected, we all just burst into tears and then immediately into peals of laughter.

"We're back," Alyssa said, holding me tightly and refusing to let go, "all four of us, like it should be."

"How are you doing, Issy?" Robin said.

"Good," I said.

She frowned at me.

"No, like, actually OK," I said, wiping tears from my cheeks. "Happy tears!"

We decided to brave the seagulls and took our gelato down to the beach so we could sit on the sand.

Pistachio—it was rich and salty and grown-up. I let it melt over my tongue. I wanted to taste it, and I could.

The housemates were there for an emergency summit, to help me with my reentry into the world. I felt like a very depressing debutante. When I'd told them that I was going to come to London for the final Outside the Lines event, that I was going to be making a speech, they rallied around me, giving me a list of things I needed to do.

"So first things first," Alyssa said, "haircut."

"I know," I said. "It's really bad."

"It's not *that* bad," Robin said.

"Robin," Alyssa said, "don't lie to her. It doesn't help anyone. That's what we said on the train here, isn't it? We've all got to be more honest with one another about how we're feeling."

"Yeah, not about *hair* though," Mo said, but Alyssa was already standing up, dusting the sand off her white trousers.

"Let's go," she said.

I had an appointment at a tiny hairdresser in town, a red-and-turquoise shop front, just two chairs. The man cutting my hair had short dark hair, a strong Polish accent, and a piercing between his eyes. I liked him immediately.

"I'm sorry that I've brought an entourage," I whispered to him, while he was washing my hair, "do you want me to tell them to go?"

"No," he said, "I like it, we are chopping off a lot of hair, it is good to have emotional support."

I sat facing the mirror like I had the last time I'd had my hair cut and watched myself transform back into someone I recognized. Someone who could make a speech, someone who had something to say.

"Babes," Alyssa said, standing behind me where the hairdresser should have been when he'd finished; I think she'd honestly shoved him out of the way. "This is so much better. Look, you're *you* again."

And I wasn't quite yet. But I knew what she meant.

We sat in a pub for hours working on my speech. It started off earnest and then became sillier and campier and more like an Oscars acceptance speech the more wine we consumed. I couldn't remember the last time I'd laughed so hard I couldn't breathe. It felt like a dream.

Once we put the speech away, once they had decided I wasn't a delicate flower who couldn't handle any piss taking, I felt a distinct energy shift as they were obviously gearing up to say something.

"Can we talk about the elephant in the room?" Mo said.

"Which elephant would that be?" I said; I tried to keep my face serious but I was already laughing, I knew exactly what they were going to say.

"An elephant called Aubrissy," Robin said, and then we all burst out laughing.

"I know," I said. "I don't even really know what to say."

"Well," Alyssa said, "if you want my opinion, I really like her."

"Literally, what are you talking about?" I said. "You hated her!"

"I never did," Alyssa said. "I like her on the show, very no-nonsense."

"Right," I said.

"You could do a lot worse," Alyssa said.

"OK," I said. "Great. Thanks."

"Do you like her?" Robin said.

"Of course she likes her," Mo said. "You've seen the show, she's *obsessed* with her. Honestly the whole thing I was just waiting for was you to kiss."

"Mo!" I said.

"What? Me and every teenage girlie in the country watching some boring art show with their parents and having their gay awakening."

"Is she going to be there when you make your big speech?" Robin asked.

I nodded.

"I think so," I said. "I hope so."

"Well, she'd be mad to miss this," Alyssa said. She tapped my phone screen and I saw the first few words.

First, I'd like to thank my gorgeous, sexy housemates, without whom I would have terrible hair . . .

"It might need some tweaking," I said.

"No," Alyssa said. "It's perfect."

Eventually, we stumbled out of the pub and bought fish and chips and ate them sitting in a row on a wall, staring at the sunset.

"This place is beautiful," Mo said.

"It is beautiful," I said.

"You're lucky to live here," he said.

"Lucky to *stay here*," Alyssa said, before I could answer him, "for now."

I smiled. I did feel lucky. I felt lucky that I had two homes that wanted me.

We walked back to the station slowly. I wasn't ready to let them go.

"Guys," I said, as I was hugging them all goodbye, "I just want to say again how much I love my blanket you made me. I sleep with it every night."

"Isn't it so good?" Alyssa said.

"Yes," I said, "it's so good. It's perfect."

I walked home with a feeling I hadn't had in a long time, like I was walking on air. Like I was lucky, like there was hope.

—————

My mum called me from the living room, and I yelled back to tell her that I'd be there in a minute, that we wouldn't miss our train, that we still had over an hour. I checked myself over one more time in the mirror and then I sat down on the edge of my bed, popped pills from a packet, and swallowed them carefully with a glass of water. I set the notification on my phone to do the same thing at the same time the next day.

Mum and I arrived at the train station early.

We ate homemade sandwiches in amiable silence on the platform. Mum watched me closely, pretending the entire time that she was not. I let her, without calling her out on it. I finished every last bite of my sandwich. She didn't remark on it, just let the relief wash over her face, the way she always did when I finished a meal. Especially one that wasn't cereal.

"Delicious, thanks, Mum."

She silently passed me an apple. I ate that too.

The train was one that stopped at every single station on the way to London. The pace felt only slightly faster than we could have walked it; still it was relaxing to sit in the quiet coach watching the world go by, listening to the click of my mum's knitting needles.

Or, I should say, it was relaxing right up until the train stopped at some small station in the middle of nowhere. No one got on the train, no one got off. The train did not move. A few minutes passed once the train doors had closed, long enough for Mum and me to glance at each other, raise our eyebrows. A sweaty man in a shiny suit on the seats adjacent to ours said, "Oh, come on," to no one in particular.

And then, ominously, the train's engine switched off entirely.

"Ladies and gentlemen and um, other passengers," a wobbly

voice with a local accent said over the crackling loudspeaker. I'd like to think he was being inclusive, but I do think he probably meant dogs and bikes. "I'm afraid I've been stopped at a red signal. I don't know how long we're going to be here, but I'll let you know any information as and when I have it. For now, sit tight and continue to enjoy your journey with us today. I would just like to remind you that there is no on-board catering on this train, I repeat no on-board catering. OK, um, speak soon. Oh, and the Wi-Fi is broken. Thanks."

"Classic," my mum said, tutting, "absolutely typical."

I didn't know exactly when she'd last been on a train journey, but I'm pretty sure it had not been in the last decade.

"Thankfully I'd prepared for this," she said, rummaging in her handbag.

She passed me a bottle of water and a packet of Jaffa Cakes. I stared at the bag, small and square, that had been tucked neatly under her arm. This woman was Mary Poppins. Or a witch.

"Maybe don't eat them all at once, Issy," Mum said, frowning as I put one in my mouth, whole, so as to avoid getting a single crumb on my white T-shirt. "You know, just in case."

"Just in case of what?" I said, my mouth full.

Mum tutted.

"Well," she said, "I suppose just in case we're stuck…indefinitely."

I smiled and shoveled another Jaffa Cake in my mouth.

"Mum," I said, orange goo gluing my gums together, "we're about thirty minutes outside of London. Worst-case scenario we'll get off the train and they'll put us on a bus, I should think."

My mum flung her hand to her chest in horror, and I could tell immediately that I'd said the wrong thing. That she'd have preferred it if I'd agreed that we might now live in this train carriage for the rest of our lives, surviving on biscuits and mineral water alone.

"Oh god, Isobel," she said, shuddering, her face pale. "I hadn't even considered that."

Fortunately, my mum did not have to brave a rail-replacement service. But we were stuck on the tracks for long enough that while sitting completely stationary, we watched the time on our phones change to when we were supposed to arrive in London and then to when we were supposed to arrive at the loft in Hackney Wick.

We were twitchy in our seats. People started to pace up and down the carriage. Children were screaming. At one point a dog started belting up and down, barking. Everyone went a bit feral.

"Pete," my mum said, speaking so loudly into her phone she may as well have simply yelled out of the window and he would have heard her, "we're still stuck."

We were meeting Uncle Pete and Auntie Jan at the loft. They'd taken the opportunity to have a day in town, gone shopping, had afternoon tea at the Ritz, an IOU Uncle Pete had been giving Auntie Jan for every birthday and Christmas since I can remember, finally cashed in.

"Babe," I heard Uncle Pete bellowing back.

My mum tensed, she hated when he called her babe and he knew that.

"You wanna hurry up, it's starting. I've been on camera, haven't I, Jan? They've interviewed me."

I groaned.

"We can't hurry up," Mum said. "Obviously, that's why I'm calling. To tell you we're stuck."

"What?" he said.

"We're stuck on the train," she said.

"What? Listen, see you soon, yeah? Chop-chop!"

He hung up. He'd clearly been enjoying the complimentary champagne.

"I've lost him," Mum said, glaring at the phone.

There was a part of me that wondered at that point whether we might simply have to turn back home to Margate.

When the engine roared back to life and we slowly screeched out of the station in the middle of nowhere, I was flooded with a mixture of disappointment and relief.

I shoved another Jaffa Cake in my mouth.

We finally pulled into London St. Pancras station and tried unsuccessfully to speedily weave our way through a sea of commuters who somehow knew exactly where to step and when to speed up or slow down, all without looking up from their phones. It would have been quite fascinating to watch were it not so utterly infuriating.

I stopped at the end of the platform before we reached the escalators because I found myself momentarily floored by the neon pink Tracey Emin sign below the clock.

I want my time with you

My mum stood for a moment and looked at it with me; we ignored the people tutting and shoving past us. And then she grabbed my hand and pulled me along toward the escalators at breakneck speed.

"Come on, Issy," Mum said. We walked down the escalators and then she raced toward the sign that read "Underground," clutching her handbag to her side and eyeing every single person who walked past her with suspicion.

"We've come all this way, and we don't want to be any later than we already are. If we're going to do it, then let's do it."

I don't know exactly what it was that she thought she had to do, but I appreciated the sentiment. I let myself get swept up in her renewed enthusiasm. We started to shove our way through the crowd.

When we arrived at the loft, thirty minutes later, red-faced and sweating, I gave my name at the door, and we raced up the stairs. People weren't milling about looking at the art as I hoped they might be, instead they were gathered around a small stage that had been erected, standing still and silently listening to Elizabeth making a speech. Of course they were, we were so late that we'd missed the milling and the free booze and the canapés. We'd arrived just in time for the awful bit.

Elizabeth was wearing a bright yellow dress that went all the way to the floor. So long that you couldn't even see her shoes. The arms were sheer and embellished with something that I thought might have been bees. She wore glasses with bright yellow frames and her bleached-blond hair was slicked back. She looked wonderful. A light. A shining sun. What she'd always been.

"Well, isn't that perfect timing?" Elizabeth looked straight at me and smiled. Horrifyingly, absolutely nightmarishly, the people in the crowd turned to where she was looking, straining their necks to get a look at me. There must have been hundreds of them. I spotted Uncle Pete and Auntie Jan; Pete gave me a thumbs-up and a wink. They were both holding empty champagne flutes.

I could practically feel the stress hives on my chest blooming in real time.

I desperately shook my head at Elizabeth. This wasn't how it was meant to go. I hadn't had time to see any of the people from the group, or from the studio. I hadn't had a chance to pull anybody aside or ease myself in. I couldn't just go up there and speak right off the bat. I wasn't convinced that I could go up there and speak at all.

Elizabeth ignored the pleas I was trying to telepathically send to her. She just smiled even more broadly and gestured for me to come up on the stage to join her. I found that my feet were glued to the spot.

"Go on, love," Mum hissed in my ear, giving me a little shove in the back. For a tiny sparrow woman with the world's jangliest nerves, she can be surprisingly strong. I lurched forward.

"Don't keep everybody waiting any more than we already have done. Remember," she said, "this is what we came here to do."

I didn't look at her but I did force my feet to unstick and slowly made my way toward the stage. I climbed the steps with the somberness of someone walking the plank.

"Everybody," Elizabeth said, "it is my great pleasure to introduce Isobel Bailey, the inspiration behind Outside the Lines. She's the person who has thrown her time and energy and love into this group even when she didn't really have anything left to give. I adore her."

She nodded at me, firmly, her cheeks rather pink.

"And I just know that you're going to adore her too. I'm so proud that she's made it here today. Come here and let everyone get to know you, Issy."

Elizabeth moved away from the microphone, grabbed me, and hugged me tightly. I was enveloped in yellow chiffon.

"Deep breaths," she whispered in my ear. "Now, what do you think I'm going to say to you?"

I smiled, my cheek pressed into a sequin bee.

"You're going to say that I'm here because I deserve to be here," I whispered back, without hesitation.

Elizabeth kissed me on the cheek, gave me a gentle nudge forward, and then there I was, in front of a microphone and a roomful of people I'd already let down or was just about to.

I didn't dare look into the crowd, for fear of who I might see, or who I might not.

"Thank you, Elizabeth," I said. I was standing too close to the microphone, and it screeched excruciatingly loudly. The audience collectively winced. I took a step back.

"Sorry," I said, "I'm really sorry."

With shaking hands, I pulled my phone out of my pocket to begin to read my prepared speech. I had read it over and over in the past couple of days, I should have known it by heart by then. But the words on the screen were an unfamiliar blur. The person who had written them didn't feel like the same person standing onstage in that too big suit, trying not to throw up Jaffa Cakes.

I slipped my phone back into my pocket, took a deep breath, and looked up at the crowd. I locked eyes with my mum, small and alone in a crowd full of strangers from another planet. She nodded at me, and it was like something shifted inside me that I didn't even realize was there, that I didn't even realize needed shifting.

"The thing is," I said—no screeching on the PA this time, no audience wincing, "I've never actually spoken into a microphone before, so I don't know how to do it. I've never worn a suit outside of my bedroom or in front of other people. I've never stood on a stage. Not even at school."

The room was quiet. No one was heckling me or laughing at me. I dared glance down at Elizabeth; she was standing with P and Olivia, and I realized I didn't care if either of them judged me, if they said mean things or smirked. They didn't though. They both smiled at me. Olivia nodded even, like she was willing me to go on.

Aubrey wasn't with them, and I felt that absence in my chest, how much I missed her.

"Elizabeth asked me to let you get to know me," I continued, "and what a huge ask that is. I have to admit that I have been struggling with getting to know myself my whole life, but in these past few months, more than ever. So, what can I tell you? My name is Isobel Bailey; I grew up with my mum in a council flat in Margate. I still live there now. I don't know my dad. I don't miss him ever. My mum is a powerhouse; she is my mum and my dad and a force of nature."

I took a deep breath, feeling slightly lightheaded.

"I was a very anxious child," I said. "I had a teacher who once said I was prone to melancholy."

I paused and then added, "Which is, incidentally, my favorite word. It sounds so lovely, doesn't it?"

There were polite titters from the audience. I let myself glance at the crowd again and saw that people were smiling with me.

"I was a happy child too, as well as a melancholy one. It came in fits and bursts, the happiness. And it usually involved animals or my mum or making something with my hands."

I paused and swallowed. My mouth felt dry. There was a loud cough to the left hand side of the stage, and I looked down to see Alyssa holding a dangerously full glass of champagne out to me. She shook it, gesturing for me to take it, and it started to spill out over the sides.

Alyssa was wearing a gold lamé jumpsuit. She looked like a Christmas tree decoration and an angel and a very shiny safety blanket, just as she always had done. I felt a deep rush of affection for her.

"Excuse me," I said, and everybody laughed politely as I reached down to accept the glass from her. My eyes met Alyssa's and filled with tears.

"You're fine, hun," Alyssa said, "keep going, we're loving it. You look gorge."

Mo and Robin were standing next to her, and they nodded enthusiastically.

"So gorge," Mo mouthed at me and then, "down it."

Robin elbowed him in the side, rolled her eyes at me. And it was like no time had passed at all.

I took a couple of sips of my drink, let the champagne run into the crevices of my mouth, felt the bubbles in my throat.

"Sorry," I said, "my . . . my friends are down there."

I swallowed again and exhaled slowly. I couldn't cry yet. Not at being given a glass of champagne.

"So, where was I?" I went on. "I was a 'melancholy child.' OK, so I was a sad kid and then I was a depressed teenager."

I placed my hand on my chest, the fat stripped away from the past couple of months of disappearing. I was down to my skin and bones now.

"To say that I felt hopeless does not do the feeling justice."

I glanced up at my mum; she was still staring resolutely at me, stone-faced. She nodded at me again to keep going, and I did, even though I knew the next bit was going to be hard for her to hear.

"And I spent years, from the age of fifteen, at home instead of at school, alone in my room, with an anxious mother and as far as I could see, no good reason to live."

I paused and took another large gulp of my champagne. I grimaced.

"I promise it's not all this bleak," I said, and the audience guffawed with laughter this time, relieved that I'd broken the tension momentarily.

"Go on, babes," I heard Alyssa say loudly. Mo and Robin immediately shushed her.

"Things got better," I said, "with a combination of therapy and medication, of changing brain chemicals, growing up, and, to be honest, for no good reason at all because that's how it works sometimes. Sometimes the sun shining is enough, and sometimes you want to close the curtains and be in the dark anyway. It's unpredictable, you know?"

I wasn't speaking to anyone in particular, but I looked down and saw that Mo was nodding. Several people were nodding. I stood up a little straighter, my shoulders back. I opened my mouth, tried to untense my jaw.

"So when I was feeling a little bit better, I started leaving my flat. I managed to get a job even. My tiny world expanded, it allowed room for something else. And that something else was Abigail."

This is the bit of my life story I'd been saving my tears for. I didn't try to stop my bottom lip from wobbling or my voice from quivering. She deserved the tears. She deserved everything. I wanted to howl.

"It sounds very silly to say that a chinchilla saved my life," I said, a tear spilling down my cheek. I didn't wipe it away. "But I am not worried about sounding silly. I can't downplay Abigail. She was consistent and nonjudgmental, and her love was unconditional. She saved my life, and she changed it irrevocably. Abigail died this year. Abigail died, and I've spent my life trying to capture her or replicate her, find a way of making her bigger and everywhere and everything and in the end, despite all that, she's just gone. I have hundreds of Abigails. And no Abigail at all."

I took another deep breath, gathering myself. I wiped my nose on the sleeve of my blazer, and when I looked up, my mum was rummaging in her handbag for tissues. Uncle Pete and Auntie Jan had made their way over to her. Pete was crying too, but also rolling his eyes at my mum.

I knew that my wiping my nose on my suit would be the first

thing she said to me when this was over—*Were you raised in a barn, Isobel?*

"I would not be standing here in front of you all today if it wasn't for Abigail. That is a fact. I also would not be standing here without Elizabeth, who saw the Abigail Project, what was then my little bedroom in Margate filled with knitted chinchillas and painted chinchillas and sketches and whatever else you can think of, and in seeing the Abigail Project, she saw me too. And she lifted me up and dropped me somewhere else entirely. And it was up to me to sink or swim."

The door slammed at the back of the gallery, and I looked up just in time to see Aubrey grimacing at the noise she'd made. She stood right at the back, pressed up against the wall, her arms folded. She looked directly at me and then nodded, impatiently almost, for me to keep going.

Nothing had changed there, then. My heart soared. I did as I was told.

"A few weeks ago, a few days ago even, I would have said I had sunk. I neglected my family. I neglected my friends. I neglected Abigail when she needed me the most. I'll regret that for the rest of my life. I let down the Outside the Lines group, who have put in so much time and energy in sharing their phenomenal talents with us. I let down Elizabeth and the team."

I looked at Aubrey again. Her arms were still folded tightly across her chest. She was too far away for me to see her eyes. Not that I'd ever been able to read her anyway. Not that she'd ever given anything away.

"I let down Aubrey Kerr, who took me under her wing and terrified me and inspired me every day. But all of that happened because I let myself down. I did not take care of myself in the way that I deserve to be cared for."

I sighed.

"Anyone here who recognizes what I'm talking about, knows that once the little things start to slip, it is only a matter of time before you're dealing with a landslide."

I paused. I let myself look at the group, huddled together, and watched as William wiped a tear from his eye. He was wearing a suit that was too big for him too, and a bow tie that was slightly wonky. His hair, thinner than ever, was combed over his head.

"But," I continued, trying my best to keep my voice steady, "now I don't see it that way. I did not sink. I might once have felt like I was sinking, but I have always, always been swimming. And I am still swimming now. And that's what the group is about. It's about doing something that brings joy in a world where some of us are expending every single iota of energy we have on trying to get through that day.

"When putting one foot in front of the other can feel impossible, it is a miracle to create something outside of your body, outside of your mind, that can not only spark joy in yourself but in others too. I am in awe of my group. I am indebted to you. I am forever grateful to have met you and for this experience. I don't really know what my life will look like after today. But then, whoever really knows what their life will look like?"

I swallowed hard, and then I really did down the rest of the glass of warm champagne. I heard Mo say, "Go on, girl."

"But I hope that I know one thing for sure about my future. I hope that I'm able to continue the group in whatever form that might take, if you'll have me. We can invite more people, make art together, and talk and laugh and cry and keep on going and going and going."

I didn't dare look at Elizabeth. I hadn't run this past her yet. I concentrated on finishing up, on getting through this last bit.

"Thank you all for being here today to appreciate everyone's work. They deserve everything. All the love and attention and praise and happiness. They're the reason that we're here today, but thank you for listening to me going on about myself. I've taken up more than enough of your time. If you have any questions, you'll find me with my mum, who will be telling me off for having no manners and trying to wipe my nose for me at the back of the room."

I looked up to catch my mum's eye, and she laughed. Laughed and wiped a tear from her cheek with an extra-large Kleenex. Uncle Pete put his arm around her and squeezed her tight. He said something into her ear, probably "Daft cow," and kissed her on the head.

I leaned forward to speak into the microphone one final time.

"This wasn't as bad as I thought it was going to be. Thank you for being so kind to me."

There was a brief moment of silence, and then the room erupted with applause. I could hear Alyssa, Mo, and Robin whooping and cheering, louder than everybody else. I blew them a kiss, and then I looked to the back of the room. I couldn't see Aubrey anymore. I scanned the back wall in case I'd missed her, but I knew I hadn't; I knew she was gone. It was OK. I guess she'd seen what she needed to see.

And I had said what I needed to say. It was over.

When I stepped off the stage, the crowd started chatting again, music started playing, the room came back to life.

I craned my neck, looking into the swarm of people who had surrounded Elizabeth. I had hoped to catch her eye, find a moment to talk about the grand plans for the group I'd mentioned in my speech but not yet mentioned to her. But before I got the chance, I was accosted by my housemates, a blur of arms around me, lips on my cheeks, hands ruffling my hair. A cacophony of glorious screeching.

"Babes," Alyssa said, holding my face in her hands like a baby. "That was amazing. I've literally been sobbing. All that stuff you said about your chinchilla."

"Hey," I said, "you said *chinchilla*; I think this is the first time you've retained that she wasn't a guinea pig."

"No, I don't think so," Alyssa said firmly, "that must have been someone else."

"Right," I said. "Must have been."

"That really was bloody great," Robin said. She gripped my shoulder and gave me a little shake. "This whole thing is incredible."

She gestured around the room. She was grinning from ear to ear, and as usual, it was infectious. I grinned back, grabbed her hand, and squeezed it.

"I'm really glad you're here," I said.

"I am too," she said quickly. "I wouldn't miss it."

Something passed between us, an understanding, a relief. I hugged her again, and she squeezed me back.

There was a tap on my shoulder.

"William," I said, and I hugged him tightly. He smelled so strongly of aftershave it took me aback for a moment.

"I'm in," he said.

"In what?" I said, pulling back from the hug, gratefully accepting the glass of champagne he'd got for me.

"The group," he said. "I'll come, wherever you are. We'll do it. Keep going and going."

"Oh, I'd love that," I said. "Even if it's just me and you."

"It won't be," he said. "We're all in. Now come and have a look at our work, will you? This is a friends-and-family exhibition, and you're both!"

For god's sake. I had to accept that I was simply going to cry nonstop all day.

The rest of the Outside the Lines lot were gathered by William's miniature house, and they rushed toward me, embracing me in a very uncomfortable, very lovely group hug.

"Wheeey," Stella said, slapping me on the back so hard I swear I heard a rib crack, "she's back in business!"

"I'm back in business," I said, "and I make speeches now, can you believe?"

I walked slowly around the exhibition, looking at the group's work—William's perfect house, like nothing I'd ever seen before; Leah's portraits, bold and striking and delicate all at once. Stella's work looked like she'd transported her workstation and dumped it there—a total mess and entirely her. I paused when I got to Aisha's work, pages and pages of a comic strip, unbound, just laid out.

"It's us," I said, eventually, tracing the lines of the loft on the page.

"What else would it be?" she said.

It was wonderful. It was heartwarming and uplifting and emotional and beautiful. It was the polar opposite of my life from the past few months in every possible way.

And I needed a break.

I managed to escape from a group of strangers, assuring them that I'd be right back, and slipped out the doors of the loft with my phone lifted to my ear, a trick I learned from the producers of the show.

When I reached the stairwell, instead of going downstairs and out the front of the building, where I assumed all the smokers would be gathered, I turned the other way instead, ran up one flight of stairs to the locked door at the top. I pulled a set of keys out of my pocket.

The rooftop was empty, and it was a relief. It was a beautiful evening, chilly still but bright. I walked to the edge, to stand next to the railing and look out at the view. I wanted a moment to pinch myself, to check that it was all real. To allow it to sink in rather than just waiting for it to end.

"Bailey?"

I jumped and spun around. And there she was.

Aubrey was wearing what looked like a handmade multicolored sweater vest, an Aubrey original, underneath a black blazer. She'd had a haircut, and yet it still looked as untamed as ever. Wild waves, and slightly flat from a bicycle helmet. Her signature look.

Now that I could see her dark brown eyes up close, I saw that I was right, they were still giving nothing away. She was carrying two glasses of champagne.

"I thought you'd left," I said.

"As if," she said, raising a glass of champagne at me, "open bar."

She walked toward me and handed me a glass.

"Of course," I said, "you can't waste that opportunity. Thanks."

We hesitated a moment and then tapped our glasses together, a silent toast.

Aubrey came and stood next to me, close enough that her hip brushed up against mine. She leaned over the railings to look down at the street below. It made my stomach turn, but I refused to say anything because I knew it would just mean she'd lean over even farther to make me squirm.

It was surreal to be standing next to her. Another bonkers layer to this magical night. I hadn't let myself believe that it would ever happen again.

"That was quite a speech you gave," Aubrey said.

"Thank you," I said.

"I'm sorry," she said, "about you know, your life."

I laughed at the unexpectedness of it, the candor. No one had ever put it like that before but of course Aubrey knew just how to put it.

"Thanks," I said. "If you want to make a donation to my sad cause, I'm accepting bank transfers."

"Oh, I think I've contributed enough, Bailey."

"Yeah," I said, "that's fair."

We were both quiet for a moment, watching the sky, listening to the traffic below and the faint sounds of the party inside.

"Are you going to come back to work for Elizabeth, then?" Aubrey said.

"Maybe," I said, "in some capacity. In a way that I can manage with the old . . ."

I tapped the side of my head, and Aubrey nodded.

"Right," she said. "I see."

"Why?" I said. "Are you going to miss me?"

I held my breath as soon as I'd said it. The champagne had gone straight to my head. Too many missed chances in my life. The magic of the night taking over.

Aubrey grinned. She was still looking out onto the city. She seemed surprised by my cheekiness. Or not surprised; maybe she was just remembering. This was, after all, a classic Aubrissy moment.

She took another sip of her drink and turned to face me.

"Well, the thing is, Bailey. I'm really hoping I won't get the chance to miss you."

And before I could respond, or even think about what was happening, Aubrey pulled me toward her and kissed me. Her soft lips on mine, her hand inside my jacket on my waist.

It was like an explosion in my head, and in my chest. A series of explosions. Kissing Aubrey was the key to a kind of happiness I didn't even know I had within me.

My theory about kissing was wrong. The fireworks *were* real.

Aubrey was surprisingly gentle. Even when she bit my bottom lip.

When she pulled away, she left her hand on my lower back, her thumb gently stroking my bare skin. I swear it felt as good as the kiss. I wanted her hands all over me. She was watching me, and my reaction to her, with tenderness and amusement. A typical Aubrey combination.

"You really do like me," I said.

"I really do," she said. "Isn't that obvious by now?"

"Not really," I said, and then, "sometimes."

Aubrey started fiddling with the gold hoop in my left ear, and for the first time in my life I experienced vertigo.

"Fuck," she said, shaking her head. "This is an HR nightmare."

"Shut up," I said, and I kissed her again, just quickly, a brush against her lips. It was the first time I had kissed someone, rather than someone kissing me. It felt good.

"Are you moving out permanently?" Aubrey said. "Of the house with the loudest housemates in the world?"

"Oi," I said, smiling, "those very loud people are my friends. And I don't know yet. I don't know what I'm doing, I'm just taking it one day at a time at the moment."

"Solid policy," Aubrey said.

"Oh," I said, patting my pockets, panicking for a moment, until my hand landed on it. I handed Aubrey a card in a brown paper envelope with her full name written on the front.

"What's this?" Aubrey said, turning it over in her hands.

"I told you, didn't I? That I'd give you your Christmas card as a surprise, when you least expected it."

Aubrey grinned from ear to ear.

"And I told you, didn't I," she said, "that nothing would surprise me about you, Bailey."

"Apart from this," I said. "Admit it, you'd forgotten."

Aubrey didn't say anything. She just opened the card.

On the front I had drawn a pencil sketch of the loft in Hackney Wick, the one we were standing on top of right at that moment. And in the window you could see the back of a sofa, the back of two heads, sitting at opposite ends but facing each other.

Aubrey studied it for a moment, running her finger over the lines, before she read the message inside. After a moment she closed the card, placed it back in the envelope, and slid it gently into her inside pocket.

"Yes," she said. "Yes."

She pulled me toward her and kissed me again. And the fireworks went off. And kept going and going.

Aubrey,

I wanted to tell you because what is there to lose now? I'm so happy that I met you.

When I'm with you I feel most like myself.

And a bit scared, obviously. You're the most frightening and brilliant person I've ever met.

When I think of the past year, despite everything, this is what I think of: me and you at opposite ends, and close together.

I hope that's what you think of too.

Yours,
Bailey

EPILOGUE

A day in the life of Isobel Bailey, three months later

It's unseasonably warm for September, again. Perhaps this is what September is now, thighs chafing and upper lips sweating and the park full of dog walkers at 7:00 a.m. before the sun gets too strong.

That's where I am now, the park. Walking slow laps, head up, my brain unknotting. There is nothing in my ears. My raw thoughts rattle around, some good and some not so good. I notice them all, and I keep going, round and round the park.

I stop at my favorite place to buy croissants and coffee and chat loudly to the barista over the sound of the machine grinding. I carry breakfast back with me, through the park, across the road.

Our landlord has painted the door with a fresh coat of canary yellow, and has finally, a whole year later, replaced our letterbox, but not before asking if boarding up the gaping hole in our door was "absolutely necessary."

I walk up the two flights of stairs as quietly as I can so as not to wake anyone else and gently push open the door to my bathroom-bedroom. My plan is to wake her gently, so that she might stir at the smell of coffee and look up at me through sleepy eyes, grateful and madly in love, but unfortunately, someone else has other ideas.

"Fuck," Aubrey says, waking with a start, "oh my god, Walter, piss off."

She says this in the kind of way someone else might say "Walter, good boy," and with her arms wrapped around him so that after his morning lick attack, he has no choice but to slump on top of her, his long snout buried in her neck.

Aubrey first thing in the morning is my favorite version of her. When she's still extra soft, before she wakes up properly and she slowly hardens into the grumpy old man I know and love.

I love her. I love Aubrey Kerr.

We said it the first night I moved back to London, in early August. We sat on the roof terrace and watched the sunset together, our hands intertwined, her legs resting on mine.

"Bailey?" she said.

"Yes?"

"You know you used to think I hated you?"

"Yes."

I tried to catch her eye, but she was refusing to look at me, squinting into the distance instead.

"Well," she said, "I don't."

"Yeah," I said, "I gathered that."

I squeezed her hand.

"No," she said, frustrated that I wasn't cracking her code, "I mean, I don't *hate* you, I *love* you," she said. Not to me, but to the space in front of her.

"You don't hate me, you love me?" I said.

"Yes," she said. "Bailey?"

"What?"

"Don't laugh at me."

"I'm laughing with you."

She looked at me then.

"Say it back."

She poked me on my thigh.

"Aubrey, obviously I love you. I'm obsessed with you; you're so weird. I can't get enough."

"OK," she said, smiling, she lifted my hand to her lips and kissed it gently, "good."

"Budge up," I say, wriggling out of my shorts and lifting my T-shirt over my head so that I can climb back into bed in just my pants.

"Issy," Aubrey says, "darling."

I love it when she calls me that. When she calls me that and she really wants to chastise me, but when she looks at me she can't help but smile. Like she's annoyed at how irresistible I am.

"Yes?" I say.

I slide into bed next to her, and she and Walter maneuver themselves so that Aubrey can sit up straight and take her coffee from me. She kisses me on my bare shoulder and rests her head on it.

"I don't think there's enough room in this single bed for the three of us," she says.

I look around us, frowning. I point at myself, Aubrey, and Walter, silently counting on my fingers.

"Weird," I say, "because . . . it seems like there's three of us in this bed right now . . ."

"One of us is slowly suffocating though," she says. Walter's entire weight is leaning back on her chest. She makes no effort to move him.

"All I'm saying," she continues, "is that maybe we could stay at my house a bit more."

"But it's so far away," I say. "Is it really worth walking those extra meters? Plus Walter likes it here."

"Walter likes it anywhere he can eat things and fall asleep," Aubrey says, patting his big, soft head. "He's a man of simple pleasures."

I know she's right, but I like sleeping in the bathroom-bedroom. I find it comforting. It's the only place I've ever left home for, and it's the only place I've ever desperately wanted to come back to. Plus Aubrey has no complaints about sleeping in a single bed usually. She's been known, when her defenses are down, when she's naked and sleepy and it's dark, to wrap herself around me and say things like, "I love being so close to you" and "let's never leave this bed."

If I point that out now, she'll flat out deny it.

We start eating our croissants, at which point Walter is ejected for gross misconduct (trying to eat the Marmite scroll directly out of Aubrey's mouth) although he doesn't mind too much because he can hear the others starting to stir. He's familiar with their morning routines now, he's been living at this house since I moved back in. When I shut the door on him I hear Alyssa start talking at top volume, so, her normal voice.

"Hi, baby boy, do you want a cup of tea, my sweet ang
Mo, MO, oh sorry were you asleep? I just need you to go upst..
and get Walter, he doesn't like walking down by himself."

I climb back into bed with Aubrey, and she slides down under
the covers, pulling me with her. I know I need to get up soon—
I have a big day ahead of me—but I let her anyway.

"Why are you wearing so many clothes?" Aubrey says, tugging
at my underwear.

"My pants?"

"Yes," she says. "Off."

I oblige, and Aubrey moves so she's on top of me, she kisses me
like it's the first time. Or like it could be the last time—urgent and
earnest. I love it. I've learned in the past few months all the things
sex can be other than silly—fun and intense and heated and slow
and lazy and surprising. It can be everything.

"Don't go," Aubrey says, into my upper thigh, "just stay here."

"Forever?" I say, running my fingers through her hair.

"Forever," she says.

I don't look at the clock until it's almost too late. I shower in record
quick time, throw on the shorts and T-shirt I wore to the park, and
fly out of the bathroom-bedroom door.

"Babe, you can't wear shorts later," Aubrey calls after me.

"Bring me an outfit," I call back.

"Your ball gown?"

"Yes."

"But which one?"

I find Walter in the kitchen, lying on his bed, eating a piece of
toast.

"Oh, mate," I say to Alyssa, "he's really not meant to . . ."

"Shhh," Alyssa says, shaking her head at me and frowning, "he'll get a body complex."

"It's not about his body though, it's about . . ."

I give up when she bends down and covers Walter's ears so that he can't hear me.

While I wait for him to finish his breakfast, I take my meds. I keep them on the kitchen counter, not squirreled away, secret or forgotten in my room.

Robin walks into the kitchen in her gym gear, one headphone in. She looks tired, her blond hair dark at the roots and scraped back. She puts one arm around Alyssa's shoulders and gives her a little kiss on the head by way of good morning.

"You walking to the station?" she says to me.

"Yep," I say, "if Walter can get a move on. Want to come with us?"

"I may as well," she says. "Get some sun. Get some Walter time."

I want to hurry but Walter sets the pace, and he is slow and steady, sniffing the ground in case there is anything nice he can eat, like used tissues or pieces of glass.

"You OK?" I say. I tap my head gently on Robin's shoulder and she rests hers on mine briefly.

"Oh, you know," she says, "fine."

This summer, Robin decided not to go back to drama school. She's in limbo trying to work out whether to get back into medicine or do something else entirely. For now, she's mainly going to the gym and sunbathing on the roof. Oh, and Kate broke up with her. So she's also listening to a lot of Phoebe Bridgers and crying.

"You're not fine," I say. "But that's OK, you will be."

"Yeah," Robin says, "I will be. Just have to keep going, right?"

Walter pushes his snout into her hand, and she looks like she might cry.

"He's too much," she says.

"I know," I say. "I sort of can't really believe he lives with us."

"Me neither," Robin says, "but I also can't really believe he didn't always live with us? When you next see Elizabeth, please thank her for blessing us with an angel."

"I thank her every day," I say.

Before Elizabeth moved to Paris, she asked whether I might do her a favor. Told me she knew nothing could ever replace Abigail. Told me he was really no trouble but that he needed a loving home and some stability and she thought she knew exactly the place, that the place wherever that might be, was with me. How could I have said no?

Robin jogs off in the direction of the gym when we get to the station, but not before kissing Walter on the mouth and giving me a hug.

"I can't wait for later," she says.

"Oh god," I say. "Don't. I feel sick."

"Well, I feel like a proud mummy."

"That's weird," I say, "but thanks, Mummy. See you later."

When I walk into the loft in Hackney Wick, it feels like nothing has changed even though everything has. I do everything Aubrey did before, when I'd needed telling what to do—arrange chairs and make tea and lay out snacks. We're not filming today, just having an informal get-to-know-you session. Filming starts next month. This is truly my project now. My entire role is working on Outside the Lines.

I buzz William up on the intercom and then run down to help him up the stairs. My assistant for the day. I don't really know how this happened because I don't remember asking him to be there, but here we are.

"Blimey," William says, looking around, "feels like only yesterday it was me coming in here with no idea what to expect."

"And a magnifying glass taped to your head," I say.

William's house has been painted white by his landlord now. He paints and repaints his miniature house all the time though, it evolves with him. He charts the changes on his very popular Instagram account. He overtook IsobelandAbigail in popularity quite some time ago.

"What do you need me to do today, then?" William says, once he's eaten a biscuit and is on his second cup of tea.

"Make everyone feel comfortable," I say. "You know what this is like, make sure they're not too overwhelmed."

One by one our new cohorts begin to arrive—nervous and shy, unsure what to expect. And we settle in to get to know one another, and the whole process starts up again. In the moments where I get a second to pause, I'm overwhelmed with a specific feeling—that I'm exactly where I'm meant to be.

I listen to people talk about their lives, how difficult things have been, how expensive things are, how you don't realize how valuable health is until suddenly it's precarious. I look at drawings and paintings and sculptures and photographs, and I see their hearts and souls poured out. What an immense privilege it is to see them, to be able to hold them in my hand.

"I'm so sorry," I say, as we're wrapping up, "I have to dash off today; it's a bit of a special one, as I'm sure you all know, because William has not stopped going on about it."

I look at him, and he beams at me, giving me a thumbs-up.

"But I'm going to leave you in his very capable hands to wrap up and lock up."

I look at him sternly, and he pats himself down for the keys.

"Next time we'll be filming, which is obviously awful."

Everyone laughs.

"But I promise we'll get through it together, and before you know it, you're going to be having fun."

As I run out of the door, William yells that he's "right behind me!"—that he's waiting for Stella to arrive to give him a lift in her van.

"Yes, but lock up first, William."

"Right you are," he says.

I decide to trust him but also to go back and check on everything before I go home.

Walter and I arrive early at the gallery that looks like a shop. It's tiny, smaller even than the place we'd visited the sex toy graveyard.

Aubrey is waiting for me, holding a bag of clothes for me to change into.

"Go," she says, after she's kissed me. "Everyone will be here soon."

"Oh my god," I say, looking around me, "this is really happening, isn't it?"

"Yes, and if you're not careful, it's going to be happening while you're wearing shorts."

I do as I'm told.

I put on the black tailored trousers that Aubrey's packed for me, the fresh dark gray T-shirt, the new white trainers. I run my hands through my hair in the mirror trying to make it do the right thing, and I whip out my eyebrow gel. I smile at myself in the mirror. I feel good but also quite sure that I'm going to pass out. A mixed bag.

When I finally emerge from the loo, the small space has filled up—my mum's there and Uncle Pete and Auntie Jan, deep in conversation with Aubrey. My housemates have arrived and are fussing around Walter, trying to wrestle a tiny knitted Abigail out of his mouth. I see Stella's van pull up outside and the whole gang—William, Aisha, and Leah—spilling out onto the pavement.

And then there are the people here who I don't recognize, who are here because they've seen *Artistic License*, or because it was advertised to them on Instagram, or because they simply walked past and were interested. And to them, I'm just a concept, to them I'm just the pieces on display around the room.

I stand for a moment by myself and watch them, my visitors, walking around slowly, reading about my life on small plaques, looking at Abigails and sketches and notes and paintings.

I walk around slowly with them, trying to see it through their eyes, trying to put distance between the me inside my head and the me in the objects in the room. I read about myself as though I am a stranger, and I feel vulnerable and moved and impressed and hopeful.

I feel everything.

I pick up a tiny Abigail, soft and gray, and hold her between my thumb and my forefinger. I stroke her head gently, and then I put her down again and move on.

You'll notice I leave this exhibition, which details the ebbs and flows of the last year—my tiny life, the way it expanded and imploded, the way it was put back together again—on a blank page. I told you at the beginning that it was not possible to know if there is a happy ending because it hasn't ended, but today I feel happy. I'm lucky to be here.

Thank you for being here too.

Isobel Bailey, the Artist

ACKNOWLEDGMENTS

Thank you to Emma Finn and Hillary Jacobson for being such wonderful champions. I am very lucky to have you two in my corner.

Thank you to Emma Capron and Anna Kaufman for "getting it" and working so hard to make my writing infinitely better than when it falls out of my head and onto the page.

Immeasurable thanks to all the people behind the scenes who make it happen:

My marketing team in the UK, Charlotte Gill and Khadisha Thomas.

My marketer in the United States, Lauren Weber.

My publicity teams, Kelsey Curtis and Ayo Okojie.

My production controller in the UK, Tara Hodgson, and my production editor in the United States, Edward Allen.

My copy editors, Erica Ferguson and Penelope Price, for making this novel far less ridiculous than it would have been.

Cover designers on both sides, Holly Ovenden and Madeline Partner.

Thank you to my friends, colleagues, mentors, and dream girlies/theylies: Emma Hughes, Bethany Rutter, and Lily Lindon.

Thank you, Emmett De Monterey, for being a ray of sunshine and for being an evil gay with me.

Thank you, Ashley Chalmers, for all the cake and the goss. Everyone is obsessed with you but especially me.

Thank you to all my other friends who keep having to put up with me writing books and then talking about them all the time.

Thank you, Merlin and Arthur, for being good boys even when you're being bad boys.

Thank you, Joey, for liking me even though this is my job. And for making me laugh every day.

Finally, thank you, Mum (my knitting correspondent), Dad, and Sarah (and Disco) for being the best fan club anyone could ask for. How lucky I am to be on Team Kay.